Dear Reader,

I am very delighted that *Heartless* (with its companion piece, *Silent Melody*, to follow next month) is being republished in this lovely edition. It has one of my all-time favorite heroes. The story is set in eighteenth-century England, an earlier era than my usual Regency setting. I made the change deliberately so that I could dress up my characters in all the splendid plumage of the time. Lucas Kendrick, Duke of Harndon, has just returned from Paris, undisputed center of the fashionable world, having unexpectedly inherited his title and position as head of the family that had spurned and exiled him many years before. Now he has power to wield and old scores to settle, and he looks upon his world with a cold and dangerous cynicism.

I enjoyed creating that very masculine aspect of his character, but I positively reveled in clothing him in all his Parisian splendor. He attends a ball early in the book in a wide-skirted scarlet coat and a gold waistcoat, both sparkling with gold embroidery, while white lace froths at his neck and wrists. He wears satin knee breeches with white stockings and jeweled shoes with high red heels. His long hair is powdered and crisply curled at the sides and bagged at the back, and he wears cosmetics and carries a fan. But he also carries at his side a jewel-hilted sword with which he is said to be more than ordinarily adept, and for all the languid grace of his manner, there is that look in his eyes—a look he soon directs across the ballroom at Lady Anna Marlowe.

And so begins a passion-fraught love story that kept me pounding the keyboard until they had found their happily-ever-after. I hope you enjoy seeing the two sides of Luke as much as I did creating them. And I hope you consider Anna a worthy heroine for him.

Mary Balogh

*continued . . .*

# ALSO BY MARY BALOGH

**THE SURVIVORS' CLUB SERIES**

*The Proposal*

*The Arrangement*

*The Escape*

*Only Enchanting*

*Only a Promise*

**THE HUXTABLE SERIES**

*First Comes Marriage*

*Then Comes Seduction*

*At Last Comes Love*

*Seducing an Angel*

*A Secret Affair*

**THE SIMPLY SERIES**

*Simply Unforgettable*

*Simply Love*

*Simply Magic*

*Simply Perfect*

**THE BEDWYN SAGA**

*Slightly Married*

*Slightly Wicked*

*Slightly Scandalous*

*Slightly Tempted*

*Slightly Sinful*

*Slightly Dangerous*

**THE BEDWYN PREQUELS**

*One Night for Love*

*A Summer to Remember*

**THE MISTRESS TRILOGY**

*More Than a Mistress*

*No Man's Mistress*

*The Secret Mistress*

**THE WEB SERIES**

*The Gilded Web*

*Web of Love*

*The Devil's Web*

**CLASSICS**

*The Ideal Wife*

*The Secret Pearl*

*A Precious Jewel*

*A Christmas Promise*

*Dark Angel/Lord Carew's Bride*

*The Famous Heroine/The Plumed Bonnet*

*A Christmas Bride/Christmas Beau*

*The Temporary Wife/A Promise of Spring*

*A Counterfeit Betrothal/The Notorious Rake*

*Irresistible*

*A Matter of Class*

*Under the Mistletoe*

*Longing*

*Beyond the Sunrise*

*Silent Melody*

# HEARTLESS

# MARY BALOGH

A SIGNET ECLIPSE BOOK

SIGNET ECLIPSE
Published by the Penguin Group
Penguin Group (USA) LLC, 375 Hudson Street,
New York, New York 10014

USA | Canada | UK | Ireland | Australia | New Zealand | India | South Africa | China
penguin.com
A Penguin Random House Company

Published by Signet Eclipse, an imprint of New American Library, a division of Penguin
Group (USA) LLC. Previously published in a Berkley edition.

First Signet Eclipse Printing, July 2015

LIBRARY OF CONGRESS CATALOGING-IN-PUBLICATION DATA:
Balogh, Mary
Heartless/Mary Balogh.
p. cm.
ISBN 978-0-451-46973-1
I. Title.
PR6052.A465H43 2015
823'.914—dc13 2015004808

Printed in the United States of America
1 3 5 7 9 10 8 6 4 2

Set in Bell MT
Designed by Spring Hoteling

# Heartless

# 1

"FAITH, child," Lady Sterne said to her goddaughter, "'tis time you gave some thought to yourself. Always it has been your family—first your mama, may God rest her soul, and then your papa, may God rest his, and always your brother and the girls. Well, now, Victor is of age and has come into his inheritance, Charlotte has married, Agnes is as pretty as a spring meadow and is like to marry as soon as we have presented her to some eligible gentlemen, and Emily . . . Well, you just cannot make yourself a martyr to your youngest sister. 'Tis time you looked to your own interests."

Lady Anna Marlowe smiled and watched her younger sister at the other end of the gallery being fitted out for fashionable clothes suitable to be worn in London. Bolts of fabric, mostly silks and shimmering satins, were piled on tables, some of them partly unrolled. There was some excitement about the scene and about the anticipation of seeing the clothes made and worn, she had to admit.

"Agnes is eighteen, Aunt Marjorie," she said. "I am five-and-twenty. On the shelf, one might say."

"And I vow that is where you wish to stay," Lady Sterne said sharply. "Life slips by fast, child, and increases in pace as one gets older, I swear. And life can become filled with regrets for what one might have done in the past but did not do. 'Tis not too late for you to seek a husband, but in another year or two perhaps it will be. Men do not look for breeders among women who are staring thirty years in the face—and men of course look for breeders when they choose mates. You have a great deal of love to give, Anna. You should now be looking to giving it to a husband and to receiving love in return—and position and security."

That last point hit home. Victor, Anna's only brother, had recently celebrated his twenty-first birthday. With university days behind him and his title still new to him—he had been the Earl of Royce since Papa's death a little more than a year ago—he was soon to return home to take up his responsibilities there. And he was newly betrothed. Where did that leave her? Anna wondered. And Agnes and Emily? Suddenly their home did not seem quite home any longer. Not that Victor would turn them out, or Constance for that matter. But one did not like to intrude on a newly married couple in their own home—especially not in the status of spinster sister.

She was a spinster. Anna clasped her hands rather tightly in her lap. But she could not marry. The thought brought with it the familiar shortness of breath and coldness in her head. She fought off the dizziness.

"I brought Agnes to London at your urging, Aunt," she said. "'Tis more likely that she will find an eligible husband here than in the neighborhood of Elm Court. If she can be settled, I will be content."

"Lud, child," her godmother said, "I urged you to *bring* your sister, not send her. I intended that you both find husbands. But you most of all, Anna. You are my godchild—my only one. Agnes is nothing to me except the daughter of my dear Lucy. For although you are all sweet enough to call me aunt, I am no such thing, you know. I see that Madame Delacroix has all but finished with her measurements." She got to her feet. "I will have you, too, decked out properly for town, my dear. Excuse my bluntness, but you look quite rustic. Even your hoops— they should be twice the size they are."

"Large hoops look quite ridiculous," Anna said. Ridiculous, but wondrously feminine and pretty, she thought treacherously. And her godmother had just reminded her that there was no real tie between her and Agnes. Could she be expected to take Agnes about to all the social events at which it was to be hoped she would attract a husband? Was not that Anna's responsibility? And would not it be wonderfully exhilarating to dress fashionably and to go about in society just a few times? Just for a short while?

*I will return. And of course you will be here when I do so. You will remember, my Anna, that you are mine? Body and soul?* The voice was as vivid in her head as if the man who had uttered them stood at her shoulder and spoke the words now. They had been spoken a year ago at Elm Court. A long time ago and a long way away. He would not come back. And even if he did, it would surely do no harm to enjoy herself a little before he did. She was only twenty-five. And really there had been very little enjoyment in her life. Surely just a little. . . . It was not as if she was going to be in search of a husband, after all. She knew very well that she could never marry.

"Well, perhaps," she said, getting to her feet to stand beside Lady Sterne, "I could have a few new clothes made so that I will not shame you if I do venture out with you once or twice."

"Lud, child," her godmother said, "'twould be difficult for you to do that when you have such beauty. Nevertheless, fashion is of importance. Come." She linked her arm through Anna's and moved her forward across the room. "Let us proceed before you change your mind."

Agnes was flushed and bright-eyed and was exclaiming that she could not possibly need all the clothes Madame Delacroix claimed to be the bare essentials for a young lady of quality making her first appearance in society. Anna's heart went out to her sister. She was eighteen years old and had been in mourning for two years—first for Mama and then for Papa. Even before that Mama had been ill with consumption and Papa had been—well, he had been ill too. And there had been the poverty. There had been very little chance for Agnes to enjoy her youth.

"Lud, child," Lady Sterne said to Agnes, "'twould not do at all, you know, for you to be seen in the same dresses time and again. Madame knows her job. Besides, she has had strict instructions from me. And now 'tis Anna's turn."

Lady Sterne had insisted from the start that she would bear all the expenses of the few months to be spent in London. It would be a dream come true for her, she claimed, to have two young ladies to take about and introduce to society. She had never had children of her own. Anna had brought some money with her—Victor had insisted that she take some from the estate though it would be years before he could expect to make it prosper again. And perhaps he never would if . . . But Anna refused to pursue the thought. She was not going to think about any of that for a month or two. She was going to give herself a chance to heal a little. She had told her godmother that she would keep a strict account of all that was spent on her and Agnes, that she would consider it a loan to be repaid when she was able.

And so, after all, she found herself being taken into the capable hands of Madame Delacroix and measured and poked and prodded and pricked and draped. It seemed that she stood still for hours while discussing with the two older ladies fabrics and trimmings and designs for petticoats, stomachers, open gowns, closed gowns, sack dresses—it was all very dizzying. She was laced into stays far tighter than she was accustomed to and looked down in some embarrassment—and some fascination—at the way they pushed up her breasts, making them seem larger and more feminine. And she was tied into whalebone hoops so wide that she wondered how she would pass through doorways.

She enjoyed every moment.

How wonderful it was, she thought, to feel young and free. Not that she was either in reality. Youth had passed her by. And as for freedom . . . well. She felt slightly nauseated for a moment when she remembered how very much she was not free. If *he* should come back from America as he had sworn he would . . . But she was not trying to break free forever. Merely for a couple of months. Surely he would not begrudge her that much time even if he knew about it.

How wonderful it would be to feel youthful and free for two whole months.

"I vow, child," Lady Sterne said when the fitting was finally over, "the years are falling off you by the minute. You have had a hard time and have remained devoted to your family throughout. Now is the time for yourself. And 'tis not too late. As I live, I am going to find you a very special husband."

Anna laughed. "'Twill be enough to attend a few balls and concerts, Aunt," she said. "I will remember it all for a lifetime. I have no need of a husband."

"Pshaw!" said her godmother briskly.

"*Egad,* but you made us all look like bumpkins tonight, lad," Theodore, Lord Quinn said, slapping his thigh with delight as he seated himself in a deep chair in his nephew's library and took a glass of brandy from a valet's hand before the man was dismissed. He laughed heartily. "'Twas the fan that really slayed 'em."

Lucas Kendrick, Duke of Harndon, was neither drinking nor sitting. He stood elegantly propped against the marble mantel. He raised the fan to which his uncle had just referred, a small ivory and gold affair, and opened it to waft it languidly in front of his face. "It serves to cool one's brow in a warm room," he said. "It has a purely practical function, my dear."

His uncle was in a mood to be amused. He laughed afresh. "Pox on it, Luke," he said, "'tis pure affectation as are the powder and rouge and patches."

His nephew raised his eyebrows. "You would have me appear in society half naked, Theo?" he asked.

"Not me, lad," Lord Quinn said. He took a sizable mouthful from his glass, savored it for a few moments on his tongue and then swallowed. "I have spent time in Paris and know how men dress and behave there. Though even there, as I remember, you have a reputation for leading fashion rather than following it. 'Tis perhaps a good thing that you also have a reputation as a deadly shot and swordsman, or it might almost be thought . . ."

"Yes?" The clear gray eyes of his nephew narrowed slightly and the fan stilled in his hands. "What might almost be thought?"

But his uncle merely laughed and looked him over from head to toe with leisurely appreciation. His amused eyes took in the powdered hair neatly set into two rolls on either side of the head, the long hair caught behind into a black silk bag and tied in a large bow at the nape of his neck—it was his own hair, not a wig—the austerely handsome face with its dusting of powder and blush of rouge and one black patch; the dark blue silk coat with its full skirts and silver lining and lavish silver embroidery and facings; the silver waistcoat with blue embroidery; the tight gray knee breeches and white silk stockings; the silver-buckled shoes with their high red heels. The Duke of Harndon was the very epitome of Parisian splendor. And then, of course, there was the dress sword at his side with its sapphire-jeweled hilt, a weapon with which his grace was said to be more than ordinarily adept.

"I refuse to answer, lad," Lord Quinn said at last, "on the grounds that I do not fancy having the tip of that sword poking out from my backbone. But it was kind of you to leave White's Club early tonight. You will be the topic of conversation there for the rest of the night, I warrant you." He chuckled once more. "The fan, Luke. Zounds, but I swear Jessop very near swallowed his port, glass and all, when you first drew it out and opened it."

"If you will remember, Theo," Luke said, fanning himself again, not participating in the laughter, "I left Paris with the greatest reluctance. You talked me into it. But I'll be damned before you also talk me into becoming the typical English gentleman, stalking about my land with ill-fitting frock coat and staff in hand and hounds at heel and English ale in my stomach and English oaths on my lips. Don't expect it of me."

"Hark ye, Luke," his uncle said, suddenly serious. "If I had to persuade you to come back home, 'twas only because you would not take the responsibility on your own shoulders and everything is like to go to wrack and ruin at Bowden Abbey in your absence."

"Perhaps," the Duke of Harndon said coldly, "I do not care the snap of two fingers what happens to Bowden Abbey and all who live there, Theo. I have done well enough without them for the past ten years."

"Nay, lad," his uncle said, "I know you better than most. Cold you may appear to be when you are not charming the ladies and coaxing the most lovely of them into your bed, and cold you may have the right to be after the unjust way you were treated. But I know that the Luke of ten years ago is still in large measure the Luke of today. You care, lad. Besides, there is such a thing as responsibility. You are the Duke of Harndon now and have been for two years."

"I never looked for such a position," Luke said, "or expected it, Theo. There was George older than me, and George married ten years ago." There was something resembling a sneer in his voice for a moment. "One might have expected there to be male issue in the eight years before his death."

"Aye," his uncle said. "But there was only the one son, stillborn, Luke. Like it or not, you are the head of the family, and they need you."

"They have a strange way of showing need," Luke said, fanning himself slowly again. "If 'twere not for you, Theo, I would not even know if any of them lived or all were dead. And if they are in need, they may be sorry if I begin to answer it."

"'Tis time for old wounds to be healed," his uncle said, "and the awkwardness of a long and mutual silence to be overcome. Ashley and Doris were too young to be held responsible for anything that happened, and your mother, my sister—well, your mother is as proud as you, lad. And Henrietta . . ." He shrugged expressively, unable to complete the sentence.

"And Henrietta is George's widow," Luke said quietly, his fan still.

"Aye." Lord Quinn sighed. "You have begun badly, lad, leasing this house instead of taking up residence at Harndon House. 'Twill be thought strange that you live here while your mother, brother and sister are there."

"You forget, my dear," Luke said, looking keenly at his uncle from beneath half-lowered eyelids, "that I care not one fig for what people think."

"Aye, 'tis so." Lord Quinn drained his glass. "But you have not even called on them."

Luke sat down at last, crossing one leg elegantly over the other. He set down his fan and withdrew an enameled, jeweled snuffbox from a pocket. He set a pinch of snuff on the back of one hand and proceeded unhurriedly to sniff it up each nostril before replying.

"No," he said, "I have not waited upon them yet, my dear. Perhaps I will do so tomorrow or the next day. Perhaps not."

"And yet you came home," his uncle reminded him.

"I came to England," the duke said. "To London. Perhaps I came out of curiosity, Theo, to find how it has changed in ten years. Perhaps I grew restless and bored in Paris. Perhaps I have grown tired of Angélique. Though she has followed me here. Did you know?"

"The Marquise d'Étienne?" Lord Quinn asked. "Sometimes known as the most beautiful woman in France?"

"None other," Luke said. "And I would have to agree with public opinion. But she has been my mistress for almost six months. I usually make three the upper limit. Mistresses are not easy to shed after three months. They become possessive."

Lord Quinn chuckled.

"Of course," his nephew said, "everyone knows that you have kept the same mistress for ten years or more, Theo."

"Fifteen," his uncle said. "And she is not possessive, Luke. She still refuses to marry me whenever conscience prompts me to broach the subject of matrimony."

"A paragon," Luke said.

"You will return to Bowden?" his uncle asked casually.

"You would make a masterful conspirator, my dear," his nephew said. "First one small step and then another until your victim has finally done all you set out to persuade him to do. No, not Bowden. I have no wish to return there. I have no love for the place."

"And yet," his uncle reminded him, "'tis yours, Luke. Many people there depend upon you, and word has it that 'tis not being run as well as it might. Rents are high and wages are low and cottages are falling into disrepair."

The Duke of Harndon fanned his face again and looked at Lord Quinn with keen eyes. "I was called a murderer ten years ago," he said. "By my own family, Theo. I was twenty years old and as naive as—well, complete the simile for yourself. What is as incredibly naive as I was at the age of twenty? I was forced to flee and all my abject, pleading letters were returned to me. I was cut off without a penny. I made my own way in life without help from any of my family, except you. Am I now to go back to make everything right for them?"

His uncle smiled, but it was a gentle smile, without any of the humor he had shown earlier. "In a word, yes, my lad," he said. "And you know it too. You are here, are you not?"

The duke inclined his head to acknowledge the hit but made no reply.

"What you really ought to do," Lord Quinn said, "is take a wife, Luke. 'Twould be easier for you to return, perhaps, if you were married, and 'tis time you set about producing heirs."

His nephew's stare had become icy and haughty. "I have an heir," he said. "Ashley may succeed me when I die as I succeeded George."

"There is frequently dissension between brothers when the one is the other's heir," Lord Quinn said.

"As there was between George and me?" Luke fanned his face slowly. "But it was not because I was his heir, Theo. And until he was four-and-twenty and I twenty, we were the best of friends. I never remember coveting the title despite what must have been said afterward. There was one specific cause of our quarrel. I very near killed him, did I not? One inch lower, the physician said. One inch. I was a poor shot in those days." There was coldness, almost bitterness in his voice.

"This is spring," Lord Quinn said. "The time when almost the whole of the fashionable world is in town, Luke. The perfect time for selecting a bride eligible for a duke's bed."

"This duke is not in search of a life's partner," Luke said. "The very thought is enough to make me shudder." He shuddered rather theatrically to prove his point.

"You may wish to consider it, nevertheless, after I have taken my leave," Lord Quinn said, getting to his feet and stretching. "'Tis time, my lad."

"And yet," Luke said, "you are almost twenty years my senior, Theo, but it has never been time for you? You have retained your bachelorhood into the fifth decade of your life."

His uncle chuckled. "I had the misfortune to fall in love with a married lady," he said. "By the time she was widowed it was too late to get my heirs on her anyway. Or perhaps it was not too late, who knows? No matter. I am a mere baron. And I do not have a passel of unruly relatives breathing down my neck."

"And I do?" Luke said, closing his fan and getting to his feet to see his uncle on his way. "They must be taught, Theo, that 'tis not to be tolerated. No one breathes down my neck unless she is specifically invited to do so."

His uncle laughed heartily once more. "Take a wife, Luke," he said. "Egad, 'twill be the answer for you. Take my word on it. And get sons on her as fast as it may be done. I will keep my eyes open and see who is available this year. I will choose you the prettiest, lad, provided she has the rank and breeding to go along with her looks."

"Thank you, my dear," his nephew said languidly, following Lord Quinn into the hall, "but I make it a habit to choose my own bedfellows. And truly, rarely for more than three months at a time." He grimaced as a footman stepped forward to open the outer door. "Must you ram your hat on your head as if to glue it to your wig? Did you not know that hats are not meant to be worn on the head but to be carried decoratively beneath the arm?"

His uncle threw back his head and guffawed inelegantly. "Pox on your French ways," he said. "You are living in an English climate now, my lad, where a hat is not an ornament but a head warmer."

"Heaven forbid!" the duke said fervently. He turned back to the library as the door closed behind his uncle.

A bride. He had never seriously considered taking one even though he was thirty years old and had unexpectedly been elevated to high rank on the death of his brother two years ago, only three years after the death of their father. At least, he had not considered taking a wife since ten years ago. He did not particularly want to think about that.

Marriage was not for him. Marriage meant commitment. It meant belonging to someone and having someone belong to him. It meant children and the ties they would bring. It meant being bound, body and soul. It meant being vulnerable—again.

He was not vulnerable now. He had spent ten years—well, nine anyway, if he remembered that for that first year he had whined and pleaded and then staggered into a life of wild, self-pitying debauchery—carefully cultivating an invulnerability. He had amassed a fortune entirely by his own efforts, first by gambling and then by careful investments. He had made himself into the complete Parisian gentleman so that he was not only accepted everywhere but even sought after in the very highest circles. He had learned how to attract the most beautiful and fashionable women and how to make love to them and how to get rid of them when he tired of them. He had acquired expert instruction on the art of swordplay and on the skill of pistol shooting and had made himself deadly with both weapons; he had learned how to be charming in manner but steely of heart. He had learned that love was not to be trusted, even when it was the love of one's own family—especially then. He had learned neither to expect nor to give love.

He knew that he had acquired the reputation of being a ruthless and a heartless man. It was a reputation he coveted. It was how he wanted to be seen by the world. It was how he wanted to be.

And was he now to consider taking a wife? Merely because his uncle thought it a good idea? When had he allowed his uncle to make his decisions for him? Actually, he thought, propping himself against the mantel again and staring absently across the room, if he was to answer that question honestly, he must confess that he had frequently taken his uncle's advice. At Theo's suggestion he had gone to France and eventually given up the hope of coming home to resume the life he had known—it seemed rather laughable now that he had been intended for the church and that he had wanted the life of a clergyman for himself. It was at his uncle's suggestion that he had gone to Paris to make a new life for himself. And it was at Theo's suggestion that he had come home—well, partly home, anyway. He had come to

England, to London. He was not sure he would be able to go all the way home to Bowden Abbey.

Henrietta was at Bowden. His sister-in-law. George's widow.

If he had a wife, perhaps he would find it more possible to go home. The thought came unbidden.

But he did not want a wife. And he did not want to go to Bowden.

Except that Theo had reminded him of his responsibilities there, of the people who depended on him even apart from the members of his own family. Devil take them all, he thought. What were they to him? They were his father's people. George's people.

And now his own.

He had never wanted to be the Duke of Harndon. He had never envied George his position as eldest son. He had been quite content to be merely Lord Lucas Kendrick. Perhaps the Reverend Lord Lucas Kendrick. He smiled ruefully, though the expression was perhaps more sneer than smile. Poor naive boy. All eager at the age of twenty to enter the church, to marry, and to live happily ever after.

Well, he decided, he would force himself to see his mother since she was in town, and Doris and Ashley too. There were apparently problems with his sister and brother, if Theo was to be believed, problems that his mother seemed unable to deal with, problems that he would have to handle. And he would handle them too, by God. But the problems at Bowden would be solved at long distance. He would appoint a new steward, perhaps, and get rid of Colby. Better still, he would summon Colby to London and allow him to speak for himself.

He would not marry. He would tell Theo so in no uncertain terms the next time he saw him. One had to be very positive with Theo or else one found oneself willy-nilly doing what the man wanted one to do. Theo really had missed his calling in life. He should have been a diplomat.

Luke had returned to England in order to make an appearance there as duke and in order to wait upon his mother and brother and sister while they were in London. He had come in order to assert his authority where it needed to be asserted—and only where there was need. He had come out of a grudging sense of duty—and, yes, perhaps out of some curiosity. But he did not intend to stay. As soon as he was decently able, he would return to Paris where he belonged, where he was happy—as far as a man without a heart could be happy, that was. Actually he did not look for happiness. If one was happy, one could also be unhappy and would be sooner or later. It was altogether more desirable to steer clear of either extreme.

𝓛𝓪𝓭𝔂 Sterne looked down at herself dispassionately. She was naked to just below the waist, where a sheet covered her. She had, she supposed, reached an age at which she should start covering herself up when there were other eyes in addition to her own to look at her. She was no longer a youthful beauty. But she turned her head on her lover's arm and noticed the signs of aging in his own sleeping face and torso. It did not matter, she decided. They were long familiar with each other. If she were to see him now for the first time, perhaps—undoubtedly—she would see him as a man of middle age. He would look even older if she saw him—as she was seeing him now—without his wig, with his thinning hair cut very short. But her eyes saw only the man she had known and loved for years.

He opened his eyes and smiled at her. "Old age creeping up or galloping up, Marj," he said, echoing her thoughts. "Have I slept away our afternoon together?"

"No, Theo," she said. "You did not sleep away the first part of it. Ah." She sighed with contentment and stretched luxuriously, feeling one of his legs firm against her own. "I do believe this gets better with age."

He chuckled. "But we used not to sleep at all," he said. He changed the subject suddenly to resume the topic of conversation that had engrossed them before they made love. "You think the older gel, then? She is not a little too old, Marj?"

"To bear him a few sons and some daughters too?" she asked scornfully. "Lud, Theo, she is five-and-twenty. Hardly decrepit. And a great beauty. She has a pleasing maturity too. She has suffered, you know."

"Maturity," he said dryly, "is not like to make Harndon foam at the mouth, my love. He might find the other gel more appetizing."

"Perhaps," she said. "I do not know his tastes. But Agnes is only eighteen. Pretty enough and good-natured but she would be a mere toy to a man of Harndon's age and experience. Anna could be a companion to him."

"Some men, Marj," he said, "want toys for wives. And breeders, of course. Eighteen sounds a good age to me."

"For my sake"—she turned her head to kiss his cheek—"let us make it Anna, Theo. She is very precious to me. I would dearly love to marry her to a duke. And to your nephew into the bargain."

He turned his head so that their lips met. "Why not?" he said. "The boy is not easily led, anyway. It has taken me two years of wheedling just to get him back to England. It may take another two to get him down to Bowden. And he insists he is not in the market for a wife. We will try to interest him in the mature beauty."

"And Anna too declares quite emphatically that she is not in search of a husband," Lady Sterne said. "It took all my ingenuity just to persuade her to have some fashionable clothes made so that she may go about in town. She looked quite rustic."

Lord Quinn grimaced. "Harndon would not like that," he said. "So, granted that we are probably embarking on an impossibility, when shall we bring them together? Lady Diddering's ball?"

"The night after tomorrow?" she said. "Yes, 'twill do nicely, Theo. Oh, if only it works. My dear Anna a duchess. And a lady of fortune. I am as anxious for her happiness as if she were my own daughter."

He stroked her hair. "Has it been a sadness in your life, not having children of your own, Marj?" he asked. "Should we have tried, perhaps . . . ?"

"No," she said. "Regrets are pointless, Theo. I have had a good life. And 'tis not over yet. Perhaps not nearly over. I am still only in my forties. In fact, 'tis not yet quite impossible . . ." She did not complete the thought.

"But this afternoon is nearly over," he said. "I am to dine with the Potters and they always begin a meal promptly. Shall we make use of what time we have left?"

"Yes." She turned to him with another sigh of contentment. "Yes, let us do that, Theo."

## 2

His mother and his sister and brother would be at the Diddering ball, which his uncle was urging him to attend. Luke had guessed it even before he knew it as a fact. It would be altogether too awkward to encounter them for the first time in ten years in such a public setting. Besides, the meeting was not to be avoided. It was to see them that he had come to England, after all. And he could not expect them to call on him, even though they must know he was in London; Theo would have seen to that. If he delayed beyond a few days of his arrival from Paris, it might be thought that he was afraid of meeting them.

He was not afraid. It was just something that he did not want to do and that he wished he need not do—ever. If George had lived, or if he had had a son to succeed him, everything would have been different. He himself could have stayed in Paris for the rest of his life and forgotten that he had been born an Englishman. He could have forgotten the fact that he still had family there. He would not have been needed by them, and he certainly would not have needed them. He had long outgrown such a need.

But George had not lived and George—and Henrietta—had had no son. And so there was the tie forever binding him to England and to Bowden Abbey, where he had been born, and to the family still living there.

It was fact and unavoidable, and so the day before the Diddering ball he made his appearance at Harndon House, his own town house even though he had rented another for a month—a foolish move, perhaps, and suggestive of a certain cowardice. The simple fact was that he did not want to live under the same roof as his mother. And he had not been invited to live there, though of course he needed no invitation. Perhaps his mother had not even known he was coming to England.

The butler who received him in the hall of Harndon House was a stranger to him. But he was a master at the art of passivity, cultivated by all the best of his breed. There was scarcely a flicker in his eyes when Luke identified himself, though the man's bow deepened and his manner became perceptibly more deferential. But clearly the man faced a dilemma. Was he to present his master as a visitor or . . .

Luke helped him out. "You will ask the Dowager Duchess of Harndon if she is receiving this morning," he said and strolled across the tiled hall to examine a rather well-executed landscape painting in a gilded frame.

His mother received him alone in the morning room since he had not announced his intention of calling. She rose to her feet as he entered the room, having been given only a minute or two in which to compose herself to receive the son she had not seen in ten years.

"Madam?" Luke made her a bow from just inside the door. "I trust I find you well?"

"Lucas." She spoke his name after looking at him for several silent seconds. "I had heard that you had changed. I would not have recognized you."

She was as he remembered her: unsmiling, straight-backed, composed. Her dark hair, unpowdered, was dusted with gray. It was the only sign that she had aged by ten years. But then his mother had never been young—or old. And she had never been smiling or warm or maternal. Duty had been the guiding principle of his mother's life. Any love she might have felt for her children had been smothered by a devotion to preparing them for the positions they must expect to hold in life. While never harsh and never neglectful, she had been humorless and unaffectionate.

"I was a mere boy, madam," he said, "when I was judged no longer fit to be your son. Ten years have passed since then."

She made no comment on his words. "You have come home to your responsibilities at last," she said, "though 'tis wrong that you have chosen to take up residence in another house when this is your own."

He inclined his head to her but offered no explanation of his decision to live elsewhere. He found himself wondering for no apparent reason if his mother had ever hugged him. He could not remember such a time. This welcome—if welcome it were—was exactly what he might have expected of her. Had he expected open arms and eager eyes and tears and fond words? He would not have welcomed them even if they had been offered. They would have come ten years too late. She had made no attempt to shield him from his father's harsh sentence. She had not kissed him good-bye or assured him that she loved him despite everything. She had been dutiful to the end.

"I trust that my sister and brother are well too?" he asked.

"Doris is nineteen, Ashley two-and-twenty," she said. "They have been without the guidance of a father for five years and without that of the head of the family for two."

Was it her way of asking for his help? Or was it a reproach that he had hitherto neglected the duties of his position? Probably the latter, he decided.

Had she grieved, he wondered, when his father died? When her eldest son died? George had been taken by the cholera, a disease that had killed only him from the family, though apparently several people from the village had been struck down by it too.

"There is a problem?" he asked. They were still standing at almost opposite ends of the room. She had not invited him to sit down, though the thought struck him again that he did not need an invitation to be seated in his own home. Nevertheless, he remained where he was.

"Doris is determined to make an ineligible match," she said, "despite the fact that I brought her to town to meet a husband worthy of her rank and she has met any number of eligible gentlemen. Ashley is—well, he has become wild and unmanageable and totally forgets his position."

"It is called sowing one's wild oats, I believe, madam," he said.

"The worst of it is," she said, "that they have heard about their elder brother's exploits in Paris and expect you to support their indiscretions or at least to ignore them. They believe that with their father gone and George gone they can do whatever they please."

Luke raised his eyebrows. "Indeed?" he said quietly.

"You have come," the dowager said. "Whether you have come to indulge or ignore them or whether you have come to assume the responsibility of your position remains to be seen. As does the question of whether you will continue to allow *the duchess*"—she put emphasis on the words—"to rule at Bowden as if she were still married to the head of the family."

Ah. So there was conflict between the two women, was there? Between his mother and Henrietta. Both duchesses but neither one of them quite *the* duchess. Neither one of them his duchess. It was another argument in favor of his taking a wife, perhaps. The thought came unbidden and unwillingly. Why should he care if they were feuding? He did *not* care.

And then, before their conversation could continue, the door behind his back was flung open. A very pretty young lady wearing a fashionable sack dress over hoops, her hair vividly dark without powder, rushed into the room and stopped short a mere foot away from him.

Doris! She had been a thin gangly child of nine when he left home. She had been the only member of his family to show regret at his leaving—Ashley had been away at school at the time. She had hidden among the trees near the gates at the end of the driveway and had hurtled out into his path as he rode down it on his way from the house. He had jumped from his horse and caught her up in his arms and held her there for perhaps a whole minute before telling her that she must be a good girl and go back home and grow into a beautiful and accomplished young lady. She had been sobbing too helplessly to say anything beyond his name, repeated over and over again.

She looked into his face now with wide, dark eyes and bit her lower lip. He had the feeling that she had been about to throw herself

into his arms but had checked the impulse. He made no move himself. He had been too long out of the habit of hugging—at least of
hugging from simple affection.

"Luke?" She looked doubtful. "You *are* Luke?" She laughed breath-
lessly. "They said you had come. You look . . . so very different."

There had been no one more unfashionable than he when he was
a boy. He had been interested in nothing but books and his future
career in the church and his family and home . . . and the woman he
had planned to marry.

"And so do you, Doris," he said. "You have grown up. And you
are as lovely as I knew you would be."

She flushed and smiled with pleasure. But the moment for spon-
taneity had passed. He knew—perhaps with a small pang of regret—
that she would not now rush into his arms. He was a stranger to her
although he was her brother. At first glance she had even doubted
that it was he.

"Why are you standing here?" She glanced uncertainly at her
mother and looked back at him. "Come and sit down, Luke. Are you
going to come and live here? It seems strange that you do not. Was
it hard leaving Paris? You must tell me about the latest styles there.
I fear we are far behind the newest fashions here. Tell me about the
ladies' fashions. I can see what gentlemen must be wearing. Oh,
Luke, you are very splendid. Is he not, Mama?"

The dowager did not reply. She busied herself ringing the bell
for tea.

It was a strange homecoming. Even though Doris chattered,
apparently at her ease after the first moments of shock, there was a
certain awkwardness and a consequent air of stiff formality in the
drawing room. He felt, Luke decided, like a stranger who was paying
a difficult courtesy call.

Which was exactly what he was, in a way.

Except that he was head of this family.

As he was about to take his leave, the door opened again and a
tall, slender, dark and handsome young man hurried inside. For one
moment Luke's breath caught in his throat. George? But George was

long dead. He got to his feet and exchanged bows with his younger brother, who gazed at him with mingled eagerness and awe.

"Luke?" He stepped closer. "Zounds, but I would not have known you. Uncle Theo said I would not. Zounds!"

"Ashley." Luke inclined his head slightly. His brother had a pleasing, open countenance. It was easy to imagine that he was indeed sowing his wild oats—an admirable activity for a man of his age, provided the wildness was not of a nature to destroy him.

"I hear you are more skilled with it than any other man in France," Ashley blurted as he took a seat, indicating the sword that Luke carried always at his side. "And with a pistol too. Is it true that you have killed your man in two duels?"

Perfectly true. But it was not a topic of conversation suitable for female ears. Under the circumstances it was in particularly bad taste. It was in a duel that he had narrowly escaped killing their elder brother.

"If it is true," he said coldly, "'tis not something of which I boast. And 'tis not something that our mother and our sister need have discussed in their presence."

Ashley flushed and Luke felt instantly sorry for the harsh rebuke. Somewhere far back in memory he could remember what it was like to be young and impulsive and rather gauche.

"I-I am sorry, Mama," Ashley said.

And conversation died.

Luke was on his way back to his rented house a few minutes later, glad to be alone again, glad that the initial visit was over, stiff and awkward as it had been. He felt nothing for any of them, he decided. They were strangers to him. Even Doris—it was hard to see in her now the child he had cared for. He was relieved.

And yet something in him ached. The tingle of long-ago memories, perhaps. The long-suppressed, long-forgotten memories of what it felt like to be rejected by everyone who had given meaning and stability to his life. The frightening emptiness of facing life alone when he knew nothing about life, when he had no defenses against it.

It was not the ache to go home. He did not want to go home.

More than anything else he wanted to go back to Paris. If he had a home now, that was it. He was comfortable there. It was a familiar world, a world that had shaped him into the man he had become, a world over which he felt he had some control.

But he had come to England again and had seen his family again—or what was left of it. And he had felt again the old mingling of hurt and anger at his mother's rejection of him and the old determination to break on his side the bonds that had held him to her, son to mother. He had seen no welcome in her during his visit and had felt nothing that would make him want to see her again.

Yet he had seen Doris again, too, and Ashley. And his mother had suggested that they needed guidance. His guidance as head of the family. And he had loved them—in that time of innocence when he had been capable of love.

Was guidance something he could give? Something he could give promptly and then return to Paris?

Henrietta was ruling at Bowden as if she were still the mistress there. But why not? She had been George's wife. She had suffered for her position. Perhaps she had suffered more than he, even though she had had a comfortable home and high rank.

As far as he was concerned she could continue to rule there and his mother could continue to fret about the fact. But if he had a wife, there would be no argument about who was mistress there.

There it was again! Damn Theo and his suggestions, which always somehow acquired the quality of a needle, pricking away at him night and day until he acted on them.

But this was one suggestion he would not act upon. Not even for the sake of family order and peace would he sacrifice his freedom and take a wife.

And so the worst was over, he supposed as he walked on. He had seen them all again, except for Henrietta, whom he had no intention of seeing at all. He would find out more of what was happening in Doris's life and in Ashley's, sort out any problems, if he was able, send for the books from Bowden and perhaps for Colby himself and find out if there were any grounds for dismissing the man and appointing another steward, and then take himself back to Paris. By the summer it should be possible for him to leave again.

In the meantime he would enjoy himself. It would be a novelty to go about in English society for a change and see new faces and hear new gossip. Theo had urged him to attend Lady Diddering's ball tomorrow evening. It was always one of the more glittering balls of the spring, his uncle had said, the place where one was likely to meet everyone who was someone.

What his uncle did not say, of course, was that it was also the place to meet eligible young ladies. But Luke understood that that was what he had meant.

He would go regardless. His mother and Doris were to be there. Doris had said so during tea. He would see how Doris behaved toward prospective suitors and whether there was any sign of the ineligible attachment his mother had mentioned. And it never hurt to look at and dance with young ladies of quality even if they were not mistress material. He enjoyed charming them and watching them smile and blush. He even enjoyed escorting the prettiest of them about once in a while.

Yes, he would go. He might have forgotten how to feel deep emotion, but he had never forgotten how to enjoy himself.

*They* were going to their first ball, Lady Diddering's, which would be a grand and magnificent affair, according to Lady Sterne. All the fashionable world was sure to be there.

Anna was dressed in her new finery—an apple green silk mantua with robings from neck to hem heavy with gold embroidery and a stomacher so covered with the same embroidery that it seemed to shimmer all of gold. The mantua opened at the front to reveal a petticoat of paler green, huge and swaying over her new hoops. She had balked at having her hair cut short and curled tight to her head in the latest style, but it was curled at the sides and back and powdered white—she had never worn powder before. The small round cap she wore far back on her head was all of fine lace to match the three deep frills of her shift that extended below the sleeves of her mantua at the elbows. And the same lace trailed from the back of her cap in two long lappets. Her shoes, pale green with gold embroidery, had heels a few inches in height, another new venture for her. She had been wearing them in private for two days in order to be sure of her balance. She wore no cosmetics or patches despite her godmother's warning that she would be more the exception than the rule.

And yet it was not of herself that she thought in the last few minutes before the carriage arrived, and it was not her own appearance or expectations that had brought a flush to her cheeks and a sparkle to her eyes. She was watching Agnes as her sister came into the salon where Anna waited with Lady Sterne, and was filled with wonder that this could be the same girl who had been a child but yesterday—or so it seemed.

"Agnes," she said, her hands clasped to her bosom. "Oh, Agnes, you look . . . beautiful." How could she fail to attract suitors? Surely there would be enough of them even after just tonight that Agnes would have a choice.

"Yes," Lady Sterne agreed. "I vow you will do, child. And we were quite right to choose that particular shade of blue with your fair coloring."

But Agnes, modest as she always was about her own appearance, had eyes for no one but her sister. "Anna," she said, stretching out her hands and taking her sister's. "You have always been lovely—oh, more lovely than anyone else I know. But now you look—ah, I cannot find the words. Does she not, Aunt Marjorie?"

"Faith, child," Lady Sterne said, "I believe I should carry a stout stick with me to the ball in order to beat back all the young gentlemen who will crowd about the two of you. But I hear someone at the door. It will be Theodore with the carriage. Perhaps he has brought his cane. He will certainly be wearing his sword. I vow he will need it."

Both sisters laughed and each eyed the other admiringly. And both felt suddenly breathless. It was true that they were the daughters of the late Earl of Royce and as such had entertained and been entertained by persons of quality and had danced at local balls and assemblies. But London seemed like a different world to them. Even after Lord Quinn had bowed over the hand of each and declared that he had not seen two such lovely gels in a month of Sundays—whatever that meant—and had ushered them into his carriage with Lady Sterne; even after he vowed that he would be challenged to a dozen duels before the night was out for greedily surrounding himself with the three most fascinating ladies at the ball—even after that there was still uncertainty. What if their manners were just too rustic for town tastes? What if their conversation was too dull? What if the dance steps with which they were familiar were different from the way the same dances were performed in town?

And what if no one wanted to dance with Agnes?

It seemed impossible to Anna, looking at her sister, to imagine that such a thing could possibly happen, especially when she was sure that Lady Sterne would see to it that she had partners, but even so it was an anxious time. Her stomach felt somewhat queasy as the carriage slowed and a glance out the window revealed a large mansion with all its windows ablaze with light. Its front doors were thrown back so that light spilled forth and splendidly clad ladies and gentlemen could be seen in the hall. A carpet had been laid down over the steps and across the pavement so that those alighting from carriages would not have to set their feet on hard ground.

Agnes's eyes were rather like saucers.

"Egad," Lord Quinn said as he handed down the ladies from his carriage, "but 'tis many a long day since I was like to be so much the focus of attention and envy. 'Tis to be wished that I had three arms, but I have been blessed with no more than two. Will you walk unescorted, Marj?"

Anna had met Lord Quinn the day before and had been introduced to him as an old friend of her godmother's. She liked him. He was of average height and inclined to stoutness. He was pleasant-looking and had kindly eyes. He must be about the same age as—as *him,* but very different in every other way. And he had a way of setting one at one's ease. At the moment, as she took one of his arms and Agnes took the other, she could think of no one with whom she would rather make her entrance to her first London ball.

"Nervous, my dear?" he was asking Agnes.

"A little, my lord," Agnes admitted.

"Some young man will dance the first minuet with you," he said, "and after five minutes, if you remember at all that you were nervous, you will wonder at yourself and settle to enjoying the rest of the evening. And you, my dear?" He turned to Anna.

"No, my lord," she lied. "I have come to observe and to enjoy the sights and sounds of a society ball. I have nothing to be nervous about."

He chuckled, and then Lady Sterne whisked the sisters away to the withdrawing room to straighten their skirts and check their hair and caps in the looking glass though there had been no wind outside to effect any damage.

And so the moment came when they stepped for the first time inside a London ballroom. It was decked out with flowers and greenery so that it smelled like a summer garden in full bloom on a hot day. But the flowers were superfluous, Anna thought, gazing about her, robbed of breath for a moment. All the most sumptuous satins and silks and laces and jewels must be assembled in this one room, decking out the persons of the guests gathered there. It was hard to say whether the gentlemen or the ladies were the more colorful and gorgeous. The ladies perhaps had the advantage in the sheer size of their skirts and the amount of fabric and decoration that could be displayed. But the gentlemen had the advantage in the elegant cut of full-skirted coats and in the long waistcoats beneath, on which all of an embroiderer's art could be displayed to full advantage.

Anna thought of the rather sober, staid styles worn at home, and looked about her at London fashions.

"Well?" Lady Sterne was asking her, a smile on her face.

"'Tis a new world," Anna said. "One of whose existence I thought I was aware but was not."

"The wonder you feel is in your face, child," her godmother said. "You are not sorry now that I persuaded you to come?"

"Oh, no," Anna said.

When she thought back over the last two years, her mind thought in color—or rather in the absence of color. Black and gray, all of it. Of course, those were the colors they had worn for two years. Only in the last two months had they put off their mourning. And there had been the grief, first over the lingering illness and death of Mama and then over the sudden death of Papa. But it was not just the mourning that had sapped life of its color. There had been everything else too. The fight to keep the family together despite adversity, the struggle to avoid ruin and to keep Papa from debtors' prison and her brother and sisters from destitution, the futile, futile efforts to pay off or redeem all the debts. And the greatest blackness of all—the web that had been woven inexorably about herself, drawing her ever inward, trapping her in a forever after of enslavement. Except that he had gone away after Papa's death. He had gone to America, promising to come back, promising to come to claim her. But he had been gone for longer than a year, and perhaps—oh, she prayed for it—he would not come back after all.

And now she was in a different world.

Anna smiled suddenly as Lord Quinn caught her eye and winked. And the smile held and spread. She felt an unexpected welling of excitement and happiness. She was in a new world, a world of splendor, a fairy-tale world that she had only ever dreamed of a long, long time ago, when there still seemed to be some point in dreaming. It was true that it was for only a brief time. It was true that he might, after all, come back to claim her and bring back the darkness. But now, at this moment, she was in a London ballroom at the start of a ball. And she was going to enjoy herself.

Oh, yes, she was. She was going to enjoy herself as she had never enjoyed anything else in her life before. She lifted the fan that hung from her wrist by a ribbon, opened it, and cooled her face with it. And she gazed about her with a wondering smile and sparkling eyes.

## 3

*L*UKE arrived as the opening minuet was ending. It was unusually early for him, but latecomers at a ball in London were frowned upon, it seemed. Or so his uncle had warned him. Actually his uncle was up to something, and it did not take a genius to guess what.

"Marjorie has her goddaughter up from the country for the spring," Lord Quinn had remarked casually the evening before. "The Earl of Royce's daughter. And her younger sister too. A pair of lovely gels, I warrant you, lad."

Which one, Luke had wondered, did his uncle intend as his bride?

"Indeed?" he had commented. "A little rustic, are they, Theo?"

"Egad, no," his uncle had replied. "Not with Marjorie to look to outfitting them. They are lovely enough and well-bred enough to make one forgive some rusticity anyway. Pox on it, lad, if I were twenty years younger—"

"If you were twenty years younger, my dear," Luke had said, "you would still be attached to Lady Sterne but somewhat embarrassed at the age gap."

His uncle had thrown back his head and laughed heartily. "And so I would, lad," he had said. "And so I would. Now in your case . . ."

"I suppose," Luke had said, "Lady Sterne is to be at the Diddering ball tomorrow evening? With her charges?"

"What?" His uncle had looked startled. "Tomorrow evening already is that, lad? Zounds, and so it is. Marjorie will be there with the gels? It is altogether possible, I suppose. Yes, they may well be there. I hope someone asks them to dance, Luke. Apart from me, that is. They are strangers and all that."

"But lovely strangers," Luke had said. His uncle was overdoing the carelessness.

"Lovely? Zounds, yes," Lord Quinn had said. "I daresay they will not lack for partners, will they?"

Luke had not replied. He had changed the subject. But it was as clear to him as a bright summer day what his uncle was up to.

He had come alone to the ball, though Angélique, Marquise d'Étienne, had hinted that she would be pleased with his escort. She had declared her own intention of spending a month or two in London soon after he had decided to come home. Life was too, too tedious in Paris at times, she had said with a sigh. And she had heard that London could sometimes be amusing. They had not traveled together and had taken only one walk together in public, though he had paid her two lengthy visits at her hotel. He had no intention of their names being linked as an established couple.

The minuet had ended. The floor was clearing. Young ladies were being returned to their chaperones. His eyes picked out the elegant figure of Lady Sterne, whom he would have recognized even if his uncle had not been standing beside her. From across the ballroom she appeared not to have aged since he saw her last, in Paris, at least eight years ago. There was one young lady with them—actually, young girl would be a better description. She looked shy and sweet and very, very young. Luke undressed her with practiced eyes and felt that he was committing some obscenity. She was a child. Theo must have taken leave of his senses.

And then another couple joined them. The gentleman bowed and strolled away, leaving behind his partner. Doubtless she was the other of Royce's daughters. Luke looked at her critically. Although he could see her only in profile, she was clearly the elder sister. She was fashionably dressed in a shade of green that made her look fresh and inviting. She was fanning her face and talking to Lady Sterne. He drew his own fan from a pocket, opened it, and plied it absently.

She turned, having finished what she had to say. Her face was smiling and animated. Ah, yes, definitely rustic. A few months in Paris—or even perhaps in London—would soon wipe that expression from her face and replace it with a look of languid ennui. She was gazing all about her with an eagerness that was almost palpable. Her foot was tapping even though there was no music playing. It set her skirt to swaying invitingly.

Her eyes passed over him and smiled impersonally. And then a few moments later they returned and held on him. Had her expression not been so bright and so open, he would have sworn that she was doing the same to him as he had just done to her younger sister. She seemed to realize suddenly that he was looking directly back at her. She smiled dazzlingly, raised her fan to cover her mouth, and continued to smile with her eyes over the top of it.

He raised his eyebrows and inclined his head a little. By God. She was a flirt.

But Angélique had found him.

"Luc," she said in heavily accented English, setting one delicate white hand against the wide cuff of his sleeve, "you 'ave come, *cheri*. This is all very quaint, *non?*"

Quaint? Was it? He looked about him. English fashions did not appear to be lagging so very far behind those of Paris, though the French were in the habit of scorning the backward English or at least of treating them with condescension. Of course, there were subtle differences—a little more hair, a little less powder and paint, for example, than he was accustomed to seeing at a fashionable gathering. And he intercepted a look of mingled shock and contempt on the face of an elderly lady whose eyes were fixed on his waving fan.

"It is all very English, Angélique," he said. "But we are in England now. A quadrille is to be next? You will do me the honor?"

Although he was to all effects a stranger to English society, there were people he had met in Paris and people who remembered his father or his brother and gentlemen he had met at White's. And of course there were his mother and Doris and Ashley, to whom he paid his respects when the quadrille came to an end. He charmed the ladies and conversed with the gentlemen and felt quite at home within an hour of his arrival. He always enjoyed balls. He liked to dance.

For longer than an hour he avoided Lady Sterne and her god-daughters—though apparently only the elder sister was that. His uncle made no move to draw him into their circle—the old devil was too cunning for that, or thought he was. He probably did not even know that Luke realized what he was up to.

But Luke kept an eye on the older sister. She continued to smile and sparkle and enjoy herself quite openly, and she did not lack for partners, though the younger girl, who might have been considered prettier by many, missed one set. And the older sister was not un-aware of him, either. Her eyes seemed to alight on his person alto-gether too often for it to be accidental, and her smile always deepened when their eyes met.

Interesting. He would meet her without reluctance when Theo considered the time right. He would discover whether her manner was as flirtatious at close quarters as it was at a distance. He won-dered with some amusement if she realized that Theo had picked him out as her future husband. And then he sobered. If Theo had set out to promote the match, it was altogether likely that Lady Sterne was a coconspirator. And it was possible that the goddaughter knew about it—if she was the one, of course. Perhaps they had chosen the younger girl for him.

He must be careful. He had no intention whatsoever of being trapped into marrying a rustic, bright-eyed young innocent. Or into marrying anyone for that matter.

*Lady* Sterne and Lord Quinn between them had made very sure that she and Agnes had partners for the opening minuet. That was very clear to Anna. And she was grateful to them. Although she had come to the ball merely to observe and to give Agnes a chance to meet eligible gentlemen, once she was there she wanted to be a part of it all too. She wanted to enjoy herself. She wanted to dance. And dance she did, with a friend of Lord Quinn's. Her feet moved gracefully through the steps; her ears appreciated the rich sounds of a whole orchestra playing the music; her nostrils breathed in the myriad scents of flowers and expensive perfumes; and her eyes were dazzled by the color and movement of silks and satins and jewels. It was surely one of the happiest half hours of her life. She thought it even though her partner was not a handsome man or a young man or one with a great deal of conversation. But he danced well.

Her eyes feasted on the sight of so much splendor as she stood with Agnes, her godmother, and Lord Quinn after the minuet was over, and she tapped her foot, almost as if she could still hear the music. She hoped—oh, she hoped someone else would ask her to dance. She wanted to dance all night without stopping. She wanted to dance until her toes were all blisters and her legs would no longer hold her up. She smiled gaily at her foolish thoughts.

She felt young and pretty, and filled to the brim and beyond with youthful energy. She had never been young, she realized suddenly. She had never had a chance to be young. At the age of five-and-twenty, it might have been thought that youth had forever passed her by. But it had not. There was tonight, this magical night in which she was young and free and pretty and . . . and happy. She was so happy that she could scarcely contain her exuberance.

And then her mind registered what her eyes had seen a few moments before. She looked back to the man standing alone in the doorway. She had thought herself surrounded by the epitome of splendor, but he was—was there a more powerful word than splendid? He was gorgeous. It seemed not quite the word to use for a man.

He was not very tall and he was quite slender. He was graceful—another word that seemed not quite suitable for a man. He wore a coat of crimson satin and a waistcoat of gold, both so bedecked with embroidery and jewels that they shimmered. His shoes had jeweled buckles and high red heels, encrusted with more jewels. The hilt of his dress sword was embossed with rubies. His hair—she was sure it was his own even though it was heavily powdered—was dressed neatly in side rolls and bagged in black silk behind. Even across the distance she could see in some shock that he wore cosmetics—powder and rouge—unlike most of the men in the ballroom.

But the feature that had caught her attention more than any other and had caused her to look back at him was the small ivory fan that he was waving before his face.

He should look effeminate, Anna thought as her eyes wandered over him. Why did he not? There was something about him that was almost suffocatingly masculine. Something about his eyes, perhaps? They looked very steadily and very directly at her from beneath rather heavy lids.

And then she realized that she had been staring and that he had observed her doing so. But if he had done so, then it was because he was staring at her too. He had been as ill-mannered as she. She felt a flutter of physical attraction to the man. And because this was a new world and not quite the real world, and because she was feeling young and pretty and free, she ignored her first impulse, which was to look away in some confusion, and instead continued to look back at him and smiled in acknowledgment of the fact that they had caught each other doing the same thing. Sizing each other up.

She went further. Some instinct—some long-suppressed, quite unsuspected instinct of femininity—made her deliberately raise her fan to her nose so that she could laugh at him with her eyes over the top of it. He did not smile back. But he raised his eyebrows and made her a slight bow with his head and held her eyes until a woman as startlingly gorgeous as he took his attention by laying a hand on his sleeve.

Anna had partners for every set and proceeded to live this magic night to the fullest, consciously enjoying every single moment of it. And yet she was constantly aware of the gentleman in scarlet and gold as he danced and conversed and moved about with an elegance and a grace that had been obvious from the start. Would he effect an introduction? she wondered. Would he ask her to dance?

She hoped so. Shamelessly she sought him out with her eyes as she danced with other partners. And shamelessly she smiled at him whenever she caught his eye. Shamelessly she flirted with him from afar.

It felt wonderful to flirt, she thought. And even the use of that particular word in her mind could not make her feel ashamed. Her moment of youth and freedom would be complete if he but asked her to dance.

_Luke_ had watched his sister dance and behave quite properly toward her partners and toward other young men who obviously had an acquaintance with her and came to converse with her between sets. He had observed Ashley dance once and then disappear, presumably in the direction of the card room. And of course he had danced himself and conversed and kept an eye on Lady Sterne's goddaughter.

Instead of dancing one set he wandered into the card room and observed that the stakes were not high and that Ashley was winning—and drinking. It was not a good combination. He had discovered that for himself early in his career. He would not have made his fortune if he had not played with all his wits about him, unbefuddled by alcohol. He would keep his eye on his brother over the next few weeks, he decided. But his attention was distracted now by two gentlemen who began a conversation with him.

It was in the card room that Lord Quinn found him. He joined the group for a few minutes and then took Luke's arm and strolled away with him, leading him casually in the direction of the ballroom.

"Enjoying yourself, are ye, lad?" he asked. "Egad, but you have turned some heads tonight. 'Tis the fan that has done it—again." He chuckled.

"I thought," Luke said, taking the offensive, "that I might get you to present me to Lady Sterne's goddaughter, Theo. She is the older one? The one wearing green?"

The look of suppressed triumph on his uncle's face was almost comical. "Aye, lad," he said. "And all my fears were for naught. The gel has not missed one set. You have noticed her, then?"

"Only because you mentioned her," Luke lied. "I will dance with her if I may, Theo—as a courtesy to Lady Sterne."

The dancing was between sets in the ballroom. Luke followed Lord Quinn across the room to where Lady Sterne was standing

with her two charges. The elder of the two stopped fanning herself
when she saw him approaching and then began again at an almost
furious speed. She lowered her eyes for a moment and then raised
them again boldly. They were large green eyes, he saw as he drew
closer, made more green by the color of her mantua.

"Well, Marjorie, m'dear," Lord Quinn said in a loud and hearty
voice, "lookee here at whom I ran into in the card room. And I was
saying to you not half an hour since that in all the crush it seemed I
was not going to have a chance to exchange a word with my own
nephy."

"Harndon," Lady Sterne said, smiling graciously, "I am pleased
to see you again. And lud, what a happy chance it was that took
Theodore past the card room."

Ah yes, indeed, Luke thought, a co-conspirator without a doubt.
"Madam?" He made his bow to her.

"May I present my goddaughter to you?" Lady Sterne asked.
"Lady Anna Marlowe, daughter of my dear late friend, the Countess
of Royce. And Lady Agnes, her younger sister. His grace, the Duke
of Harndon, Anna."

He bowed deeply while both young ladies dipped into curtsies.
He included both in his bow, but it was on the elder that his whole
attention was focused. "Charmed," he murmured.

A Parisienne would have considered herself half naked without
cosmetics quite heavily applied and without patches artfully placed.
Lady Anna Marlowe wore none. Her complexion was delicate and
clear and healthy, he noted. Her lips were curved in a smile and her
eyes sparkled. There was no pretense of indifference now that he was
close. A flirt she might be; a coquette she was not.

"His grace has recently returned to England after spending a
number of years in Paris," Lady Sterne was explaining.

"Lady Anna has recently arrived from the country after a
lengthy term of mourning for her parents," Lord Quinn was explaining almost simultaneously.

Lady Anna, looking as if she had never mourned or entertained
one sad thought in her life, smiled at him.

"My condolences," he said, including both sisters again in his bow.

"How fascinating that must have been," Lady Anna said at the same moment. Her voice was light and as eager as her expression.

She smiled. He inclined his head.

His dealings for years past had been almost exclusively with sophistication. The woman's open appraisal of him and her very obvious delight in her surroundings made him feel slightly dizzy. Slightly dazzled. Lines were forming for the next dance, a set of country measures.

"Madam." He bowed once more, but directly to Lady Anna this time. "May I hope that you have not promised this set? May I have the honor of leading you out?"

"Thank you." Her answer was made almost before his question had been completed and she was reaching out a hand to set in his. "Yes, thank you, your grace." The whole of the sun seemed to be behind the smile with which she favored him.

"How fortunate," Luke heard his uncle say. "'Tis the supper dance."

Ah, yes, of course. His uncle, the consummate schemer. Luke led his partner to the end of the line of ladies and took his place opposite her in the line of gentlemen. The music was beginning.

She danced with a light grace. He was accustomed to partnering graceful dancers. Dancing was an accomplishment much cultivated by the fashionable. But Lady Anna Marlowe danced with more than grace. It was almost as if she took the music inside herself as it played and became music and harmony and rhythm as she moved. Dancing was more than an accomplishment with her. It was a delight and a self-expression. And all the while she danced, except for the occasions when the patterns of the dance took her away for a few moments with other partners, she kept her eyes on his and smiled into them.

And how did he know that? he asked himself before the set ended. How could he know it unless his eyes were upon her too? She had a loveliness and a directness that he found rather refreshing, rather different. He did not know how old she was though he guessed that she had passed the age of majority. She had been kept in the country by a double bereavement. That must have been sad for her, especially if they had been a close family. But apart from that, he judged that she was a woman of little experience and therefore of little depth of character. She did not look like someone who had suffered a great deal in life.

And yet there could be something dazzling about innocence and simplicity when it was combined with smiles and exuberance. He was not sorry that his uncle had maneuvered him into leading her into the supper dance. He looked forward to the opportunity to talk with her. He hoped she had some skill at conversation. He hoped she would not merely blush and giggle, the common malady of girls with no experience in life and society.

$\mathscr{It}$ was an evening Anna knew she would remember for the rest of her life. It was an unexpected and priceless jewel in the dark path of her life and she clutched at it greedily, knowing that it might be the only one that would ever come her way. Tomorrow life would return to normal and though she would be spending almost two more months here in town, she would not expect any more evenings like this one. There could be no more like this.

He had lived for years in Paris. That explained a great deal. It was said that the people of Paris were years ahead of the English in fashion and in frivolity. The lady who had approached him soon after his arrival and had proceeded to dance with him was also from Paris. Anna had found that out in the course of the evening. She was the Marquise d'Étienne. Her hair was shorter and more tightly curled than anyone else's and her cosmetics were worn strangely. Her powder was white and heavy, her rouge very bright and worn in large circles on her cheeks, with no attempt at blending. Her lips were a corresponding red. It was the French way, Anna had been told. It was very hard not to stare at the woman.

He had lived in Paris. He was a duke. And she had been right about his eyes. Everything about him was graceful—a sort of languid grace. Everything except his eyes. They were dark gray and they were very keen despite the fact that he frequently drooped his eyelids over them. She suspected that his eyes did not miss much. And she had been right about something else too. There was an indefinable but quite unmistakable air of masculinity about him despite outer appearances. And it was not just his eyes.

He made Anna breathless. She had always thought that her dream man would be tall. This man was no more than a few inches taller than she. And yet she found herself imagining how much more comfortable it would be to be held in this man's arms than in those of a tall man. So much more comfortable on the muscles of the neck.

She was briefly appalled when she caught the direction of her thoughts. She was not given to lascivious thinking. Besides, it was all quite pointless and only likely to give her more pain when the night was over and she realized again how very alone she was and would be for the rest of her life. And yet—she shivered inwardly— she should be thankful for aloneness. If *he* came back, she would not even have that. But she would not think of him. Not tonight on her magic night.

It was their turn—hers and the Duke of Harndon's—to twirl down the full length of the empty space between lines. She would remember this, she thought, feeling his warm hands clasping hers, forever and beyond forever. They were strong and handsome hands. When she smiled up into his eyes, her lips were only inches from his. Her eyes dropped to them for a brief moment.

He was, she judged, a man who had spent his adult years in fashionable society. In Paris. A man of sophistication and charm—she had felt his charm even though she had not spoken with him yet. A man of frivolous character. Someone with whom she had flirted and was flirting without fear. Someone with whom she could relax and talk for the half hour of supper. An unthreatening man.

Someone so very different from—*him*. She thought for a moment about that other man, about his tall, thin body and narrow handsome face, his soft, pleasant voice. On first acquaintance she had liked him. Everyone had liked him and probably still did. She had thought him her savior. She had expected him to offer her marriage and had been ready to accept—not out of love, perhaps, but out of respect and liking and out of what she had thought would develop into devotion. But it had not been marriage that was on his mind—or seduction either. And that latter point puzzled her and disturbed her perhaps more than anything. If he did not want to marry her and did not want to use her body outside marriage, then why . . .

But no. No! He had controlled her life and haunted her to the core of her soul for two years even though he had been absent for one of those years. But not this evening. This was her magic evening and she was not going to allow another thought of him to intrude.

Anna listened regretfully as the music drew to an end. But there was still supper. Still perhaps the best part of the evening, which was already perfect. How could anything be more perfect than perfect? She smiled.

"Madam." The Duke of Harndon held out an arm for hers. "Will you honor me by taking supper with me?"

She set her own arm along the shimmering satin of his sleeve and felt the warmth of his body heat. "Thank you, your grace," she said.

Prince Charming, she thought, and smiled gaily at her own fancies. She wondered if Cinderella's prince had worn scarlet and gold. And then she wished she had not remembered the old fairy tale at all. At midnight all of Cinderella's finery had turned to rags and her prince had been left behind and she had found herself sitting on a pumpkin. And there was no point in reminding herself that Prince Charming had retained one of the glass slippers and had been able to use it to find his princess again.

Cinderella had lived in a fairy tale. Lady Anna Marlowe lived in the real world.

# 4

"I vow 'tis succeeding," Lady Sterne said, laying a hand on Lord Quinn's sleeve. "Just look at them, Theo."

Lord Quinn had been looking. His nephew and Lady Sterne's goddaughter were sitting at a table some distance away from their own and were focused entirely on each other even though they were surrounded by other guests. It was something he had observed before. It was perhaps what had always made the lad more sought after than almost any other gentleman in Paris, both as a husband and a lover—that ability of his to give his whole attention to the lady of the moment, almost as if he had forgotten the existence of all others. But usually his attention was given to some beauty of high rank and easy morals, some beauty he could reasonably expect to lure into his bed for as long as he cared to keep her there.

For all the animation of her ways, which might almost be described as flirtatious. Lord Quinn did not believe his nephew would have mistaken Lady Anna Marlowe for an easy or even a possible conquest. Not as a mistress, anyway.

"I warrant you, Marj," he said, "he will have her brought to bed of a boy before ten months have passed."

Lady Sterne sighed with contentment, too long accustomed to her lover's manner of speaking to be shocked by his bluntness. "Lud, Theo," she said, "I hope you are right. Anna has had a hard time of it, as witness the fact that she is almost past marriageable age despite beauty and rank. Lucy would never countenance my coming to visit her when she was ill and I never forced myself on her, but I have often wished since that I had. I wished it especially when I knew about the other troubles. Certainly Royce lost all his money and almost brought the family to ruin. By gambling, word has it."

"Aye," Lord Quinn said, "and word has the right of it there, Marj, though I never knew the man personally. One must not judge others, but it does seem criminal for a man to indulge in reckless living when his children are still unsettled in life. There are the boy and three gels?"

"Four," Lady Sterne said. "There is the one young girl still at home and Charlotte, who was married to a rector just recently, a year almost to the day after Royce's passing. It was a decent match, I believe."

"A nasty business, that," Lord Quinn said. "Falling off the roof and all that. Messy."

"There is a walk up there," she said. "I remember it well from years ago. The house is at the top of a rise and there is a splendid view in all directions from the roof walk. But the balustrade, I recall, is no more than waist high. I would never walk too close to it. It seems that Royce did. I suspect, Theo, though it may be slanderous to say so and dear Anna would never admit it even if I asked straight out, that he drank more than was good for him."

"Aye, very like," Lord Quinn said.

"He doted on Lucy," Lady Sterne said. "My guess is that he went all to pieces when she became consumptive and then died."

"Aye," he said. "'Twould be hard to lose someone one had long loved, Marj." He set a hand over hers on the table for a moment and patted it. But he did not keep his hand there. They were ever discreet in public.

"I do believe," she said, "that Anna, the eldest by four years, was forced to bear all the burdens alone. She has been weighed down by them, Theo. Not just by the grief of having lost both parents in such a short time, but by more than that. I wish I had known sooner so that I might have gone there to Elm Court and given her some assistance."

"You are helping her now, Marj," he said. "You have brought her

to town and decked her out in fashionable rig and presented her to
the most eligible bachelor in all England. If the lad can but be
brought to heel!"

"Will you but look at him," Lady Sterne said with a laugh. "The
fan, Theo. 'Tis outrageous. 'Tis an affectation, would you not say?"

"Aye, as I live," Lord Quinn said. "All is affectation with Luke.
'Tis what is behind the artifice that matters, though, Marj, but it is
never easy to know with Luke. By my life, though, he seems taken
with her. She is a lovely gel."

"Yes." Lady Sterne sighed. "'Twould do my heart good to see her
hold her own child, Theo, and to know her settled happily for life."

He patted her hand again.

*Anna* was feeling flushed and hot after the vigorous country
dance and it must have shown. After filling her plate and his own
and seating himself beside her at one of the long tables in the supper
room, the Duke of Harndon drew out his fan, opened it, and cooled
her face with it. She laughed at him.

"Do all gentlemen in Paris use fans, your grace?" she asked.

"By no means." His eyes roamed her face. "I do not follow fashion, madam. I set it."

"So I am like to see more fans in gentlemen's hands in London
during the coming weeks?" she asked.

"I do not doubt it," he said.

"It must be wonderful," she said wistfully, "to live in Paris. Is it?"

"If you enjoy a life of glittering frivolity," he said, "there is no
place on earth to compare with it. Do you?"

She laughed. "I have no idea, your grace," she said. "I have lived
in the country all my life and am but recently arrived in town. I am
what one might call a country bumpkin."

Ignoring the food on her plate, she had set an elbow on the table
and rested her chin on the back of her hand. She smiled at him. She
was deliberately fishing for a compliment and felt no doubt that it
would come. She had never before done anything nearly so shame-
fully brazen. It felt wonderful.

"If that is true, madam," he said, "then it seems I have been spending my days in the wrong place. Perhaps I too should have been in the country."

"Ah, but," she said, "'twould have been a different part of the country, your grace. That is the problem with the country. It is too vast."

"Yes." He paused in his gentle fanning of her face for a moment. "After all, madam, it appears that I did the fortunate thing in coming to town on my arrival in England instead of going into the country."

She had had her compliment and tingled with the joy of it right down to her toes. He closed his fan and they began to eat. But though she knew that her godmother was sitting some distance away with Lord Quinn and that Agnes was seated with one of the dancing partners Lady Sterne had selected for her, she was not fully aware of her surroundings. The Duke of Harndon talked exclusively with her, telling her about Paris, amusing her with details of fashion and anecdotes of gossip, and it seemed to her that his attention was as fully focused on her as hers was on him. There was something in his manner—she found it impossible to identify what it was—that made her feel special, that made her feel almost cherished.

It was an exhilarating game that she played—something entirely uncharacteristic of her and beyond her experience. It was something she would have thought herself incapable of even a few hours ago. It was a game for one evening only—until, that was, supper was at an end and guests around them began to drift back in the direction of the ballroom.

"I shall do myself the honor of calling on Lady Sterne tomorrow afternoon," the Duke of Harndon said, "if I find from enquiry that she is to be at home. Perhaps, madam, if the weather is favorable, you would care to walk with me in the Mall of St. James's Park afterward. It is the strolling grounds of the fashionable world, as you are probably aware."

She was not. But it was an invitation she could not—must not—accept. She must not try to carry the fantasy beyond this one night.

Doubtless it would mean nothing to him to dance with her tonight and walk with her tomorrow; there would be no declaration of attachment in his doing both. But it might well mean something to her. She was already in love with him in much the way all females are in love with Prince Charming while reading "Cinderella"—in a warm, detached way that would bring sighs but no real pain tomorrow. But if she walked with him . . .

She did not wish to fall in love. Indeed, she dreaded doing so. Life, which had been barely supportable for several years past, would be finally and totally unbearable if she were indiscreet enough to fall in love. All her instincts and all her common sense told her that it would be so. She must not be tempted to continue this flirtation beyond tonight.

"Then I must pray fervently tonight, your grace," she heard someone—herself—say, "that the weather tomorrow afternoon will be favorable."

He pushed back his chair, got to his feet, and reached out a hand to assist her to hers. He bowed over her hand as she rose and set his lips lightly against her fingers. She barely restrained herself from snatching them back as if she expected to be burned.

Five minutes later she was back in the ballroom, dancing a quadrille with someone else. And still smiling. And still feeling that welling of happiness that had carried her through the evening. Much as she tried to scold herself for the answer she had given the duke in the supper room, and much as she tried to tell herself that she would be sorry, she could not feel regret. Just a few days ago she had promised herself a couple of months of enjoyment, though she had not expected enjoyment to be quite this vivid or all-encompassing. Why, then, had her vision narrowed to just one evening? Why should she not give herself longer? One more day? Perhaps even the two months? It would be wonderful to live this fully for two whole months.

Would life in the future, when she had returned home, be any more dreary if she allowed herself to live now when she had the chance? Yes, a little demon somewhere in her mind told her. It would be unbearable once she knew that life could be so very different. And yet perhaps if she denied herself now, she would be forever sorry that she had not grasped more tightly the jewel she had discovered tonight.

And perhaps life in the future would be only dreary. She would be thankful if that was all it was. It might be so much worse if *he* returned from America. Surely he would not. There was panic in the thought that he might—he had promised to come back. She would not be able to bear it. She would want to die.

The Duke of Harndon was not dancing. He was standing near the door in conversation with two gentlemen and the Marquise d'Étienne. But he was watching her. Anna, catching his eye, gave him a dazzling smile before concentrating her attention on her partner and the quadrille once more.

*Luke* was up early the following morning, as he always was, regardless of the time he went to bed. He had been out for a lengthy and vigorous ride and had breakfasted before his unexpected visitor arrived, unfashionably early.

But then there was nothing fashionable about his visitor, instantly recognizable despite the gap of ten years since they had seen each other last. He was a little more ruddy of complexion and a little more portly about the middle so that he looked every one of his nine-and-twenty years, but he had not really changed. He wore a carelessly powdered bob wig, loosely curled, a somewhat ill-fitting frock coat, a waistcoat that was unfashionably long, and stockings rolled over the tops of his knee breeches instead of the more fashionable breeches buckling over the stockings. He was clearly a man who lived in the country and cared not a fig for town styles.

"Will!" Luke said as William Webb, Baron Severidge, strode into the morning room hard on the heels of the butler, who announced him. "My dear fellow."

Lord Severidge stopped abruptly and gaped inelegantly. "Luke?" he said. "Egad, man, is that you?" But he must have been convinced of the identification for he grasped his former friend heartily by the hand and pumped it up and down several times. "What the deuce has Paris done to you?"

"Ah, this, apparently," Luke said, looking down at the silk morning robe he had donned after returning from his ride.

"Zounds!" William said. He reached into an inner pocket. "We heard that you had come to England. I am a messenger boy, Luke, though I had business that forced me up to town for a couple of days anyway. It brings me here about twice a year, which is twice a year too many for my liking. I have a letter from Henrietta."

"Ah," Luke said, ignoring the feeling that a heavy fist had collided with his stomach and taking the offered paper from his friend's hand. He slipped it inside a pocket of his robe. "That was good of you, Will. How is she? And how are you? Married with half a dozen hopefuls in your nursery already?"

William's already ruddy complexion flushed. "Not married," he said, "and not really looking. The only place to do that properly is London, and I cannot bear the thought of spending time here and trotting off to balls and such all done up like a painted maypole. Oh, sorry, Luke."

Luke motioned to a chair and rang for refreshments as Lord Severidge seated himself. "I appear like a . . . ah, painted maypole to you, Will?" he said. "Goodness me, and I am not even dressed in all my finery."

William looked distinctly uncomfortable. "Henrietta is well," he said abruptly, answering an earlier question.

Luke sat down and crossed one leg over the other. It had seemed incredible to him even as a boy that William and Henrietta could be brother and sister. Henrietta was exquisitely small and slender. He wondered if she was still as slender.

"She was never happy," William said. "She lost the child, as you doubtless heard. They never appeared close and he changed— became more morose." He paused to cough. "You do not want to hear this, do you?"

Luke's hand was opening and closing on the arm of his chair. "'Tis old news, Will," he said. "Very old news."

His friend was mopping at his forehead with a large handkerchief. "She has been restless since we heard you were back in England," he said. "She thinks perhaps it is she who is keeping you from coming home."

"Ah," Luke said quietly. "No, Will. I have as great an aversion to the country as you do to the city. I belong in Paris, or at the very least in London. No, she is wrong."

They sat in silence while a footman carried in a tray and poured them each a drink—wine for William, water for Luke.

"I do not know what she has written in the letter," William said, nodding his head in the direction of the pocket into which Luke had put it. "Though it looked to be long enough. Pox upon it, but women can ramble on when they have a pen in their hands, Luke. I point the quill at the air when I try to write a letter while my mind draws a total blank, and I end up squeezing out two stiff sentences in an hour if I am lucky."

"I shall read the letter later," Luke said.

"But she would insist on my bringing it in person," William said, "and delivering it into your own hand, Luke. She would have me tell you in words, too, that Bowden is yours, that you belong there, that she is pleased you do, and that it would hurt her to feel she is keeping you from what is rightfully yours."

"She is not," Luke said. "You may tell her that, Will."

"It hurts her to know that you are in England but have made no move to go to Bowden," William said. "She might have come here with me, Luke, but she would not force you to meet her again. She seems to feel that perhaps you blame her . . . Ecod, but this sort of thing is not to my liking. As I live, this will be the last time I carry messages for anyone."

"If you will give me time to change," Luke said, "we may proceed to White's together, Will. Are you a member? I have been newly accepted there."

"Aye." His friend was visibly relieved at the changing of topic. "There is frequently good conversation to be had there."

"Land and crops and cattle and such?" Luke asked. "One shudders at the very prospect. Give me half an hour, Will. I will rush for your sake."

"Half an hour?" William asked, frowning. "What the deuce is to do, beyond throwing on a coat and taking up a hat?"

"We painted maypoles take a little longer about our toilettes," Luke said as he left the room.

He did not need all of half an hour. But he did need to read Henrietta's letter. Ten years of silence and now he held a part of her in his hands again. The temptation was to tear it up, to keep the distance of ten years between them. But he knew he must read it, that he could not even wait until later in the day.

She had made a mistake, she had written, coming straight to the point. Her handwriting looked startlingly familiar. Even after what had happened, she should have married him, not George. She had been promised to him, after all, and she had loved him. And he had still wanted her to marry him. She had made the wrong choice, believing at the time that it was the only possible one. She had been wrong. She had been very unhappy.

Well, Luke thought, pausing in his reading. Well. But he could not blame her for the decision that had changed the course of several people's lives, including his own. She had been carrying George's child, however unwillingly, and she had married George. She had been little more than a child herself, only seventeen years old. But what she wrote was all pointless now. She was George's widow and was now free again to pursue happiness and to marry whomever she chose—except him. A woman could not marry her dead husband's brother.

But she wanted him to come home. He was needed there, she wrote. The affairs of the estate had not been running smoothly since George's death and neither she nor his mother knew anything about the running of an estate. Laurence Colby appeared to be doing much as he pleased and was glorying in his power as steward of an absentee landlord. And as for the running of the house . . .

Henrietta, it seemed, wished to change almost all the furnishings and draperies of the house. What was there was old-fashioned and dreary. But her mother-in-law held with tradition and opposed all change. Yet she, Henrietta, was merely trying to carry out the renovations that George had approved before his death.

Luke must come home. It was where he belonged. He had always loved Bowden Abbey. Did he not remember? Did he not remember their growing up there together? Did he not wish to see it all again?

She sent him her duty and her love.

Luke folded the letter deliberately into its original folds. He wished Will was not waiting downstairs for him. He wished he had left the letter to read later.

He had killed deep feeling inside himself long years ago. He had killed his love for her, his misery over his loss of her, his agony over the life she must lead through no fault of her own. He had put it all from him. They had loved each other. They had been going to marry, young as they both were, and she was to go with him when he took up his first church living. And then George had come home from the two years of his Grand Tour and had seduced and impregnated Henrietta. She had wailed hysterically in Luke's arms while telling him. George, when confronted, had been tight-lipped about the whole thing, neither denying nor confirming the story Henrietta had told Luke—though he had made haste to offer for her. She had chosen to marry her seducer rather than the man she loved, though Luke would still have married her.

And so there had been the duel, fought with pistols, and George ostentatiously deloped, shooting into the air, then watching unflinching as Luke, who had never before shot a pistol, aimed with shaking hand. He had aimed to miss by six feet—and ended up hitting his brother in the shoulder and almost killing him. They had all thought that he had shot to kill. In those days he had been an even

worse marksman than they had given him credit for. They had ac-
cused him—and convicted him—of trying to kill for the heirship to
the title and the fortune and for Henrietta. They had not known the
true story: they thought that Henrietta had preferred George to him
and had been indiscreet with him, ignoring her promise to marry
Luke. They had assumed that the challenge had been made out of
jealous rage. In reality he had issued the challenge for the mere sake
of making a point. For the sake of honor.

And because he had been devastated by a sense of betrayal.
George, four years older than he, had always been his idol. And he
had returned from his Grand Tour looking very grand and dashing. George had always been extremely handsome—as Ashley was
now. Luke had spent time with him, drinking in the accounts of his
brother's travels, reveling in the pleasure of his company again.
And then George had stolen his woman in the cruelest possible
manner.

No, it was not a memory to be revived. Luke was not surprised
that he had suppressed it so ruthlessly. But Henrietta had been forced
to live with it for ten years—or for eight, rather, until George's
death. She had found no happiness with him—both William and her
letter told him that.

But she was still the Duchess of Harndon. And she had plans for
sweeping renovations at Bowden Abbey, plans of which his mother
disapproved. He was being invited home so that he could take sides.
So that he could take Henrietta's side. He hated the thought of becoming involved in such a dispute.

He did not care what they did with Bowden. They could burn the
house down and lay waste the land for all he cared. And yet, unbidden, the memories came back of the home he had loved as a boy. He
did not know quite what Henrietta had in mind, but he could not
picture Bowden renovated. There was a fine air of antiquity about
the old abbey even though architectural changes down the centuries
had almost totally obscured the ecclesiastical origins of the house.
He feared that if he must take sides, he would take his mother's.

And clearly Colby was not doing a good job and must be replaced. Yet how could he replace the steward unless he observed for himself what the man was doing or not doing? Would it be fair to discharge him on hearsay evidence or on the evidence of the books for which he was planning to send? Or even on a personal visit by his steward to London?

He was going to have to go down there himself, Luke thought with a dull certainty. Devil take it all, he was going to have to go.

If he went home he would be caught in the middle of a petty squabble, the duchess, his sister-in-law, on one side and the dowager duchess, his mother, on the other.

Unless . . .

He held the completion of the thought at bay while his valet helped him into his coat and he picked up his tricorne hat and his cane.

Unless he took home with him a third Duchess of Harndon. A wife.

His mind shifted to the evening before and the ball he had attended. She was fresh and charming and innocent despite the flirtation she had engaged in quite boldly. There was a sparkle about her and an unmistakable enjoyment of life—qualities to which he was unaccustomed in a woman. He had been unexpectedly dazzled by them. He had stopped at a florist's on his way home from his ride this morning and arranged to have a dozen red roses delivered to her. And he was to take her walking in St. James's Park this afternoon. He had thought about it throughout his ride and at breakfast and had looked forward to it more than he could remember looking forward to anything for a long time.

She was of suitably high rank. She was the daughter of an earl. He did not know if she had a fortune, but that point was immaterial to him. He had two vast fortunes, one that he had earned for himself and the one that had come with his title and properties two years before.

She was the bride Theo had picked out for him. Doubtless Theo had chosen her because she was his mistress's goddaughter, but even so his uncle would not have been swayed by that fact alone. And she had a body that he could contemplate with some pleasure having beneath his own on a bed.

If he had sons, preferably more than one, there would be greater stability in the family because the succession would be assured.

Luke sauntered downstairs only a little after his half hour was up and entered the morning room to find a visibly impatient Lord Severidge pacing the floor. Of course, Luke thought as they left the house together, William ramming his hat onto his wig while Luke more fashionably carried his beneath his right arm, he had no wish to marry, now or ever.

But sometimes one's personal wishes seemed to count for little.

## 5

"I DID enjoy the ball," Lady Agnes Marlowe protested. "Oh yes, of course I did, Anna." She gazed down at one of the two nosegays she had been sent this morning from two of last night's dancing partners and twirled it between her fingers.

"But . . . ?" Anna prompted, smiling gently.

"But nothing," Agnes said. "It is lovely to be in town, Anna. 'Tis something I shall always remember with pleasure. I merely remarked to you that I cannot imagine how some people make a life of such frivolity."

Anna sighed. "I want you to find a husband here, Agnes," she said. "Someone of your own rank. Someone with whom you can be happy. There is no one of any interest at home. Charlotte was fortunate, but there is no one for you."

"No, I know," Agnes said. "But I am only eighteen. I am not past marriageable age yet." She flushed and looked anxiously into her sister's face to see if she had hurt her. "When Aunt Marjorie was urging us to come, Anna, and you were so eager to accept her invitation, I agreed because I thought perhaps you would find someone here. I believe you enjoyed the ball. You looked wonderfully happy and ten times prettier than any other lady present. Did you see that French lady? With her great circles of rouge? She looked . . . strange."

"The Marquise d'Étienne," Anna said.

"And the Duke of Harndon?" Agnes said. "I thought he must be French, too, until Lord Quinn presented him to us as his nephew.

Anna, you had to dance with him and take supper with him. I would have been terrified."

"Terrified?" Anna looked at her strangely.

"I have never seen a gentleman dressed as he was," Agnes said. "Actually he was rather splendid, was he not? But there was something about him, Anna. Something about his eyes, I believe. I think he must be different as a person from what his appearance indicated."

Anna smiled. "He was very charming," she said. "And very amusing. He is to call on Aunt Marjorie today and take me walking in St. James's Park afterward. Apparently it is the fashionable place to stroll."

"Oh," Agnes said. "A duke. And young and very handsome, Anna, despite the powder and rouge. I am glad for you. I am glad that important gentlemen are noticing how lovely you are."

Anna laughed. "I do not believe he is on the verge of declaring undying love for me, Agnes," she said. "'Tis just a walk we are taking— if he has not forgotten, that is."

Agnes set down her own nosegay and touched one of the red roses that had been delivered for her sister. "They are from him?" she asked. "I was so surprised by my own nosegays that I did not even ask about your bouquet. It is from him?"

Anna nodded.

"Well, then," Agnes said, "I do not believe he will forget to take you walking. I will be so happy for you if you find someone, Anna. You deserve happiness more than anyone else I know. We all thought at one time that Sir Lovatt Blaydon . . ."

*That name.* "No!" Anna said hastily, getting to her feet and picking up her bouquet to take upstairs to her own room.

"I know he was old enough to be your father," Agnes said. "I always thought that rather a pity. But he was very kind to us all, and he was very particular in his attentions to you."

"He was merely being neighborly," Anna said. She bent her head to smell one of the blossoms, feeling slightly dizzy. "And he had been acquainted with Mama's family."

"It was always you he asked for first when he came calling,"

Agnes said, smiling, "and he was always disappointed if you were from home. He used to take you for drives and walks and he used to dance only with you at the assemblies. We all thought he had a tendre for you, Anna."

"No," Anna said. "These roses need water. I must take them up and have a vase brought."

"I am sorry," Agnes said. "I have upset you. Did he offer and you refused, Anna? Is that why he left so soon after Papa's death, when we all thought he might have stayed so that you would have had someone to lean on?"

Anna repressed a shudder. "No," she said. "There was nothing, Agnes. Nothing at all. As you said, he was an older man. He had no interest in me beyond a neighborly friendliness, or I in him."

"Well, 'tis as well," Agnes said. "He was too old for you. The Duke of Harndon is a much younger man. Perhaps he has a tendre for you." She laughed as her sister effected a hasty retreat.

Anna hurried upstairs as if to outdistance demons at her heels. She lowered her face close to the roses again as she entered her dressing room, and breathed in their scent. A dozen red roses. Roses as red as the coat he had worn last night. And the card. She read it again and noted the boldness of his handwriting: "With the compliments of your obedient servant, Harndon." Purely formal and conventional words. They made her heart race.

She could not shake off last night's mood. She could not bring herself back to sober good sense. She could not feel the regret she knew she should feel that she had agreed to walk with the duke this afternoon. She wondered how he would look today. Away from the glitter and splendor of the ball, would he look quite ordinary? Would he no longer resemble Prince Charming in her mind? She must hope so. She must hope that after this afternoon the magic would be gone.

Sir Lovatt Blaydon. Anna closed her eyes and bowed her head, the roses clutched against her long after they should have been put into water. Yes, everyone had liked him—everyone in her family and everyone in the neighborhood, except perhaps Emily, but then Emily

very often did not react as other people did. He had deceived everyone with his elegant good looks and warm charm.

He had arrived in the neighborhood only days after Mama's
death, having leased a house that was going to be empty indefinitely.
He had known Mama's family and Mama, too, a long time ago. It
was pure coincidence, he had said, that he had come to that particular
place to take up his abode and had then discovered that he had once
been acquainted with the recently deceased Lady Royce. His concern
and sympathy had appeared very genuine. He had been so very kind
and so very comforting, especially to her, Anna. She had nursed her
mother for years and had scarcely left her bedside for weeks. She had
been physically and emotionally drained after the death and funeral.

Sir Lovatt Blaydon had been someone on whom to lean. There
had been no one else. Her father had already been a broken man, and
Victor had returned to university after the funeral. Besides, Victor
had been only nineteen years old.

She had leaned on Sir Lovatt. She had come to look forward to
his frequent visits. She had even confided some of her worries to
him—worries about her father, worries about the girls and their future. He had been kind and understanding.

Anna opened her eyes and stared blankly at her roses for a few
moments. And then she crossed her dressing room with resolute
steps and pulled the bell rope. They must have water. They were
beautiful. And they were from him, her Prince Charming. She smiled
at the thought.

Yes, she would concentrate on today. Today might be all she ever
had. Then she smiled again at the rather self-pitying thought.

*Luke* had wondered if perhaps he would be less dazzled by Lady
Anna Marlowe in the light of day, without the trappings of a grand
ball surrounding her. But she was as brightly lovely and as vivacious
this afternoon as she had been last evening.

They strolled along the straight, treelined Mall in St. James's
Park, acknowledging among the crowds also walking there those
people they knew, occasionally stopping to exchange pleasantries

with acquaintances, but mostly walking and talking exclusively to each other. One thing experience had taught him was that women liked to feel that they had the whole of a man's attention. He never allowed his attention to stray appreciatively to any other woman when he was with one in particular.

But it was not difficult to focus all his attention on Lady Anna. She sparkled as she had done the night before and her green eyes danced with merriment as she described to him the agony and the absurdity of standing for hours while a mantua maker fitted her out for a whole new wardrobe.

"It seemed that the clothes I brought from the country were fit for nothing but the dustbin," she said, "though I made very sure that they were not put there. Even the servants, Madame Delacroix hinted, would be insulted to be presented with garments so far out of fashion." She laughed merrily.

A woman who could laugh at herself, he thought, was one not overly given to conceit.

"I would wager, madam," he said, "that you looked more lovely in your country clothes than many a lady decked out in the latest Parisian mode."

She laughed again.

She looked very handsome indeed in her new clothes. His eyes appreciated the wide-brimmed straw hat she wore tilted slightly forward over her frilled lace cap and tied with blue ribbons at the nape of her neck. And he admired the graceful flow of the loosely pleated back of her sack dress, the bodice fitted tightly over her neat figure in front, English fashion, and opened to reveal an embroidered stomacher.

They talked on easily about trivialities while his mind returned unwillingly to the thoughts he had had during the morning. What would it be like, he wondered, to live permanently with this woman? Was she always so brightly cheerful? So amusing and even witty? Would he tire of the brightness, the frivolity? Were there any depths to her character that were not apparent on first acquaintance?

And what would it be like to have her as a bedfellow for the rest of his life? She was lovely. He felt a definite stirring of desire as he unclothed her with knowing and expert eyes and mentally placed her back against the mattress of his bed. Yes, he would certainly enjoy making love to her. But for a lifetime? He had had some of the most lovely and most sexually accomplished beauties of France to bed and yet had tired of every single one of them after a few months. Although he had spent two satisfactory afternoons in Angélique's bed since their arrival in England, in truth he was tired of her. He had neither expected nor wanted her to follow him to London.

Would he not tire of an innocent far sooner? She would know nothing. She would have no idea how to give him pleasure beyond submitting to having her body penetrated. He would have to teach her everything. And teach her how to receive pleasure without guilt or embarrassment.

She smiled brightly across at him in response to a story he had told about his rather stormy crossing of the English Channel and its effect on his fellow passengers. Oh yes, but there was some appeal in the thought of giving instruction to such lovely and sprightly innocence.

But it was a lifetime he was thinking of.

He was the Duke of Harndon, he reminded himself. That fact and the fact of his vast fortune must be common knowledge. And of course so would be the fact that he was thirty years old and unmarried. He was, he supposed, one of the biggest matrimonial prizes in London this spring, if not the biggest. He had never had to consider those facts before in the two years since he had succeeded his brother. He had never before considered matrimony.

And was he seriously considering it now? Part of his mind rushed into an instant denial. But another part of his mind . . .

It was altogether possible that Lady Anna Marlowe, who was somewhat past the age of twenty if his guess was not quite wide of the mark, had set out to net him. She had her godmother and his uncle on her side. And she had gone out of her way last evening to attract his notice and to hold it. She had been quite openly flirtatious. Perhaps the real Lady Anna was quite different from the one who sparkled and laughed up at him now. Perhaps she was a shrew. Perhaps after they were married she would show herself in her true colors.

*After they were married?*

He needed to be exceedingly careful.

He took his leave of her an hour later in the hall of Lady Sterne's house, bowing over her hand and kissing it as he did so. "I have enjoyed this afternoon's walk more than anything else since my return to England except for one hour of last evening's ball," he said. "For which I have you to thank, madam."

"And I you, your grace," she said. "I had no idea that life in town could be so—so very enjoyable."

He spoke from impulse. "I plan to escort my mother and my sister to the theater tomorrow evening," he said, "and to invite a few other guests to join us in my box there. Would you do me the honor of being one of their number, madam? And your sister and godmother, too?" he added hastily as an afterthought.

He was given again the impression that Lady Anna Marlowe was no coquette. She leaned slightly toward him, her lips parting, her eyes coming alight, and answered almost before he had finished speaking.

"Oh yes, your grace," she said. "That would be lovely. I have never been to the theater and have always longed to watch a play being performed. It is a play?"

He inclined his head. *"The Beggar's Opera,"* he said. "A very successful work by the late Mr. John Gay."

"Oh, yes," she said. "I have heard of it."

He made her one of his deepest bows. "Until tomorrow evening, then, madam," he said. "The hours between now and then will crawl by."

He left her standing in the hall, smiling. What the devil was happening to him? he wondered. *The hours between now and then will crawl by.* He was accustomed to uttering such gallantries to women who clearly knew that he was trying to maneuver them into a liaison. They were not the sort of words he was in the habit of speaking to innocent young ladies of quality whom he could neither wish nor hope to bed this side of a wedding ceremony.

And yet he had spoken the words to Lady Anna Marlowe— one scant hour after he had cautioned himself to be very careful.

And what had prompted him to say he planned to take his mother and Doris to the theater? Some responsibility for the latter he might reluctantly acknowledge, but he desired no social inter-course with his family. He had planned to go to the theater himself since *The Beggar's Opera* was a play he wished to see and since the subscription on his family box at the theater had been kept up even after George's death. But he had not planned to take a party there. Thank the Lord that at least he had thought to include the sister and Lady Sterne in the invitation.

He supposed that he should call on his mother again to issue the invitation.

Damnation, he thought. His mother, in particular, was someone with whom he did not really wish to renew relations. He had not forgiven her and doubted that he ever would or could. And during his own brief visit to her and the meeting at last evening's ball she had shown no sign of wishing forgiveness. Perhaps she still believed he had tried to kill George. Damnation. He wished he had stayed in Paris and consigned them all to hell.

He turned his steps in the direction of his ducal town house.

*Anna* sat with Agnes and Lady Sterne in the Duke of Harndon's box at the Covent Garden theater the following evening and gazed about her in wonder and awe. Her desire to see London, to attend balls and concerts there, to sit in a theater and watch a play or listen to an opera, had been so suppressed in her during her youth and the early years of her adulthood that she had been scarcely aware of them before coming here. It had all, she supposed, seemed to be such an impossibility.

She was here, she told herself. She was really here. And it was all more wonderful than anything she might have imagined. She had given up all caution during the past few days. It was silly, she had persuaded herself, to stop herself from enjoying these two months only because she knew they must come to an end. She was going to enjoy them and she was going to enjoy the company of the duke and flirt with him, too, for as long as he gave her the opportunity. Once she had returned home, she would never see him again. It would not matter what sort of an impression she left behind with him.

She looked over her shoulder to where he was standing, greeting Lord Quinn and a tall, handsome young man, who had just entered the box together. The duke was wearing a gold coat tonight and a scarlet waistcoat. He was wearing his cosmetics again, something he had not done on their walk yesterday. She wondered how long his hair was inside the black silk bag. She wondered what color it was in its natural state, beneath the carefully applied white powder.

The handsome young man was Lord Ashley Kendrick, the Duke of Harndon's younger brother. He smiled at her and bowed deeply when he was presented. He shared his brother's charm, Anna thought, though he smiled more easily than the duke. Apart from that they were unalike. He greeted Lady Sterne and took a seat beside Agnes, who looked painfully shy, Anna thought, despite his charm.

The duke's mother and his sister, who had come with the two gentlemen, would arrive any moment. They had stopped outside in the corridor to exchange a few words with a friend, Lord Quinn explained as he sat beside Lady Sterne.

She and her family and he and his. It was very significant, Lady Sterne had commented when she knew of the invitation. She had smiled and nodded knowingly. And it was extremely satisfactory. It was what she had hoped for from the first. The Duke of Harndon was, of course, Lord Quinn's nephew, and very wealthy with vast estates, Bowden Abbey in Hampshire being the principal one. And he was going to present her to his mother. Very promising indeed.

Anna had felt instant alarm. And yet there was no need to do so, she had told herself. It was ridiculous. He had danced with her and taken supper with her at Lady Diddering's ball. He had walked with her during an afternoon in St. James's Park. And he was escorting her to the theater—with her sister and her godmother. There was hardly cause for alarm there even though the other members of his party belonged to his family. After all, he must be the most eligible gentleman in London. He was also the most fashionable and one of the most handsome. It would be absurd to imagine that he was even beginning to think of her in terms of courtship. She would not become alarmed and run from him out of any such fanciful imaginings.

And then the door of the box opened again and two ladies stepped inside. Anna rose to her feet and curtsied as she was presented to the Dowager Duchess of Harndon, an elegant, regal lady who was still handsome, and to Lady Doris Kendrick, a thin-faced, pretty girl with a petulant mouth—or what Anna, who had three younger sisters, thought was probably a petulant mouth.

The dowager acknowledged Lady Sterne's presence and Agnes's with a slight inclination of the head before looking closely at Anna and nodding graciously. "I am pleased to make your acquaintance, Lady Anna," she said. "You are the sister of the young Earl of Royce?"

Anna inclined her head.

"I am sorry for the double bereavement you suffered quite recently," her grace said. "You must be enjoying your visit to town now that your official term of mourning is over."

Lady Doris seated herself to one side of Anna and smiled at her. "I wondered if it was you," she said. "I saw Luke dance with you at Lady Diddering's ball and I thought how lovely your gown was. I wondered if 'twas you he was escorting here tonight. 'Tis wonderful to have him back home from Paris, Lady Anna. You cannot imagine. I was but a young child when he went away ten years ago." She leaned a little closer and spoke more quietly. "Papa was very strict and George—my oldest brother who was duke for three years—was aloof. And now Luke has the title. I have been hoping beyond hope that he would come home to stay. We have all been hoping it."

He had been in Paris for ten years and had not returned home even on the death of his father or that of his brother? Or since then until now? He had not seen his young sister for ten years? It seemed strange to Anna. Had his life been so devoted to frivolity that he had no use for his family or home? Or for his responsibilities as the Duke of Harndon? She could not imagine anyone so frivolous or so heartless that he could turn his back on his family.

But he was with them now.

"Perhaps," Lady Doris whispered, "you can keep him in England and bring him home to Bowden Abbey, Lady Anna."

Anna was relieved of the necessity of answering by one more arrival, that of a slightly portly, florid, flustered young man, who looked as much out of place in this London theater as Anna and Agnes had looked just a couple of weeks before. He was presented as Baron Severidge, who lived close to Bowden Abbey. He acknowledged his new acquaintances with a quick bobbing of the head and plopped himself down on the chair next to Agnes that Lord Ashley had briefly vacated. Anna felt uncharitably annoyed for her sister's sake.

But she soon forgot all else when she became aware of a stirring of heightened interest in the theater. The play was about to begin. The Duke of Harndon seated himself on her other side. Anna turned her head to smile at him and then concentrated her attention on the stage.

The music and the action enthralled her. For an hour or more she saw and heard nothing else. She forgot about herself and about her surroundings. She had never experienced anything so wonderful in all her life. But finally the need to share her wonder caused her to turn her head in the duke's direction.

He was leaning back in his chair watching her, not the stage. She looked into his face a little uncertainly. He was holding his fan, closed, in his lap. He lifted it and ran the tip of it lightly along her hand, which was resting on the velvet edge of the box, from her wrist to the end of her middle finger. He did not take his eyes from hers. He did not smile.

It felt as if some deep intimacy had passed between them. If she had to get to her feet at this moment, Anna thought as she turned her eyes but not her attention back to the stage, she would not be able to do it.

For the rest of the evening, she was aware of him seated close beside her with every single fiber in her body.

Anna sat beside the duke and opposite her sister and godmother in the darkened carriage on the return journey, her heightened awareness of him making the space seem smaller and almost suffocating. He did not touch her though she could feel his body heat with the arm closest to him.

"You enjoyed the play?" he asked her.

She turned a dazzling smile on him though she could barely see him in the darkness. "Oh, yes," she said. "It was wonderful. Even more wonderful than I imagined it would be. Did you not think so?"

Her godmother, Anna noted, was talking rather animatedly to Agnes. Anna suspected that Lady Sterne was tactfully trying to give her some semblance of privacy.

"I enjoyed the *evening*," the duke said quietly, emphasizing the last word. "I am afraid my mind was distracted from the play."

"Oh," she said. The word came out as a breathless little sigh.

He said nothing, but held her eyes for a few moments before she smiled at him again and turned her attention to the seat opposite.

When they arrived at Lady Sterne's house, the Duke of Harndon stepped inside with them. But he set a staying hand on Anna's arm as her sister and godmother proceeded upstairs. He waited until they had reached the top of the staircase.

"I would ask leave, madam," he said, "to call on you tomorrow morning to discuss a matter of some importance with you."

Tomorrow morning? A matter of some importance? Anna's heart began to beat uncomfortably and her mind began to race too fast for rational thought.

"Yes, of course, your grace," she said. She sounded, she thought, as if she had just run a mile against a stiff wind.

There was a further short silence.

"You are of age, madam?" he asked.

"Yes." Her eyes widened. "I am five-and-twenty, your grace. I am perhaps older than you expected." Suddenly she was desperate to make herself seem quite unattractive to him. Perhaps she had misunderstood him. Surely she had. But why had he asked if she was of age?

"I would not, then," he said, "have to talk with your brother in advance of discussing any matter with you?"

She stared at him wide-eyed. "No," she said, her voice a whisper.

And then Lady Sterne reappeared on the stairs to invite the duke to come up for refreshments. He refused politely, bowed to both of them, and took his leave.

"Faith, child," Lady Sterne said, coming the rest of the way down, linking her arm through Anna's and leading her back in the direction of the stairs, "you look a handsome couple. And I declare, he had eyes for no one but you all evening. I believe 'tis not being overfanciful to expect a declaration before summer."

"Aunt Marjorie!" Anna exclaimed in dismay. Though in truth— why was he going to call tomorrow?

"Agnes is waiting in the drawing room," Lady Sterne said, leading her goddaughter up the stairs. "We will all three plan the wedding over tea before retiring for the night." She laughed merrily.

Anna, entering the drawing room with her, wished more than anything that she could go directly to her room and lock her doors, even against her mind. She felt slightly sick to the stomach.

# 6

*L*UKE had the distinct feeling that he had started something he could not stop and that he had started it from a wholly mad impulse without giving it due thought—or any thought at all. He ate his way doggedly through breakfast, though he felt as much like eating as he would feel like jumping into a pit filled with vipers.

He thought carefully back over what he had said last night. Had there been any ambiguity in his meaning? Anything that would enable him to withdraw honorably? Could he perhaps make it seem that he had merely intended to ask her to walk with him again? Or drive with him?

The answer to all his questions was a decisive no. He had said he would call on her this morning. The afternoon was the more normal time for social calls. And he had said he had a matter of some importance to discuss with her. A walk? Hardly. He had asked if she was of age. And then—Luke grimaced and gave up the effort to finish eating the final slice of toast—he had said that he need not, then, consult her brother before discussing the important matter with her.

No, indeed. The lady would have to be an imbecile not to have understood his meaning, and he suspected that Lady Anna Marlowe was not that even if she did not have any great depth of character.

He had done it, then. Having spent ten years building a life for himself in which he was independent and a law unto himself, he had capitulated within three days—*three days!*—under the burdens of ducal and family responsibilities. He did not want any of them. He wanted to go back to Paris and resume the way of life which had suited him for many years. He wanted to forget England and his family. He wanted George alive again and the father of ten healthy sons. He wanted to be simply Lord Lucas Kendrick again.

But one could not always have what one wanted. He could not go back. Worse, he could only step forward now in the direction he had set for himself last night with an impulsiveness that had been foreign to him since his boyhood. And yet not so impulsive after all, perhaps. Events had been pushing him toward it since before his return and certainly since then.

He could only wish that he could go upstairs now to dress and proceed on his way to Lady Sterne's with all haste. He wanted the matter over and done with now that he had made it inevitable. But one could not call on a lady this early in the morning. He did not know how he was to fill in the hour or so until he could decently go.

But the problem was solved for him by the announcement that his brother had called and was begging the favor of a word with him. Luke got gratefully to his feet and tossed his napkin onto the table.

"Ah, Ashley," he said, strolling into the hall, where his brother was standing, examining a sculpted Venus, whose flowing and transparent draperies were so molded to her body by an unfelt breeze that she might as well have been naked. "Come into the library and tell me to what I owe the honor."

Lord Ashley Kendrick grinned at him and strode toward the room indicated. "I was not sure you would be up at this hour, Luke," he said. "Egad, but that is the devil of a fine morning gown you are wearing. 'Tis almost as bright a red as the coat you wore to the Diddering ball."

"Have a seat." Luke indicated a chair beside the fireplace and took the one across from it. His brother, he noted, tall and slender and handsome, wore his fashionable clothes with a somewhat careless air. A typical Englishman.

"That was the devil of a fine play at Covent Garden last evening," Ashley said. "Fine music too."

"I thought so," Luke agreed. "But then, I do not believe I have ever seen a poor production of that particular play."

"Zounds, no," Ashley said. "And Lady Anna Marlowe is the devil of a fine lady. Doris said so on the way home and Mama agreed. I believe she has hopes." He flashed his brother a charming and mischievous smile. "Hopes of your becoming respectable at last, Luke."

"Indeed?" Luke said softly, raising his eyebrows. He had been watching his brother's hands opening and closing on the arms of his chair. There was a general air of tension about him despite the bright geniality. "But you did not call here to discuss the play or to compliment me on my taste in women, my dear. What is on your mind?"

Ashley grinned again. "Nothing of any great import," he said. "Colby has been overstepping his bounds."

"My steward?" Luke said. "What has he done that affects you?"

"He has returned all my bills to me in a neat bundle, that is what," Ashley said. "Pox on it, Luke, can you imagine the insolence of the man? Said I had overspent this quarter's allowance again and he could not pay 'em without your permission—for which I was to ask, not he."

Luke held out one hand, at which his brother stared blankly.

"The bills?" Luke said.

Ashley flushed. "I did not bring them," he said. "All you have to do, Luke, if you will, is instruct Colby to pay 'em and not be such an ass in the future."

"Bills of what nature?" Luke asked.

"Coats, waistcoats, shoes, canes, hats—how the devil should I know what they are for?" Ashley said perhaps a little too casually. "Be a good fellow, Luke. I never wished harm on George, I swear, but there was one thing I was glad of when he passed on and that was that you were then head of the family. You were always easygoing. I remember how you used to have the patience to play with me and with Doris too when we were children even though you were years older than us."

"And any other debts?" Luke asked, refusing to be diverted. "Gaming debts, for example?"

Ashley's flush returned. "As I live," he said, "you are trying to get me to bare my soul, Luke. I suppose there are some. A fellow wins and a fellow loses. It is in the nature of gaming."

"When one consistently loses more than one wins," Luke said, "perhaps it is in the nature of the player, my dear."

"Pox on it," Ashley said, shifting position uncomfortably in his chair, "must you call me 'my dear' in that soft voice, Luke, as if I was a girl? Are you saying I am not a good player?"

"I made a statement," Luke said, "not an accusation."

"Egad, you are not going to cut up funny, are you?" his brother asked, frowning. "You do not know what it is, Luke, to have to live on a pitiful allowance when there are appearances to keep up. You spend a fortune on clothes—I've seen some of 'em. I don't need any expert to tell me they are Paris's finest. Do you want your brother to look like a pauper?"

Luke took a snuffbox from the pocket of his gown and proceeded to take some snuff. He looked inquiringly at his brother and offered the box, but Ashley shook his head.

"Perhaps you forget," Luke said, "that until two years ago I was also a younger brother, Ashley."

"You have expensive tastes," Ashley said. "I will wager Colby never refused to settle any of your bills."

Luke looked at him steadily from beneath lowered eyelids. "No, he did not," he said. "None of my bills were ever sent to Colby—or to Father or George. My allowance was stopped the quarter after I left home."

His brother gaped at him.

"You will send me your bills later today," Luke said. "I will pay them, but I will see them first. I will also make enquiries about the nature and amount of your allowance and increase it if I deem an increase to be called for. Beginning next quarter I will expect you to live on it."

"Live on it?" Ashley had turned quite pale. "Impossible, Luke. I would have to live at home."

Luke raised his eyebrows.

Ashley got to his feet. "Word travels," he said. "We have heard all sorts of things about you over the years, Luke—about your prominence at the French court, about your duels, about your fine women. I believed it all except for one thing. Word has had it that you are a heartless man, that you have feelings for nothing beyond your own pleasures. I always refused to believe that. I remembered the older brother who used to play with me and whom I used to worship. Deuce take it, I am not sure that brother is still alive."

"He is not," Luke said softly. "He died a violent death ten years ago. George was the only survivor of that particular duel."

Ashley strode across the room to the door. But he stopped with his hand on the knob and looked at the back of his brother's head. "I'll send the bills," he said. There was a short silence. His voice was stiff when he spoke again. "I thank you for taking care of them."

Luke heard the door open and close again. Ah. He set his head back against the high back of his chair and closed his eyes. He had just made an enemy and in the worst possible way. He had humiliated his brother. Ashley had already been embarrassed at having to come to him, begging to have his unpaid bills settled. And instead of waving a careless hand and saying that yes, of course he would send the required note to Colby, and then changing the subject, he had reached out a hand to take the bills he had known Ashley would not have brought with him.

Why had he done it? To try to teach his brother some sense of responsibility? To try to punish him because he, Luke, had not had a chance in his twenty-third year to be the pampered, irresponsible younger brother?

He could recall those times Ashley had referred to. He had been very much the older brother, at home far more often than George. The younger ones had always adored him, much as he had adored George. And he had responded to them in kind, giving them his time and his patience and his affection. The tall young man he had just allowed to leave, angry and shamed, was that same eager boy he had climbed trees with and taught to swim and taken fishing.

A long, long time ago. A lifetime ago.

The point was he had forgotten how to love. More than that, he had taught himself not to love, not to lay himself open to hurt and humiliation and betrayal. He had been happy for almost ten years— as happy as one could be when the dimension of love had been cut from one's life.

And yet now, having hurt and humiliated his brother, he felt almost guilty. But there was no need. A man had no business living beyond his means and then expecting someone else to foot the bills without question—even when the paying would not put even the smallest of dents in that someone's fortune.

Ashley had something of life to learn, and the sooner he learned it the better for him. The better he would be able to survive in a hard world. Sentiment had been all very well between a child and a youth. There was no room for sentiment between adults.

No, he need not feel guilty for the way he had handled this particular situation, Luke decided.

And then he sat up abruptly and got to his feet. He had something else to think about this morning. He glanced at the clock on the mantel. It was high time he got dressed and was on his way to Lady Sterne's.

At least Ashley's visit had served one purpose, he thought as he climbed the stairs after giving directions that his valet was to be sent up to his dressing room promptly. It had taken his mind off what was perhaps to be the most fateful hour of his life.

He would not think about it, he decided. He would merely think about his appearance. Something a little more formal than usual for morning wear but not vulgarly ostentatious for the time of day.

He longed suddenly for Paris and the pleasurable routine of his days there. Ashley's visit and his own handling of the situation had depressed him more than he cared to admit.

*Anna* was sitting in the morning room with Lady Sterne. They were working on their embroidery and talking about the social events that were coming up in the next week. Most notable was another ball—Lord and Lady Castle's—this evening. Agnes was out shopping with one of her new friends and the girl's mama.

"Perhaps Agnes will meet someone at the ball more to her taste than anyone she has met so far," Anna said. "Several gentleman have looked as if they might be interested, given a little encouragement. But Agnes has not given any. I did think last evening that perhaps Lord Ashley Kendrick . . . But when he got up for a moment, Lord Severidge took his place beside Agnes. I felt quite provoked, though the poor man appeared perfectly civil."

"One must remember that Agnes is only eighteen years of age," Lady Sterne reminded her. "But she is a sensible girl nonetheless. She is one little lady, I vow, who will not grab the first opportunity for matrimony that presents itself unless the gentleman is to her liking. You must not be anxious on her account, Anna. She will do very nicely, given time."

"Oh, but I am anxious," Anna said with a sigh. "Victor is so very young himself and about to marry. He will not wish to be encumbered with two unmarried sisters and the duty of finding them husbands—not that Emily is of marriageable age yet and not that it is likely that anyone will be willing to marry her despite her great sweetness. Not at least without a large dowry, which she just does not have."

"Two unmarried sisters," Lady Sterne said, clucking her tongue. "I notice you do not include yourself, child, having concluded, I vow, that you are too old to be marriageable."

Anna flushed and thought of what she had been trying desperately to forget all morning. Not that she had forgotten for a single moment. She glanced down at the new dress she wore even though it was only morning—her godmother had commented on how grand she looked for so early in the day. And she had not told her godmother. It was something that ought to be told.

"I-I almost f-forgot," she said, hearing in dismay that she was stammering, something she had not done for years. "The Duke of Harndon said he might call this morning."

"*Might?*" Lady Sterne looked up sharply, her needle suspended

above her work. "This *morning?* Lud, child, 'tis as I have thought and
hoped. He is coming to declare himself."

"Oh, no," Anna said in some distress. "Merely to pay his compliments, Aunt Marjorie. I daresay he thinks to ascertain that we enjoyed the visit to the theater last evening."

"Faith, child," Lady Sterne said, folding her embroidery away
and setting it on the table at her elbow, "you are the cool one. He said
no more? No more about the purpose of his visit?"

"N-no," Anna lied. "No more. Perhaps he will not even come. He
merely said he might—in a very offhand manner. I daresay he will
not come."

*I would ask leave, madam, to call on you tomorrow morning to discuss
a matter of some importance with you.*

His words had burned themselves into her memory. And if there
had been any possibility that he had meant something different from
what had seemed his obvious meaning, his following words had dis-
pelled all doubt. He had asked if she was of age. When she had told
him her age, he had commented that he did not then have to speak
with Victor before discussing the matter with her.

He was going to offer her marriage.

Her certainty that that was what he had meant had given her a
largely sleepless night, a night of waking nightmares.

He must be refused, of course. She had no choice at all in the
matter. Even if Sir Lovatt Blaydon never returned from America, she
had no choice. She could never marry. But the truth was that he
might return, that he had said he would. And if and when he returned, she was bound to him more closely than ever slave was
bound to master. Lying in bed, alternatively sweating from the heat
and shivering from the cold, she had remembered—and could not
stop remembering—his setting his hands loosely about her neck on
one occasion and slightly, ever so slightly tightening them as he had
described to her how a rope was tied about a condemned criminal's
neck, the knot beneath one ear, and how the rope, after the trapdoor
had been released, did not always break the neck but often strangled.
She had well nigh fainted.

The Duke of Harndon must be refused. This morning should not even be difficult to face. He would ask; she would refuse; he would take his leave. It was all very simple. Except that she knew that during the few minutes of his visit she would be faced with perhaps the greatest temptation of her life.

The longing—oh, the desperate, desperate longing—to escape from herself and from the reality of her life was almost beyond bearing. She had been wrong to give in to the temptation to taste life. Now that she had tasted it, she was ravenous for the whole feast. But like a deadly poison it could only kill her.

Literally kill her.

"I daresay he will not come," she said more briskly to her godmother, and she smiled. "'Tis the sort of thing gentlemen say, I think, when escorting ladies home."

"Mercy on me!" Lady Sterne said, shaking her head.

But she had no chance to say more. The butler opened the door to ask if her ladyship and Lady Anna would receive his grace, the Duke of Harndon.

Anna closed her eyes very tightly, but she opened them quickly. Dizziness felt worse with closed eyes.

He was wearing emerald green and gold. He looked to Anna's eyes more splendid and more handsome than she had ever seen him. But perhaps that was because he was no longer a Prince Charming with whom she dared to flirt, but a man who had come to tempt her. A man she must reject and send away forever. Gone already, after only a few brief stolen days, was the wonderful exhilaration of stepping outside her own character and circumstances to flirt with London's most dazzling beau. The fairy tale was at an end.

She thought for a while that she had been mistaken after all. He sat and conversed with both her and Lady Sterne for perhaps fifteen minutes, displaying an easy grace and charm that seemed to belie any further motive for his visit. But finally, just when Anna was beginning to relax, he spoke the words she had dreaded to hear. For a moment they scarcely registered on her mind. He had turned to address himself to her godmother.

"Madam," he said, "might I beg the favor of a few minutes alone with Lady Anna to discuss a private matter?"

Lady Sterne got immediately to her feet, smiling warmly and graciously. "Since she is past girlhood and does not need to be so carefully chaperoned, yes, Harndon," she said. "But not for longer than ten minutes. I shall return."

Anna got to her feet while the duke crossed the room to open the door for her godmother. She walked to the window without realizing what she did and gazed out with sightless eyes. She could hear her heartbeat loud in her ears. She could feel it in her throat, robbing her of breath.

God. *Please, dear God. Please, dear God,* she prayed silently and frantically. But she knew such prayers to be futile. God had been silent in her life for years. God had not been kind to her. Or perhaps God was testing her, as he had tested Job, to see how much she could endure before breaking. Sometimes she felt that she was teetering on the brink.

His voice came from close behind her. "Madam," he said softly, "I believe you must know why I have come this morning and what it is I have to say to you."

*Turn. Tell him now. Look puzzled and tell him that no, you have no idea. No, not that. Look serious. Look troubled. Tell him that it distresses you to know that he has misunderstood the situation. Tell him there is some-one else. Someone at home, waiting.* But she shuddered at the thought of the man who might even now be there, waiting for her to return.

She turned. But in doing so, she donned her mask. She had not thought of it as a mask before but merely as the manifestation of how she felt and how she wanted to feel until it was time to go home again. But now it was a mask. She smiled brightly and parted her lips and made her eyes shine.

"But no, your grace," she said. "No woman dare know any such thing. What if she is wrong? Consider her embarrassment." She laughed at him. She wanted to see one more time that answering gleam in his own eyes. She felt the deep feminine need to feel power over a man, the power to attract. For one last time.

And she watched herself and listened to herself, dismayed and confused. And desperately unhappy.

"You are quite right." His eyes looked at her keenly from beneath their lazy lids, an incongruity that had the power to turn her knees weak. "Forgive me. This sort of situation is not in my everyday experience."

He took her right hand in his and turned it palm up to rest in his left hand. He set his other hand flat on top of it. Hands touching. Her own sandwiched between his. It felt impossibly intimate. Anna felt a sudden ache in her throat.

And then he startled her by going down on one knee and not looking even remotely ridiculous as he did so.

"Madam," he said. "Lady Anna, will you honor me and make me the happiest of men by becoming my wife?"

The words had been spoken. The words she had expected and prepared herself for. Words that would not somehow form themselves into any meaning inside her brain. She gazed downward into his eyes and leaned slightly toward him. And then the meaning was there, the code of his words unscrambled.

They were the words she had expected and prepared herself for. And as new and as wonderful as the sun rising over and over again each morning. She could become his wife. She could step out into freedom and happiness and leave everything behind her, like a snake shedding an old skin. She could be his wife.

No, she could not.

She tried. "Your grace," she said, her voice little more than a whisper, "I have no fortune. Perhaps you did not know. My father lost almost everything through n-no f-fault of his own, and my brother is young and has not yet had a chance to recover. I have no dowry."

"I ask only for you," he said, getting to his feet again but not relinquishing her hand. "I have fortune enough. It does not need to be augmented."

He wanted her. Her. With no other inducement. Just her.

She tried again. "I am five-and-twenty, your grace," she said. "You must want a younger bride."

"I want a bride exactly your age," he said. "Whatever that age happens to be. I want you."

He wanted her. Oh, dear God, dear God, he wanted her.

"I-I have sisters," she said. "Two sisters, for whom I feel responsible now that my mother and father are both dead. My brother is too young to take responsibility for them except financially. I must go home to look after them."

"Your sisters," he said, "may live with us if it is what you wish. And if it is their lack of a dowry that makes you fear for their future, then I will supply them with a dowry."

Her fears for Emily went far beyond the lack of a dowry. But he was willing to give Emily a home and Agnes too, and dowries in return for her marrying him. He wanted her that badly.

"Are there other reasons," he asked, "why I should hesitate to press my suit? Any other dark secrets, Lady Anna?"

Only the fact that she might be thrown in prison for a number of offenses. Or hanged for others—including murder. And the fact that even apart from those reasons, she could never, never marry.

"No," she whispered.

"Well, then." His hands were warm, she realized suddenly, and strong and steady. Comforting and sustaining. "Will you have me? Will you be my duchess?"

If he removed his hands, she would be unable to stand. She would crumple to the floor. And if he removed his hands, there would be no source of heat to her body. She would freeze. If she said no, he would remove his hands. The foolish thoughts teemed through her head, not pausing long enough to be judged for common sense.

"Yes."

The word was whispered but the volume and power of it felt as if they would shatter Anna's brain and her very existence. She could not believe that the word had come from her, and yet no one else could have spoken it. And she was doing nothing to retract it. It floated in the air about her head like a tangible thing.

He had removed his right hand from hers and was raising her hand and setting his lips against her palm, holding back her fingers with his thumb.

"Then you have made me the happiest of men, madam," he said.

The conventional words caressed her like a velvet glove. And sliced into her like a sharp blade.

She smiled dazzlingly at him. Her mask, it seemed, was a mobile thing.

$\mathcal{L}$UKE was thankful for the busy nature of the rest of the day. Lady Sterne, as good as her word, returned to the morning room ten minutes after leaving it. She was delighted at the news, of course. He was convinced that she had planned it all with Theo and was now congratulating herself on the speedy fulfillment of their hopes.

Lady Anna Marlowe did not want a large wedding, the sort that might take a month or more to plan. She wanted only that her brother be summoned; he was less than a day's ride away at the home of his betrothed. She did not want to wait for her youngest sister to be brought—it would take too long.

He was relieved. Now that he had taken the momentous step, without having given himself time for proper consideration, he wanted it all over and done with. He did not want to have to live through weeks and perhaps months of wondering if there was still a way out. There was no way out. He might as well be married so that he could become accustomed to the new fact in his life.

They would marry, he suggested—and she agreed—by special license in three days' time. They would marry in London and remain in London for a while afterward. He could not yet commit himself to going to Bowden. Perhaps it could still be avoided. Yet he knew deep within himself that it could not, that the inevitability of his return there had played a large part in his decision to marry. He was not marrying from personal inclination.

And yet, looking at his betrothed—*his betrothed!*—he was not sure that was strictly true. She smiled and glowed and looked vibrantly beautiful. For the first time he noticed that she must have dressed for the occasion, rather more grandly than was normal for the morning. She was so very obviously happy, though she had been quite honest and open about her disqualifications to be his bride. He wondered if she loved him.

He always felt a distinct unease when he suspected that a woman was in love with him. He had no such emotion to give in return. He always put a decisive end to a liaison when it happened even if he had not yet grown tired of the woman concerned. And yet with Lady Anna Marlowe matters were different. She was to be his wife. And though he could not love her, he felt a certain pleasure in the knowledge that he was to possess that beauty and that happiness and vivacity.

If he must marry someone, he thought as he got to his feet to take his leave—and it seemed that he must—then he would rather marry her than any other woman he had ever met.

Except Henrietta, an inner voice prompted, uninvited. But that had been a lifetime ago.

He bowed over Lady Anna's hand, taking it in both of his again. "Madam," he said, "I trust you will do me the honor of dancing the opening set and the supper set with me at Lord Castle's ball this evening?"

Her smile was radiant. Seen up close, it made him almost take an involuntary step backward.

"Thank you, your grace," she said. "I shall look forward to both sets."

"And I," he said, "will look forward to no others but those two. Your servant." He raised her hand to his lips.

The visit to Harndon House was necessary, he decided reluctantly. He might regret having returned to England and having renewed his acquaintance with his family. But he had done both. It seemed that now he could only go forward. There was no point in wishing that he could go back and decide not to leave Paris or his familiar life there.

His mother and his sister were both at home. They talked to him about last evening's visit to the theater. Doris commented on the fact that he had paid far more attention to Lady Anna Marlowe than to anyone else in his box. She smiled mischievously as she said so.

"I think her rather beautiful," she said. "More so than the Marquise d'Étienne for all her Parisian magnificence."

"Doris!" the dowager duchess said sharply while Luke raised his eyebrows. "Do watch your manners."

Doris winked at Luke.

"Lady Anna Marlowe seems a well-bred young lady," the dowager said to her son. He noticed now, as he had noticed before since his return, that she rarely looked directly at him. "And she is the daughter of the Earl of Royce. She is of suitable rank, Lucas."

"Suitable for what, madam, pray?" he asked, his eyebrows still raised.

"The succession has been uncertain for too long," she said. "And 'tis time Bowden Abbey had an undisputed mistress again—someone who is the wife of the present duke. 'Tis time you set duty before pleasure, Lucas."

"To please you, madam," he said, "I will marry the lady. How will three days from today suit you?"

She looked at him then—suspiciously and somewhat tight-lipped.

"I have come directly from Lady Sterne's," he said, "where I made my offer and was accepted. I am to marry Lady Anna in three days' time."

Doris shrieked and hurtled across the room quite inelegantly to throw herself into his arms and kiss his cheek.

"Luke," she cried, "I knew 'twould happen. I knew you would fall in love with her and marry her and come back home to live. And now everything will be as it used to be. I am so happy I could scream."

"Pray do not, my dear," Luke said faintly.

"Doris!" his mother said sternly.

But Doris was not to be cowed. She linked her hands behind Luke's neck and leaned back the length of her arms. "He is my brother, Mama," she said, "and he is coming home. For all your fine clothes and elegant ways and pretense of ennui, you are still the person you used to be, Luke. I know it and I am glad of it. Oh, la, I am going to like *this* sister-in-law, I declare."

The emphasis she put on the one word suggested that perhaps she did not like her other sister-in-law. Had Henrietta been difficult to get along with? Had she passed her own unhappiness on to other people?

"'Tis to be hoped that you will, Doris," he said, feeling a little uncomfortable with such an open display of affection. And yet Doris had been thus as a child. She had liked to hug and be hugged. She had liked to hold his hand when they walked. She had liked to ride up on his shoulders, clinging to his hair, when she was very young. His last encounter with her had been that desperate hug on the driveway.

Doris, he thought, was going to be disappointed with him. He was not the brother she remembered. That man no longer existed.

His mother appeared pleased. But Luke wondered if she really wished him to stay in England and return to Bowden or if she merely wished to see Henrietta supplanted and hoped that perhaps Anna would be more easily ruled.

Ashley was not at home. Luke wondered if he would be pleased with the news or if he would wish his brother in Hades, or back in Paris at the very least.

Luke took his leave and went to White's to eat and to relax for a while after the tensions of the morning. At White's he met his uncle and told him his news. Lord Quinn, as might have been expected, greeted the announcement with such hearty good humor, pumping Luke's hand as if to shake his arm from its socket, that the attention of other gentlemen was attracted. Soon half of those present knew of his betrothal. All of polite society would doubtless know of it by the start of the Castle ball, Luke thought ruefully.

And having thought so, he took himself off to have the announcement of the betrothal and the impending marriage placed in tomorrow morning's papers. Then he went on his way to procure a license.

• • •

$\mathcal{I}t$ was late in the afternoon when Luke arrived at the hotel at which the Marquise d'Étienne had taken a suite of rooms. She had just recently returned from a walk with some newly made acquaintances though she had already changed into a loose negligée. She greeted Luke with outstretched hands and her rather haughty smile.

"Ah, *cheri*," she said, turning her cheek for his kiss, "I am furious with you, *non?* Last night you took an English lady to the theater, I hear, because your maman was to be there, too, and you were ashamed to take a French marquise. And today I wait an hour for you to come and then I say *non*, I will wait for that faithless lover no longer. I will perhaps return to Paris and grant my favors to some other eager lover, *non?* There are many begging for them most pitifully."

"I know, Angélique," he said. "The honor of having been your lover is more coveted and more boasted about in France than that of receiving some favor from the king."

"Ah, shameless flatterer," she said. "Luc of the golden tongue. I will forgive you immediately, *cheri*, though I should punish you with my anger for at least an hour. It would be an hour wasted, *non?* I will take you to my bed, and you will boast about it to the oh so slow Englishmen that inhabit London. Come, you must be the lion for me today—you do it so well. I am ready to submit to the attack, mon *amour*." Her eyes had half closed; her voice had become husky.

He had half intended to have her before telling her his news. Angélique was so very thorough and so very skilled at what she did. But it would be unfair to her to keep her in ignorance of a fact that might well change her attitude toward him. She was not, after all, a woman he paid for her favors, a woman who would have no right to any feelings about his marital state.

"Angélique," he said, "perhaps you should not have left Paris. There you shine, my dear. Here you are wasted. Perhaps you should return."

She made a kissing gesture with her mouth. "We will return together," she said. "Now we will not talk. Now we will do. You will touch me and caress me and make me beg for mercy and cry out with ecstasy. Touch me, my lion!"

"The lady I escorted to the theater last evening," he said, "Lady Anna Marlowe, this morning consented to be my wife, Angélique. We are to be married in three days' time."

She stared at him blankly for several silent seconds before her hand whipped unexpectedly and painfully across his face.

She became a wild thing, fighting him, coming at him with fists and fingernails and teeth, kicking him, and cursing him with language straight from the gutters of Paris. He would not hit back, but it took all his strength and a not inconsiderable amount of time to overpower her. He did it eventually by forcing her back against the bed and down onto it so that he could immobilize her body and legs with his own and trap her wrists above her head with his hands.

She fell silent finally, her body heaving beneath his own.

"Luc," she said, the hatred dying out of her eyes as they gazed into his own, only inches away. "Luc, I 'ave made a shameful fool of myself over you. I 'ave followed you 'ere when you did not invite me to come. I forgave you this afternoon when I should 'ave 'ad my servants slam the door in your face. I showed anger instead of disdain when you told me you are to be married. All this I 'ave never done before. I am the Marquise d'Étienne. I am the one who breaks 'earts, *non?*"

"Yes," he said. "Paris is strewn with them, Angélique. The whole of France is strewn with them."

"But finally I make a fool of myself," she said. "Finally I allow my 'eart to be broken. I would 'ave been your wife, Luc. Did you think I would not leave France to live here the rest of my life? With you I would 'ave lived anywhere on earth. I would 'ave been your duchess."

He had no answer for her. He continued to look down into her eyes.

"Make love to me," she whispered. "Make love, *mon amour*, as only you know how."

But he rolled off her, got to his feet, and straightened his clothes.

The room seemed suddenly a great deal smaller than it had seemed at first or on any of his other visits, and quite airless. He could think only of getting away, out into fresh air and space.

"I cannot, Angélique," he said. "It would be unfair to you. I am sorry, my dear. I thought it was for mutual pleasure we came together."

"Ah, Luc." She lay on the bed as he had left her, her arms still stretched above her head. "It was, *cheri*, it was. Always for pleasure more pleasurable than any other I 'ave known."

He picked up his tricorne and his cane and made for the door. He had to get out of there. But her voice stopped him as he opened the door.

"It is true what they say of you in Paris," she said. "I should 'ave listened, but I thought it did not matter. I thought I was the same as you. They say you are a man without a heart, *cheri*."

He forced himself to walk unhurriedly down the stairs of the hotel and out onto the street. That was the second time in one day that someone had said that to him—first Ashley and now Angélique. And of course they were both right.

How foolish people were to allow themselves to love, he thought, quickening his pace and filling his lungs with cool spring air. Love only ever brought heartache and humiliation and wild, impotent fury. Love deprived a person of rationality and control of his own destiny.

He turned his thoughts determinedly to the coming evening and the two sets he would dance with Lady Anna Marlowe. She was something like a breath of fresh air in his life. He hoped she would smile at him again tonight and flirt with him again even when he was not dancing with her. He knew he would spend the whole evening in the ballroom even if he danced only the two sets, merely for the pleasure of looking at her and observing her uncomplicated exuberance for life.

*The* three days prior to her wedding passed so quickly for Anna that there seemed no time to catch her breath. She kept promising

herself that she would think things through, find some way out of
the dilemma that temptation and impetuosity had got her into. But
she never seemed to find the time.

The Duke of Harndon danced with her twice at Lord and Lady
Castle's ball, as promised, and watched her all evening long with his
deceptively lazy eyes, his absurd fan alternately clasped, closed, in
his hand and waving, opened, languidly before his face. He was
wearing cosmetics again, powder and rouge, and a black patch high
on one cheek. He looked very different from that first night, dressed
all in pale ice blue and gleaming white with a quantity of diamonds
sparkling in the folds of his cravat and on his fingers and on the hilt
of his dress sword.

Anna watched him all evening too, though she danced every set,
and she flirted with him over the shoulders of her partners, over the
top of her fan, and with open smiles across the room. She did not
believe she once stopped smiling.

But it was different tonight. It seemed that the fact of their betrothal was general knowledge. This time they watched each other
and flirted with each other in public, under the interested and indulgent scrutiny of fashionable society. It was exhilarating and wonderful. And the very fact that he gazed at her, surely knowing himself
observed, felt wonderful. He wanted her, he had told her. And she
could feel that it was true. He wanted her.

The next day he drove her in the afternoon to take tea with his
mother and his sister. The announcement of their betrothal and im-
minent marriage had been in the morning newspapers so that now
it was all very official—as if it had not been so before.

The Dowager Duchess of Harndon greeted her graciously, and
Lady Doris Kendrick actually hugged her and kissed her cheek. It
seemed she had been approved. She was, of course, she reminded
herself, both the daughter and the sister of an Earl of Royce, a bride
of suitable rank for a duke even if she was without fortune.

While the duke sat in near silence and his sister smiled warmly,
the dowager proceeded to tell her about Bowden Abbey and the busy
round of duties that awaited any Duchess of Harndon there.

"You will, of course, supersede all others who share your title once you marry Harndon," the dowager explained. "That will be my daughter-in-law and myself. You will be Lucas's duchess, Lady Anna, and mistress of Bowden."

She did not sound sorry about the fact that she would be superseded, Anna thought. But then of course that had happened to her when her husband died and her eldest son had become duke. Anna had learned that the duke—*her* duke—had had an elder brother, married, who had held the title for three years after the death of his father. But the elder brother had had no children, no sons.

She would be expected to bear the present Duke of Harndon a son without delay, she thought, and her stomach did a somersault.

Lord Ashley Kendrick came striding into the room before they had finished tea. He had just come in and had been told that she was taking tea with his mother, he explained to Anna, smiling his boyishly handsome smile and making her a courtly bow before taking her hand and kissing it.

"I could not be more delighted," he said. "If I had had the choosing of my own sister-in-law. Lady Anna, I could not have chosen better."

She laughed with him and with Lady Doris while their mother looked on graciously and the duke watched her with those sleepy eyes that were not sleepy at all and she felt excitement curl inside her.

Lord Ashley turned to shake his brother by the hand and wish him well and assure him that he was a lucky devil, though his mother reproved him sharply for his language before ladies.

He was a very handsome and eager young man, Anna decided, and her thoughts moved to Agnes and the annoyance she, Anna, had felt at the theater when Lord Severidge had prevented Lord Ashley from resuming his place beside her. They would be perfect together and were surely not far apart in age. Lord Ashley was considerably younger than the duke, she guessed. Surely he was not much older than Victor. Perhaps she would be able to encourage a match between her sister and her husband's brother.

Her husband. Her stomach lurched and she felt panic grab at her. But she put it ruthlessly aside. It was not for public moments.

The next day Victor arrived, alone. He had left Constance at home with her parents, he explained, since there had not been enough time to arrange to bring her with proper chaperonage and to find suitable friends with whom she might stay. He was delighted for Anna, he said, hugging her tightly and kissing her on both cheeks. He had been very afraid that in the course of nursing their mother and caring for their father she might have lost her chance for an advantageous and happy marriage.

"Of course," he said, "there was the expectation for a while that Blaydon would offer for you and that you would accept, but I was never much in favor of it. He was a pleasant enough fellow but too old for you, Anna. Almost as old as Papa, I warrant you."

She had made no comment but had asked about his own wedding plans, set for later in the autumn. Constance's parents wished her to celebrate her eighteenth birthday before she wed.

The Duke of Harndon came during the afternoon to meet Anna's brother and to take tea. The two men withdrew later to talk privately together. There was no dowry to discuss, of course, and there was no question of consent since she was of age, but it seemed that the two men still deemed it necessary to go apart to discuss some business aspects of the marriage. It seemed absurd that Victor should be discussing her marriage with her betrothed. He looked so very boyish still despite his bag wig and his fashionable clothes.

And tomorrow, Anna thought, left alone with her godmother and Agnes, was her wedding day. Tomorrow at this time she would be Anna Kendrick, the Duchess of Harndon. Panic rushed at her again and had to be quelled as she smiled and agreed that yes, Victor had grown into a very handsome young man and that he was carrying his new title with sense and dignity.

Sometimes, she thought, concentrating her mind on those facts, everything that had happened seemed worthwhile. Victor, of course, would have succeeded to the title anyway on the passing of Papa, but there might have been nothing else. There was precious little now beyond the property itself, but at least there was that to build upon. And Victor had intelligence and sense and the ability to work hard.

Oh yes, she must remember that she had done some good. She must remember that.

The three days rushed by and dragged by. When she was with other people she could keep the panic at bay. When she was alone, it assaulted her from all sides like very real demons from hell. She could not go through with the marriage. She could not. She must tell him. The very next time she saw him she would tell him.

She had been mad, utterly mad to have given in to the temptation. But it seemed that the madness gripped her every time she saw him, and clad her in the mask of smiles and flirtatious ways so that she felt sometimes that she clawed at it from the inside, desperate to get out so that he could see her—see her as she really was before it was too late. But she could not tear away the mask.

It had to be madness, she told herself. In reality there were no demons and there was no mask. All she had to do was tell him. It was not too late and would not be too late until they had been through the marriage ceremony. Ghastly as it would be to break the betrothal now when everything had been made so public, when the license had been procured, when Victor had come, it could still be done. It was not too late.

But every moment that passed brought her one moment closer to too late.

She could not marry him. She could not. And yet tomorrow she was to do just that. Tomorrow morning. The clothes she was to wear had already been chosen and laid out. Her godmother had already had a talk with her, explaining what she could expect to happen tomorrow night in her marriage bed and how she was to respond. But she must not be afraid, she had been told. The Duke of Harndon was a man of thirty years and had doubtless had a great deal of experience. He would know how to calm her fears and cause her the minimum of pain as he broke through the barrier of her virginity. And Anna was fond of him and he of her. Lady Stern had smiled. Anna would come to enjoy it after the shock of the first night or two.

During that last night—the night before her wedding day and the night before her wedding night—Anna knew that she was going to do what could not be done. She was going to marry him. She closed her eyes after lying for hours staring up at the canopy of her bed and pictured him, only a little taller than she, graceful and handsome and gorgeously fashionable almost to the point of effeminacy, except that there was nothing remotely effeminate about the man himself.

He was a man she wanted. She admitted it to herself at last.

And he wanted her. He loved her.

Perhaps . . . oh, perhaps the great impossibility might after all be just possible. Perhaps.

By this time tomorrow night . . . Anna swallowed convulsively. By this time tomorrow night he would have done to her body those things Aunt Marjorie had described to her in quite graphic detail. Perhaps.

By this time tomorrow night she would be a married lady. And perhaps, too, by this time tomorrow night her marriage would be over.

She wondered where Sir Lovatt Blaydon was at this precise moment. Still in America? On his way back to England? In England? Dead? She wished he was dead. She wished only one thing more than that. She wished he was dead and she could know about it.

She waited for guilt to assault her at wishing for the death of another human being. But it did not come.

She wished he was dead.

*Sir* Lovatt Blaydon was sitting up late, alone, a decanter of brandy at his elbow and an empty glass in his hand which he had not refilled for longer than an hour. He stared into the dying embers of the fire his valet had built up a long time ago.

Beside the decanter was a morning newspaper that was almost two days out of date. It was opened and folded at the page of announcements. He knew the announcement by heart.

He had accomplished what he had gone to America to do. He had bought property and a house and had furnished the house with care and taste. He had hired servants recommended for their domestic skills and their air of gentility. And he had stayed to establish himself in the neighborhood, to be accepted and liked and sought after. He had always found it easy to make people like him. As far back as his childhood his mother had used to say that he could charm the birds from the trees if he so chose.

He had got everything ready. For her. For Anna. And then he had come back for her. She would be waiting. He was confident of that. Poor Anna, he had made sure that she would wait. But it was time now for her to be weaned of her family. They no longer needed her. They were no longer dependent on her for everything in life. His dear, strong Anna, who had borne all the burdens alone, keeping her family together while Royce crumbled before her eyes, afflicted by an addiction to alcohol and gambling, loving him and caring for him while keeping the worry off the shoulders of her sisters and even of her brother, doing everything in her power to repay the debts so that they would not all face total ruin, so that the brother would have something to inherit.

Well, now it was all over for her. Now she was free. And now was the time he would take her to the life of plenty and ease that she had earned. She would never have to know another moment of anxiety. Now she would be able to reap the rewards of her efforts. For the rest of his life he would lavish on her everything that was his to give, including his undivided devotion. And even beyond his life he would care for her. He had made provision for her.

His Anna was going to be happy.

Or so he had thought until he returned and found that she was not at home, that there was no one there except the youngest girl. Anna had gone to London with one of the other sisters—Agnes—to spend a couple of months with her godmother.

He had arrived in London to find this—he half turned his head to the newspaper, but he did not pick it up. He knew it by heart. She was betrothed to the Duke of Harndon, to be married to him two days after the announcement. Tomorrow.

Something inside Sir Lovatt Blaydon had died. And something else had turned to icy fury. Had she not understood? Had he not seen to it that she knew beyond any doubt that she was his, that he owned her? He owned her mind. He owned her body. He had left her in no doubt of those facts. Had he not been quite convinced that she understood beyond any doubt, he would not have gone to America without her. He would not have allowed her the year to mourn for Royce and to see her brother and sisters well on the road to recovery.

She had not understood. But yes, she had, of course. His Anna did not lack for intelligence. Neither did she lack for courage. She had not seen the whole picture of her life and had concluded that he only wanted to destroy her. She did not know what he had planned for the rest of her life. She had thought to escape him.

His dear, courageous Anna. Surprisingly he could not hold on to his anger against her. He could feel only a reluctant admiration for her defiance. And with the admiration had come a decision. His first instinct, of course, had been to see to it that she did not solemnize this marriage. But he had decided that he would allow it. And for a very good reason.

Oh, yes, he was surprised he had never thought of it before. It would be perfect. It would make an already happy future utterly perfect. He would have to wait for it, of course, and for her. But he was used to waiting. It seemed to him that his life had been made up of waiting.

He could wait a little longer for perfection.

Dear Anna. He set his head back against the chair and closed his eyes. He wondered if she realized that he loved her, that she had become the consuming love of his life, that the focus of all his remaining days had become Anna and her happiness and prosperity. He guessed that she did not realize it. He had had to be cruel to her. He knew he had been cruel. But no longer.

By allowing her to marry her duke, he was ensuring that her ultimate happiness would be even greater than he had originally planned. Even after his own death she would be happy—she would not be lonely.

But the wait was going to be hard on him. Ah, Anna. It was going to be torture.

## 8

URIOUSLY, standing at the front of the cold, almost empty church with his bride, speaking and listening to the words that were binding them together for life, Luke did not feel sorry.

She had smiled her usual dazzling smile a few minutes ago when her brother had brought her to him before the altar, and she was still bright-eyed and flushed even though the smile had gone. She looked lovely enough to catch at his breath with her white satin open gown with the wide gold embroidered robings and cream-colored petticoat, and stomacher so heavily embroidered with gold thread that it seemed to be made of pure gold. Even her lace cap with its long lappets at the back and the three lace frills of her shift that fell from her elbows beneath the cuffs of her sleeves glittered with gold thread.

And yet it was not just her beauty or her vitality that made him almost glad he was marrying her. He had had many beautiful women and had felt no inclination to make permanent his connection with any one of them. But Lady Anna Marlowe, he had learned, was not as frivolous or as superficial in character as he had thought. She was capable of loyalty and love and self-sacrifice.

Her brother had told him everything. For years she had nursed their consumptive mother and run the home and cared for her younger brother and sisters. And after their mother's death she had continued her care of them all despite the fact that their father had collapsed with grief and had faced ruin after a series of reversals in his fortune. Anna had not thought of herself at all, Royce had explained, turning down one perfectly eligible offer of marriage at the age of one-and-twenty rather than abandon her family to their fate. By the time their father died a little over a year ago, she had been four-and-twenty.

Luke guessed, though Royce had not once stated it, that the father had been a drinker and a gambler and that the physical, mental, and financial collapse had had its roots in years of weakness and self-indulgence. Near financial ruin rarely came overnight.

But through it all, through what must have been difficult and oppressive years, Lady Anna had held the family together, allowing the younger children, the present Royce included, to grow up with a feeling of some security. In the process she had almost lost her own chances for personal fulfillment. She had rejected a chance to marry and leave all her burdens behind her.

Yes, he thought, looking at her now as the rector spoke, he might have done a great deal worse. She would doubtless do an admirable job as his duchess. And she was beautiful and desirable too. Perhaps—in the quietness of the church and the strangeness of the moment he dared to think it—perhaps sometimes life offered second chances even when for ten years one had done little, if anything, to deserve them.

Perhaps after all there would be a return of some feeling to his life. Affection, loyalty, devotion, trust—most of all trust. He realized in some surprise, but without real alarm, as he slid his ring onto Anna's finger that he had fallen a little in love with her.

And then words the rector had spoken registered on his mind. They were man and wife. She was his wife, his duchess.

He took both her hands in his, bowed over them almost reverently, and raised them one at a time to his lips. He looked into her eyes as he did so—wide, green eyes in which something flickered for a moment before she smiled. Fright? Yes, undoubtedly fright. She was five-and-twenty years old. He would soothe her fears tonight. It would be his pleasure to do so. His great pleasure.

His mother laid her cheek against his for a moment. Doris hugged him tightly and kissed his lips. Ashley shook his hand and grinned at him; perhaps he knew that all his debts had been paid, including the rather extravagant ones dealing with ladies' clothes and jewels and the renting of a house and servants that could be kept for only one obvious purpose. Theo pumped his hand and slapped him heartily on the back. Lady Sterne, claiming a mother's privilege, she said, kissed both his cheeks. Royce shook his hand warmly. Lady Agnes Marlowe looked at his chin with wide eyes and curtsied and looked distinctly frightened when he took her hand and kissed her fingers.

His wife in her turn was being hugged and kissed. She was even more flushed than before and she was laughing. She looked wonderfully happy. She deserved happiness, he thought. And he wondered if he was capable of giving it to her, if being his duchess and the mistress of his home and the mother of his children would be enough. He was not sure he had love to offer even though he had been reckless enough to fall in love with her. But she seemed to have a naturally sunny nature.

He found himself counting back the days to the night he had first seen her at Lady Diddering's ball. He could not remember the day of the week on which the ball had been held. Today was Monday. Incredibly, he thought, having performed the calculations twice in his mind, the ball must have been held on a Tuesday. Last Tuesday. A week ago today he had not even set eyes on Lady Anna Marlowe, now the Duchess of Harndon.

The fact was somewhat dizzying. What did they know about each other? Practically nothing. And yet they were man and wife.

And then he was leading her outside into daylight and sunshine, her arm resting formally along his. His carriage was waiting for them there.

There was the usual small crowd of the curious gathered in the square outside the church. Somehow word had spread that there was a society wedding being solemnized inside. Almost all the spectators were members of the lowest classes and many of them were loudly vocal in their admiration of the bride's appearance and the groom's, though some wag—male—informed Luke and an appreciative audience in a falsetto voice that he was as gorgeous as a girl. Someone else—female—made loud and ribald predictions about the coming night and someone else again—also female—added that the bride would regret tonight's fun come nine months from tonight.

Luke took little notice, and from her expression as he handed her into his carriage it seemed that neither did his wife. And yet he half noticed the one spectator who was not of the lower orders. Spectator he appeared to be, though he was partly hidden behind the trunk of an ancient oak tree in the center of the square. He wore a long dark cloak, and his tricorne hat was pulled low over his brow—a tall, rather thin, rather handsome man of middle years.

Luke only half noticed him and yet he frowned slightly as he climbed into the carriage to take his seat beside his wife. Something fleeting nudged at his memory and was gone. He did not reach for it to bring it back and recognize it. It was not important enough. The matter was forgotten even before the carriage lurched into motion on its well-oiled springs.

No one else in the wedding party who might have recognized Sir Lovatt Blaydon even glanced in the direction of the old oak.

*Anna* had not known that the Duke of Harndon did not live at Harndon House. Even when he had escorted her there to take tea with the dowager duchess, she had not realized that he did not live there with her and with his sister and brother. She had not realized it even today when they went there for the wedding breakfast—until late in the afternoon when he had risen and suggested that he take her home.

For one foolish moment she had thought that he intended to take her back to her godmother's house. And for the same even more foolish moment her heart had leapt with gladness.

It seemed strange to her that he did not live in his own house in London but had gone to the great expense of renting another. And it was no small establishment, she saw when they arrived there. She wondered about his relationship with the rest of his family. And she realized suddenly that she knew almost nothing about him. She knew appallingly little about him, in fact. He had talked to her during their meetings, charming her and amusing her, but he had told her almost nothing at all about himself.

She had dreaded the embarrassment of being in a house with his family on her wedding day and her wedding night. And yet now, released from that embarrassment, she longed for other company. She was alone with him, with the man who was her husband, and she was so filled with dread that she scarcely knew how to draw breath.

They dined late and alone together, though she noted that he had dressed as if for another ball, changing from the royal blue and silver he had worn at their wedding to brown velvet and gold embroidery and lace. And he conversed with her with as much easy charm as usual, dispelling the atmosphere of awkwardness she had been expecting. She was, she realized with some surprise, making her own contributions, smiling at him and laughing with him and talking to him just as if she were any bride on any wedding day.

Except that most brides would be tense and nervous at such a time, she thought. But if she stopped smiling and laughing she would—oh, she would crumble altogether.

He took her to the drawing room when the meal was at an end and they talked more over their tea. He did not drink, he had told her when she had asked if he wished to be left alone in the dining room to take port. The toasts he had drunk at their wedding breakfast earlier had merely been a concession to the festive occasion. It was another unexpected fact she had learned about him. She did not know any other men who did not drink alcohol.

But he got to his feet far too soon and far too early, it seemed to her, though a glance at the clock on the mantel showed her that it was after ten. He held out a hand for hers.

"Come, madam," he said, those keen eyes of his looking steadily at her from behind the lazy lids. "I shall escort you to your dressing room. We have a wedding night to celebrate before we sleep."

He might as well have curled his outstretched hand into a fist and slammed it into her stomach, she thought. It could not more effectively have robbed her of breath than did his words. As she set her hand in his and rose to her feet and smiled at him, she found herself thinking foolishly and frantically of headaches and tiredness after a busy day and wrong times of the month.

"Yes, your grace," she said. "We have."

He left her outside the door of her dressing room after opening it for her. He would do himself the honor of visiting her in her bedchamber in half an hour's time, he said.

She smiled her assent.

*By* the time he came to her a little more than half an hour later, she was almost screaming with hysteria because he was late, because the terrible denouement was delayed. Condemned criminals, she thought, must not savor their last moments on earth. They must eye the approaching gallows with longing, willing the slow process of the law to speed up to an indecent haste. But the unfortunate intrusion of the thought of hangings only succeeded in making her almost blind with terror. Breathing had become a conscious and a painful process.

He was wearing a pale blue satin dressing gown. She could see that without his heeled shoes he was indeed only three or four inches taller than she. Without the heaviness of his waistcoat and full-skirted coat, he looked very slender. And yet the breadth of his shoulders and chest suggested strength. His face had been washed clean of cosmetics and his hair brushed free of powder. She saw in some surprise that it was dark brown. It was tied loosely at the nape of his neck with a black ribbon, but not bagged. It fell thick and wavy from the ribbon tie almost to his waist.

Anna noticed all the details of his appearance and his attractiveness without emotional response. She noted the details almost clinically, desperately trying to focus the teeming, uncontrolled workings of her mind. She wondered if she should have had her maid tie back her own hair instead of leaving it to hang loose down her back. She was not even wearing a cap.

She reached for a smile. But drawing up the corners of her mouth proved to be a physical impossibility. Her mask had eluded her. She stared mutely at him.

He had stepped up close to her and taken both her hands in his. "'Tis as I thought," he said softly. "Two blocks of ice. And a look of blank terror. Anna? What has happened to all your smiles? Am I so fearsome? Is the marriage act with me so much to be dreaded?"

It was the first time he had used her name without any title to go along with it. She concentrated her mind on the curiously comforting sound of her name on his lips, while an uncontrolled part of her brain presented her with images of herself forced down onto a bed and her arms spread wide above her head and her wrists tied firmly to opposite bedposts.

"Silence?" he said, releasing her hands in order to raise his own to cup her face. His thumbs lightly caressed her cheeks. "Anna, I am no monster. There will be pain, I have heard, the first time—a little pain for a few moments only. I will be gentle, my dear, and try to make it nothing at all. Come, let us lie down, shall we?"

There would be no pain. Oh, dear God, there would be no pain. And it was not a little pain for a few moments only. It was sharp and searing pain and it blistered the soul for a lifetime.

"Yes, your grace," she whispered.

"Luke," he said. "My name is Lucas, though only my mother has ever called me that."

"Luke," she whispered.

He blew out the candles after she had lain down on the bed, moving over to one side to make room for him. He joined her there after a few seconds and she realized almost before he touched her that he was naked.

One arm slid beneath her neck while the other hand turned her onto her side, facing him, and then cupped her cheek. And he kissed her, his lips warm and firm against her own. His hand moved downward again and behind her waist and lower to draw her against him. Loosely. Unthreateningly. She felt his man's powerful body, warm and naked, only the thin lawn of her nightgown separating them.

His mouth moved an inch back from hers. "Anna," he said, "every muscle is tense. Relax, my dear. There is no hurry. We have all night. We have a lifetime. I will give you time to accustom yourself to the feel of me. I will not enter you until you are ready. Come, you will find it not such an ordeal after all."

*Don't delay. Do it now. Get it over with. Do it now.* Her mind screamed at him. Her body tried to obey his command.

He kissed with parted lips. He kissed all parts of her face and her throat. His hands moved lightly, unthreateningly, over her back, both above and below her waist. And then one hand touched her stomach and the side of her hip and waist. And then her breasts, circling them so lightly that he scarcely seemed to touch her at all.

By the time he opened the buttons of her nightgown her eyes were closed but not clenched, her lips were parted, and her body rested against his from the hips down. And she waited for him to touch her again, there, where it had felt so good. On her breasts.

It felt doubly good to feel his hand against her flesh, first circling lightly as before and then massaging almost as lightly and then brushing with his thumb against a nipple, causing a rush of tightness there and a stabbing of pain that was not really pain at all.

She could hear whimpering sounds but paid them no attention. She could feel against her lower abdomen his growing hardness and she pressed closer against it. He made a sound of appreciation in his throat.

And then he lifted himself onto one elbow and turned her onto her back and was lowering her unbuttoned nightgown over her shoulders and down her arms.

"Let us dispense with this, Anna," he said, his face bending close to hers again. "'Tis a mere encumbrance, is it not?"

She lifted her hips obediently as he stripped the garment away from her and tossed it over the side of the bed. She had been jolted back into herself again. It was time. She knew it was time. She was on her back. And she had relaxed for him. And she had felt his readiness.

He kissed her again, warmly, almost languidly, open mouthed. His palm moved over her breasts again and down to lie flat on her stomach—or on her womb, she supposed—for a few moments more.

And then he moved across her and his whole weight was on her.

He kissed her again and murmured words whose sense her mind could not unscramble while his knees spread her leg wide and his hands came firmly beneath her buttocks to hold her steady.

She drew breath in and held it as she felt his hardness against her and coming into her—coming in where there was no barrier and would be no pain—slowly and inexorably coming inward.

He was deep, her mind told her when he finally stopped coming. Far deeper, far harder than she had ever imagined. She felt stretched wide. Man. For the first time in her life her body was possessed by a man. By him—by Luke. She saw him just behind her closed eyelids gorgeous in scarlet and gold, with his rouged and powdered cheeks and his powdered hair, his gold and ivory fan cooling his face, his gray eyes steady on her. And now she felt him, naked against her own nakedness, deep in the intimacy of the ultimate embrace.

Despite herself she reveled in the feel of him there as she waited for the end. And she was not sorry after all. For this moment in time she was not sorry. For this moment—for this one moment—she felt like a woman.

He lay deep and still in her for a long while before he broke the silence. When he did, speaking quietly against her ear, it seemed to her that his voice was without expression. Though she could not in reality tell what his voice sounded like.

"Let yourself relax," he said.

It was only then she realized that every muscle in her body had tightened again and that she was still holding her breath. She obeyed him.

He withdrew from her slowly so that her heart died a little in her and she almost cried out in anguish. But he paused at the entrance to her and thrust deeply inside again. And repeated the action again and yet again. She remembered suddenly what her godmother had told her, though the reality bore little resemblance to what she had imagined from the verbal description. The reality was far more . . . physical. Thrust and withdrawal became steady and rhythmic and were soon being performed against the unexpected comfort of wetness so that sound and movement became together part of a dance into which her own body gradually relaxed and then responded.

He was completing the marriage act with her, her mind told her while her body opened and yielded to him and shared his rhythm and followed his pace.

Pleasure sighed out of her a moment before he held deep in her and she felt heat gush at her core. The marriage act was completed. Her womb was receiving his seed.

Anna felt tears hot against her eyelids.

Perhaps, she thought as his relaxed weight bore down on her and she turned her head to rest her cheek against his damp shoulder, he had not noticed. Perhaps it had not been so obvious after all.

He drew himself out of her body, leaving her feeling bereft for a moment, lifted himself off her, and lay at her side. She closed her legs and then lay still. She wanted to turn onto her side. She wanted to pull up the bedclothes, feeling chilly now that the blanket of his warm body had been removed from hers. But she lay still, afraid for some reason to move. She could make herself comfortable after he had gone back to his own room. She willed him not to say anything before he did so.

She was on the brink of sleep when she felt the warmth of bedclothes being lifted over her and settled about her shoulders. She turned onto her side, facing him, relaxing into the warmth of the blankets and of his body heat, though she did not touch him or he her, and let herself slip all the way into the luxury of sleep.

*He* never slept with women. For that reason he conducted his liaisons almost exclusively in the afternoons—as well as for the reason that he liked to see the women to whom he made love. He liked to make love twice, sometimes three times, merely relaxing between times and then taking his leave when his body and the woman's were sated. Sleep seemed to him one of the most private of activities. He liked to do it alone.

But he awoke, feeling disoriented, to find that he had fallen asleep in his wife's bed. He could hear her deep, quiet breathing. He could feel the heat of her down his left side, though they were not touching. He was surprised that he had slept. He turned over onto his back and rested an arm across his eyes. He should be angry, he thought. Was he? It seemed somehow foolish to be angry. She was, after all, five-and-twenty. Disappointed, then? Yes, definitely that. He could remember feeling enchanted by her vivacity and her innocent charm. He could remember feeling just today—or yesterday, he supposed it was—that perhaps life gave second chances once in a while. A second chance for innocence . . . and peace.

Well. And maybe life did give such chances. But not to him.

He thought of his unpardonable foolishness in allowing himself to fall in love and to begin to trust. His heart—and his eyes—were cold as he stared upward. His teeth were clamped together, his jaw hard.

He had intended to have her only once tonight. The combined shock of performing such an intimate and unfamiliar act and pain at having had a sealed physical passage newly ripped open would be enough for her to cope with for one night, he had thought. He would not take her again until tomorrow night and even then perhaps only once and gently.

Well, there was no reason now to deny himself. And her body was as beautiful and as inviting without her clothes—though he had experienced it only through the senses of touch and taste and smell and not of sight—as it was with. She was his wife. He was entitled to have her whenever he wanted her and however he wanted her. He wanted her now.

Despite his denials, the anger came. And, still denied, the hurt. And the unrecognized need to hurt back.

He set a hand on her shoulder and turned her onto her back, moving with her. He spread her legs wide with his own, lifted her with his hands, and mounted her with one firm stroke. She came awake with a little cry and her legs slid up beside his until her feet were flat on the bed beside his upper thighs.

Making love had always been a shared experience of give and take, a taking of pleasure and a giving according to the sensed needs of his partner. It was a matter of pride with him never to leave his bed partner unsatisfied. He knew that he had acquired some fame in France as a skilled and considerate lover. But this encounter was all take. He drove his anger and his hurt and his need into her for several long minutes before the blessed release came. He was surprised by her cry, which came almost simultaneously. A cry of sexual satisfaction.

He felt instantly guilty. But he hated feeling guilt. He hated feeling any strong emotion. He lifted his face from her hair—the long, almost blond, wavy hair that had excited him when he had first seen it without its careful curls and powder—and set his mouth to hers, kissing her softly and with mute unrecognized apology. Her arms came about his shoulders and held him warmly. Her legs slid down the bed so that he could feel their slimness against the length of his.

He stayed in her bed all night. He had her once more in the darkness and once in the dim light of early dawn when he raised himself on his forearms to look down at her and at what he did with her.

She was still sleeping when he left her bed and her room in order to take his morning ride in the chill of drizzling rain.

# 9

*A*NNA knew as soon as she awoke that she was alone and that she was far later than usual getting up. It did not matter. It was the morning after her wedding day, the morning after her wedding night. She would not be expected to rise early. The servants might wonder what was wrong if she did. She smiled at the thought.

She stretched luxuriously beneath the warm bedclothes, feeling their unfamiliar softness against her body. She had never slept naked before. It somehow felt good though she felt a moment's embarrassment to realize that her maid must already have been in the room—there was a cup of chocolate covered with a grayish film beside the bed—and must have seen her nightgown tossed onto the floor.

It did not matter. At least the word would be spread belowstairs that the Duke of Harndon had indeed slept with his new duchess.

All her fears had been for nothing, she thought. Well, all her immediate fears, anyway. There were others that she would not think of any longer. If and when Sir Lovatt Blaydon returned to England, he would find that she had defied him. He would find her a married lady. Perhaps he would admit defeat, perhaps not. But she was not going to worry about it any longer.

It had not been obvious after all. He had not noticed. He had made love to her four times. Anna laughed out loud. She had had no idea it could be done more than once in a night, as if there were some law. He wanted her. He loved her. She had known that before their marriage, but terror had destroyed some of the wonder of it for her.

No longer. He had made love to her four times, and the fourth time
the room had been almost light and he had raised himself on his
forearms and deliberately looked at her. She had felt embarrassment
for a moment, but he had been inside her and loving her. She had
known that she was beautiful to him. She had felt beautiful. And so
she had let her eyes roam over him, over the powerful muscles of his
dark-haired chest and shoulders and arms, and downward. She had
watched what he did to her.

Anna stretched again. This morning she felt like a woman. No,
that was not quite it. She always felt like a woman. This morning she
felt like a *married* woman, something that even three or four years
ago she had given up hope of ever feeling, something that for two
years she had considered an impossibility. She had reconciled her
mind—or tried to do so—to the fact that she would live her life as a
spinster. That she would never know a man.

Yet now she had known a man and had been known by him—in
the biblical sense. And her body knew it this morning. Her breasts
felt sensitive and sore-tipped. Her legs were stiff from having been
pressed wide for long minutes at a time. There was a soreness inside
where he had loved her. And there was an overall feeling of—of being known.

He would do it again tonight, she thought with a quickening of
her breath. And tomorrow night and the next. He would do it regularly for perhaps the rest of her life, only abstaining for a few days
each month and when . . . She rolled onto her side. Four times. He
had performed the marriage act with her four times last night. Perhaps she was already with child. Something somersaulted inside her
at the wonder of the thought. Every time he made love to her, her
body would be filled with his seed. She was his wife. She was his wife
forever and ever.

She bit her upper lip suddenly and laughed again at the tears
that were trickling diagonally down her cheeks. She had not known
that happiness could feel like an agony. She felt so happy this morning that it hurt. She wanted to see him again. She wanted to see his
eyes. She wanted to see the awareness in them that she was his wife

and that they had shared the intimacies of marriage for a whole night.

Anna threw back the bedclothes and reached for the bellpull.

He was not in the breakfast room, of course. He must have eaten hours ago. He had probably taken himself off to his club or wherever else gentlemen went during the day. She hoped he would come home before evening. Perhaps he would since it was the day after his wedding day. Anna filled a plate from the warming trays on the sideboard and sat down to eat, determined to enjoy the day even if she must do so alone.

But she was not long alone. Luke joined her there a few minutes later, looking immaculate and gorgeous in a dark red silk morning gown worn over his shirt and knee breeches. His hair was carefully rolled at the sides and bagged at the back and powdered. The dress was informal, she thought, but the effect was not. He bowed over her hand and raised it to his lips before seating himself and indicating to the butler with the raising of just one forefinger that he would take coffee.

Anna gazed at him, her body pulsing with the awareness of what he had done to her during the night and of how he felt and looked without his clothes. She smiled warmly at him.

"Have you been up for hours?" she asked. "I was ashamed to see how far advanced the morning was when I awoke."

"I always rise early," he said. "I like to ride before there are any crowds abroad to slow me down. But you must sleep as long as you wish in the mornings, my dear. This morning you had every reason for doing so."

She could feel herself blush but did not care that he saw it also. She held her smile. Early-morning rides had always been her habit too. It had been the only time of day she had felt belonged to her alone. Since coming to London, she had neglected the exercise. Perhaps she would suggest riding with him one morning. Would he mind? But she was his wife and he loved her. Of course he would not mind.

"Your food will be getting cold," he said, indicating her plate.

She turned her attention back to it while he amused her with an account of an unfortunate maid in Hyde Park this morning who had been walking five dogs on leashes. All had been sedate dignity until he had come riding by. Anna smiled and chuckled at his graphic description of how each dog had reacted and of how the maid had responded. Luke, it seemed, had had to ride back and dismount in order to restore order and harmony among the excited canines and to free the maid from imprisonment by five tangled leashes.

He talked on lightly, amusingly, until Anna had finished her breakfast. Then he drew back her chair and offered his arm for her to take.

"We will go to the library, my dear," he said.

He was going to spend the day with her. She knew she could not expect it every day. Doubtless it would be undesirable for them to be always together. But today was special. Today was the day after their wedding night. She linked her arm through his instead of laying it more formally on top and smiled at him.

"'Tis your own special sanctuary?" she asked.

"'Tis the room from which I do business," he said.

Business. There must be letters to write and domestic and financial matters to discuss. Mundane matters that would bind them together more closely as man and wife. Yes, it was how today should be spent.

He seated her on a leather chair at one side of a great oak desk and walked around it to take the more imposing chair on the other side. He sat down and looked at her. And she knew in that instant, before he spoke, that she had been wrong—wrong about everything.

"I believe, madam," he said, his voice almost frighteningly quiet, "that you have some explaining to do."

She felt the remnants of her smile drain away as she stared back at him. She had not fooled him after all. He had known, just as Sir Lovatt had warned her that any man would know.

"It seems to be a generally acknowledged truth," he said, "that a man has a right to a virgin bride. It may seem a little unfair since a woman does not have the same rights in a bridegroom. But such is the nature of our world and our society. You did not come to me untouched, madam."

Oh, but she had. She had.

"Perhaps," he said, "you would care to explain." The pleasantness of his tone was more frightening than open anger would have been. There seemed to be something steely behind it.

Explain? How could she explain? She could not explain that one fact without explaining everything. The simple truth would make no sense at all outside the context of the whole of it. Ravishment would have been easy to explain. Ravishment could stand alone. But it had not been ravishment—not really. It had been worse. More cold-blooded. She had never understood why he had not simply ravished her. No, she could not tell everything—or anything. It was an impossibility.

"Let me make it easier for you," he said. "Did it happen once or several times?"

She stared at him. Once? Not even once.

"With one man or with several?" His voice was softer.

She wished he would yell at her. She wanted suddenly to scream at him to yell at her. When the silence stretched, she wanted to rush from the room and from the house in search of air. She was suffocating. She continued to look directly into his eyes.

"Did you love him?" His voice was almost a whisper. And when she still did not answer him, "Do you love him?"

She thought of Sir Lovatt Blaydon standing beside that bed, talking soothingly to her while they tied her wrists to the bedposts, the man and the woman, and then her ankles, one to each of the posts at the foot of the bed, and while the woman lifted her petticoat and her shift to her waist, folding them neatly as if it mattered that they not crease. Love? Love? Had there been a moment in her life more devoid of love?

Her husband's face blurred before her eyes suddenly and she realized in humiliation that her eyes had filled with tears.

He got slowly to his feet a few moments later and walked across the room to stand at the window, his back to her. She bit her upper lip hard, willing the tears to return to their source. He came back toward her after what seemed like an hour and was in reality perhaps two minutes. He did not go back behind the desk. He came to stand in front of her chair.

"I will not condemn you," he said. "I suppose that a woman's sexual urges can be as insistent as a man's and that when a woman is past the age of twenty and family circumstances make it difficult for her to marry and satisfy those urges in the usual manner, she might be tempted to take comfort where it can be found. Especially if there is some modicum of love involved. I will not condemn or insist that you answer my questions. You may keep your secrets. But I will say this, madam. Look at me."

She had closed her eyes and kept them closed. She opened them now and looked into his. She wished he would take a step or two back.

"You are my wife," he said. "You belong to me. I cannot command your affections, but I can and will demand that your body be my exclusive property. While we both live, mine will be the only body to penetrate yours from this moment on, mine the only seed to enter your womb. Be clear on this, madam. Do not mistake my decision not to punish what is past and what preceded our marriage as weakness. You will disobey this command at your own peril. You would be punished. Your lover would die. Anyone who knows me would be able to assure you that I do not make idle threats."

For the first time it occurred to her that there was a great icy coldness behind his eyes. She gazed at him, tense and terrified. And yet a part of her mind was rebelling. They were all the same, she thought bitterly. Men were all the same. Power was everything to them and the need to possess, to control. She had thought this man different. She had been foolish. He was no different from Sir Lovatt Blaydon. And yet something in her screamed a protest at the comparison. It was not true. It could not be true.

But was there no man in this world with a heart? Yet that, too, was unfair. She had refused to answer his questions—she had been unable to answer them. He had a right to be a great deal angrier than he was.

"You have been silent long enough, madam," he said. "I will hear from you now, if you please."

"Yesterday," she said, her voice blurting far too loudly. She swallowed. "Yesterday, I made vows to you, your grace, and to God in the hearing of my family and yours. I do not make vows that I have no intention of keeping."

"Very well," he said after a short silence. "We will say no more on the matter, then. We will proceed with the marriage we contracted yesterday."

She closed her eyes tightly again. "Thank you," she whispered.

She did not know if her marriage had been saved or if her soul had been destroyed—again. Only time would tell, she supposed. But at least he was not putting her aside, publicly shaming her after just one day of marriage. She did not know yet if she was glad or sorry. She had seen steel in his eyes and had heard it in his voice. She had been frightened of him, terrified of him, of this man she had thought quite unthreatening just a few days ago.

Perhaps after all he had not been making love to her last night. Perhaps, having made his discovery at the start, he had been taking her as he would a whore. It was a possibility to chill her to the very heart.

And yet—*we will proceed with the marriage we contracted yesterday.* He had said those words to her.

*He* could not accept the fact that he had been hurt by the knowledge that she loved the man who had had her virginity. Hurt? In what way? He had made himself invulnerable to pain.

He had had to get to his feet and walk away from her to the window when he had seen the lost, deeply pained look in her eyes, which usually sparkled so brightly, and when the tears had welled in them.

She loved the man whoever he was, God damn his soul. Her face and her unshed tears had spoken far louder than words could have done.

It was only his pride that had been hurt, not his heart. He had no heart. He knew, conceited as the admission was, that any one of his French lovers and any one of the countless women who would have been his lovers if he had given the slightest encouragement, would have jumped at the chance to be his wife. He had chosen a brightly happy woman, a woman of purity, and he had been duped. Not only had she been touched, but her heart was given elsewhere. Or so her reaction to his question strongly suggested. She had refused to speak.

He did not care about her heart, he told himself as he stood at the window, his back to her and to the room. But by God, no other man would ever touch her body again. Not unless he was prepared to make it his final act in this life.

And so he walked back across the room to tell her just that. And he realized something else as she looked up into his eyes when he commanded her to do so. He realized that the smiles, the sparkle, the flirtatious ways had all been an act. He realized that she was a woman who had worn a mask during the week of their acquaintance.

Or perhaps not. Perhaps he was overreacting. He was not even sure why he hoped he was mistaken since he had just established his ownership of her and she had accepted reality.

He turned to walk back around the desk and sat down behind it again. He had felt the need when they had come from the breakfast room to set some distance between them, some formal distance. The width of a desk was impersonal and indicated a symbolic separation between master and servant.

She was not his servant. She was his wife.

"Anna," he said. She was looking steadily back at him, her face pale, no trace of her earlier smiles remaining. "'Twould be as well if there were plain speaking between us. There already has been some despite the secret you have refused to tell and I have refused to insist upon sharing. Let there be more so that we may begin our marriage with no misunderstandings, no false expectations. Tell me why you married me and I will tell you why I married you. The full truth even if it may seem hurtful. Tell me."

He thought she was going to remain silent again. He sat waiting. This was something he would insist upon. If they left the room now and went their separate ways for the rest of the day, they might never be able to establish a working relationship. But she spoke finally without further prompting.

"I am five-and-twenty years old," she said. "Since my mother's death, and even before it to a degree, I have been mistress of the home into which I was born. No longer. My brother is now master there and will be taking home a bride later this year. I preferred to marry than be a spinster sister in their home. I had a chance to marry you, a man of high rank and comfortable fortune. I took the chance."

*And did you connive at it?* he wanted to ask her. Was that what the flirtation at Lady Diddering's ball had been all about? But did it matter?

"That is all?" he asked.

She hesitated. "My sisters," she said. "I spoke with you about them before. But I did not mention that my youngest sister is—is . . . My brother does not have the gift of handling her though he is fond of her, I believe. And his betrothed has expressed her concern over having Emily live in her home."

"What is the matter with Emily?" he asked.

"She is a deaf-mute," she said. "It is difficult to communicate with her. And she—she wanders. She does not behave as other young girls behave."

"You married me partly so that you could give her a different home, then?" he asked.

"Yes," she said.

He wondered what else she had kept from him, this uncomplicated woman he had thought he was marrying, this woman he had thought he could trust. A lover whom she loved but for some reason had been unable to marry—perhaps the man was already married. A deaf-mute sister. Did she have any more secrets?

He waited for more and wondered if he could ever now trust this woman—his wife—to tell him the full truth.

"I have been away from my home and family for ten years," he told her when she said no more. "I had no intentions of ever return- ing to either, even after the death of my brother two years ago pre- sented me with the unwelcome burden of my title. But responsibilities cannot be so easily ignored, it seems. Problems are clamoring at me in the form of every one of my family members and my chief prop- erty, Bowden Abbey. It seems altogether likely that I am going to have to go there sooner or later. When one is a duke and has all the responsibilities that come with the title, one can no longer follow inclination even in one's personal life. I needed a wife."

He had intended to be honest, not brutal. When she lowered her eyes for a moment before raising them again, he realized what he had implied by his words. But they were spoken now, and they were the truth. If he had for a brief moment imagined himself in love with her, then the feeling was gone without trace.

"It was desirable to choose a bride of no lower rank than earl's daughter," he said. "I told you before that fortune was of no impor- tance to me. I have two, one that I made for myself, and one that I inherited. You were recommended to me by my uncle as a woman of suitable rank. I did not see any point in looking farther."

Her eyes dropped before his.

"It is not a good situation for brothers to be heirs to one another once they have passed a certain age," he said. "It has become clear to me that fathering sons is my main duty to my position. I needed a wife to bear those sons for me. If I prove capable and you fertile, I will be keeping you with child with suitable intervals between for the recovery of your full health until there are at least two sons in our nursery. Daughters will not be unwelcome, but I will want sons."

"Yes." She was still not looking into his eyes but at the desk be- tween them. "And so will I, your grace."

He got to his feet again and came around the desk to hold out a hand for hers. He was feeling relieved, as if some burden had been lifted from his shoulders. They had spoken openly to each other and now had something practical on which to base their marriage. It seemed unimportant now that he had been enchanted by her warm vivacity and that after years of cold cynicism he had forgotten the lessons of ten years ago so far as to hope that there might be more than practicality between them. That had been fantasy. This was reality. And not such a very dreadful reality after all. She might love her secret lover, but she was his duchess and would be true to him and capable in the performance of her duties. Her training had been a thorough one, according to her brother.

"Anna," he said as she rose to her feet. He kept his hold on her hand and took the other one, too. "I know this is an hour you have not enjoyed. But 'tis as well that we have spoken frankly to each other, that we have got to know each other a little better. We did marry rather in haste, did we not? If we always practice openness and honesty with each other, I believe we will deal well together. 'Tis as well too that there is no deep sentiment between us. Sentiment leads inevitably to pain, as I discovered years ago."

Something flickered in her eyes. Yes, she had doubtless discovered it too, else why was she not married to the man she had loved and lain with?

"I have always found that a better guiding principle in life is pleasure," he said. "Although we were strange to each other last night, I believe we found pleasure together. I found delight in your body, and I have had enough experience with women to know that you found delight in mine. We will aim, then, for the performance of duty by day and for the indulgence of pleasure by night—as well as duty. I will teach you to satisfy my needs and you will teach me to satisfy yours."

"Yes," she said.

He held her hands a little tighter. "And I would see you happy again," he said, "and smiling again. The smiles were not all artifice, Anna? I liked them. I would see them again."

"Yes," she said.

He raised his eyebrows.

"But not now," she said. "Later, your grace, but not now. I would be alone if I may."

He raised her hands one at a time to his lips and looked closely into her wide, green, unsmiling eyes. He inclined his head to her and released her hands. He strode across the room to open the door for her and closed it quietly behind her.

Was she regretting, he wondered, that she had given up love, even an unhappy love, for rank and wealth and duty and pleasure?

Well, if she was, the problem was hers. Perhaps she had not yet learned the lessons of love, but she would. He would give her and her sisters the home they needed. He had already given her the dignity of married status, which was obviously important to her and the security of rank and fortune. And he would give her pleasure, so much pleasure that she would forget the foolish love that had put the sadness into her eyes a little while ago and made it impossible for her to smile.

He would fill her nights with pleasure. And his own too.

Yes, despite the discovery he had made last night and her refusal to be completely open with him this morning, he was not sorry he had married her. Perhaps he was even glad that he had learned so soon that even in his marriage he was essentially alone. That he was to expect no real love, no real trust. He had learned the lesson too early in his marriage to feel betrayed by the knowledge.

Luke got restlessly to his feet. He would go to White's and endure all the bawdy remarks that would doubtless greet him there. He needed something to dispel the inexplicable depression of spirits that had not quite lifted despite a thoroughly frank and satisfactory talk with his wife.

*The* note had been brought by personal messenger, the butler informed Anna with a bow as she turned to hurry upstairs to her own apartments, with strict instructions that it was to be delivered into the hands of no one but her grace. The butler had taken the liberty of persuading the man that he himself would see to the matter.

Anna took it upstairs into her private sitting room to read. A premonition of disaster set her hands to shaking as she unfolded the single sheet of paper.

"This was very naughty of you, my Anna," he had written. "It saddens me to know that perhaps you are having to endure a severe beating this morning. Your duke has a reputation as a proud and a ruthless man. I allowed the marriage to proceed—you looked more beautiful in your white and gold than I have ever seen you look—and will do nothing for a time to interfere with it. But Anna, you are merely on loan to the Duke of Harndon. It would be a grave mistake to become attached to him. I will come for you when the time is right and take you home. You will be happy there eventually and for the rest of your life. My promise on it. Your servant, Blaydon."

She folded the letter slowly and carefully into its original folds and stared down at it in her lap, dry-eyed, for a long time.

"Why did you not stop it?" she whispered at last. "Oh, why did you not stop it?"

## 10

ENRIETTA had written again. She wanted a fountain constructed in the formal gardens—George had approved it before his death but had not had time to implement his decision. Mr. Colby was unwilling to allow her to proceed without his master's permission. It was too bad of the steward to behave in such a high-handed manner, she had written. He frequently got above himself and forgot that she was still the Duchess of Harndon.

But the tone of the letter changed just when Luke was being given the unpleasant impression that the years must have changed her into an imperious, peevish woman.

"Come home, Luke," she had written. "In truth, I care nothing for altering the house or building a fountain or for the tyranny of Mr. Colby. They are merely excuses to lure you home. Ah, how can I be anything but honest when lures have not brought you thus far? Come home. It has been a dreary lifetime since we saw each other last. Do not punish me longer for a single wrong decision I made ten years ago. I suffered for it, Luke, both before and after."

Henrietta, Luke thought as he set the letter down on the desk and sat back in his chair, had obviously not heard about his marriage. Will had returned home the day he proposed to Anna and so had not carried the news with him. Not that the marriage would make any difference in anything. Not as far as the two of them were concerned, anyway. Of course, it would take all semblance of power away from her. He was not sure how badly affected she would be by that.

She regretted her decision. Her feelings for him had not died over the years as his had for her. Perhaps she had not made the effort to kill them that he had made. Poor Henrietta—losing the child must have seemed unusually cruel. And now she wanted him back even though she must know that they could not marry. The law was clear on that point.

He had killed his feelings for her. They were dead. Why, then, did he dread going back to Bowden Abbey? Why did he dread seeing her again?

But he was going to have to go home, Luke thought, drumming his fingers slowly on the desktop. Sometime. Sometime soon. He had made that inevitable when he married. There was no possibility now of returning to Paris and his life there. And he could not live in London indefinitely with a new duchess. He had taken only a three-month lease on this house. Once he had Anna with child, she would need to be in the country.

Yes, it was something that would have to be faced sometime soon.

But not too soon. He wanted to enjoy the pleasures of London with Anna for a while yet. And they were to be enjoyed. He had expected yesterday after his talk with her and after the manner of her leaving him that she would stay alone in her rooms for the rest of the day. He had assumed that they would have to cancel plans to attend Mrs. Burnsides's rout in the evening, that it would be a long time before he saw her smile again.

But she had appeared at dinner, gorgeously clad in a deep pink satin sack dress he had not seen before, her hair tightly curled and powdered, her cap all frivolous lace and ribbons, its lappets reaching halfway to her waist. She was obviously ready for the rout. And she had glowed, her cheeks flushed becomingly—he was glad she wore no cosmetics—her lips smiling beguilingly and eagerly, her eyes sparkling with what he had always interpreted as happiness.

And perhaps it was happiness too, he had thought, watching her appreciatively and listening to her witty and quite frivolous chatter as they dined. Perhaps she had thought over their talk and had con-

cluded that they had worked everything out very satisfactorily. Perhaps it was a relief to her, as it was to him, to have had plain speaking
between them.

She had continued to sparkle at the rout and had appeared to
revel in the fact that she was the main focus of attention there, since
it was her first appearance in public as his duchess. His mother, at
her regal best, had taken Anna about, presenting her to people who
were strangers even to Luke. He had found himself watching his wife
quite as closely as he had during the week before their marriage,
enchanted by her beauty and vivacity again.

Mainly duty by day, he had told her, and mainly pleasure by
night. Luke absently set Henrietta's letter to one side, on top of a
small pile of other letters and cards of invitation, and sat back in his
chair again, his arms on the rests, his fingers steepled before him.

She had been waiting for him, naked, in bed. And she had given
him a night of vigorous pleasure. There had been very little sleep. He
had even woken late for his ride in the rain this morning. She did not
possess many skills—or she had not at the start of the night, anyway. Luke had wondered briefly about her lover, but he had suppressed the thought. He had to forget about the lover. But what she
had lacked in skill she had made up for in an eagerness to please and
in a willingness to allow him any liberty he chose to take; he had
taken a few but had decided to be patient, leaving for another night
some of the delights that might shock her most deeply. And she had
displayed, too, a willingness to be pleased and to show her
pleasure.

It was a night he had thoroughly enjoyed, a night he looked forward to repeating, though before too many more nights had passed
they were going to have to think of getting enough sleep to carry
them through the following day. He was not accustomed to sacrificing sleep for sexual gratification.

Of course—he tapped his forefingers against his chin—there
was nothing to stop him from taking his wife to bed during the afternoons, was there? He laughed softly. Yes, this morning he was
feeling well pleased with his marriage.

But his larger family was clamoring for attention, and they were the reason for his return to England, the reason for his taking a wife. His butler announced Lord Ashley Kendrick. Ashley had been sent for and came striding into the room, looking a curious mixture of confidence and wariness. Luke ruefully remembered certain interviews with his father, the man always seated behind a large desk and he immediately became conscious of where he himself now sat. It was still difficult to adjust his mind to the fact that he was now the figure of authority in his family. He got to his feet, came around the desk, and extended his hand.

"One remembers England as a country of green grass, leaf-laden trees, and colorful flower gardens," he said, shaking his brother's hand and motioning him to a chair. "One forgets the infernal rain that makes it all possible."

"Good old England." Ashley flashed his boyish grin and sat down.

He was nervous, Luke noticed, turning back to the desk and picking up the paper that lay beneath Henrietta's letter. He might as well dispense with the small talk, which they would both know was just that. A man might be invited to make an afternoon call. He was summoned to make a morning call. This was morning and Ashley had been summoned.

"You will doubtless have an explanation for this," he said, handing the paper to Ashley. "It came yesterday after the others had all been paid. Perhaps it came late? As you will see it is the bill for a rather extravagant sum in payment of a . . . ah, emerald bracelet. A gift, perhaps, for our mother?" He seated himself and crossed one leg over the other.

Ashley laughed. "For Mama, as I live," he said. "That is a good one, Luke. 'Twas for a lady who likes baubles. For a lady I like to please."

"A *lady?*" Luke raised his eyebrows. "The same one for whom you have rented a house and hired servants? The same one you clothe in the finest silks and satins?"

"She is worth it, Luke," his brother said. "Word has it that you always had the loveliest women in Paris. And you have taken one of the loveliest women in London to wife. 'Tis merely that I am keeping up the family tradition, you see. And I have never had a better woman on the mount."

"I feel constrained to inform you that she is too expensive, my dear," Luke said.

"Zounds!" Ashley exclaimed, his face paling, his jaw setting into a hard line. "But you are no different from Papa and George, Luke. I am two-and-twenty. Am I to live like a monk? And don't call me 'my dear.' You sound like a damned . . ."

"I assume," Luke said after waiting politely for a moment to allow his brother to complete the sentence if he wished, "that there are reputable whorehouses in London as there are in Paris, where one may be assured of finding satisfaction for one's needs with girls who are both clean and skilled and who are not encouraged to wheedle silks and jewels out of the more naive of their customers."

"Pox on it," Ashley said, "I do not want a whore, Luke. I want a mistress. I am brother and heir to the Duke of Harndon, deuce take it, and have your reputation to live up to."

"Ah," Luke said softly, "you are very young, my dear. Pardon me. I forget that I am in England where men must be men and live in terror of suggesting femininity by word or deed. But to continue. One has nothing to live up to except one's own expectations. Especially when one is free of responsibilities. Are you bored? Do you have any other plans for your life apart from living up to my reputation? And that might not be quite what you think it is—I have never employed a mistress and I have touched alcohol only rarely since my twenty-first year."

"You do not need to keep mistresses," Ashley said with bitter sullenness. "'Tis said that ladies of highest quality rush to your bed if you but look at them and raise an eyebrow. 'Tis said that the Marquise d'Étienne came to London to—"

"Have a care," Luke said quietly. "The lady moves in the highest court circles. She goes where she wills. What are your plans?"

"Not the army," Ashley said firmly. "That was Papa's plan for me. George for the title, you for the church, me for the army. I am no coward, Luke, but I have no fancy to be fodder for enemy cannon whenever statesmen take it into their heads to quarrel. And not the church, either, though George and Mama were keen on the idea after you disappointed them. I go to church when I have to, and I give alms whenever anyone appeals to me in a good cause, and I have not stolen or murdered as far as I can recall, but I don't fancy being a clergyman, even with the prospect of being a bishop one day through the ducal influence. So do not try to force either of those on me, Luke, there's a good fellow."

"And yet," Luke said, "you seem to be a man of energy and one who chafes against restraints, Ashley. You have an independence, but you live beyond it. Will you enjoy having to come, cap in hand, to me or to my steward for the rest of your life?"

"As I live, no," Ashley said, surging to his feet. "You are the worst of the lot, Luke. At least they would rant and rave. You sit there, striking an elegant pose, your eyes as cold as ice, calling me your dear as if I was a girl. Sometimes I believe that you must have killed my brother Luke ten years ago and taken his place. Sometimes you do not even look like him. The Luke I knew was warm and generous."

"You may leave that bill on the desk," Luke said, getting to his feet too. "I will settle it. But pay heed, Ashley. It will be the last of such bills I will pay. If you must satisfy your sexual appetites with an expensive mistress, you must do so within the bounds of your allowance. 'Twill not be easy even with the increase I will implement next quarter. 'Twould be much better to let her go and follow my advice. Indeed, I will amend what I just said. You may wish to make some settlement on the woman. You may bring me the bill for that settlement."

"Zounds, but this is insufferable humiliation," Ashley said, clearly not hearing the library door opening behind him. "Cold eyes and cold, cold heart. I wish you had stayed where you were, Luke. No, I wish more. I wish you had taken yourself to the devil instead of coming here."

"Good morning, my dear," Luke said over his brother's shoulder to his wife, who was standing, startled and embarrassed, in the doorway.

Ashley spun around and strode toward her. "Madam," he said, making her a hasty bow and taking her offered hand to raise to his lips, "your servant. From the bottom of my heart I pity you." He hurried from the room without looking back.

"Come inside, my dear," Luke said.

Anna looked after Ashley before hesitantly obeying. "I am sorry," she said. "I did not know there was someone with you. I should have had myself announced or found out that you had company and gone back to my rooms."

He crossed the room to close the door behind her. He set his hands on her shoulders and kissed her continental fashion, first on one cheek and then on the other.

"This is your home, madam," he said. "You may go wherever you will in it, without asking anyone's permission, my own included. Did you sleep well?"

"I slept far too late," she said. "The morning is all but gone."

"If you had not slept late," he said, "you would not have slept at all." He enjoyed watching her blush. The other women with whom he had been intimate had been far too blasé about life ever to blush. "Thank you, my dear, for a night of great pleasure."

"Lord Ashley was upset?" she asked.

"Family matters," he said. "I have been taking him to task about certain bills that are beyond his own means to pay. He has been accusing me of heartlessness—a familiar accusation."

"You will not pay the bills?" she asked. "You will let him come to ruin? Perhaps even end up in debtors' prison? You are very wealthy, are you not?"

He remembered that her father had been deep in debt, that he had perhaps been a compulsive gambler. It must be a subject on which she was more than usually sensitive.

"The bills have been paid or will be paid," he said. "And certain commands have been given. I am head of this family, madam, and

have recently taken the reins into my own hands. It is only fair that
all those dependent upon me be told where certain lines are to be
drawn and what the consequences of stepping beyond those lines
will be."

"Yes," she said. "But it is love that binds families." She looked
down at her hands and her voice dropped almost to a whisper. "But
you do not believe in love." She looked up into his eyes again, but did
not raise her voice. "What is wrong in your family? Why do you not
live in Harndon House? Why have you been estranged from your
family for so long and never intended coming home or seeing any of
them again? Forgive me, but do not say 'tis none of my concern. It is.
Your family is mine now. And you said we must always speak frankly
to each other." She frowned suddenly and flushed deeply. She looked
away from his eyes.

"I was a wild young man," he said. He had begun with an un-
truth. He had been anything but wild. "Sweet" and "even-tempered"
had been the descriptions of himself he had heard most often. He had
been exuberant too, but never in any destructive way. And he had
been utterly, incredibly naive. He had been in love—with his calling
to the church and with his boyhood sweetheart. "I fought a duel with
my older brother over some unremembered offense"—over Henrietta, whom George had ravished and impregnated and then offered
for—"and came literally within an inch of killing him. He was in a
high fever for a few weeks, I heard. I did not see it. I was gone. Ban-
ished. My brother was judged to be the one in the right, of course,
since he was the one near death. He was noble enough to delope—his
bullet was lost in the air above our heads. Is that frank enough for
you, my dear?"

She was staring at him, pale faced. "*Was* he in the right?" she asked.

She was deeply shocked he could see. He withdrew from her
emotionally, something that was quite unconscious, something he
had become quite expert at over the years. "As I said," he told her,
"'twas over some quarrel I cannot remember. Doubtless at the time
I believed I had the right of it. But he was more noble than I." Only
because Luke had not even heard the word "delope" until after the

duel. And only because at that time he was such a lamentably poor shot that the bullet had hit six feet from its intended target—a willow tree well to one side of his brother.

"You see, my dear," he said, quite unaware of the slight edge of bitterness to his voice, "what you overheard my brother say a few minutes ago is quite true. I am without a heart. It is as well that you and I decided yesterday to settle for pleasure, is it not?"

"Your mother wishes me to accompany her and Lady Doris this afternoon when they pay some calls," she said. "She sent a note. May I go, your grace? Do you have other plans?"

Only to take her to bed to satiate himself again.

"You must send an acceptance," he said. "You must become well acquainted with them, Anna. As you just observed, they are your family too now."

"Thank you." She looked uncertainly at him for a moment and then turned to leave.

But he reached for her hands and held them. He had found himself wanting to—to defend himself? To tell that story as it had really happened? To tell her about Henrietta? But he had long ago developed a confidence in himself that demanded no self-defense. He did not care what people believed of him or said of him. They would believe what they wanted, even if what they believed was not the truth. Only a weak man—a man to whom the regard of others mattered—worried about his reputation.

"Enjoy your visits," he said, bowing over her hands. "I shall see you at dinner. The hours between now and then will seem endless."

The conventional gallantries, spoken without conscious thought. And yet nevertheless true, he thought ruefully after she had left the room. He wanted her. Even after two nearly sleepless nights of energetic lovemaking, he wanted her.

For a moment the yearning was so great that it seemed to him it was more than just physical. But only for a moment. He knew better today than to walk into the trap that those thoughts could lead to.

• • •

"*Do* tell me," Lady Doris Kendrick said, taking Anna's arm and leaning her head close. They were at Lady Riever's, taking tea, their third call of the afternoon, and several other ladies had arrived after them. Lady Doris had contrived to take Anna a little apart to sit side by side on a small sofa. "Is marriage quite, quite wonderful? I will wager it is. Luke is very splendid, is he not? I enjoy watching the way all the ladies look at him at balls. Marriage to someone like Luke must be very wonderful. There are always whispers among women when they are talking about marriage and believe one is not listening about that which has to be endured at night as the price of position and respectability, but I will not believe that it is so very dreadful. I long for it, I make so bold as to say. Do tell. Is it exciting?"

Anna had quite alarmingly inappropriate memories of long, sensitive male fingers stroking her where it should have been too embarrassing to think of fingers being at all and of the raw sensation they aroused there. "It is pleasant," she said.

"Oh, fie, pleasant!" Doris stifled a giggle and looked consciously at her mother, who was not observing her. "How refined you are, Anna. Are you deep in love? 'Tis said that half the ladies of Paris were hot in pursuit of Luke when he was merely Lord Lucas Kendrick and that three-quarters of them were after he became duke. Are you in love with him?"

Yes. Oh yes, she feared she was very much infatuated with a man about whom she was having more and graver doubts. But it was too late to doubt. He was her husband. And perhaps he was right about one thing. Perhaps the pleasure he gave her in bed was worth it all. Perhaps it was better than love. Love of her family had caused all the impossible tangles in her life. Perhaps it was as well that he did not love his own family, herself included. She wondered if he would love their children.

"I have an affection for his grace, Doris," she said.

"Affection," Doris said. "His grace. La, I will feel more than an affection for my husband when I marry, and I will call him by the intimacy of his Christian name or some other endearment. But perhaps you do in the privacy of your own . . . apartments." She giggled again.

Doris was a year older than Agnes, Anna thought, yet far more of a child. Perhaps Agnes had been forced to grow up faster by the precariousness of their situation for a few years, though Anna had done her best to shield her younger sisters and even Victor from anxiety. She had sold her soul to the devil in order to shield them.

*You are merely on loan to the Duke of Harndon.* She shivered quite involuntarily. No. No, she had decided not to think of that. She had burned the note. She smiled warmly.

"Have you met anyone to whom you would wish to attach yourself?" she asked. "You must not have lacked for interested suitors. You are very pretty."

"And the daughter and sister of a duke," Doris said with a sigh. "And the possessor of an enormous dowry. But yes, Anna, I have met the man of my dreams and I am going to marry him and live happily ever after."

"Tell me about him." Anna sensed that she had been led aside for just this purpose. Perhaps she was the only youngish woman in whom the girl had had a chance to confide, though there was a sister-in-law at Bowden Abbey, was there not?

"Mama does not approve," Doris said. "In fact, Mama has expressly forbidden me to see him. Because he is poor, Anna, if you can imagine a more ridiculous reason for disapproving. He was hired to paint my portrait several months ago. He was considered good enough for that, you see, even though he has not yet attained any great fame or fortune. But he will. Oh, one day he is going to be the most famous, most sought after portrait painter in England. In all of Europe. We fell deep in love, Anna. And we will marry. The violence of my attachment will make it impossible for me to give him up."

Oh dear. Anna, who was accustomed to having her ears assailed with confidences from sisters, had never had to deal with anything like this. She was suddenly very thankful that Charlotte's attachment had been a perfectly eligible one even if not brilliant. And Agnes had shown no attachment to anyone yet.

"I suppose," she said, "that your mama is thinking of your happiness, Doris."

"Oh, no, she is not," the girl said emphatically. "She is thinking of family pride. 'Tis just not the thing for the daughter of a Duke of Harndon to marry a penniless painter."

"Poverty is not a pleasant thing," Anna said quietly. "Especially when one is not accustomed to it. There is certainly no romance in it."

"Oh, fie," the girl said. "We will have my dowry to live on until Daniel grows rich. And I do not fear poverty. Luke will let me marry him."

Anna recalled the scene in the library that she had walked in on earlier in the day and the humiliation and distress she had seen in Lord Ashley's face as he had greeted her. All because he had acquired some foolish debts. Not that debts were ever foolish. Luke had perhaps been right to take him to task over them.

"You have spoken to him?" she asked.

"There has not been the chance," Doris said. She giggled. "He has been distracted since coming home to England with marrying you. But that is all for the better. He will understand how Daniel and I feel. I will talk to him and he will tell Mama that I am to be allowed to meet Daniel and to marry him before the year is out. We cannot possibly wait longer. Oh, Anna, we are going to be the happiest couple in the world."

Anna felt less sure.

Doris leaned toward her again. "Luke will agree," she said. "Luke was always my favorite person in all the world. I thought my heart would break when he went away. But you might speak to him, Anna. You might explain that I am quite, quite sure about Daniel, that I can be happy with no one else, that wealth and position mean nothing to me. You will explain? You will help me?"

"Doris." Anna touched her hand. "This is a matter for your mama to advise on and his grace to decide upon. You must talk with

them. I am a stranger to all intents and purposes even if I am your
sister-in-law. I have been married to your brother for only two days."

"But that is the best part of it," Doris said. "He will be so deep
in love still that he will give you whatever you ask, Anna. Though
he will do it for me, anyway. Talk to him. Please?"

"I will see what I can do," Anna said unhappily. "But I will not
interfere, Doris."

The girl did not seem disappointed. She smiled with satisfaction.
And there was no more time to talk. The dowager duchess was getting to her feet and signaling them that it was time to take their
leave.

Luke would cut the girl to pieces, Anna thought. He had admitted to her quite openly that he had no heart, and she had seen for
herself that it was true. He would not countenance his sister's marrying a penniless nobody. Anna had to admit to herself that he would
be quite right to object or at least to have the deepest misgivings
about consenting to such a match. But she feared his methods.

There was no love in him. Least of all for the family who had
rejected him—with very good reason, from what he had told her—
ten years ago.

## 11

*F*OR a month Luke succeeded in clinging to a life with which he was almost familiar. For a month he succeeded in keeping family problems more or less at bay, convincing himself that all had been solved. For a month he succeeded in making of his marriage what he had suggested they try to make of it—something wholly pleasurable. For a month he succeeded in staying away from Bowden Abbey.

He wrote to Henrietta, telling her of his marriage, though probably she had already heard about it from some other source. He wrote only of business matters, careful to keep his tone quite impersonal. Under the circumstances, he wrote, any changes to the house or park should perhaps be postponed for a while. It was a tactful way of informing her that his wife was now mistress of Bowden Abbey. Henrietta did not write again. He hoped she would not. He hoped that somehow he could avoid seeing her. He felt the gulf between them as an almost tangible thing, wider than ever, though it had been insurmountable even before his marriage.

He wrote to Colby, instructing him to increase Ashley's allowance by a substantial amount and to pay him a certain sum to see him through to the next quarter. He did not see a great deal of his brother during the month, and when he did, Ashley was scrupulously polite to him, gallantly charming to Anna. Luke understood from a certain large bill that arrived on his desk one day without explanation that the expensive mistress's services had been dispensed with.

For ten years Luke had cut himself off from family ties, feeling

nothing for any of them except his uncle. And yet there was something whenever he saw Ashley. Some unidentified heaviness.
Some . . . regret. He remembered the eager, mischievous little boy to
whom he had been a hero. And he saw the handsome, eager, rather
wild young man whose life might go either of two ways at this early,
impressionable stage of his development. A young man who needed
guidance. Luke was not sure he could give it—or wanted to even if
he could. But if not him, who else?

He asked no questions of his brother during that month and
hoped that the irresponsible extravagances were at an end. He shied
away from any emotional involvement, even with a brother.

He made a little more effort in Doris's case. A few days after his
wedding he called on his mother for the express purpose of finding out
about the ineligible connection she had mentioned during the first
visit. It seemed that a portrait painter had been engaged to come to
the house in London to paint Doris. There had been several lengthy
sittings, at which the dowager herself or else Doris's maid had always
sat as chaperone. Or so the dowager had thought. Later, when Doris
claimed that she and the painter were in love and intended to marry,
it was discovered that the maid had often been sent out of the way.

"He is the son of a publican," the dowager explained disdainfully.
"He has had some small success as a portrait painter and is convinced that he will become fashionable and wealthy within the next
year or two. Or so Doris claims. At present I believe he lives in shabby
poverty."

"You have talked with him?" Luke asked.

"About this matter?" his mother said haughtily. "Mercy, Lucas,
what do you think of me? Of course I have not spoken with him. I
have merely forbidden any communication between them. It is a connection that is quite out of the question."

"And yet," Luke said, "you are still concerned, madam? They are
still seeing each other?"

The dowager was tight-lipped. "I fear there is some communication," she said. "Doris is a headstrong girl and has not had the guidance of a father or older brother for more than two years."

"I will see him," Luke said. "His name?"

"Daniel Frawley," she said, making it sound as if she were naming a worm.

Daniel Frawley, Luke decided after he had called at the man's studio and wandered unhurriedly about, examining his paintings, was a man of very mediocre talents. He would probably scratch a living by painting portraits that grossly flattered his sitters without in any way grasping the essence of their individual characters. If he aspired to be another Joshua Reynolds, he was doomed to disappointment.

Frawley was closemouthed about his relationship with Doris. But Luke was coldly and haughtily persistent. They were in love, the painter admitted at last. They wished to marry. He would support her on the proceeds of his work. Already he was receiving commissions from influential people—the Dowager Duchess of Harndon, for example. Soon he would be in fashion and would move in high society as if he were a born member. Besides, Lady Doris would have her dowry.

"Lady Doris Kendrick is an impulsive, immature young lady blinded by romance," Luke said, seating himself without invitation on a hard and lumpy sofa and taking a pinch of snuff from the box he had withdrawn from a pocket. "The idea of starving in a garret with an as-yet-unappreciated artist doubtless has irresistible appeal to her. But she is accustomed to another manner of life entirely, Frawley. She would be unable to make the adjustment, even if I were willing to allow her to try. She would be desperately unhappy within a few months."

"I see," the artist said, gazing at him with hostile eyes that did not conceal the contempt he felt for the Parisian splendor of his guest. "But I am not so sure that I could adjust to life without her, your grace."

"Ah," Luke said softly. His eyebrows rose and he regarded the artist from beneath half-lowered eyelids. "I did wonder." He looked Daniel Frawley up and down before speaking again. "How much?"

Frawley licked his lips. His eyes roamed restlessly about the studio. "Five thousand pounds," he said.

Luke took his time about answering. "Lady Doris's dowry is larger," he said. "You might have asked more, Frawley. Ten thousand, perhaps even twenty."

The painter tried unsuccessfully not to show his chagrin. "I am not greedy," he said stiffly. "It will not be easy to give her up. I love her."

"Then you might have put a higher price on your love," Luke said pleasantly, getting to his feet and strolling languidly toward the much taller and larger man. "But no matter. My answer would have been the same whether you had asked five, ten, twenty, or fifty thousand. This is my answer."

The next moment, Daniel Frawley crashed backward to the floor. His face contorted with pain, he lifted one hand to cup about one side of his jaw.

Luke flexed his right hand and looked down ruefully at his reddening knuckles. "You will, of course," he said in the same pleasant tone he had used a few moments before, "stay quite away from Lady Doris Kendrick from this moment on."

The artist lay silently where he was on the floor while his visitor let himself out.

And then Luke called on Doris and asked for a private word with her when their mother would have joined them.

"You have *what*?" His sister stood wide-eyed in the middle of the room after he had spoken to her.

"I have forbidden him to have anything more to do with you, Doris," he repeated.

"Have you?" Her voice was quiet, but her bosom, he saw, was heaving. "Have you? Because he is a struggling artist, I suppose, and because his father was not a gentleman. Because he has not yet achieved fame or fortune. I am to marry a man who has wealth and rank, regardless of my ability to love him or be happy with him. Is that it, Luke?"

"My dear," he said, regarding her coolly, "grant that I have an older and wiser head than you and that our mother does too. Grant that perhaps we can see better than you what or who could *not* make you happy. Daniel Frawley could not do so."

Her bosom still heaved. Her eyes flashed. With an inner sigh he prepared himself to deal with feminine hysteria, something he loathed doing and normally avoided at all costs since women did not fight fairly. They might claw and scratch and punch and kick and bite and use blistering language. But let the man retaliate with even the mildest oath or the lightest slap and they were screeching murder. And the whole world—male and female—took their part.

But Doris did not explode as he expected her to. Her eyes filled with tears, which spilled over onto her cheeks. "You too, Luke?" she said in a near whisper. "You too cannot see that I am a person with feelings and dreams of my own? Because I am a duke's daughter and your sister, you must see to it that my future reflects the family position and pride? My preferences are of no importance at all? You must order my life as if I am a thing, and not a breathing, feeling, thinking person?"

He realized his mistake immediately. His mistakes. He should have spoken with his sister before going to Frawley's. He should have tried to get her to see for herself that such an attachment was quite ineligible and very unlikely to bring her lasting happiness. And he should have conducted this interview differently. He should not have spared her feelings by withholding the information about her true love's perfect willingness—even eagerness—to withdraw his suit for a price. But he would not change course now. He had taken the path of authority and would keep to it. She doubtless would not believe him anyway. He had never had to deal with a younger sister before from a position of authority. What was as clear as day to him was obviously not clear at all to her.

"Did Anna not speak with you?" she asked.

"Yes," he said. "She did."

Anna had told him that Doris had fallen in love with all the hot impetuosity of youth and that the object of her attachment might well be ineligible. But it was a real attachment, she had added. Young people's feelings might sometimes be misguided but they were nevertheless intense. And young people could feel as much pain as older people— sometimes more. Anna had asked him to deal gently with his sister.

He knew nothing about gentleness. And he was not sure it was the answer to anything. Life was a harsh business with harsh lessons to learn. He had learned the hard way himself and was none the worse for it.

"I feel sorry for Anna," Doris said very quietly, "married to you." Ashley had said that too—directly to Anna.

"One day, Doris," he said, "you will realize that I am doing what is best for you."

"I wonder," she said, "if parents and older brothers really believe that when they say it. I never ever expected to hear it from you. Not from you, Luke."

"I will have your promise now," he said, "that you will no longer communicate with Frawley."

"Or what?" she asked. "What will you do to me, Luke, if I refuse to give any such promise? Or if I do not keep it? Take me over your knee and beat me?"

"I do not make silly threats, Doris," he said. "It is only fair, however, that you understand that you will be very sorry for disobedience on this matter."

"That is not a threat?" She looked down at her hands and then up into his eyes. "What did they do to you in France, Luke? If I could tear open your coat and waistcoat and shirt, would I find a scar on your left breast where they removed your heart?"

She did not wait for a reply, though the questions were, of course, purely rhetorical. She turned and hurried from the room, her promise not given.

Luke sighed. He had given up wishing that George had not died or had fathered a dozen sons before doing so. And he had given up wishing that he had stayed in Paris and allowed his family members to find their own way to heaven or to hell. But sometimes he still felt angry—deeply, impotently angry—over a fate that had given him responsibilities he had never asked for. He had been happy as he was, in the life he had forged for himself.

But over the following weeks all seemed to be well in the sense that his mother believed the connection with Frawley had been brought to an end. Doris was subdued whenever she was forced into his company and never looked directly at him or addressed a word to him if she could avoid doing so. But she did not look as if she were pining for a lost love. She danced every set at the balls they attended and conversed with gentlemen at routs and concerts. She had a court of admirers, several of them eligible enough to be encouraged if she so chose.

Perhaps by the summer, before it was time for her to return home, she would fall in love with someone else. She was young enough to forget easily. Though unwillingly he remembered someone—himself—who had not found it at all easy to forget. There had been a year of hell . . .

As for his marriage, Luke found himself regretting it less as the month progressed. Anna was an interesting and witty companion in the privacy of their own home, a dazzling and charming one in public, and a warm and passionate lover in bed. Sometimes he made love to her during the afternoons—so that they might get some sleep during the nights, he told both her and himself. She was embarrassed and rather stiff the first time, finding neither darkness—or even semidarkness—nor clothing nor bedclothes behind which to hide. But it did not take him long to persuade her—with his hands and mouth and body rather than with words—to accept her own beauty and her own sexuality and to know that he found her in no way wanting.

And yet, strangely, even on the nights when they did not make love, he found himself going to her bed to sleep almost as if it were his own. They never touched except when they were making love, but he found her soft breathing and her body heat and the womanly smell of her soothing. He slept better than he had ever done alone. It was one surprising—and not at all unpleasant—discovery about his marriage.

She gave him pleasure and he knew that he gave it to her, too. Pleasure in their sexual life and pleasure in their social life. They attended almost all the many social functions of the spring season and did some entertaining themselves, having close acquaintances to dine more than once, and hosting a card and informal dancing party one evening. Always Anna sparkled with warm gaiety as she had during that first ball. She was widely admired. Other men envied him, Luke knew. He found that he watched her in public far more than other men watched their wives. It pleased him to watch her— and to note that she watched him almost as much. He wondered if she drew as much pleasure from his appearance as he did from hers.

Pleasure, he decided, made for a far firmer and more lasting basis to a relationship than love. He was glad—very glad—that there was no love between himself and his wife. He was glad that his discovery on his wedding night and her refusal to answer his questions the morning after had killed the foolish infatuation he had felt for her. He was glad there were no real depths to their relationship. Only pleasure.

His first month in England had brought with it a new way of life, with which he was not entirely dissatisfied. If only it could continue thus, he thought sometimes, he could be almost as well content as he had been in Paris.

But then came the evening of the masquerade at Ranelagh Gardens. By the following morning he knew that his return to Bowden Abbey could be postponed no longer and that his life was about to change again.

It was not a happy prospect.

*Ranelagh* Gardens in Chelsea had been opened only a few years before and was still all the rage among people of fashion. There was the large rotunda, inside which one could stroll or take tea or coffee while listening to music. More popular, there were the gardens to walk in and the artificial lake and canal with boats and a picturesque Chinese pagoda. The treelined walks on either side of the canal were favorites with lovers, particularly during the evenings, when the gardens were lit by hundreds of golden lamps.

Anna had never been there before. Nor had she ever attended a masquerade. She was enormously excited and despised her excitement when she was a twenty-five-year-old married lady. Sometimes she felt as if all the youthfulness she had been deprived of at the appropriate time in her life was finding its way out of her now. And yet Luke never seemed to mind. It excited her that he watched her at balls and other assemblies just as he had before they were married, his fan usually waving absently before his face.

She flirted with him still when they were in public, even though they had been married and lovers for a month.

She dressed as a Turkish princess for the masquerade—or rather as a member of a Turkish harem, Luke told her when he saw her. He also told her that she could be a member of his harem any time she chose. She laughed and batted her eyelashes at him over the top of the heavy gold veil with which she had covered her face from the eyes down, in place of a mask. And unseen by him she blushed at the naked desire she saw in his eyes for a moment.

She felt deliciously comfortable and feminine—and slightly wicked—in her loose scarlet damask drawers with gold embroidered flowers and in her fine white silk gauze smock edged with gold damask. She felt almost undressed despite the red, gold-belted caftan she wore over all. It felt strange to be without the armor of her hoops—though she was still tightly laced, of course. On her unpowdered hair she wore a small red velvet cap, decorated with pearls.

Luke had refused to be a sultan to please her. If he were one, he had explained, he would certainly not be escorting her to a masquerade for all to see and admire. He would have her behind locked doors, guarded by six-foot eunuchs with large muscles. He wore a domino and half mask. But since the domino was scarlet, lined with gold, and his waistcoat and mask were also gold, he looked quite gorgeous enough to Anna to be her sultan.

Agnes was also at the masquerade, dressed as a shepherdess, with Lady Sterne and Lord Quinn. And Doris was there as Diana the huntress with her mother. Anna loved all of them and spent time talking with them between dances in the rotunda. It was amusing but not at all difficult to guess the identities of most of the masked revelers. Some gentlemen, most of them in dark dominos and masks, kept in the shadows or out of doors. Men who were not well received in society, perhaps, Anna thought, but who had nevertheless been willing to pay the entrance fee.

But not all the evening was spent inside. She walked beside the canal with Luke for a whole hour first and wished they could stroll there for an hour longer before going inside and being forced apart by the demands of sociability. It was lovely to walk alone with him in such magical surroundings, to feel all the romance of it, to know that they belonged together, that they were lovers, and that . . . But she hugged entirely to herself the secret and exciting hope that had been growing in her for several days.

They did not talk a great deal as they walked, and it pleased her, as she watched the shimmering reflections of the lamps in the water, to imagine that he felt the romance of it too, that perhaps there was coming to be a little more than just duty and pleasure to bind them. With his free hand he covered her own as it rested on his arm. She felt it as a touchingly intimate gesture.

She sat with Doris after they had entered the rotunda. The musicians were not playing. She had remained friendly with the girl even though there had been a certain rift with Luke—if "rift" was the right word. Luke was not close to his family at all. Apparently he had handled the business of Doris's romance rather badly. He had called on Doris's Daniel and forbidden him to see or communicate with her again. He had told her that much himself. But when the man had protested his love for Doris, Luke had threatened him. And then Luke had offered him money—twenty thousand pounds—to stay away from Doris. When Daniel had refused, Luke had knocked him down. Those last details had been supplied by Doris.

Anna always tried not to think of Luke's part in what had happened. For there it was again—that total lack of respect and feeling for a woman's point of view, that overpowering male urge to control. What he had done had perhaps not been wrong in itself, but there had surely been a kinder way of discouraging Doris from making what would surely have been an unwise marriage. Men never took the kind way, though. Men seemed to know nothing about kindness, only about power.

But the very story Doris had told Anna seemed to prove that her young man had not heeded the warning. There had obviously been at least one more communication between the lovers. It bothered Anna to know that the inflexibility of the commands Luke had given might drive them to desperation. She would have liked to confide in him. But she did not do so. How would he punish his sister for receiving a forbidden letter? Perhaps it had been a harmless letter of good-bye.

Doris seemed full of suppressed excitement tonight.

"'Tis a wonderful occasion, is it not?" Anna said, taking a seat beside her. "So many costumes, such an imposing building, such beautiful gardens. They must be lovely by day. They are enchanted by night."

Doris's eyes were searching the shadows of the interior of the rotunda and the outdoors as seen through the open doorway. "I care not for any of it," she said. She leaned forward as someone in a dark domino passed outside, and then sat back again. "I care nothing for this life of wealth and endless and meaningless pleasures. They mean nothing to me. I mean to renounce them. I mean to be happy."

Perhaps she did not intend to make her meaning quite so plain. But it was instantly obvious to Anna that a tryst had been arranged. What better place for it than Ranelagh Gardens at night during a masquerade? But what did she mean to do? Just meet Daniel for a few minutes? Her words had suggested more.

"Doris." She set a hand on the girl's arm. "What have you planned?"

Doris looked at her. "The least said the better," she said. "I like you, Anna, and I pity you being married to Luke because he has become a monster without a heart—I wish you had known him a long time ago when he was my favorite person in the whole world. I like you, but you are his wife, and perhaps you would feel constrained to tell him any confidence I placed in you. 'Tis better if you know nothing."

Oh, the foolish girl. Her meaning was as plain as if she had put it into words.

"Doris," Anna said, "do not do anything you will regret."

"La, I do not intend to," the girl said, leaning a little closer and speaking intensely. "I will never regret what I will do tonight." She laughed suddenly. "Dance with all the most handsome gentlemen, that is."

Lord Quinn bowed over Anna's hand at that moment to ask her for the honor of leading her into the next set of country dances. She smiled at him and rose to her feet.

"Egad," he said, "but I can never resist treading a measure with a gel newly escaped from the harem. My nephy is a lucky fellow, I warrant you."

Anna laughed and sought out her husband with her eyes, as she was in the habit of doing. He was standing talking with a few other gentlemen, his eyes looking at her through the slits of the golden mask, his ivory fan, closed, tapping against his chin. He would not be able to see her smile behind the veil. She widened her eyes at him.

What was Doris planning to do? Spend so much time with her Daniel that Luke would be forced to consent to her marrying him? Elope with him? Anna very much needed to talk to her husband, and yet she hesitated. What if it were merely an innocent meeting that was planned? Was there any great harm in that when the girl was young and fancied herself in love? And yet Anna knew that more than that was planned. But what if the young man did not come? She would get Doris into trouble for naught. But if he did not come tonight, would they make plans for another night?

The worst of it was, Anna thought, that in a month of marriage that had brought her and Luke close physically and that had established a light flirtatious relationship between them, there had been no closeness of minds. She felt a reluctance, almost an embarrassment, about talking to him on any serious matter.

Anna danced and talked and made her eyes sparkle and . . . worried. What should she do? The only thing she could do, she decided at last, was keep a careful eye on Doris herself and make sure that she did nothing irreparably foolish.

It was during the next set, a minuet, that Doris, who had refused two would-be partners and stood near the door, was approached by a tall man all in gray. They did not dance. They disappeared through the door so quickly that even Anna, who was watching for such a move, hardly saw them go.

Anna was dancing with Mr. Hatwell, an acquaintance. She looked around quickly for her mother-in-law. The dowager was talking with a couple, her back to the door. Anna turned her glance back to where her husband had been standing a few minutes ago. He was still there and still looking at her. He seemed to realize that something was amiss—she had stopped dancing and turned completely away from her partner, she was suddenly aware. He came striding toward her.

"My wife is feeling unwell, Hatwell," he said with a polite bow to her partner. "You will excuse her?"

Mr. Hatwell bowed in return and murmured his concern for her health.

"Something is wrong, my dear?" Luke asked after he had taken her arm and skillfully steered her past dancers to the door.

"'Tis Doris, Luke," she said. "I feared from something she said earlier that she had planned a meeting with her young man tonight. She just left hurriedly with a tall man in a dark gray domino and mask. I do not know if it was he. But she should not be alone with anyone anyway."

They were outside in the cool, lamplit darkness. He took her by the shoulders and squeezed hard. "Stay here," he said, his voice steely enough to make her shiver. "I will be back." He turned to stride away in the direction of the outer gates. He was not going to waste time, then, searching the paths along which his sister might be strolling with a beau.

Anna hesitated and then hurried after him. "Luke," she said, "do not be too harsh with her. She is young and fancies herself in love. She believes this is the only chance for happiness she will ever have."

He did not answer her. Neither did he order her to go back. His eyes were looking keenly in all directions. Anna shivered again. Had she done right to appeal to him? He looked coldly murderous.

The lovers had not had enough of a start to escape completely.

They were approaching the gates when Luke hailed them. They swung around, hand in hand, and Doris let out a little cry. Her eyes, round with terror and dismay through her mask, moved from Luke to Anna and turned reproachful. Despite herself, Anna felt her eyes drop.

"You are going somewhere?" Luke asked, his tone ominously pleasant.

"Yes." Doris was the one who spoke, her voice defiant. "We are going away from here. We are going to be married."

"In a few minutes' time, my dear," Luke said, "you will be going home with our mother." He turned his attention to the tall and silent young man. "You are a glutton for punishment, Frawley?"

"This is what your sister wants," the young man said, his voice intense with anger. "And 'tis what I want."

"Yes, I have no doubt of it," Luke said. "I informed you, after all, that her dowry is worth more than the five thousand pounds you asked for in return for breaking off communication with her."

"Oh, 'tis a lie!" Doris cried. "'Tis you who offered money, Luke— twenty thousand pounds—and Daniel who refused."

"Ah," Luke said, his eyes still on Daniel Frawley, "that detail had escaped my memory."

Anna, listening to the pleasantness of his voice, shivered once more.

But suddenly the other man dragged a sword free of its scabbard at his side and pointed it directly at Luke. Anna felt her knees turn to jelly.

"You will not stop us," he said. "Stay just where you are, Harndon, if you do not wish to take harm. Doris and I are leaving."

Luke neither moved nor changed his tone of voice. "Extremely unwise, my dear," he said to Daniel Frawley. "Put it up while you have the chance."

Daniel made the mistake of sneering. It seemed to Anna that she saw the sword in her husband's hand before she heard the scraping sound of its being drawn from its scabbard. And then somehow—her eye was not fast enough to follow the exact sequence of events—Daniel Frawley's sword was flying in an arc through the air and clattering down onto the path a dozen feet away and the point of Luke's sword was at his throat. Anna, too horrified to move, watched in fascination as a dark bubble beaded there and began to flow in a thin trickle down his neck.

"What you will do," Luke said, his tone still unchanged, "is leave alone, Frawley. With your life and most of your blood if you are a good boy. I shall relieve you of a little more of the latter if you ever come within hailing distance of Lady Doris Kendrick again. I might have allowed you to meet her occasionally under strictest chaperonage had you not shown yourself quite as prepared to take my money as to marry my sister. I might have allowed it in the hope that she would come to realize that such a change in her style of life would not bring her the happiness she expected. But now you will communicate with her on peril of your life. You may retrieve your sword before leaving." He lowered his sword unhurriedly and replaced it in its scabbard.

Daniel Frawley did as he was told.

Doris, who had stood frozen, both hands over her mouth, lowered them finally as her lover disappeared from sight. "I hate you," she said dispassionately to Luke. "And I will do all I can to defy you. I will elope with him at the earliest opportunity."

"Anna." Luke kept his eyes on his sister. "Will you be so good as to hurry back to the rotunda and ask my mother if she will come here? Explain that she will be taking Doris home, if you please. Stay there with Lady Sterne until I come to you."

Anna hurried away. She knew for once in her life what Judas Iscariot must have felt like when he left the Garden of Gethsemane. The betrayer. Except that Doris had been saved from a disastrous future, especially if what Luke had said about the money was true.

Somehow she was more inclined to believe Luke's version than Doris's, which had come from Daniel Frawley. Perhaps because she wanted to believe Luke's.

Five minutes later the Dowager Duchess of Harndon was on her way to the gates, having heard enough from Anna's brief explanation to understand exactly what had happened.

Anna, watching her leave, stood for a few moments outside the rotunda, welcoming the darkness and coolness and relative privacy, calming herself before following her husband's instructions and joining her godmother inside.

But before she could do so, a tall black shadow stepped between her and the nearest light. "Ah, alone at last," a horrifyingly familiar voice said. "Well met, my Anna."

# 12

*I*T seemed that all lights had gone out and all air had been sucked away. Panic—sheer raw panic—froze her to the spot on which she stood.

"Your husband is otherwise engaged for the present," he said. "'Twill be my pleasure to give you my company, Anna. I will walk with you beside the canal." He extended an arm for hers and in doing so stepped slightly to one side so that the light of a single lamp streamed over his shoulder.

"What do you want?" Her lips were stiff and unwilling to move.

"I want to walk alone with my Anna for a few quiet minutes," he said. "Take my arm."

The thought of touching him was deeply nauseating. "Please." She could hear the abject, pleading note in her voice and could seem to do nothing about it. "Please leave me alone. Please. I am married now. All that is in the past." Pointless words and untrue. Nothing was in the past.

"Take my arm, Anna."

She took it and squeezed her eyes tightly shut. She knew suddenly why she liked Luke's height. This man was tall; her head reached barely to his chin. She felt overpowered by him, enveloped in him, robbed of personal identity by him.

He strolled with her in the direction of the canal and the tree-lined path on the far side of it. Other masked revelers moved to either side of them, chattering and laughing. One or two of them greeted Anna. She walked past them in the darkness, in the shadow of the tall, black-cloaked, black-masked man at her side. It was impossible to believe that this was the same enchanted path she had taken with Luke earlier.

"What do you want?" she asked again.

"Just this, my Anna," he said, indicating the pleasure gardens about them and touching her hand. She dared not snatch it away. "I longed to be back home with you. It was a severe disappointment when I finally returned and found you gone and knew that there would be the delay of coming to London to claim you. And yet when I came here, I found a further complication. Well, I chose to allow you to continue with your very naughty plans to marry. I chose to stand back and allow you a little time with your duke. 'Tis not easy. These few moments will soothe the emptiness."

"What are you going to tell him?" she asked.

"Nothing at all," he said, looking down at her with eyes that glittered through his mask. "'Twill be unnecessary. You will come to me when the time is right, my Anna, and he will need to know nothing but the fact that you have tired of him. He will not need to know that you are a cheat and a thief and a murderer—and a whore— unless you prove difficult."

"I intend to repay every one of my father's debts," she said. "Then you will have no more reason to terrorize me."

"Terrorize?" he said. "Do you still not believe that I love you, Anna? That when the time comes I will take you away and make you happier than you ever dreamed of being? And do you not know that the debts mean nothing to me? That I assumed them only to lift an intolerable burden from the shoulders of my beloved Anna?"

"I will pay them all," she said. "In money. I will no longer accept even the smallest of them as gifts for favors rendered. In time I will pay them all."

He patted her hand. "Let us not talk of such things," he said. "Let us enjoy a quiet stroll. Ah, the wonder of seeing and feeling you beside me again."

She could remember the deep gratitude she had felt toward him when he had first come to live in the neighborhood very soon after her mother's death. He had seemed solidly calm and kindly and re-assuring in contrast with her father, who had lost himself in drink and self-pity for years and then had collapsed almost completely when Mama died. Sir Lovatt Blaydon had visited often and, without ever seeming to insinuate himself into her confidence, had won her trust. She could remember strolling with him one afternoon in the garden, her arm through his as it was now, comforted by his tall solidity and his sympathy, telling him about her father's debts, about their closeness to total ruin. She had not known what would happen to the children—even Victor had still seemed a child though he was nineteen at the time. And Emily was a deaf-mute.

Even unburdening her anxieties to someone else had been an enormous relief. She had not asked herself why she would do so to a stranger. He had not seemed to be a stranger. He had seemed more of a father figure—a dependable father figure.

He had bought all her father's debts. She could remember his telling her, also in the garden. And she could remember being speechless with gratitude and relief. She could remember stretching out her hands to him and squeezing his very tightly and lifting them to her cheeks. She could remember biting her upper lip to stop the tears from flowing and then laughing because they had spilled over anyway and because she had been quite unable to speak even the words "thank you."

She had thought he had done it because he loved her. She had expected him to return the next day to offer her marriage. She had pictured his making her a wedding present of those debts—a most precious gift. She had liked him so well that it had felt almost like love. It had not seemed to her that she would be sacrificing herself by marrying him. She had wanted to marry him. She had wanted to spend the rest of her life showing her gratitude.

But he had not wanted marriage. Only power over her. Though he had begun to call her "my Anna." And he had begun to talk about the future life they would live together. He had begun to claim to love her. The further he drew her into his net, the stronger had grown his claim to love her.

Sometimes she wondered why he had chosen her as his victim. Simply because she had been there? Because making her a victim had been almost laughably easy? Probably she would never know.

"Ah," he said now as they strolled back along the shabby path, "the husband awaits."

Luke, she saw, was standing still below the rotunda, watching them. She wondered if the two men would meet. She wondered what would happen. Panic had long ago disappeared to leave in its place a dull sense of fatality. It was out of her hands.

But Sir Lovatt Blaydon stopped when they were a little distance away from Luke, took her hands in his, and bowed over them. Anna closed her eyes, but he did not kiss them.

"You may enjoy him a while yet, my Anna," he said. "I will communicate with you from time to time to make sure you keep in mind that you are merely on loan to him at my pleasure. But you need have no fears for your reputation. I love you more than anyone else possibly could."

She drew her hands from his, breathed air slowly into her lungs, and turned from him. She moved toward Luke, who was still standing where he had been before. She tried not to hurry, though she felt suddenly that devils' claws were about to tear at her back. She smiled and let her eyes sparkle above the veil until she remembered that for more than one reason the smile was inappropriate. She let it die.

*Luke* watched her come. He had felt a rather foolish and uncharacteristic alarm when he had returned to the rotunda to find that she was not there, either with Lady Sterne or with anyone else. For one moment he had imagined that she too had flown. But of course she was outside strolling, as were more than half the other revelers at Ranelagh.

He did not recognize the man who accompanied her, though he might have been an acquaintance. His black cloak and mask and the fact that his hood was up made identification difficult.

It was perfectly acceptable for his wife to be walking with another man. He should return to the rotunda, Luke thought, lest both she and others think that he spied on her. He spent enough time watching her in ballrooms and drawing rooms, and he had no doubt other people had noticed. He had no wish to be known as a man besotted with his own wife.

However, he stayed where he was, watching them, having the inexplicable feeling that he might be needed. But they had seen him and the man was taking his leave of her, bowing over her hands. For a fleeting moment Luke felt that he must know the man, but full recognition eluded him.

Her eyes smiled at him as she approached and then turned serious again.

"Anyone I know?" he asked.

"Oh." She laughed. "No. Just a rather distant neighbor from home. I used to know his daughter quite well. I am amazed he recognized me. I did not know him until he identified himself. Did you send Doris home?"

"Yes," he said. "I saw them on their way. I regret that you were a witness to violence, Anna."

"'Twas not your fault." She looked closely at him. "Where did you learn such skilled swordplay?"

"In Paris," he said, "among other things."

She shivered suddenly and sagged toward him in such a way that he had to reach out a hand to steady her.

"I want to leave," she said. "Please, Luke?"

"I came to suggest it," he said. "'Tis not easy to rejoin the revels after one's sister has just narrowly escaped ruining her life when she is too young to know what she does."

They took their leave of Lady Sterne and Anna's sister and Theo and were in the carriage on their way home five minutes later. Luke set his head back and closed his eyes, glad that his wife seemed indisposed to talk. Ruin would be so much more disastrous for a woman than for a man. He had been only a year older than Doris was now when his own life fell to ruins about his ears. Because he was a man, he had been able to make a new life for himself. It would have been far more difficult for Doris to do likewise.

His cold anger had receded though he was not sorry for the decision he had made while he had waited with Doris for their mother to come to take her home. Tomorrow she would be sent all the way home—to Bowden Abbey, where she could be watched more closely. His mother would go with her. He had told them of his plan and had told them too that he would call on them in the morning to see them on their way.

"And to beat me before I leave?" Doris had asked defiantly and bitterly. "You are not going to let me escape without a beating, are you, Luke?"

"Be quiet, girl," their mother had said coldly. "I would stand by without a word of protest if Lucas should have the good sense to discipline you in such a way, even if he were to use a whip. It is something that should have happened to you long ago."

Luke had made no comment. He had been too angry. But remembering his mother's words now, he found himself wondering if it was whippings that Doris had lacked through her childhood and girlhood—or if it was love. Perhaps if his mother had hugged her a few times . . .

But he did not believe in love. Love would have destroyed Doris just as surely as its absence seemed to be doing. Not that he could accuse his mother of a total absence of love, he supposed. It was just that she had always put duty and propriety first, as if a display of love were a foolish weakness. And yet Doris perhaps needed more open love than she could get from her mother—or from him. He could remember what an affectionate child she had been.

Luke swallowed. And he realized suddenly that he was holding his wife's hand rather tightly on the seat between them. It was not something he was in the habit of doing. It was almost as if he had reached for her, needing her. He did not need her or anyone else. He had learned to be strictly self-sufficient. He must never allow himself to need Anna in any other way than the sexual. He slid his hand from hers.

She sat quietly beside him for a few moments, and then she swayed toward him so that her arm was against his and she rubbed her cheek hard against his shoulder. Startled, he opened his arms to steady her as she got awkwardly to her feet and moved across him to sit on his lap. She yanked her veil beneath her chin, wrapped her arms about his neck, rubbed her breasts suggestively against him, and found his mouth with her own in the darkness.

Good Lord! His arms closed about her, his mouth opened appreciatively, and he thrust his tongue into the warmth of her mouth. She moaned and he felt the stirrings of arousal in himself.

"After all"—she drew back her head and laughed—"why waste a perfectly decent carriage ride?"

Anna as innocent flirt he was familiar with. Anna as seductress was a new pleasure to him. She feathered kisses over his face. "I want you," she whispered between each one. "I want you."

He could feel the warmth and shape of her legs through the flimsy drawers. Her breasts were pushed high by her stays, an armor that kept the rest of her body from his seeking hands, and yet somehow an excitement in itself.

"Here in the carriage?" he said. "I am very ready to oblige you, madam, if you can stand the relative discomfort."

"Here and now." Her voice was low and throaty. "Not a moment later. Give it to me now."

He would have made the peeling away of her drawers an erotic part of their foreplay. But her hands joined his to tear impatiently at them and toss them to the floor. He undid his own buttons and brought her astride him on the seat. She was on fire, almost frantic with desire. She had fired him too. He was glad she wanted it now. He did not believe he could wait until they reached home.

"Now it will be, then," he said, spreading his hands over her hips and drawing her down onto him.

She was hot and wet and so ready that she cried out and exploded into release even as he mounted her. He let her shudder into relaxation before enjoying his own pleasure in more leisurely fashion and to the accompaniment of satisfied murmurings from his companion.

He held them coupled until he feared that they must be nearing home. What a wonderful treat, he thought drowsily. He had never made love in a carriage before. It was a step in his education that he was very glad he had not missed. Very glad. He kissed Anna's cheek.

"My coachman might well have an attack of apoplexy if he finds us like this when he opens the door," he said. "Shall we make ourselves respectable and resume the unrespectability in the privacy of our own apartments later?" He would want her again, he knew. This had merely whetted his appetite.

She chuckled in that throaty manner he had noticed earlier and sighed as he uncoupled them. She bent to retrieve her drawers and wriggled into them. They were seated side by side, not touching, when the carriage drew to a halt and the coachman opened the door and lowered the steps.

Luke escorted her to her dressing room and stepped aside after opening the door.

"Soon, madam?" he asked, raising his eyebrows.

She smiled dazzlingly. "Sooner, your grace," she said and swept into her room, all floating gauze and sparkling embroidery and fascinating femininity.

Soon. Ah, yes. Or sooner. He strode away to his own dressing room.

*Hopelessness* had given place to panic, a panic she had tried to control in the carriage. Unusually, miraculously, he had taken her hand in his and she had concentrated all her being on the contact, rested all her sanity on the touch of his hand. When he had removed it, her sanity and her control had gone with it and she had hurled herself at him, only one need driving her. The need to climb right inside him. The need to become so much a part of him that no one would ever find her again.

The feel of him coming into her, hard and long and solidly real, had been so wonderfully reassuring that it was everything. It was all. She had allowed herself the luxury of losing herself in him. And then of letting him hold her, warm and utterly safe, his body still a part of hers.

But the panic had not gone, she discovered when she was in the safety of her own home and her own rooms. She was alone and terrified even while her maid was with her. She fought hysteria while she waited for him to come. He came much sooner than usual though it seemed she had waited for him for hours. She smiled at him from the bed and pushed the bedclothes back from her naked body as he let fall his dressing gown.

*Hold me. Save me.*

She reached up her arms to him. "Make love to me."

"It is my full intention, madam," he said, "as I am sure you can observe." He bent over the candles to blow them out.

The sudden darkness brought a wave of panic, and then he was beside her and reaching for her and beginning the growingly familiar, but always new, ritual of lovemaking.

"Anna." He liked to proceed slowly, making every move excruciatingly agonizing, excruciatingly pleasurable. "You are very hungry?"

"Ravenous," she said. "I am starved, Luke. Fill me."

"An invitation not to be resisted," he said.

She parted her legs for him as he moved over her, frantic to be filled with him again, hot and panting with her need. But it was his fingers that touched her first, his marvelously skilled fingers, which could bring her to the edge of madness with their stroking and probing sensitivity. But tonight they met sore and pulsing need as he kissed her breasts and sucked gently on them.

She could hear herself begging as her hands pulled loose the ribbon at the nape of his neck and spilled his hair about her breasts.

And then his mouth was where his hands had been, shocking in its unexpectedness, his tongue more sensitive, more erotic than his fingers. His hands covered her breasts, her nipples squeezed between thumb and forefinger.

"Harder," she heard herself beg and the increased pressure of his fingers had her crying out in unbearable pain and desire.

She shattered about him, felt the ache build again and shatter again and build yet again.

By the time his body covered her and he came inside her, she was whimpering with a need that had been satisfied time and again but had not been put to rest. She relaxed gratefully against his driving hardness for several minutes until he reached so deep into her soul and became so much one with her there that no conscious thought, no conscious feelings or emotions were left.

Only perfect peace. Perfect love.

When she awoke she was alone. Oh, not alone in bed. He was there beside her, as he always was at night. He was sleeping. But she was alone in the sense that they were not touching. She did not know what time it was, but she guessed that she had slept for several hours. It was amazing—she had not expected to sleep at all.

She was safe. She was in her own bed with her husband beside her. She tried to keep her body relaxed and relive in her mind the way he had made love to her earlier—the most wonderful lovemaking in a month of wonderful lovemakings. She tried to convince herself that he would eventually come to love her as she loved him and that they would live happily ever after.

But it was coming back and she could not keep pushing it away. The panic. And the nightmare memory of how she had lived with it for weeks and months on end for the whole year after his leaving before she had met and married Luke. The bed suddenly seemed a mile wide and he and she perched on opposite ends of it. She felt surrounded by cold emptiness, the cold threat of reaching hands.

She rolled over onto her side and pressed herself close to the reassuringly warm and solid body of her husband and burrowed her way past his arms so that she could snuggle her head against his chest beneath his chin. *Hold me. Please hold me.*

His arms came about her and he muttered sleepily. And then woke up.

"Anna," he said, "what is this? Would you have me lame and impotent from so much use? Give me a few moments and I will be ready for you."

"No-o," she wailed. It was not pleasure she wanted now, but comfort. Love. "Luke, take me home. Please take me home. I want to go home." Perhaps there she would be safe.

"To Elm Court?" he said. "You are feeling homesick? You are missing your youngest sister? I will take you there if you wish it."

"No," she said, "not there. Not there ever again. Take me home. Home to Bowden Abbey."

He held her close for a while, saying nothing. She felt almost as if he had retreated somewhat from her.

"To Bowden?" he said. "Anna, what is all this? Has something happened?"

"Nothing," she said against his chest. "Nothing at all. But I am tired of London. I want to go home. Please let us go home."

"Home," he said. She could feel him draw breath slowly. "Yes, it is home, is it not? But there is something, Anna. What is it?"

She swallowed and pressed closer. "I am going to have a child," she said. She had not intended to tell him yet. She was not even sure yet.

"Already?" One hand had moved up to her head. His fingers stroked through her hair and massaged her scalp.

"I am a week late," she said. "I am never late. I think I must be with child. I want to go home."

He said nothing for a long time. He continued to massage her head soothingly while her hand clung to a thick lock of his hair that had fallen over his shoulder and across her face.

"Yes," he said at last very quietly. "It is time. Our first child must be born at Bowden. You must have the quiet of the country while he grows in you. We will go home."

Safety and peace closed in about her again and she felt very close to sleep once more.

"Anna," he said softly, "it pleases me that you are with child. I thank you."

She smiled drowsily. In a month of physical closeness and passion and of emotional distance, they were the first words that seemed to reach across the distance. They sounded almost like a declaration of love. For tonight *almost* was good enough. She let herself fall the rest of the way into sleep, held safely in her husband's arms.

• • •

*He* was frankly terrified. He rode faster than usual in the park early the following morning. He had created a new life. He and Anna together. They had created a new life inside her body. And for the rest of his days he would be responsible for that life he had started and for the life of the mother.

He was bound inextricably to life and its duties and responsibilities and to at least two other people—his wife and the child who was growing in her womb. He had thought the marriage bond to be the one that would always weigh most heavily on him. He had not expected that the knowledge she had given him last night would bind him so much more. The material needs of his child he could supply with no worry whatsoever. But he would be responsible also for the emotional needs of his child. His mind touched on the idea of love and veered away again.

It was something he could not do. He had spent ten years detaching himself from human ties, from emotional entanglements. And he had been well content with the results. Could he now go back? Could he become again the person he had been? Only to be destroyed again? Only to be vulnerable again and reminded of his essential aloneness?

He was terrified. Terrified. What if Anna should die? What if he had killed her by putting new life inside her when he was in no way equipped to nurture that life beyond the womb? What if he had killed all the beauty and all the joyful vivacity that was Anna?

He eased back on the reins when he realized he was risking his horse's safety as well as his own. And he could no longer afford the luxury of risking even his own safety. A child and its mother depended upon his life and safety. He felt a wave of dizzy nausea at the thought. He did not want anyone emotionally dependent on him. He would be unable to handle the responsibility.

What if, like his mother, he could not give his child love?

But he was incapable of love.

He did not want to be capable of love. He did not want to be capable of feeling pain.

Fortunately, he had something else on which to focus his mind as he rode home. Doris. He knew that she suffered and that she would suffer for some time to come—he could remember something of what that kind of suffering felt like. But despite a lingering uneasiness, he was still convinced this morning that he had handled the matter in the only possible way. And he had not relented about sending her back to Bowden. He would go this morning, as promised, and see her on her way with their mother.

Luke thought again of the child she had been and the youth he had been. A long time ago. He sighed as he sat down to breakfast and looked through the pile of letters and invitations neatly stacked beside his plate.

There was a voucher for an enormous sum of money enclosed in a letter that asked payment of the gaming debt by the Duke of Harndon since his brother, Lord Ashley Kendrick, appeared unable to meet it himself. Ashley's signature was scrawled at the bottom of the voucher.

Ashley was still in bed when Luke arrived at Harndon House. Before seeing his mother and sister, Luke went himself to his brother's room, took a glass of water from the dressing room, and trickled its contents over Ashley's face. His brother sputtered into wakefulness.

"Zounds! What the deuce!" he said.

Luke tossed the voucher onto his chest and his brother picked it up and regarded it silently for a few moments.

"Pox on it," he said, "he had no business sending it to you, Luke. I shall see to settling it. Go away and let a fellow sleep."

"I shall give you a choice," Luke said coldly, and he could almost hear his father speaking through his voice—though his father had given him no choice ten years ago. "You may keep this voucher and go to the devil with it with no further allowance to help you along, or you may hand it back to me for payment and get out of that bed and have your bags packed in time to accompany Doris and our mother to Bowden, where you will stay until you can satisfy me that you have good reason for leaving again. You have five minutes in which to decide." He crossed the room to the window, flung back the heavy curtains, and stood looking out at the sunny square. He had forgotten that the sun was shining.

He had offered a choice between the devil and the deep blue sea. A choice of being tossed out without any means of living—as he himself had been tossed out ten years ago—or of facing total capitulation, total humiliation. But Luke hardened his heart and said nothing more.

"What time are they leaving?" his brother asked from somewhere behind him after perhaps four minutes had passed.

"As soon as you are ready," Luke said without turning.

He heard the door into Ashley's dressing room open and close again a few moments later. The gaming voucher, he saw when he turned, was on the bed. Luke walked over with a stony heart to pick it up.

So it was back to Bowden Abbey, he thought, folding the paper and putting it in a pocket. Back into his past. Taking his present and his future with him.

He went to find his mother.

## 13

*❊❧ ⚬͡⚬ ☙❊*

BOWDEN Abbey. Luke watched for it with some dread. As a boy he had loved the house and the park, the farms and the village. He had hated the thought of ever being away from it. School and university were tolerated only because there were the holidays to look forward to. And perhaps he would not have had to move away if all that mess with George had never happened. His father would have given him the living at Bowden.

But then it was not so much the place he dreaded, he knew, as the memories that had become associated with it. It was a pity, perhaps, that it was the last memories that had stuck with him ever since, almost obliterating the good ones. He could remember feeling great pleasure at George's return from his Grand Tour. Although he had always been enormously fond of his older brother, the four-year age difference had sometimes been an impediment when they were boys. Now it seemed to have narrowed. They were young men together and brothers. There had been a few weeks of endless talking and of riding together, fishing together, playing billiards together, visiting together—they were always together. Or so it had seemed. Obviously there had been some time when George was not with Luke, else what had happened would have had no chance to happen.

The betrayal had shattered something in Luke that had never mended. George and Henrietta. George raping Henrietta. But no, the mind of the thirty-year-old Luke shied away from that particular word. Seduction maybe. Surely he must have believed Henrietta willing—Luke knew how sexual desire could sometimes blur one's judgment. But even the idea of George the seducer could still bring an empty ache to the pit of his stomach.

There was the unwilling memory of George when confronted, ashen-faced and tight-lipped, refusing to make any comment on the story Henrietta had told, refusing to defend himself and his actions, refusing at first to accept Luke's challenge—and ultimately refusing to fight him by deloping and watching steadily as Luke took aim at the willow tree. And dropping without a sound when hit.

Luke drew a slow breath. He had never seen his brother after that. And never would now. And only now—amazingly—did he recall a long-suppressed memory. A package had arrived from George after six months. Inside was nothing but a piece of paper with his brother's scrawled signature and a rather thick wad of money. Luke had returned it without comment. Olive branch or blood money? He had not known which. He had repressed all memory of the package until now.

All his own letters—written to his mother and father—had been similarly returned. He had been turned off, cast out.

And yet now by the supreme irony of fate this all belonged to him—they were approaching Bowden land—and he was coming back to it as the Duke of Harndon. Back to duties he had never asked for. Back to Henrietta, his brother's widow.

Instinctively he turned to his present and his future. His wife was sitting beside him in the carriage, quietly watching the scenery through the window. He might have reached for her hand if her sister had not been sitting opposite her. He was glad that her sister was there to prevent him from showing such weakness. Agnes, against Anna's advice and despite the protests of Lady Sterne, had begged to come with them. The girl, though very pretty, was equally shy. London and its gay round of balls and parties was not to her taste, Luke guessed. He had sent for the other sister, too, the deaf-mute, knowing that Anna was fretting about being away from her for so long.

His present and his future. In the three days since she had begged him to bring her home she still had not bled. It seemed almost certain that she was with child.

She felt his eyes upon her and turned her head to smile at him. There was sunshine in her smile again and relaxation in her posture despite the tedium of a long journey. It surprised him that she had grown to hate London. She had seemed to be enjoying to the full the social life there, and her company had been much sought after. But in the last three days she had been almost frantic to leave, urging the servants on to speed up their preparations. Perhaps she was the sort of person who, once she had an idea, had to act upon it now if not yesterday.

"We will be passing through the village within the next few minutes," he said. "We are almost home."

"Are we?" Excitement lit her eyes and she leaned away from the back of her seat, the better to see from the window.

And then they were in the village, slowing for the sake of possible pedestrians or domestic animals. It all looked shockingly the same as it had always looked. What had he expected? Luke wondered. That everything would have changed beyond recognition in ten years?

But one thing had changed. Ten years ago he had been merely a younger son of the duke and little more than a boy. He had not attracted a great deal of notice when his carriage passed through the village. This time he was the Duke of Harndon, and he was returning after a long absence. There were no crests on his carriage, but that did not appear to matter. Word must have spread that he was expected any day, and cottage doors were being flung open and tavern and shops were spilling forth their few customers.

Caught by surprise, Luke leaned forward and raised a hand in greeting to those who waved at him, their faces for the most part wreathed in smiles of welcome.

"Luke?" Anna said. She laughed with delight. "How wonderful." She, too, had a hand raised and was looking from the window on her side of the carriage.

But he leaned back sharply as they approached the end of the street and the church. He averted his head. No, he had no wish to see the church or the churchyard. He realized suddenly that it was not just the memories and not just Henrietta he had dreaded returning to. There was something worse than them. There were the graves in the churchyard, the graves of the two men he had not had chance or inclination to forgive in this life and could never now forgive.

"Ah," he said in some relief as the carriage made the almost immediate turn through the tall and imposing stone gateposts into the park of Bowden Abbey. "The villagers must have heard that a new and lovely duchess was arriving. Those standing on your side of the street will be able to boast of having seen you, my dear."

She laughed again. "'Tis more like," she said, "that they wanted to see what Paris has done to you. Oh, the trees! They are very ancient, are they not? And oh, look, Agnes. Deer. A whole herd of them. 'Tis shady here, a pleasant break from the sunshine."

It had seemed like black night to him as he rode down the driveway for the last time. They had already passed the spot where Doris had waited for him.

"Ohhh!" There was a shared gasp from both Agnes and Anna as the carriage suddenly left the trees and the shade behind and all the splendor of the open park came into view—the double arched stone bridge over the fast-flowing river; the long, smooth lawns sloping upward; the four-tiered terraces of the formal gardens, carefully cultivated and ablaze with color; and the massive house, all turrets and mullioned windows, an indescribable mess of architectural styles, but imposing and splendid.

Luke gazed on it, as he had gazed at the village a few minutes ago, with surprise to find it looking so much the same. It could have been yesterday, he thought. Or a century ago.

The carriage crossed the bridge and made its way up the driveway past the lawns and then beside the long formal gardens before turning onto the topmost, cobbled terrace before the marble steps and the great doors. The doors had been flung wide by the time the carriage had drawn to a halt and the coachman had opened the door and set down the steps.

Luke stepped resolutely out and turned to hand first his sister-in-law and then his wife down. Anna had lost her smile, he saw, though her eyes were still wide with wonder and her cheeks were becomingly flushed. He offered her his arm and she set her own formally along the top of it. He should have offered her encouragement, but he had none to offer. This was perhaps, he thought, the most difficult moment of his life. No, hardly that—*one* of the most difficult.

He led his wife into the great oak-paneled hall, two stories high, with its huge portraits of family ancestors and its massive twin fireplaces at opposite sides and its tiled floor. Dwarfed by the magnificence surrounding them, the servants were lined up on both sides of the door to welcome him home and to be inspected by their duke and his new duchess.

His mother's doing? Luke wondered.

His father's old butler, Cotes, presented him with the stiff bow Luke remembered well to the housekeeper, Mrs. Wynn, whom Luke had not seen before. Luke presented his duchess and Lady Agnes Marlowe. And then he and Anna walked the lines of the servants. They were standing stiffly to attention, many of them with brightly curious eyes. His wife, as Luke expected, rose to the occasion with all the ease of her experience. She smiled warmly at each servant and had a personal word for most. Tired as she must be, from the journey and perhaps from early pregnancy, she did not rush this first duty as mistress of Bowden Abbey or show any sign that it was anything but a delight to her.

He had chosen well, he thought. She would do her job thoroughly and with grace. He was proud of her.

"The family is waiting abovestairs in the drawing room, your grace," Mrs. Wynn said when the inspection was finally over, addressing herself to Anna. "Will you greet them first or retire to your apartments first?"

"Oh, we will go to the drawing room first," Anna said, turning a smiling and inquiring face toward Luke.

He inclined his head.

"But Lady Agnes would probably prefer to rest for a while," Anna said.

Agnes looked relieved.

Mrs. Wynn nodded and turned to lead the way through the pointed archway to the grand oak staircase.

Luke, following behind her with his wife on his arm, felt rather as if he had lead weights in his shoes. It had been home once. And was to be home again, if that were possible. His family awaited him abovestairs—his mother, who had turned away from him when he had most needed a mother's love; his brother, whom he had humiliated and dealt with almost as harshly as his father had dealt with him; his sister, whose heart he had ruthlessly broken even though once upon a time he had known all about broken hearts. And Henrietta.

And in the village, in the churchyard, his father. And George.

The family was assembled in the drawing room. And though they had all met in London—all but one—just a few days before, there was the formality of greetings to be dealt with now that he had come home with his duchess. Luke kissed his mother on the cheek and returned Ashley's stiff bow and bowed in response to Doris's curtsy. He watched as Anna hugged them all more effusively and asked about their journey and mentioned, her voice bright with amusement and delight, the welcome they had received in the village.

But there was someone else in the room, someone who stood quietly watching close to the window. Someone Luke had been throbbingly aware of since he stepped into the room. He had not yet looked at her though he knew that she was as tiny, as slim, as dainty, and as exquisitely lovely as she had been as a girl.

His mother turned to Anna to present her. "This is Henrietta, Duchess of Harndon and my eldest son's widow, Anna," she said and turned to Henrietta. "The *new* Duchess of Harndon, Henrietta, Anna."

Finally Luke looked at her. Her heart-shaped face with its blue eyes looked scarcely older. Her dark hair was powdered and she was dressed fashionably.

And her rather low musical voice jolted him, so little had it changed. "Anna." She smiled and reached out both hands. "How lovely you are. But what else could one expect of Luke's wife? I have been looking forward so much to your coming. 'Tis going to be lovely to have a new sister—and a new friend, I trust."

"Oh." Anna laughed as Luke's eyes watched the hands of the two women join. "You are young, Henrietta. Why did I expect someone older? Yes, we are sisters. And so I have two new sisters and one new brother. How fortunate I am." She turned her head to include Doris and Ashley in her smile, and then Luke.

And then finally Henrietta turned to him and he found his eyes on her and all else receding. God! His boyhood love. So cruelly torn from him. She would have been his wife now for nine years or more. They would have had children. Henrietta!

"Luke." Her smile had softened and her hands, removed from Anna's, were stretched out to him. "Oh it has been a long time. They told me you had changed. 'Tis as well they warned me. But you are ten times more handsome than the boy I knew when I married George. Welcome home, brother."

"Henrietta." He took her outstretched hands and felt the shock of familiarity. He raised one of them to his lips and both felt and saw the jewels of George's ring glittering on her finger. "'Tis good to be home."

He lied smoothly, with practiced good manners.

"Ah, here is the tea tray," his mother said, bringing him back to reality. "Would you like me to pour for today, Anna?"

Anna. His wife and his duchess. Foolish as it seemed, he had almost forgotten her for a moment. He went to take his place beside her and allowed her to warm him with her sunny smile as his mother poured the tea.

*They* stayed in the drawing room for half an hour over tea and succeeded somehow in conversing together almost as a family. It was not, Luke thought, a happy atmosphere to bring a new wife into, but then it was precisely for this that he had married. And Anna coped well, conversing with a brightness and a charm that drew them all into talking and that even squeezed smiles out of Doris and Ashley.

It was, Luke thought as he and his wife were shown to their apartments, the sort of homecoming he had expected, no better and no worse. And somehow he had survived the meeting with Henrietta.

She was more lovely, more fascinating, than she had been at the age of seventeen, a treacherous part of his mind told him.

They had the master suite at the front of the house. Not many of the house's apartments looked out over the front since, according to the design of the old abbey, the house was far longer than it was wide. Most rooms looked out on side lawns and gardens and distant trees.

Luke joined his wife in her bedchamber after inspecting his own. Her maid and another were busy in her dressing room as he passed through it, both of them pausing in their busy job of unpacking to drop deep curtsies. Anna was standing at the mullioned window, looking out. She looked over her shoulder and smiled at him, and he joined her there.

"'Tis so magnificent that it has quite taken my breath away," she said. "If I had known, Luke, I would have urged you sooner to bring me here." She laughed.

He felt suddenly an overwhelming relief to have the worst part of the homecoming behind him and once again to be alone with his wife. He took her hands in his and turned her toward him.

"Welcome to Bowden Abbey, Anna," he said, raising first one of her hands and then the other to his lips. "Welcome home, my duchess."

"Home," she said and her eyes brightened suddenly with unshed tears. "Oh, Luke, you have no idea how wonderful that sounds. I never thought to have a home of my own. I expected to live as a spinster in my brother's."

He almost released her hands in order to draw her into his arms. She had helped him face the ordeal of coming home and she herself was pleased with the homecoming. He could see the tears in her eyes. But he was living through a rare vulnerable moment, and experience had taught him that vulnerability was to be fought.

Anna had once belonged to someone else, as he had. But Anna

was still capable of shedding tears over her remembered love—as he was not.

He squeezed her hands more tightly instead. "I certainly could not permit your brother that pleasure when he is soon to have a bride of his own," he said.

She drew her head back and smiled at him. "I like Henrietta," she said. "I was afraid that perhaps she would resent me, but she was very kind. It is sad that she was widowed so early in life. But perhaps she will remarry. She is very young. She must have been a child bride."

He kissed her. He did not want to talk about Henrietta, or even think about her. Anna sighed and wrapped her arms about his neck and kissed him back. They shared a deep and lingering kiss that was strangely unsexual. Alarmingly unsexual. They kissed, not for pleasure but for something else. Luke's mind shied away from putting a name to that something else even if he might have been able to do so.

The kiss must be brought back to its more familiar purpose. Luke raised his head and looked down at his wife through half-closed eyes before allowing them to stray suggestively to the bed. "That will do nicely, madam," he said, "until I can give you a more thorough welcome home tonight."

He always found her laughter utterly delightful. It was so much more spirit-lifting than the sophisticated titters to which he was more accustomed. "Your grace," she said, "I can scarce wait."

Comforting desire came at last—comforting because it was familiar and it required no real sentiment. It also could not be satisfied immediately. "I believe," he said, thinking ruefully about the maids busy in the adjoining dressing room, "we must keep early country hours now that we are in the country. An early bedtime, that is."

She laughed again.

Their relationship had been restored to its safe, light flirtatiousness.

*Anna* felt cautiously happy during the week following her arrival at Bowden Abbey. It was a beautiful place and the early-summer sunshine was showing it off to best advantage. It felt wonderful to be in the country again, free from the constraints of London living. Not that she had disliked living there at all until the night of the masquerade at Ranelagh. But after that she had felt suffocated by it.

She felt free again. She knew that the sense of freedom was illusory, that she had not escaped from Sir Lovatt Blaydon and never would, but the illusion was there and she clung to it. There was air to breathe at Bowden and space to move in. There was happiness to know.

Perhaps.

Bowden was not an entirely happy place. Part of the reason was obvious. Ashley and Doris had come home against their will, both of them in disgrace and sullen, even hostile, to Luke. And he did nothing to try to improve matters. He was stiff and distant with them and made no effort to talk with them, to justify his treatment of them. There was justification for what he had done in both cases. But there should also have been love, love that had always been so strong in Anna's own family that it puzzled her to realize that it was not so in all families. Love might have soothed bruised pride and emotions. Love might have mended broken fences.

And there seemed to be no love in Luke.

Anna tried not to put the idea into words in her mind.

Other reasons were not as obvious. The dowager, Anna's mother-in-law, was kind, if not exactly warm, to her. She spent time explaining things to Anna, making it easy for her to adjust to her new role as Duchess of Harndon and mistress of Bowden Abbey and social leader of the neighborhood. But between Luke and his mother there was no warmth at all, and almost no communication. And yet they had a common cause in their concern for the well-being of Ashley and Doris.

And even with Henrietta, Luke was stiff and ill at ease. Henrietta, who was so lovely and so gracious and so very friendly to Anna. She had been his brother's wife. Had he hated his brother so much that he could barely be civil even to his brother's widow?

His brother, George, the late Duke of Harndon, was the key to it all, Anna supposed. Luke had almost killed his brother in a duel. He could not remember the cause of the quarrel. It amazed Anna after a few days at Bowden that she had ever believed him. How could one forget the cause of a quarrel that had resulted in a duel between brothers and the near death of one of them?

The past, whatever it was that had happened, hung over Bowden almost like a visible, tangible pall. And yet Anna could ask no one about it. To ask any of his family would be disloyal to Luke. To ask him was impossible. In over a month of marriage they had rarely talked about anything but trivialities. They enjoyed each other's company, they spoke to each other lightly and wittingly, they teased each other. But they had never shared anything of themselves with each other, except their bodies. They were essentially strangers to each other. The pattern had been set. She did not know now how she would ask him such a question, though she had tried once at the start of their marriage—*what happened ten years ago? Why has it blighted your whole life?*

It had blighted Luke's life. He had once been different. Doris had told her so.

And yet there was a sense of freedom and happiness at Bowden. Her relationship with Luke was good if she could be content with its basic superficiality. He welcomed her home to Bowden the night of their arrival as he had promised he would, with slow and thorough expertise, and told her afterward that now that it seemed almost certain she was with child, he must allow her more sleep at night.

"Once a night will have to satisfy my voracious appetite," he said.

He kept his word in the coming nights.

It might have been a disappointment to Anna since her own appetite appeared quite as insatiable as his, but it was not. His decision suggested something almost like tenderness. It suggested a concern for her health and a concern for the well-being of their child.

Almost as if he cared. On one level she believed he did.

And she began to get up in the mornings to go riding with him. He laughed at her when she first asked, not believing that she could get out of bed early enough. And the first time he aroused her indignation by having an ancient hack saddled for her use. And then he laughed at her wrath before changing his orders.

The early mornings became their special private time—or so she described them to herself. They talked and laughed and teased. And he often rode slightly behind her—to admire her splendid seat, he explained with an appreciative leer at it when she looked back at him in inquiry one day.

One morning they raced their horses when they were on their way back to the stables and he allowed her to win by a head and then denied that he had done so. He also announced as he lifted her to the ground that there would be no more racing until after her confinement. His son and heir must be protected from reckless harm.

"Or your daughter," she said, smiling at him.

"Especially my daughter, madam," he said. "She is, perhaps, of delicate sensibilities, unlike her mother, and is afraid of speed."

Her freedom was being curtailed. He would not allow her to make love more than once a night. He would not allow her to gallop her horse. It felt very like tenderness. It felt wonderful.

Henrietta became her friend. It felt good to have a friend. In the last several years, Anna realized, she had had no time for friendship, only for family.

It was Henrietta who spent several hours with her the day after her arrival at Bowden, explaining the running of the house, showing her parts of the house that would be relevant to her running of it, going over the household accounts with her, and accompanying her on her first daily consultation with Mrs. Wynn. And Henrietta insisted, with what appeared to be warm sincerity, that she was not at all unhappy to relinquish control.

"I enjoyed my duties as duchess, Anna," she said as they strolled arm in arm through the formal gardens. "I will not deny it. But the enjoyment has gone since George's passing. And look what I have in return for a little loss of power. I have Luke home where he belongs. I have you—I have so longed for a close friend and for another sister. And I have Agnes, who is so pretty and so sweet, and Emily coming soon. I just know I am going to love her, too." She squeezed Anna's arm. "Perhaps I can be happy again. I believe I can."

Yes, Anna thought as the days passed, perhaps she, too, could be happy again. Sometimes she believed she could.

She tried constantly not to think of those words that sometimes haunted her dreams, over which she had no control: *Keep in mind that you are merely on loan to him at my pleasure.* She was in control of her waking mind, and she chose to be happy. Or at least to try.

## 14

*P*ALE little face was pressed close to the window of the old carriage, gazing anxiously out, first at the house itself and then at the people gathered on the cobbled terrace, awaiting her arrival—Luke, Anna, Agnes, Doris, and Henrietta. The anxiety in her face increased for a moment until her eyes alit on her sisters. And then she smiled.

She smiled as Anna did, Luke noticed, with all the sunshine behind her eyes. He had been feeling rather wary at the prospect of having a deaf-mute living in his house, having never had to deal with any person with a handicap. She was difficult to communicate with, Anna had said. How did one communicate with her? Apparently the girl could neither read nor write—how could she when she did not hear or know the alphabet? So one could not write down what one wanted her to know.

He had consoled himself with the thought that she was Anna's concern. Anna had wanted her and had dealt with her all her life. Apparently a nurse-companion was coming with the girl. He need not concern himself with her at all beyond providing her with a home and his protection. Yet, knowing the day of her probable arrival, he had stayed at home out of courtesy to his wife and he had come outside with her when word was brought that a strange carriage was approaching up the driveway. Anna was brimming with pent-up excitement.

He would normally have stepped forward to help a guest alight from a carriage at his doors. But he held back when the footman who had ridden up beside the coachman set down the steps and held out a hand for hers.

Lady Emily Marlowe was fourteen years old, of medium height and thin, her body only just beginning to bud into womanhood. She wore a closed gown over full petticoats, but no hoops. Her hair, fair and unpowdered, was pinned back from her face but rippled free down her back. She wore no cap. She set Luke rather in mind of a young colt.

And then she was in Anna's arms, and Anna was laughing and crying. The girl made a few incoherent sounds. Agnes joined her sisters, her arms going about both. They stood huddled together in a close hug.

Anna took the girl by the hand eventually and spoke to her. "Emmy," she said, "I want you to meet my husband, the Duke of Harndon."

She neither slowed her words nor yelled. And yet the girl turned her head in his direction. Huge gray eyes in the thin, flushed face looked him over slowly—rather as her sister had done in the Diddering ballroom, he thought. He expected to see fright in her face as he always saw in Agnes's—though fright was perhaps rather too strong a word. He had made very little concession to country fashions since moving to Bowden Abbey and realized that young girls were sometimes overwhelmed by his appearance.

He took a step toward the girl and reached out his hands toward her. She looked at them one at a time and then raised her own to place in them. Small, cool hands. He felt an unexpected tenderness for the child. He also felt a certain foolishness. What now? It was pointless to say anything, and yet silence was unnatural in such a situation.

"Emily," he said, just as if she could hear him, "welcome to your new home. I am Luke, your new brother."

Her eyes, he noticed, were intent on his lips. She looked up when he stopped talking and smiled slowly and radiantly into his eyes. He squeezed her hands more tightly. Good God, he thought, she had been listening to his lips. He drew her arm through his—she did not resist—and turned her to present Doris and Henrietta to her. Doris smiled, looking as awkward as he had felt a few moments ago. Henrietta called her a dear, sweet child, who was bound to bring happiness to her sisters and indeed to all of them. But she addressed her words to Anna, not to Emily. The girl was clinging to his arm rather tightly, he realized.

He patted her hand and she looked up into his face immediately. "Come into the house for tea," he said.

She smiled slowly again and then nodded.

"She does not usually take to strangers," Anna said, moving to her sister's other side as he led her into the house. "I believe she likes you, Luke."

He felt curiously pleased. He had felt very little liking from his own family since his return home. Not that he had done much to court it. He was content that there had been no open unpleasantness.

His mother was gracious to the new arrival but made no attempt during tea to pay her any attention. Lady Emily was, of course, a child and should have been in the nursery according to his mother's strict notions of what was correct. The girl sat on a sofa between her sisters, gazing occasionally at Agnes, sometimes at him, but most of the time at Anna. Always it was a gaze, never a glance. But then he supposed that to someone who could not hear, the sense of sight was more precious than to those who could.

Ashley arrived late for tea. He was often late for meals or did not appear at them at all. Luke did not know where or how he spent his days. There had been almost no communication between them since their return from London and almost never any eye contact. But Ashley was not made for general sullenness. He was always polite with the rest of the family, often cheerful. He was cheerful now.

"Anna," he said as soon as he had nodded to everyone else in the room, "'tis said that your sister has arrived, and sure enough, I see a stranger sitting beside you. Present me, if you please."

Anna did so and Ashley stood directly in front of them. "As I live," he said, grinning and making his bow, "a beauty in the making. Your servant, madam." He took the girl's hand and raised it to his lips.

He spoke with his usual careless charm, Luke noticed. He knew, of course, that Anna's youngest sister was a deaf-mute. Perhaps he had spoken, like Luke, because silence would have seemed unnatural. But Luke watched the girl's reaction to the introduction. She did not smile, as she had smiled at him, but she watched his brother's lips as she had watched his, and her eyes followed Ashley across the room to where he took a seat and accepted a cup of tea from Doris. She continued to gaze at him even after he had caught her eye and winked at her.

Ashley, Luke thought in some amusement, had made a conquest.

*In* the weeks after his return to Bowden, Luke spent a great deal of time about estate business, talking with Laurence Colby and going over the books with him, riding about his farms and visiting those who worked them, calling on his tenant farmers.

Adjustments would have to be made. Colby was a humorless, efficient, closefisted man, Luke found, far more eager to bring money into the estate—and it was extremely prosperous—than to spend. And perhaps there was some foundation to the charge that he had acted for the past few years more as if he was the owner than the steward. But there were no signs of dishonesty in the man, and he had undoubtedly guarded Luke's inheritance from the extravagance of those who might have spent it for him. On the other hand, he had kept money from those who needed it badly with the result that there was some small suffering and certainly some discontent on his farms.

Reluctantly, Luke was going to have to set about asserting himself, getting involved in the lives of those dependent upon him. The very idea made him shudder. He began to realize how very much for ten years, at first deliberately and then unconsciously, he had cut himself off from involvement with others. He had involved himself only for pleasure.

He was pondering both the changes in his life and the changes he must begin to institute in the running of his estate as he rode home from one of his farms one afternoon. Anna, he had discovered there, had already been visiting the cottages and sampling home-made cider and promising to share her own recipe and suggesting that perhaps she could look into the organizing of a school for the younger children. He was going to have to prove himself worthy of his duchess, he realized ruefully.

And then his attention was caught by a splash of pink among the greenery surrounding him and he looked up to find Henrietta sitting on a stile that separated a hay field from the path along which he rode. She looked quite achingly pretty perched there, an open book in one hand. Something inside him lurched uncomfortably.

He had managed to avoid being alone with her. He had even convinced himself that there was nothing to avoid. His initial meeting with her had been easier than could have been expected and she had been friendly toward him and more than friendly to Anna. Everything that had been between him and her was obviously dead, ancient history. Except that there had been those letters she had sent him in London and his own dread of coming home. And so he had avoided being alone with her and would continue to avoid it if he could.

He drew his horse to a halt for a moment, but she had seen him, of course. He moved reluctantly forward.

She closed the book and looked at him unsmilingly. "Luke," she said uncertainly. "I thought you were spending the afternoon in your study with Mr. Colby."

"No," he said, drawing his horse to a halt close to the stile. He had a vivid memory of lifting her down from that very stile one day long ago and deliberately sliding her body down his before stealing a quick kiss as her feet touched the ground. She had scolded him and then swayed against him and raised her mouth for another kiss. Having grown up together, they had found it easier than it should have been to wander away unchaperoned, sometimes for a whole hour. He had never done more than kiss her, with closed lips. He had known nothing in those days about even the most basic skills of making love— unless kissing with closed lips was considered the most basic. He had known nothing else. It had been a time of incredible innocence.

"Oh," she said now, and flushed. There was an awkward little silence before she rushed on. "Luke, forgive me for the letter I wrote you in London. I swore to myself that I would never either speak or write those words to you, that I would go to my grave guarding the secrets of my heart. But I wrote them and sent the letter on its way with William. I thought he was leaving a day later than he did. I rode over to Wycherly to get it back from him, but he had left already. I was frantic. I wished I could die."

He could think of no answer to give. He gave none. There was nothing to be said and nothing to be done. Besides, it was the second letter, not the one Will had brought, that had been more personal. But it was dangerous to be alone with her and talking of such things. And dangerous to be gazing into blue eyes huge with misery. "You wish to continue reading?" he asked her after another short silence. "Or are you ready to go home?"

"'Tis time to go home," she said. "But you ride on ahead, Luke. I will come at my own pace. If you will but help me down?"

He wished he had taken a different route home. But a different route would have added miles to his journey. He wished she had not asked him to help her down from the stile. He did not want to touch her. And of course, once descended from his horse's back, he could not possibly mount up again and ride away from her while she walked home.

She looked delicately, innocently lovely sitting there with her book. God, how he had loved her, that innocent, long-dead young man of his memory. She was dressed, he realized suddenly, very fashionably in a formfitting sack dress with dazzling white petticoat and stomacher. Her straw hat was trimmed with real flowers. She wore hoops. All for wandering out to sit reading on a stile?

He dismounted and walked closer to the stile. She made no move to hold out a hand so that he could assist her to descend the two steps to the ground. She looked sorry that she had asked for assistance. And yet he wondered how chance a meeting this was. He reached out both hands, set them at her waist, and lifted her down while she set her hands on his shoulders to steady herself. A waist as small as it had been when she was seventeen. A body light as a feather. A special fragrance that assaulted his nostrils and his memory.

He had loved her with all a young man's romantic idealism, with all a young man's ardent passion. For a moment, before he released her, he held the memories and the past between his two hands again. For a moment the years rolled away. He heard her inhale and exhale rather unsteadily. He did not look at her.

"Would you like to ride while I walk?" he asked her. He could hear the strain in his voice. But how could she ride in hoops?

"No." She spoke very quietly. "I will walk with you, Luke."

He wanted Anna with him suddenly and foolishly. Anna with her bright smiles and her amusing, witty chatter. Anna, his wife, his present, with their child, his future, in her womb. He did not care to admit to himself that he was afraid. Or tempted.

"Luke," Henrietta said, her voice as strained as his, "you made a wonderful marriage. I love Anna. She is just right for you—pretty and charming and devoted to duty. I hope she will be able to do for you what I was unable to do for George." She drew breath and let it out rather raggedly. "I hope she will be able to give you sons."

He had an irrational longing for a daughter. For a little girl to pamper and be proud of. He would not mind at all if it were a daughter Anna was carrying. The realization surprised him. He had married her for heirs. All that really mattered in their marriage was that she give him sons, at least one, preferably two or more. But he wanted a little girl.

"All I was able to give George was one stillborn son," Henrietta said, her voice very low. "If only I had known . . ."

"I am sorry about that, Henrietta," he said. "It must have been a painful experience for you." Doubtless an incredible understatement.

"If only I had known," she said again. "I could not have married you, Luke, though you urged me to do so even after you knew. If it had lived, it would have been his son. Everyone would have known that. And yet I would have been married to you. It would have been impossible. You must have realized that. Have you hated me all these years?" Her voice was thin and shaking.

He could remember having contrived to be alone with her up at the falls. He could remember trying to kiss her and her turning her head sharply away. He could remember it all coming spilling out, how she had been out walking alone, how George had met her and walked with her, how he had waited until they were in a secluded place before taking her into his arms and trying to persuade her to let him further embrace her, how he had grown more ardent and insistent at her refusal until he had forced himself on her and got her with child, how she had discovered the terrible truth and confronted George with it so that he had been obliged to offer for her, how she had felt she had no choice but to accept, how she had decided to break the news to Luke before anyone else knew.

And he could remember her collapsing into his arms and sobbing her heart out while he cried with her. He could remember pleading with her, begging her to marry him anyway. He had not had a chance to think through the implications of what she had told him. All he had been able to think of was losing her, losing the love of his heart, losing his reason for living. At that moment he had not even started to think of George . . .

The pain was something he would never want to live through again. And he had spent years hardening his heart so that he never would.

"I have not hated you, Henrietta," he said. "I made a new life for myself in France. And now I have come back a different person. And I have come back with a wife. All that seems like something that happened in another lifetime to another person. I am sorry if you suffered longer than I, my dear."

"I suffered every day while he lived and I have suffered every day since," she said so quietly that he scarcely heard the words.

He heard her swallow twice but kept his eyes resolutely on the path ahead. He did not look to see if she was crying. If he saw her crying, he knew what he would do, what any gentleman would do.

But he did not trust himself to hold her in his arms. He did not trust the invulnerability of his heart. He wished they were closer to home. They were still a mile away.

"I am glad you married before coming home," she said at last, her voice more normal. "And I am glad you married someone like Anna, someone worthy of you. You chose well, even though you married her because of me. You did, did you not?"

Had he? Had that been his primary motive? He knew it had been part of it. He hoped it had not been the whole of it. "I married," he said, "because it was time and because I had met someone I wished to marry." Yes. He remembered Anna at Lady Diddering's ball and the way she had flirted with him and enchanted him. Yes, that was at least partly true. He suddenly, desperately wanted to feel that he had married Anna for herself. And he had, he remembered with some bitterness. He had allowed himself to fall in love with her—briefly.

"Forgive me," Henrietta said. "Forgive me for even suggesting otherwise. Who could wonder at any man's falling in love with Anna and marrying her all within a week? I am glad you love her. If you did not, it would be dangerous for you and me to be together. We should not be together now. I wish I had known that you were from home this afternoon. I would not have strolled away to be alone and to read. You ought not to have stopped when you saw me, Luke. You should have ridden on by."

But she had known. It had been a planned meeting. Could not even Henrietta be trusted to speak the truth?

"You are my sister-in-law, Henrietta," he said firmly. "All that happened between us happened a long time ago to two children who no longer exist." And yet they did exist. Somewhere deep inside himself, despite the effort of years, was the boy he had been. Somewhere deep within there was still Henrietta. And George.

"Yes," she said. "That is the truth. It must be the truth."

The path along which they walked disappeared as they emerged from the trees to the east of the house onto the top of the long lawn that sloped for more than a mile from the formal gardens before the house. They were quite close to the gardens in which Anna was strolling with Emily and Doris.

"Oh, dear," Henrietta said quietly and then she raised a hand to wave gaily at the three in the garden. "I will never walk with your husband again, Anna, I vow," she sang out cheerfully as they came within earshot. "He has done nothing but sing your praises and declare his love for you since I met him as I was climbing over the stile back yonder. He has not even complimented me on my new straw hat."

Anna looked briefly at Luke, her eyes startled, before smiling at Henrietta and moving close to the low hedge that separated the bottom terrace from the lawn. "And it is such a becoming hat," she said. "I will compliment you on it, Henrietta." She laughed gaily.

Luke acted from impulse. He leaned over the hedge, took his wife by the waist, and lifted her over despite her startled shriek of protest. She laughed again as he set her down.

"You will not find that so easy to do in a few months' time, your grace," she said and then flushed and caught her lower lip between her teeth.

"Oh, Anna," Henrietta said, clasping her hands tightly at her bosom, "does that mean what I think it means?"

Emily was stooping down to smell the flowers, Luke noticed, but Doris was an interested listener.

"Anna is with child," he said, offering her his arm, drinking in the sight of her, as he always did, as he always had. Now it was a relief to see her, to touch her, to speak aloud his deep, irrevocable involvement with her. His mind clung to the present, firmly relinquished the past—yet again. His horse snorted with impatience to be moving again.

But Henrietta had to hug her and kiss her first and Doris had to do likewise across the width of the hedge. All three of them were laughing and talking together. Luke grimaced and caught Emily's eye. She was observing the excitement, obviously not understanding it. He shrugged and raised his eyebrows and she smiled at him.

"'Twill be a son," Henrietta said. "I know it will, Anna. It must be a son. How happy I am for you—and for Luke, of course, even though he would not compliment me on my hat. Perhaps I will even forgive him." She laughed and moved toward the gap in the middle of the hedge so that she could enter the formal garden. "I shall return to the house with Doris and Emily. I know when three is a crowd."

He watched her go, feeling curiously depressed. For a few minutes he had wanted her again. Oh, not really physically but nostalgically. He had wanted to be that boy again and he had wanted her to be that girl again. He had wanted to change the world. He had been right to dread coming home.

Anna took Luke's arm and walked with him in the direction of the stables. "I am so sorry," she said. "The announcement was yours to make. You would have liked to make it in a more formal manner, I am sure."

"Mine to make?" he said. "It seems to me, madam, that my part in the making of our child was a singularly small one in comparison with yours. So I will be unable to lift you in a few months' time? Is that a challenge to my strength?"

She laughed. Anna's laugh was all sunshine and happiness.

He wished suddenly that there was not the necessity to go to the drawing room for tea with the family. He wished he could take it privately with his wife in her sitting room. Not necessarily to make love to her there, though the idea had its definite appeal, but just to be alone with her so that he could gaze exclusively at her without being ill-mannered and so that he could talk only to her and listen only to her.

He was shaken for a moment when he realized how much he had come to depend on Anna's sunny nature and uncomplicated placidity. Especially here at Bowden. He was not sure that even now he would not bolt back to Paris if it were not for Anna.

And why not come to depend on her? he thought. She was his wife. And despite her past and the secret she had refused to reveal—

did not he have a past and unrevealed secrets too?—she had given him no reason since their wedding night not to trust her.

"And how many months will it be, madam, before my strength is to be put to the test?" he asked.

She laughed again. "Before I am fat and ugly?" she said. "At least two more, I hope. 'Tis not even two months yet."

"Fat and *what?*" He frowned sidelong down at her. "Ugly, Anna? With my child in you? Ugly to whom, pray?"

He liked to tease her. To make her laugh. He was learning how it might be done and she was learning how to do it to him too. The time was, and not so long ago, when he would have whipped out his sword if any man had dared try to tease him—or looked stony and haughty if any woman had tried it.

"I am begging for a compliment, you see," she said. "Since you did not give one to Henrietta—how unkind of you, your grace!— perhaps you will have one to spare for me. Will I be ugly?"

"Madam." He paused to bow over her hand and raise it to his lips while her eyes sparkled up at him with mischief. "I can conceive of only one possible way you can appear more beautiful in my eyes than you are at this moment. That will be when you are nine months swollen with child."

"Oh." The mischief disappeared to be replaced with what looked very like wistfulness. "Do you speak truth, your grace? Or is it mere Parisian gallantry?"

"Madam." He bowed again. "I vow 'tis not a speech I am in the habit of delivering to ladies. I do not enjoy having my face slapped."

She threw back her head and laughed with glee.

"'Tis teatime," he said. "We will be frowned upon if we are late, Anna."

"Yes, indeed," she said. "And I am hungry. I am reminded that I am now eating for two. While I may be willing to deny myself, I do not feel 'twould be fair to deny the person who cannot speak for himself."

"Or herself," he said.

"Or herself," she agreed.

Anna had a gift for happiness, he realized suddenly. And a gift, too, for passing it on to others. He had indeed made a fortunate choice.

*Anna.* Henrietta caught up with her sister-in-law and friend on the stairs after tea and they ascended the rest of the way together, arms linked. "I was hoping for a private word with you with as little delay as possible."

Anna looked at her inquiringly.

"You must not misconstrue what you saw," Henrietta said. "You really must not. 'Twas perfectly innocent."

Anna looked puzzled.

"Oh." Henrietta bit her lip. "You did misconstrue it, did you not, and are pretending that it does not matter. Believe me, I thought Luke was at the house this afternoon. I took a book outside to be alone for a while, and he came upon me sitting on a stile as he rode home. I suggested that he ride on while I walked, for I did not want anyone to see us and misunderstand. But of course Luke is ever gallant. He insisted that we walk together. 'Twas nothing more than that, Anna, I swear. Please believe me."

Anna gazed at her in amazement. "Henrietta," she said, "how foolish of you. Of course I know 'twas nothing more."

"Ah." Henrietta exhaled in obvious relief. "You are very generous. And of course you are secure enough in Luke's love to trust him. And I hope secure enough in your friendship with me to trust me. You understand that what is past is past and there is an end of the matter. As Luke observed while we walked, we were little more than children then and it all happened more than ten years ago."

Anna felt suddenly chilled. "*What* happened more than ten years ago?" she asked.

Henrietta's hand flew to her mouth as she looked at Anna in dismay. "You did not know?" she whispered. "He did not tell you? Oh." She closed her eyes. "I wish I had known. I wish I had known."

Anna felt sorry for her sister-in-law. She knew how it felt to say something and then wish it unsaid, knowing that it was impossible to unsay. But at the same time she felt wary. And not at all sure she wanted to know. She opened the door into her sitting room and smiled. "Come in and sit down," she said. "Perhaps you had better tell me what happened, Henrietta."

Henrietta sank down onto a chair and set both hands over her face. "What a fool I am," she said. "Of course he would not have told you. Why did I assume he had?" She looked up resolutely. "'Twas really nothing, Anna. We grew up together, Luke and I, and when we reached a certain age we fancied ourselves in love with each other. We were to be married."

Luke and Henrietta. Growing up together. Falling in love. Two beautiful people. Yes, of course. Of course.

"What happened?" Anna asked. She did not really want to know what had happened. Now that the time had come and she was being offered the knowledge she had ached to know, she no longer wanted to know. Pandora's box was perhaps best left shut. But it had already been opened. Luke and Henrietta.

Henrietta sat with eyes closed and hand pressed to her mouth for a long time. "How can I tell you?" she said at last. "But how can I not? Your imaginings will be worse than the reality—if anything could possibly be worse. George ravished me and got me with child. Luke begged me to marry him even so—he cried in my arms, Anna—but I could not. I was with child by his brother. And so I married him—after Luke had challenged him to a duel and almost killed him. He was sent away. George nearly died, but I thought I had killed Luke too. Word came back of a terrible wildness in him for a long time, and then word that I had indeed killed a part of him. Word had it that he no longer had a heart. Do not believe it, Anna. He does have a heart. He loves you. He must have told you that. It all happened so long ago."

No. He had not told her any such thing. Quite the opposite, in fact. He had told her there was no love. He had married her so that she would breed his sons. She had known that from the start. There was nothing chilling in hearing confirmation of that fact now.

But once he had loved. Loved deeply enough to try to kill his own brother over it. Deeply enough to kill all love inside himself after the tragedy hit. He had loved Henrietta. And even a few weeks ago he had not wanted to come back to Bowden. He had not wanted to come back to Henrietta. He had been afraid to come back.

And now they had met again, the two of them, and walked alone together long enough to upset Henrietta. Yet they were forever divided by the facts that she had been married to his brother and that he was now married to Anna.

"I am glad you told me, Henrietta," she said. "'Tis something I needed to know and something I was curious about. I knew about the duel, you see." She smiled. "Don't feel bad about letting it slip."

"Oh, but I do," Henrietta said earnestly. "'Twill come between us, Anna, and I have so enjoyed having a friend."

Anna got up from her chair and rushed over to hug her. "And so have I," she said. "Nothing will come between us, silly goose. You are my sister and my friend." She hoped desperately that she spoke the truth.

Henrietta hugged her in return. "I swear to you, Anna," she said, "that 'tis all in the past. For both Luke and me. It has to be. Even if he had not married you, he could not possibly have married me. So you must not fear. There was not a word of impropriety this afternoon."

"Silly goose," Anna said. And yet, she thought unwillingly, her sister-in-law's protestations were almost too vehement.

## 15

ASHLEY was horribly bored. He had been home for two months and had never in his life felt more idle. He had read and ridden and walked and fished and visited neighbors and flirted with neighbors' daughters and bedded one laborer's daughter, who was both pretty and eager. He had ended that liaison almost as soon as it had begun. He did not fancy facing the embarrassment of having a bastard to support on the family estate. His father had always been strict about such matters.

He was estranged from Luke. They had scarcely exchanged a word in two months. And the worst of it was that Ashley knew himself to be in the wrong. He had been living recklessly in London and quite beyond his means despite the fact that he had a large income for a younger son—and Luke, true to his word, had enlarged it. Ashley had been at school when his father died and at university when George died. But he knew for a fact that they would have come down on him as hard as Luke had if he had lived as wildly while they were alive. Perhaps harder. Ashley had not known that Luke had been cut off altogether after the duel. He had assumed that he had continued to receive his income.

The trouble was, Ashley was finding, that it was not easy to admit publicly that one was in the wrong. Doing so would be too hurtful to one's pride. And it was not easy to feel fond of the person who had put one in the wrong. He was not feeling fond of Luke.

He still felt betrayed by the changes in his brother. He remembered the good-natured, always smiling, always indulgent and patient older brother who had been his idol. George had been too far distant in both age and position for any close relationship during their younger years and too unhappy in later years. But Luke had always been there, willing to play, to help with lessons, to listen, to sympathize when the younger boy had been punished for some offense. It was to Luke he had looked most for approval and love, Ashley realized now. He had not thought of it in quite those terms at the time.

He had known that Luke had changed. For years, all through his youth and young manhood, he had listened avidly to any fragment of news about his brother that had reached his ears, usually from Uncle Theo, and he had built a mental image of a fashionable, attractive, daring, and devil-may-care brother. When he heard that Luke was coming to England, he had expected that his brother would be his greatest ally. He had pictured them drinking, carousing, gambling, and womanizing together. He had pictured his friends envying him such a dashing older brother.

But Luke was nothing like he had been and nothing like he was reputed to be. Oh, he was fashionable to an extreme and doubtless very attractive to women. But there was a reticence, a coldness, a hardness about him that had bewildered Ashley at first and then alienated him. Luke seemed even more sternly devoted to duty and the preservation of his heritage than their father or George had been. There was no love in him, no compassion. Consider what had happened to poor Doris. And to himself. It just did not seem right coming from Luke even though both he and Doris had behaved rather badly.

He could leave home, Luke had told him, when he had satisfied his brother that he had good reason to do so. Ashley knew himself to be in the wrong, but at the same time he felt a stubborn determination never to go begging—never again, that was. And what good reason could he find for leaving? He did not know what he wanted to do with his life. And so he remained at home with nothing to do, bored and unhappy.

One afternoon he was wandering aimlessly along the river, which looped around to the west of the house among trees, flowing faster and faster, until he came to the falls, a long and rather steep slope over which the water tumbled and bubbled. The sight of flowing water and particularly the sound of it was always soothing. He would sit on the dry rocks beside the falls, he decided as he approached them, and miss tea. He was not hungry.

But someone else was there before him. She was standing on the flat rock that jutted out over the falls. She was barefoot and her dress had been tucked up at the waist to expose her ankles and the lower part of her legs. She wore no hoops beneath her closed gown and no full petticoats either. Her hair was loose and in tangled waves about her face and down her back. Even though she was of only medium height, she was too tall for her weight and shape. She was only beginning to bud into womanhood. She was holding up her dress and reaching out one foot into the rushing water.

"You had better be careful not to tumble in," he called. He did not believe there was any danger of anyone's drowning in the falls unless a head was hit on the rocks. But he knew from experience that the water was very cold. Falling in would not be a comfortable experience.

There was no response, and he remembered that the child could not hear. He walked slowly toward her so as not to startle her. She caught sight of him eventually and returned her foot to the rock before turning to smile at him. It was a sunny smile, rather like Anna's. She stepped down from the rock, clambered down over the others, and looked up at him. The top of her head reached barely to his chin.

"Have you escaped too, little fawn?" he asked. It was pointless to talk and yet one felt foolish remaining silent and grinning like an idiot.

Her eyes were going to slay men by the dozens when she was a few years older, he thought, deafness or no deafness. They focused on his mouth as he spoke, and she smiled again and nodded. She could understand what he said?

"Are you supposed to be alone?" he asked. "Where is your nurse?"

The smile became rather impish and she pointed through the trees in the direction of the house.

"You like being alone?" he asked.

She turned her head to look at the water and the trees and the falls. She set both her hands over her heart and then made a wide gesture all about her. She looked back at him.

"You love all this?" Who would not love such beauty and such solitude? But what would it be like not to be able to hear the water? "And you prefer to escape and come here alone?"

Deafness, he supposed, would lock a person up in a very private world. It would lead to loneliness or at least to aloneness. He wondered if this child was lonely. Yet she had a happy smile.

"I have disturbed you," he said. "I will go away. But be careful." He pointed to the rock on which she had been standing and turned to leave her.

But she caught at his hand with both of hers and shook her head. Well, he thought in some surprise, someone needed him, if only a child.

"What is it, little fawn?" he asked.

For answer she tugged on his hand and led him back toward the rocks. She bounded up them and onto the one that jutted over the water and he scrambled up after her. She sat down, motioned to him to sit beside her, and lowered her feet over the edge of the rock to dangle in the water. She turned her head and smiled at him.

"Is that a challenge?" he asked.

She leaned over, her hands cupped together, and scooped up a palmful of water. He expected that she would hurl it at him and braced himself for the shock, but she lifted her hands, closed her eyes, and dipped first one cheek and then the other in the water. There was a look of near-ecstasy on her face.

Did the other senses come more alive when one was absent? he wondered.

The temptation was irresistible. Ashley removed his shoes and set them behind him and then pulled off his stockings, tugging them from beneath the tight bands of his knee breeches and rolling them down his legs and off. He swung his legs gingerly over the edge of the rock and into the water, gasping as he did so.

"Zounds!" he said.

Emily was looking at him and laughing at him, the sounds she made strange and rather ungainly.

He pulled his feet up again and rested his heels on the edge of the rock. He draped his arms over his knees. She drew her feet up onto the rock too, clasped her arms about them, and rested one cheek on her knees. She looked steadily at him.

"What are you looking at, little fawn?" he asked her. "The water is cold."

She smiled rather dreamily. A sweet child. How old was she? Fourteen, had he heard Anna say? Fourteen to his two-and-twenty. An eight-year difference—the same age span as between him and Luke. Had he seemed such a child to Luke? And yet his brother had never shown impatience with him, had never given the impression that he had better things to do than spend time with a nuisance of a younger brother.

He turned his face fully to her. "You can understand me," he said, "but you cannot express yourself to me. Is it painful, little fawn?"

Her eyes—those wonderfully expressive eyes—grew wistful. He wondered if she had any way of communicating with the people in her life. There had been the few hand gestures she had used earlier. Did anyone—Anna, perhaps—care enough to build on those signs, to make something of a language of them? Even then, would it be possible for her to express any of her deepest feelings?

He smiled at her. "Answer my question," he said softly.

She nodded her head against her knee, her eyes still wistful.

He reached out a hand and gently smoothed back a lock of hair that had fallen across her face. She smiled again and lifted one hand. She pointed at him, made a flapping movement of her four fingers against her thumb, and then pointed to herself. She did it again when he made no immediate response.

"You want me to talk to you?" he asked.

She nodded.

And so he talked, telling her about his childhood, telling her about coming home from school one holiday to find Luke gone, telling her about his stupid, immature behavior in London—though he did not mention the mistress whom he had been unable to afford—and about his boredom at home. He told her about his feeling of betrayal, about his feeling of guilt.

There was a sense of great relief in unburdening himself to another person, he found, even if it was to a person who would not understand much of what he said and would be unable to do anything about it even if she did. It was soothing to feel human sympathy. Soothing to his loneliness.

"I am a poor, abject creature, little fawn," he said finally, grinning at her.

She shook her head slowly.

"And you are a good listener," he said, aware of the irony and yet the truth of his words.

She smiled back at him.

He said no more but listened to the soothing rush of the water and looked into its sparkling, fast-moving depths. And when a little hand stole into his, he clasped it, drawing comfort from it, giving comfort. She was a child in need of love, and he was an adult in need of company.

"Ashley! What the devil is going on?"

The voice, cold and haughty, cut into his peace like a knife. He turned his head sharply to see his brother standing several feet away, close to the trees.

Luke strode closer. "I suppose it did not occur to you," he said, "that Anna would be almost frantic with worry? Did you bring her here? She is a child who should be with her nurse."

But Emily had realized that there was someone behind them and had turned her head to look. She rose to her feet and bounded down the rocks like some wild and graceful woodland creature, holding her hands out to Luke. He took them and smiled at her. Ashley real-

ized that it was the first time he had seen his brother smile in over
ten years.

"Anna is worried about you, my dear," Luke said to her.

So he, too, must have realized that the child could read lips.

"Come home for tea?" Luke asked her.

She linked her arm through his and turned back to Ashley to
reach out her other arm for his. He shook his head.

"You had better come," Luke said stiffly.

Ashley pulled on his stockings and shoes and got slowly to his
feet. Emily was still reaching out an arm toward him, her face eager
and smiling. He wondered as she took his arm and he was forced to
begin the long walk back to the house with his brother, only the
deaf-mute child between them, how much she had understood of
what he had poured out to her.

"Deuce take it, Luke," he blurted after a few silent minutes,
"what do you think of me? That I am a spendthrift and a gamer and
drinker and womanizer? You are right. But as I live, I am not a child
molester."

He glared across the top of Emily's head at his brother, who
looked as cold and composed and immaculate as ever. His hair was
even powdered and he had dressed for tea in a green silk coat over a
paler green waistcoat.

"Damn you, Luke," he said. "Say something."

"I know you are not," Luke said without looking at him. "But she
is a child in my care, Ashley. She is dear to my wife. She has a handicap
that would make it impossible for her to hear searchers calling to her
and impossible for her to call for help. And it is late afternoon with the
evenings growing darker as autumn approaches. I was annoyed—
angry—that you appeared careless of those facts and of how Anna
would be worrying. But I put too much on your shoulders. Emily is
not in your care. And I trust you to behave toward an innocent child
as I would expect any brother of mine and any gentleman to behave."

Was it an apology? Ashley was not sure. But the words did cast
him in the role of younger brother, who could not be expected to

behave responsibly. The words irritated and hurt him and struck him with their truth. He should have realized that someone other than her nurse would be looking for the child.

"I am sorry," he heard himself saying. The words came out sounding as if he was anything but sorry. But he had spoken them at least.

Luke did not reply for a while. "I trust you, Ashley," he said. "That was not my meaning when I saw you with her."

Although he had been holding the child's hand? Oh, yes, deuce take it, it had been his meaning. But Ashley supposed it was as close as he was going to get to an apology from his brother.

Emily, walking quietly between them, holding on to an arm of each, looked up at them, one at a time, and smiled her serene, sunny smile at each.

Did she know. Ashley wondered, what had been going on across the top of her head? He was given the strange impression that she did, that she had maneuvered it. An impossibility, of course. She was a deaf-mute child.

*Dealing* with a family was not at all easy, Luke was finding. He was out of the habit. Indeed, he had deliberately cultivated independence. He was not enjoying being part of his family again. He especially resented being the head of it. Sometimes he longed for his life in Paris with a deep nostalgia.

Anna spoke to him about Doris one morning while they were out riding. He resented the introduction of the topic at a time of day that he was beginning to think of as all their own, just for themselves. He liked to ride a little behind her, admiring the graceful picture she made in the saddle, wishing that they could be alone together somewhere, perhaps in Paris, with no one to concern themselves over except themselves. And he consciously enjoyed each such morning. Soon her pregnancy would be far enough advanced that he must forbid her to ride altogether. Then he would be able to ride alone again. The prospect was surprisingly unappealing.

He resented her introducing a serious topic into their conversation. He relied on Anna to add light to his life.

"Luke," she said abruptly, "Doris is unhappy."

Just as if he had not noticed for himself. Just as if he did not feel uneasy about it, though he had nothing for which to blame himself. "She is sulking like a sullen child, waiting to be noticed," he said more coldly than he had intended.

"That is exactly what your mother says," Anna said quietly.

So his mother, too, was coldly ignoring Doris? It was like her to do so. Was he like his mother, then? Had he grown to resemble her over the years? He could remember Doris's riding up before him on his horse as a child though their parents had always scolded her when they knew and told her that only babies had to share a horse with their brothers. He had encouraged the child because he had enjoyed her chatter. Only now did he realize that he had been a lonely boy who had basked in the adoration of his much younger brother and sister. He could remember Doris's telling him on one occasion, her head snuggled against his chest, that she was going to marry him when she grew up. She had been maybe five years old at the time.

"I do not believe there is anything I can do to help her, madam," he said to Anna now. "Putting an end to that association and sending her home to prevent clandestine communications and a possible repetition of the attempt to elope were the only things to be done. I am not sorry that I did them."

"No," Anna said, "you were quite right to save her from herself, Luke. But—"

"But what?" He did not need Anna as his conscience. He hoped she was not going to adopt that role.

"I believe she feels that it was your own consequence and the pride of the family you were safeguarding," she said. "I believe she feels that you do not love her, Luke."

*You cannot marry me, Dor,* he had told his five-year-old sister with a chuckle. *I am your brother. But I love you more than anyone in the world,* she had protested, gazing up at him with hurt eyes. *More than Mama and Papa and George. A little bit more than Ashley.* He had hugged her thin little body with one arm. *I love you too,* he had told her. *More than anyone else except Ash*—though he had adored George too. *I love the two of you equally. We will always love each other in a special way because we are brother and sister.* She had snuggled against him as he guided the horse. *I am going to ask the king,* she had said. *He will let me marry you, Luke.*

There had been a lengthy silence between him and his wife. "Do you?" she prompted, her voice rather tense. "Do you love her?"

"I know nothing about love, Anna," he said. "I made that clear to you the morning after our wedding. I can only perform my duties here to the best of my ability. You would do well to remember that it is pointless to appeal to sentiments I do not feel."

She did not reply but after another short silence spurred her horse, first into a canter and then a gallop. He kept pace with her and lifted her silently down when they were back in the stables. He did not know if the gallop had been a deliberate defiance of his order. But he did not scold her. He would be ripping up at the wrong person. She had shown him his own inadequacy and he resented being made to feel guilty.

He resented the fact that she had set herself to arouse his conscience. Doris was his sister, his family. He would deal with her as he saw fit. He did not need Anna to prompt his actions. He needed Anna only for . . . But he frowned. No, that was unfair. He needed Anna for more than just that. *Needed?* He frowned again over the word his mind had chosen.

He did try to talk with Doris. But he made the mistake of summoning her to his office and retreating behind his desk when she came. She did not help matters, of course, when she refused the offered seat at the other side of it. She preferred to stand, she told him, and did so, establishing a sort of parent/child disciplinary relationship before anything of any significance had been said.

"You are unhappy," he said.

She laughed.

"Doris," he said, "it was intolerable. Even if you could have adjusted your life to poverty and to a loss of status and all the luxuries with which you have been surrounded since birth, you could not have been happy with Frawley. He wanted your fortune more than he wanted you."

"Perhaps even so he wanted me more than I am wanted here," she said, her eyes and her voice cold.

"You belong here," he said. "You have family here. You are my sister. Do you not believe that he was willing to take money—five thousand pounds—in return for giving up his courtship of you?"

"Perhaps," she said, "you have never known a poverty so extreme that five thousand pounds can be an overwhelming temptation. Doubtless it seems a paltry sum to you."

"Zounds, Doris," he said, frowning, "are you defending him?"

"I hate him," she said calmly, "because I believe you. But I hate you more for tempting him and exposing that weakness in him."

He drummed his fingers on the desk. "You hate me for saving you from an unspeakably dreadful future," he said.

"Yes." She added no further explanation.

*I hate you*, she had told him once; she was perhaps eight years old at the time. An elderly dog of which she was passionately fond had been ill and suffering and Luke had deliberately taken Doris out of the way while the poor animal was shot and buried. She had been distraught on their return, especially when she discovered that he had known and had kept her away. *I hate you. I'll never ever love you again.*

How had he handled the situation then? He had grabbed her and hugged her tightly to him while she struggled and kicked and screamed. He had held her until she had finally dissolved into tears and then he had rocked her and cried with her despite his nineteen years. And then he had carried her up to her room and sat with her on his lap until she fell asleep and he could set her down gently on her bed.

That was what he had done then. But then was not now. Now he drummed his fingers on the desktop and looked at her with shuttered eyes.

"You will remain here over the winter," he said. "Perhaps next year I will permit you to go back to town. You will have forgotten

Frawley by then and will be ready to make a more eligible match."
He had intended the words to sound conciliatory.

She half smiled at him. "Am I dismissed now?" she asked.

He nodded.

She turned away, but she stopped before proceeding on her way
to the door. "I always thought," she said, "that the worst thing in the
world would be never to see you again. I was very wrong. The worst
thing has proved to be your coming home. I hope that Anna has a
son. I hope she has many sons. Because if Ashley ever becomes duke,
perhaps I will lose him too."

*And* then there was Henrietta.

"Luke," Anna said to him one day after she had lain down on her
bed and he had covered her with the blankets—he had seen that she
was tired after an afternoon call and had insisted on bringing her
upstairs to rest. "Henrietta feels that the furnishings and draperies
should be changed in some of the rooms. She feels that the house
should reflect the fact that this is the middle of the eighteenth century. She wanted me to speak to you about it."

He seated himself on the side of the bed. "And what do you feel?"
he asked her.

She hesitated. "I like the atmosphere of antiquity and elegance
here," she said. "I hate the thought of changing anything. But I can
see her point."

"We will follow your wishes," he said.

"But it is what she planned with her husband," she said, looking
unhappy. "I think she finds the situation difficult, though she is always very sweet about it and swears she is happy to have me here.
Perhaps we should . . ."

He leaned toward her. "Perhaps we should remember," he said,
"that you are my duchess, madam, and not Henrietta. There will be
no changes in the furnishings or draperies of the house. The decision
is mine, made on your recommendation, and will not be changed."

She looked at him uncertainly. "She is my friend," she said. "I do
not want to make her unhappy, Luke. She told me what happened."

She bit her lip. "About why she married your brother rather than you."

He straightened up. "I suppose," he said, "it was inevitable you find out sooner or later. 'Twas all a long time ago. 'Tis all ancient history."

She smiled rather wanly.

And rather than discuss the matter further, as he supposed he ought, he got to his feet and strode from the room without another word. There was really nothing else to be said and he preferred not to talk about such matters with Anna. Anna was his present and his future. He did not want her entangled in his past.

But there was still Henrietta. Always Henrietta. If he was out riding alone, he met her. If he was out walking alone, he met her. If he was in the library or some other room alone, she joined him there. Always accidentally. She was always distressed to find that he was in that particular place at that particular time.

He realized that it was all deliberate, just as that first meeting at the stile had been. Henrietta had not hardened her heart as he had. She had suffered every day during her marriage and every day since, she had told him. And now, even knowing him married and knowing he could not marry her even if he were not, she could not stay away from him. She was unhappy having him close but could not stay away.

And what about his own feelings? Was he still attracted to her? Yes, certainly there was that. She was a very attractive woman. Even a dispassionate mind would be forced to admit that. But deep down did he still love her? Was he still capable of love?

He honestly did not know the answers. But he lived in dread of discovering them. And he lived in dread of those arranged meetings, fearing what might come of them if he lowered his guard for even one moment. Yet he would not express his displeasure to Henrietta. There had been so much pain in her life.

*Henrietta* had ridden alone to Wycherly to call on her brother. She was in the habit of riding alone, of visiting alone. Restlessness

had been a part of her nature since—since she had made some foolish
and disastrous choices many years before.

Having Luke back home was intolerable, she had just told William. Once he had been hers, entirely hers, clay in her hands. She
remembered him crying in her arms when she told him she must
marry George. She remembered that he had challenged George to a
duel for her sake and almost killed him, too. She had always wondered what would have happened if he had succeeded. Could she have
married him? Would she have?

But it was intolerable having him back. She had known they
could never marry, but she had pictured them living together at
Bowden, the duke and duchess, though not married to each other.
She had pictured herself as mistress at Bowden, doing what she
wished there, as George had never allowed her to do. She had pictured Luke, indulgent and loving her. She had never believed all
those stories about him.

But he had brought home a wife. It was impossible to know if he
was fond of Anna or not. But he clearly meant Anna to be mistress
at Bowden. And he had got Anna with child.

Henrietta, riding homeward down the dark, winding driveway
leading from her brother's house, gazed down at the road ahead. She
would never forget her disappointment at giving birth to a stillborn
son. She would never forget George's telling her, brutal as always,
that he was glad, that he had never been more happy of anything in
his life. That he would make sure she had no more chance to bear a
child of his.

Luke would be his heir, he had said with a curious, twisted smile.

And now Luke had succeeded to the title.

And then Henrietta's head snapped up, the unpleasant memories
gone. There was a horse on the driveway ahead of her, standing
perfectly still. On its back was a tall, slim man completely covered
in a long black cloak, and his face was more than half covered with
a black mask. His tricorne was worn low on his brow.

"Madam," he said softly, "I have startled you."

A highwayman on William's land, Henrietta thought indignantly. She lifted her chin and glared at him. She would be damned before she would show fear.

"What do you want?" she asked. "I have nothing of value beyond my rings and a few coins in my purse. My brother will see you hanged."

He looked rather attractive when he smiled.

"I want nothing that is yours, your grace of Harndon," he said, causing Henrietta to raise her eyebrows. "Perhaps I wish to restore to you something that is rightfully yours."

"Oh?" Henrietta was intrigued—and indignant. "Be off with you, fellow," she said briskly. "You will get nothing from me today."

But he leaned forward in the saddle and smiled again. "I do not wonder," he said, "that the duke is enamored of you, madam."

"I believe," she said, "you have the wrong duchess, fellow. Now if you will excuse me."

But he only rode closer, bringing his horse to the side of hers so that their knees almost touched. His eyes observed her keenly through the slits of the mask.

"What I do need from you is some assistance, madam," he said.

There was an aura of unmistakable masculinity about a masked and mounted highwayman, Henrietta thought. And he was looking at her with open appreciation. Henrietta had been starved for male admiration for such a very long time. She did not count the local landowners who were quite beneath her notice.

"The duke has a wife," the highwayman said, "who married him under false pretenses."

"Anna?" Henrietta said.

"Anna, yes," he said softly. "She will be leaving him sooner or later, your grace."

Henrietta frowned and forgot her air of aloof disdain. "She is your—?" she began.

"Ah, no." His eyes caressed her, from her riding hat to the low neckline of her riding habit. "There is no romantic attachment between the lady and myself. I merely wish to free the duke of an encumbrance in the interests of justice. You can help me, madam."

"I?" Henrietta wore no handkerchief at her bosom to preserve modesty. She was proud of her bosom. And she was glad now that she had neglected to wear the handkerchief. "How so, sir?"

"Allow me to explain," he said. But before he did so, he took her right hand in both of his, drew back her glove, and set the bare skin of her wrist to his lips—first the back then the front. She felt the tip of his tongue against her inner wrist.

Henrietta shivered with pleasure. "Who are you?" she asked.

He smiled at her. "But that is question upon question, madam," he said. "Shall we deal with the first? The second is of no importance."

# 16

*A*NNA had succumbed to temptation. When Luke had slid his arm from beneath her head and untangled his body from hers in order to get up for the usual early-morning ride, she had grumbled into wakefulness.

"Go back to sleep," he had suggested as he did most mornings.

And this morning she had rolled over into the warmth his body had left behind on the bed and done just that. And so she had missed their ride together, always her favorite part of the day.

She stood at the bedroom window, looking absently out at gardens that were rapidly losing their color and at distant trees that were giving hints of the changing season. Someone had been in and built up the fire and lit it. She must have been sleeping like the dead not to have heard. But she was sleeping for two, she reminded herself as excuse for her laziness.

She spread a hand over her abdomen. Through the thin fabric of her nightgown, which she had put on after rising from bed, she could feel the satisfying swelling. Luke had touched her there last night, as he frequently did now, and commented that she must have lost her waist somewhere.

The months of her marriage had brought a measure of contentment. The child in her had become a real being, felt not only with her mind now but also with her body. There was the tiredness, the insatiable hunger, the movements, the swelling. She was enjoying her impending motherhood with the deep gratitude of a woman who had expected to be a spinster and barren all her life.

It had been longer than three months. They had been home for more than two. She was beginning to believe in freedom. She was beginning to believe in happiness.

The house was running smoothly. She had made herself busy carrying out her duties as Luke's duchess and she believed that her husband's dependents liked her. She had made friends of all their neighbors. She organized dinner parties and card parties with informal dancing for the young people. She eagerly accepted the invitations that came in return. And Luke, she felt, of whom his neighbors had appeared wary at first, was being accepted again.

Emily seemed happier here than she had ever been at home. Luke was unexpectedly kind to her, and Emmy had taken to him. And Emmy had found a hero in Ashley and followed him about whenever she had the opportunity. Anna had told him apologetically that he must not allow the girl to make a nuisance of herself but he had replied that he liked the child and enjoyed her company. It was often not necessary for Emmy to follow him about. Often he took her walking or even riding, always with her nurse's knowledge and Anna's permission. They made a strangely touching pair, the deaf child and the lonely, unhappy man. They seemed to find contentment in each other's company.

Anna had been unable to spark any sort of romance between Agnes and Ashley even though she had tried subtly to bring them together. Agnes, pretty as she was, was just too shy of handsome men—and Ashley was excessively handsome. There were other handsome young men in the neighborhood, some of them interested, but Agnes seemed to prefer the very ordinary, rather portly, and dull Lord Severidge, Henrietta's brother. He was a man who had no conversation other than his farms and his horses and hounds, and yet Agnes could sit quietly at his side during a dinner and listen and talk with him with apparent interest.

It would be a good match, Anna supposed, if ever it came to the point. But, oh dear, such a dull one. She smiled at her own thoughts. Whoever Agnes married would be a man of her own choice. If she chose to marry a dull man, then so be it. But how could anyone prefer

William to Ashley? Not that Ashley had shown any particular interest in Agnes either, of course. Ashley, Anna suspected, was too
young to fix his interest anywhere yet. And unhappy and unsettled.
Poor Ashley!

Doris, too, was unhappy, though less restlessly so than Ashley.
There was no communication between her and Luke either though
Anna had tried once to explain to him that Doris probably felt un-
loved. She did not care to remember the chilliness of his reply. It was
all very sad. Between Doris and Anna a friendship had resumed.

Doris had even raised the subject of Ranelagh with her and admitted that none of what had happened there had been Anna's fault.

Anna's friendship with Henrietta had not cooled despite Henrietta's anxiety on the afternoon when she had told Anna about the
past. And Anna had tried to put the past resolutely out of her mind
though she had once mentioned it to Luke himself. It had nothing to
do with the present.

And Anna tried, too, not to think of her own past. Her new
home, her advancing pregnancy, her deep contentment helped her.
She felt sometimes like someone who had recovered, pale and weak,
from a long illness and was slowly but surely convalescing. She felt
health of body and mind being gradually restored.

And yet, of course, it could not last.

On this particular morning she heard her maid in her dressing
room even before the girl had been summoned and turned from the
window as the girl tapped on the door of the bedchamber and opened
it hesitantly.

"There is a letter here for you, madam," she said, holding it out.
"It came by special messenger, to be delivered into your hands."

Anna remembered then that an unfamiliar rider had come up the
driveway to the front doors while she had stood at the window and
had emerged after a few minutes and ridden away again. She had
hardly noticed at the time. He was probably scarcely out of sight
among the trees even now.

She knew. She did not need to take the letter and look at the
writing on the outside to know, though she did both. She knew.

"Thank you, Penny," she said. "I will want to dress soon. Return in half an hour, will you?"

"Yes, madam," the girl said, bobbing a curtsy and withdrawing. She closed the door into the dressing room.

"It has been a long time, my Anna," he had written. "Sometimes I regret my decision to allow your marriage. But patience will bring us both ultimate and endless happiness. You are to bear Harndon an heir, I hear."

Anna spread a hand over her womb and closed her eyes for a few moments. She felt dizzy and very, very cold.

"But you are beautiful even in your impending motherhood," the letter continued. "Your green morning gown—the satin one with the darker robings—made you look a part of nature as you strolled in the garden in it two mornings ago. And young Collins admired you almost to the point of indiscretion in your blue sack dress *à l'anglaise* at his mama's rout the evening before last. You see, I am never far away, my Anna."

She thought she might faint. But her muscles were too rigid to allow her to fall. Or to move away from the window. She felt eyes on her from behind every tree. She felt eyes on her from the room behind. But she could not turn.

"You must not forget," the letter continued, "that you are merely on loan. A little test, then, my Anna—forgive me. There is the small matter of an outstanding debt that must be settled. Two hundred pounds, not a great deal, you see. There is an old gamekeeper's cottage a hundred yards west of the gates into Bowden park. There is a large stone on the doorstep. The bill will be beneath it today. You may take it, my Anna, and replace it with the money. I will then consider the debt paid. Before nightfall, if you please. Your servant, Blaydon."

After several minutes, Anna folded the letter with hands that trembled only slightly. She was used to such letters. In such ways had she redeemed many of her father's debts though she knew that there were enough left that he would be able to hold her in thrall for the rest of her life. Though it was not just the debts. If it were, she knew that she would go begging to Luke. Luke would pay them for her sake, though now it was her brother who would benefit, not her poor father, who was dead. And not any of the girls. Charlotte was married. Agnes and Emmy were safe here at Bowden.

Yes, she would go begging if it were only the money. She would salvage her pride by insisting on paying it back little by little out of her allowance. And she would tell Victor, who knew nothing of the extent of the debts and who believed that by some miracle their father had paid them all before his death. Victor would pay Luke back gradually.

Luke would not miss the money, huge as the debts were. He had told her that he had two vast fortunes. And he would not refuse her, she was sure.

But it was not just the debts. Or even mainly the debts. She had redeemed many of them, although almost none of them with money. She had redeemed them by doing what he had told her to do. She had chatted brightly to neighbors and distracted them at parties and assemblies while he stole priceless ornaments and jewels. She had charmed gentlemen with whom he played cards, flirting her fan at them or showing an accidentally indiscreet amount of cleavage or smiling with warm eyes, distracting them while he cheated them of small fortunes. Once she had even accompanied him into a town where she was not known and haggled alone with a jeweler over the sale of some jewels—jewels he had stolen from her neighbors and friends.

After such occasions, he had returned one or more of her father's bills to her, sometimes wrapped about a gift.

The mystery of the disappearance of so many valuables in the neighborhood was never solved. But Sir Lovatt Blaydon had many "witnesses" to the fact that Anna was the thief. And he had two witnesses willing to testify that she was a murderer, that she had pushed her father to his death from the roof of their house. It would seem that she had motive for all those crimes. Everyone had known that her father was close to ruin. Everyone would believe that she had stolen in order to prevent it from happening and that she had killed him in order to stop the piling up of more debts.

Everyone knew how fiercely devoted she was to her brother and her sisters.

And so she could never go to Luke. For it was not a matter of paying off the debts. The debts were only the means by which Sir Lovatt had got his hold over her for reasons of his own that eluded her understanding.

The debts would never be paid off. Even if she went to Luke and persuaded him to pay them all, doing so would not help her. If she went to Luke, she would risk having Sir Lovatt angry at her and finally carrying through on all his threats. Luke would believe that he had married a woman whom witnesses could prove to be a thief and a murderer—and indeed she was an accessory to many of those crimes. All of Luke's wealth and position would be unable to save her from the gallows.

Anna went into her private sitting room. There was money in a drawer of the escritoire, enough money. Luke had insisted she have it though she had told him she had nothing on which to spend it here at Bowden. She sat down and counted out two hundred pounds.

She set her forehead down on the desk, closed her eyes, and drew several breaths, fighting both faintness and nausea. Her green morning gown. She had strolled in the garden with Henrietta and Emmy wearing it. And she had worn her blue dress to the Collinses', where young Cecil Collins had touched and rather embarrassed her—and amused Luke—with his calflike admiration. How had he known? She got resolutely to her feet and hurried to her dressing room to ring for her maid. Why wait for the full half hour to pass?

*It* was a beautiful day, with the slight nip of autumn in the air. Emily was outside as she so often was and as she loved to be. It was not difficult to escape from her nurse especially now that she was fourteen and almost grown up. She was alone this morning, Ashley having ridden off to visit some friends. Emily loved Ashley as she loved her own soul, but she never minded being alone. Most of her life she had been alone, though rarely was she lonely. She had always known herself loved, especially by Anna.

Even as she thought it, she saw Anna in the distance, emerging from the house. Emily's face lit up and she took a few hurried steps in the direction of her sister. It was rare these days to have Anna to herself. Anna was usually with Henrietta or another member of her new family or with Luke. Emily loved Luke too, though she was sorry that he was such an unhappy man. She was glad that her dearest sister had married a handsome and splendid and kind man. Ashley did not believe he was kind, but he was.

But Emily stopped before she was spotted. Anna, she could see, did not want company. She looked about her as she stood on the upper terrace, almost furtively, and then she hurried away through the formal gardens, head down, not at all enjoying her surroundings. She was on her way to some definite destination without company and without a carriage of any sort to take her there.

Emily frowned. There was something about her sister's bearing that reminded her . . . She had almost forgotten. She had seen Anna's great happiness. Anna loved Luke dearly and she was going to have a baby. Emily had forgotten Anna's great unhappiness or at least she had pushed it back into memory, assuming that it was all at an end. But there was something about Anna now . . .

Emily found herself following her sister, careful to keep out of sight. That was not easy to do on the long lawn beyond the gardens, but Anna did not look about her again. She hurried onward, her eyes on the ground ahead of her. When they reached the woods, Emily could follow more closely.

Where was Anna going? She was hurrying through the trees with a purpose and yet she was too far from the drive and the gates to be going to the village. There was an old cottage close by, Emily knew. She had discovered it during her wanderings and had thought it would make a cozy little hideaway in which she might sit and think on chilly or damp days. But the door was locked and though it was an old and dilapidated building, she had been afraid to break one of the small windows.

It was Anna's destination, she saw to her surprise, though Anna did not find it easily. She wandered about for a few minutes before she came upon it. Emily hid behind a tree and watched as her sister walked hesitantly up to the door, looking almost as if she expected to be shot at from a window or from the surrounding trees, and then stooped down quickly to lift one corner of the heavy stone that lay on the doorstep.

There was something underneath, Emily could see. It looked like a piece of paper. Anna picked it up, looked hastily about, and fumbled beneath her open gown to reach through the slit in the side of her petticoats to the pockets taped about her waist beneath them. But she brought something out in place of the paper, stooped down again, and stuffed it beneath the stone. She stood up, turned away, and half ran back in the direction of the house. Emily pressed herself close to the tree so that she would not be seen, but she saw Anna's face. It was pale and frightened.

Emily's heart sank and she closed her eyes and leaned her forehead against the trunk for a moment. It was true, then. It was all going to start again. She felt it.

Her first instinct was to hurry over to the cottage to find out what it was that Anna had put beneath the stone. But she hesitated and caution made her stay where she was. She was glad a couple of minutes later that it had. A man stepped out of the woods opposite—a stranger—and hurried to the cottage, where he stooped down on his haunches, lifted the stone, drew out what was beneath it, and inspected it. Emily could see that he was counting money that he had tipped out of a small cloth bag. He stood up, slipped the bag into a pocket, darted a quick look about him, and disappeared again into the trees.

Emily returned her forehead to the trunk and closed her eyes again. She felt sick. She felt like crying. She had been so happy here. Anna had been so happy. But it was starting again. And though she had never before seen the man who had collected the money, she knew that somehow *he* was behind it all as he had been behind all of Anna's misery. Emily had always known it even though she did not understand why it was and even though everyone else appeared to like him.

She wanted Ashley suddenly. She wanted his strong hand holding hers, his tall man's body close beside her, keeping her safe. If only she had some way of telling him. He would make things all right. Or Luke. He would make things all right for Anna.

But she had no way of telling them.

*Ashley* was not the only one who sometimes sought out the falls for the sense of peace the seclusion of the wood and the rushing of the water brought. Luke liked to go there too. On that particular morning he had been on his way home after spending an hour with one of his newly satisfied tenants when he had paused on the bridge and looked down into the water and succumbed to the temptation to steal a further hour for himself. He had turned his horse's head along the riverbank and had been lost to sight among the trees by the time Anna emerged from the house.

He tethered his horse to a tree and stood looking into the falls, one foot raised on a rock, his arm draped over his leg. He breathed in peace and the coolness of autumn and the special smell of damp autumn leaves, which could always evoke a whole host of boyhood memories. He must bring Anna here soon, before the trees lost all their leaves. She would like it here. They could be alone together for a short while. It was difficult to find time alone together outside their own private apartments.

He turned his head when the snapping of twigs warned him that someone was approaching. Perhaps she had found the place for herself and was coming there now. He had left her in bed, but that had been more than two hours ago.

But it was Henrietta.

"Oh, Luke," she said, stopping, a hand to her heart. "You startled me. I thought you were out on business. You like to come here too?"

No, not again. It was one too many times. One too many contrived meetings. He had made one of the saddest—and one of the most relief-bringing—discoveries of his life during the past month. He no longer loved her. There was nothing except a certain nostalgia for what had been and what might have been. And a certain pity for what she must have suffered and still seemed to suffer.

He had put aside strong emotions ten years ago—very success-fully, it seemed. He was content with his life as it had become—strangely, unexpectedly content.

He returned his foot to the ground and turned to face her. "No, Henrietta," he said, "you did not think I was out. You saw me and followed me here."

She flushed and bit her lip. "Oh, Luke," she whispered, and tears welled in her eyes.

"It will not do," he said. "I will escort you back to the house."

She closed her eyes. Her face was pale in the shadows of the trees. She looked youthfully, delicately beautiful. He felt nothing but pity.

"But you feel it too," she said. "I know you do, Luke. You pretend to have no heart because you do not want to admit even to yourself that the past is not over. But you feel it too."

"No," he said. "No, there is nothing, Henrietta. You must realize that. And these contrived meetings must end. What happened was painful to us both. We were both victims of—of fate. But it is long in the past."

"You swore you would love me forever," she said, tears standing in her eyes.

"Yes." He sighed and reached for his snuffbox, which he had not brought with him. "But it has proved not so, Henrietta."

"You love Anna," she said, the tears spilling over onto her cheeks. "And I am sure I cannot blame you. She is lovable and blameless. I am sure she has never done anything you could possibly censure. I love her myself. Have you told her you will love her forever?"

"My marriage is a private matter between Anna and myself, Henrietta," he said as gently as he could.

She spread her hands over her face and he stood where he was, his hands clasped behind his back. He would not go to her. She might misconstrue such a gesture.

"You have been stronger than I," she said. "And wiser. I suppose, then, Luke, I must look elsewhere for admiration and love. I have been lonely, you know."

"Yes," he said. "There will be worthy men willing to love you, Henrietta."

She lifted her head. "There is one . . ." she said.

"Is there?" He smiled.

"But he will never be you." She gazed wistfully at him. "I wonder if you had not married Anna . . ."

"No," he said firmly.

Her chin came higher. "No," she said. "You would not forget that I was George's, would you?"

He did not answer. He offered her his arm and they strolled through the trees in the direction of the house. He led his horse with his free hand.

As they emerged from the trees, they could see Anna hurrying, head down, across the long lawn in the direction of the house, looking rather as if she thought herself pursued. She was alone. She did look up and see them as she entered the formal gardens and hurried onward, but she bent her head again and seemed to increase her pace.

Luke frowned.

"I shall leave you," Henrietta said, "and go and take tea with Anna. I am sorry, Luke. I am sorry that I had less self-control than you. Forgive me?"

But she did not wait for an answer. She hurried across the lawn toward the house while he turned with his horse in the direction of the stables.

Where had Anna been, he wondered, so uncharacteristically alone? Why had she been in such a hurry? And why had she not smiled and changed direction to come toward them?

He was disappointed. He had missed their morning ride together.

# 17

THEY were to take tea at the Wilkeses': Luke and Anna, the dowager, Doris, Henrietta, and Agnes. It was no informal afternoon call. An invitation had been issued and accepted. The Wilkeses had cousins from London staying with them.

Luke's mother, then, showed open annoyance when one of their number had still not come downstairs ten minutes after they should have been on their way. To the dowager duchess punctuality had always been an important attribute of good breeding.

"I do not like to be kept waiting, Lucas," she said. "Your wife must learn that in this part of the world we do not make ourselves deliberately late merely to convince people that we are of superior rank. Perhaps where she comes from . . ."

"The world will not end, madam, because we are a few minutes late," Luke said. "I shall go up and see what is keeping her." He had been five minutes late himself. In Paris it was considered almost a mark of ill breeding to be early or even on time. Being early was a sign of overeagerness and one must never show oneself to be overeager.

But it was unusual for Anna to be late.

There was no one in her dressing room, he saw in some surprise, and no one in her sitting room. He tapped on the door of her bedchamber and opened it. She was standing at the window looking out. She was wearing a silk morning gown wrapped simply about her with a sash at the waist and no hoops. Her hair had not been dressed but hung loose and unpowdered down her back.

"Anna?" He stepped inside the room and closed the door behind him. "Have you forgotten that we are to take tea at the Wilkeses'?"

"No." Her voice was quiet and toneless. She did not turn from the window.

He crossed the room toward her.

"Go without me," she said. "I want to be alone."

She sounded quite unlike Anna. Her voice was lifeless. Her shoulders were slumped.

"What is it?" he asked, frowning.

"Nothing," she said. "I just do not feel like going out."

"You are unwell?" he asked. A glance down at her body showed him that she was not wearing stays. She was quite noticeably losing her slim figure.

"No," she said.

He continued to frown. "You are absenting yourself from tea for no apparent reason after we have accepted the invitation?" he said. "Is it not somewhat discourteous, madam? And discourteous, too, to leave my mother and my sister and yours downstairs without informing them that they need not wait for you?"

"Go away," she said.

His eyes glinted dangerously for a moment. But he had heard about the various maladies that could accompany pregnancy, moodiness among them. Anna had been so remarkably well that sometimes he forgot that her body and her mind were having to cope with unfamiliar changes and functions. He reined in his temper.

"Come and lie down," he said, setting his hands lightly on her shoulders. "You need rest, Anna. I will send for your maid to bring you a hot drink. I shall make your excuses to Mrs. Wilkes. Your condition is generally known, I believe."

She shrugged her shoulders, pulling free of his hold. "Go away," she said again. And then she was shrieking at him. "Leave me alone. Is this not my own room? Is there no privacy to be had anywhere?"

He had never seen Anna in a temper. He gazed at her in some amazement for a few moments, eyebrows raised. And he had never tolerated temper tantrums in any woman. A few of his women had tried and had found themselves swiftly and firmly cast off. He turned on his heel and strode toward the door.

"Luke!" Her voice stopped him as he was turning the handle. It was no longer shrieking, but sounded almost panicked—and shaking. He turned slowly and looked across the room at her, his own expression cold and haughty. "Don't leave." The words were whispered. Her eyes were tightly closed.

He walked slowly back toward her and she opened her eyes and looked at him. They were large with unhappiness. There was something wrong, and it was not her health.

"What is it?" he asked. "Tell me what has happened, Anna."

She shook her head slowly and reached for him. "Nothing," she said as he took her in his arms. She shivered. "Nothing. 'Tis just that I am not feeling well. I am tired and lacking in energy."

It was not that at all, he knew, but clearly she was not going to tell him what it was. "You must lie down, then, and rest," he said. "I have to go. The others are awaiting us downstairs and my mother is less than pleased by the delay. Come, let me help you off with your gown."

But she grabbed for him when he would have let her go. "Don't leave me." She pressed herself against him. "Don't leave me. Don't leave me." She whispered it over and over again as her arms came tightly about his neck and her eyes closed and she sought for his mouth with her own.

He gave it to her and tightened his arms about her again. There was a familiarity. She had been like this before. It did not take him long to remember. She had been like this in the carriage on the way home from Ranelagh Gardens, intensely, almost wildly amorous, throwing herself at him, so that he had been persuaded to the almost incredible indiscretion of coupling with her inside an unlocked carriage on the public streets of London. And she had been as wild and as clinging after they had got home. It was the night she had told him she was with child, the night she had begged him to bring her home to Bowden.

He kissed her opened mouth deeply, opening his own, thrusting his tongue inside, leaving it there while she sucked inward on it and while her hands tore at the ribbon holding back his hair and closing the silk bag that held the length of it at the back. He felt his hair spilling over his shoulders and about her face. He thought about his mother waiting downstairs even as he felt himself harden into arousal.

"Make love to me." Her lips were rosy and swollen, her eyes heavy with desire. "Make love to me, Luke. Please. Please make love to me." Her body was taut with desire, taut with desperation.

"Come." He led her to the bed, untied the sash of her gown, and slipped it from her shoulders. She was wearing only her shift beneath. She lifted her arms as he removed it, and reached for him as he drew back the bedcovers and lowered her to the mattress. But he did not join her there immediately. He crossed the room to lock both the door into the corridor and that into the dressing room. He shrugged out of his heavy silk coat and stepped out of his buckled shoes but did not stop to remove the rest of his clothes. He unbuttoned his breeches and went down into her reaching arms.

He could read well the needs of her body. He had carefully taught himself the skill many years before. And he was familiar with Anna's body after more than three months of almost daily intimacies. He knew that foreplay was not what she needed now. She needed to have him inside her. He freed himself from the fabric of his breeches and put himself there, firm and deep. She sighed and almost immediately relaxed beneath his weight and his penetration.

She needed him in her for as long as he could keep himself there. He could sense that need. In some strange way she was not aroused and did not want or need to be brought to climax. She needed his body, his closeness. His body instinctively recognized her need and set about satisfying it. He stroked into her slowly, reaching deeply and carefully inside her—he had been loving her with shallower strokes lately, conscious of her pregnancy. But he knew that she needed depth today. She moaned with every inward thrust.

She seemed quite oblivious to the fact that someone came into her dressing room and knocked quietly, first on her sitting room door and then on the bedchamber door. She did not even seem to hear when Henrietta called her name softly and then tried the handle rather hesitantly. He set his mouth wide over hers to absorb the sound of her moans until he heard the outer door of the dressing room close again.

He gave himself to her for as long as he was able before his control went and he spilled into her with a sigh. But he kept his arms firmly about her after he had turned her onto her side against him and lifted the bedclothes so that they almost covered her head. She pressed her face into the silk of his waistcoat at his shoulder and wrapped an arm about his waist. He smoothed one hand lightly over her hair and felt her slipping slowly and deeply into sleep.

He stared over the top of her head at the window.

Something had happened. Just as something had happened at Ranelagh. At the time he had concluded that it must have been a combination of factors—her anxiety over Doris, the violence of his confrontation with Frawley, which she had witnessed, her new awareness that she must be with child. He had looked no further. That last fact had seemed to explain her pleas to be brought home.

Could there possibly have been something else? As there was something now, today? He frowned and cast his mind back to that evening. He had not spent a great deal of time with her after that long walk outside the rotunda with her in the gardens. But then it was not the thing to spend all one's time with one's wife when out in company. But he had watched her when she had danced with other men. She had sparkled with gaiety and vitality as she always did; it was that brightness in her that always drew his eyes to her even when he was surrounded by other beauties. Apart from the few minutes during which she had run back to the pavilion for his mother while he stayed at the gate with Doris, he had scarcely taken his eyes off her all evening. Nothing could have happened.

Except . . . he remembered now that he thought more carefully. Except that when he had returned from seeing his mother and Doris on their way home, Anna had been strolling with the dark-cloaked, dark-hooded masked man who was a neighbor of hers from her home. The man had not brought her all the way back to him. She had made no attempt to introduce the two of them. Was that not strange if he was a neighbor, father to one of her personal friends? It had not struck him as strange at the time. It did now that he was looking for something strange in that evening.

There had been something rather sinister about that man. But of course they had been at a masquerade. Everyone had been masked. And she had not appeared at all upset when she had returned to him. Except that it was at that moment, was it not, that she had asked him if they might leave? He had assumed that the upset over Doris and Frawley had taken the enjoyment from her evening as it had from his.

And perhaps that was all it had been about.

Except that he knew there had been something else.

And what about today? What had happened to bring on the misery, the flash of temper, the clinging, the almost desperate need to have him as close to her as it was possible for him to be? It was so unlike Anna. She was a passionate and an uninhibited lover. There was no form of intimacy she would not allow or show delight in. But she liked her pleasure to build slowly and to climax explosively, as he did. And she never initiated lovemaking, only eagerly accepted it when he did so. Never except on two occasions, that was.

What had happened? Henrietta? Had she seen them together coming from the trees that led to the falls? Had she imagined that it was a clandestine meeting? But no, it wasn't that. It was something that had preceded that. He remembered that she had been hurrying homeward. He remembered his surprise that she had not waited for them or come to meet them. And his surprise that she had been walking alone when there was always someone clamoring for her company. It had not been a pleasure walk. He knew that now.

Was it anything to do with the letter she had received by special messenger? He had met the man at the gates while on the way to his tenant's house and had offered to make his delivery for him. But the man had explained that he had received strict instructions to deliver the letter only into the duchess's hands or into those of her personal maid. Luke had raised his eyebrows and ridden on without comment.

Was there a connection between the letter and the walk and this mood of hers?

And yet when he had asked Anna about her letter after luncheon, before she had disappeared upstairs, presumably to get ready for tea with the Wilkeses, she had smiled brightly and told him all the news and gossip Lady Sterne had sent her. Lady Sterne's letter had come with the regular post—he had seen it himself. She had made no mention of the other letter and he had not questioned her further. It had seemed unimportant at the time. It had been from one of her new lady friends in the neighborhood, he had assumed. She had several. Anna was well liked wherever she went.

Luke drew her naked body even more snugly against him and she sighed against his shoulder. He must find out what it was that had so much power over her emotions. So much negative power. He did not like it when the sunshine went out of her. Some light died in him, too, when she was unhappy.

The thought, consciously worded in his mind, brought a frown to his face. No, that was not true. It could not possibly be true that his mood was affected by that of his wife. That would mean that she had some power over him, some control over him. That in some way he was dependent on her.

Never! No, absolutely never in this life again. What he liked best about Anna was the comfort of the fact that she made no demands on his emotions. So different from Henrietta.

Anna stirred in his arms, whimpered, clung closer, and relaxed into sleep again. He cradled her close.

At Elm Court Anna had always had to bear the burden alone. There had been no one to confide in, no one to cling to, no one to give her the illusion of security. It had been better so. She should never, never have given in to the temptation to marry.

She did not know how long she had slept, though she felt that it had been for some time. But he was still with her, still holding her against his fully clothed body. She had the feeling he was awake. She did not know how she would look at him when she finally moved her face from the warm hollow between his shoulder and neck or what she would say to him.

She looked back on her behavior, appalled. She could hear herself begging. She could hear herself moaning as he had given her exactly what she had begged for and in exactly the way she had needed it. He seemed always to know what she needed. He had been dressed in his royal blue and silver for the Wilkeses' tea. His appearance had been perfectly immaculate, as it always was. She could remember tearing at his hair ribbon so that she might feel his hair about her face. His long hair always excited her.

She felt deeply ashamed.

She drew back her head and looked warily up into his face, hoping that he was asleep. But he was looking back steadily from beneath half-closed eyelids, and she knew somehow that he had not slept at all. She knew that he had been lying there for an hour or longer. She had kept him from rejoining his mother and the others or from sending down an explanation. She had kept them from an obligation to their neighbors. Luke took his obligations seriously. She had kept him by begging him to go to bed with her, to make love to her.

What could she say? *I was feeling unwell? I was feeling depressed because I am growing fat and heavy? I did not have energy enough to dress for the Wilkeses'? I am sorry?* She opened her mouth to speak, but she could not decide which to say or what else she might say instead. He gazed back silently so that eventually she hid her face in his shoulder again.

"Are you afraid, Anna?" he asked quietly. "Is there something or someone you fear?"

*Losing you. Sir Lovatt Blaydon. A prison cell. Hanging by the neck until I am dead. Losing you.*

"No," she said.

"Something happened today," he said. "Something that upset you."

*Someone knows how I dress in a private garden and what happens to me indoors—someone who is not even there. He is watching me. Who knows when?*

"No," she said.

He held her a few moments longer and then drew free of her and got out of bed. He buttoned his breeches with his back to her, slipped his feet into his shoes, and stooped to pick up his coat. His gloriously embroidered waistcoat was horribly creased. He turned to look down at her.

"I will protect what is my own, Anna," he said, "with my life if necessary. I do not boast, perhaps, when I assure you that my reputation as a superior shot and swordsman has been well-earned. You are my own. You need have no fears for your safety. Unless it is childbirth that you fear. That is the only danger against which I cannot protect you, alas. Do you fear it?"

Not pain. Or death. Only losing her child. She feared losing the child.

"Only a stillbirth," she said. "I would . . . For a while I would want to die too, I think."

He nodded, watching her. "Sleep again if you can," he said. "You have not been having enough rest. I am going to have to insist on more in future." His eyes were keen on her.

She bit her lip. "Perhaps I will," she said. "Thank you, Luke."

There was the ghost of a smile about his lips for a moment. "'Twas my pleasure, madam," he said. "'Tis always my pleasure to be of service to you." He turned and left the room, closing the door quietly behind him.

Yes, it had been better at Elm Court, when she had been alone. She had not been so prone to self-pity then. She lay on her back now, unmoving, trying to ignore the hot tears that had squeezed past her eyelids and were trickling down her cheeks and dripping onto the pillow on either side of her head.

*You are my own. You are my own.* He had not meant the words in that way. He had been talking strictly about possession. But oh, the longing for his love was an unbearably painful ache in her.

Anna lay still with closed eyes. She was frightened again without him. She felt eyes watching her. It was impossible. There was nowhere to hide in her room. But if she got up to stand at the window, where she had been standing when Luke came earlier, she would feel the eyes again, watching her from behind every tree.

She was afraid to get out of bed.

How much longer would it be, she wondered, before there was another letter and another demand for money or something else? How much longer would she be "on loan" to Luke? Until after the birth of their child? Longer? And then what? Would she go meekly when the time came? Or would she fight?

*I will protect what is my own . . . with my life if necessary. You are my own.*

What would have happened if she had confided in him? If she had blurted the whole truth as she had been on the verge of doing? But she had never fooled herself into thinking that physical passion and the protectiveness a man felt for his possession indicated affection or more. He would have to love her dearly to accept what she had to tell. And even then . . . But Luke was no longer capable of love. It was something he had killed in himself years ago.

Besides, Luke would not be able to protect her.

*I will protect what is my own . . . with my life if necessary.*

*The* visit to the Wilkeses' had been made. The ladies from Bowden Abbey had arrived half an hour late. Tea had been held back for them. And then the dowager duchess had had the unspeakable humiliation of having to make excuses for the absence of the duke and duchess, who were, understandably, to have been the guests of honor. She had explained that her daughter-in-law was indisposed, an excuse that would be easily accepted since her delicate condition was generally known, though of course most women of her rank would have made the effort to overcome indisposition. But how could she excuse her son's absence? That he was tending his sick wife? Such an excuse would be an insult.

Luke listened, tight-lipped, to his mother's tirade. It was the first confrontation they had had since his return.

"And so I said nothing," she concluded coldly when the family was all gathered in the drawing room before dinner—everyone with the exception of Anna, who was late again. "I allowed them to draw their own conclusions. I was and am most displeased, Lucas."

He allowed her her say. But cold fury, far in excess of the provocation, balled in his stomach. How dared she? How dared she censure Anna. But the time when he might have exploded with uncontrolled anger was long past.

"Madam." He favored his mother with the direct force of his coldest gaze. "My wife had need of me this afternoon. That is all the explanation that needs to be made to you or to anyone else. 'Tis the explanation I sent to the Wilkeses an hour ago."

Luke's acquaintances in Paris would have recognized the look and the tone of voice. They would have been wise enough to hold their peace.

"Anna is in a delicate state of health," the dowager said, her face stern, "as she doubtless will be at regular intervals during the next ten years or so. There is nothing unusual in that. Her maid is quite able to minister to her needs, and the physician if necessary. You need to understand, Lucas, that your duties are primarily to your position and that personal inclination and the imagined needs of a weak woman must be denied when they conflict with your responsibilities as Duke of Harndon. And you need to teach your wife the same lesson. Regrettably it appears to be something that was not taught as part of her upbringing."

The rest of the family had fallen silent and were listening to the altercation with varying degrees of interest and trepidation. Agnes was gazing at Luke with terrified eyes—and with a flush of indignation on her cheeks.

"I beg your pardon, madam." Luke's voice was soft and quite icy. "My wife is answerable only to me for her behavior. *Only to me.* As for myself, I will always place personal inclination before duty to my position if seeing to my wife's needs and safeguarding her well-being are to be so described. It must be remembered that I am responsible for the delicate state of her health."

"Lucas!" She glared at him coldly. "Remember, if you will, that you speak in the hearing of two unmarried young ladies. But 'tis what I would expect of you. Self-indulgence has always been your besetting weakness."

"Madam," he said quietly, "I came home against my inclinations to take up my responsibilities here. I came because my uncle suggested that my presence was necessary here and my visit with you in London persuaded me that you all had need of me. I married Anna because a duchess was needed here, my own duchess, and sons for my nursery. I wish it to be understood that she will always be first in my life, before any other member of my family or hers and before all my other duties. I will not tolerate criticism of that fact even from you. I will hear none from you ever again."

He listened to his own words almost as if someone else were speaking them. He was surprised by the truth of them. He had not wanted to leave Paris. He had not wanted to change his way of life. He had done both. And if there was something—or someone—who was making his present life bearable, it was Anna.

His mother stared at him in shocked disbelief, proud and haughty as he.

"And I will have it understood," he continued, "that for better or worse I am the Duke of Harndon and Anna is my duchess. She is mistress of Bowden Abbey. As such her behavior is irreproachable by anyone except me. There can be only one mistress in any home, I believe, if there is not to be constant conflict and bickering. Anna is mistress here."

His mother had nothing to say. Neither did anyone else for a few tense, uncomfortable moments. But Luke was not sorry he had had his say. He had come, against his will, because he was needed. They had thought to use him, all of them—his mother, Doris and Ashley, even Henrietta—to get the life they wanted. And so they were all in varying degrees responsible for his coming. Well, he had come and he would stay. But it would be on his own terms. Those terms had now been stated, not just for his mother but for all of them.

Anna came into the room before anyone had found anything to

say. She was still rather pale, Luke thought, but she was immaculately dressed—and tightly laced—and she was smiling her usual sunny smile.

"Am I very late?" she asked. "I am so sorry. I slept longer than I intended. And I am very sorry about this afternoon, Mother. Did Luke tell you I was not feeling well? I hope our absence did not upset Mrs. Wilkes. I will call on her tomorrow."

Luke crossed the room to her, took her hand, and raised it to his lips. "You are not late at all, my dear," he said. "And if you were, then we would simply wait for you. Are you feeling better?"

"Yes, thank you," she said, "much better." She smiled warmly at him and then about the room at each of its occupants. "You must tell us both what we missed at the Wilkeses'. Were the London cousins entertaining? And, Ashley, you played truant, as we did? For shame. You must tell us about your afternoon."

Tension seemed to drain away almost visibly. Luke wondered if Anna had even noticed it. But she had a gift for bringing sunshine into a room with her and for setting everyone at ease. Only his mother was still tight-lipped.

And Anna was pale. Holding on to her secret. Another secret—unless it was linked somehow with the other. But *within* their marriage this time.

Oh no, he must remember not to begin setting her on any pedestal. He must remember not to expect perfection of her. He must not grow too fond of her. He must not allow himself to depend upon her or to trust her too deeply.

She kept secrets from him. And not trivial secrets, he believed.

# 18

ENRIETTA was bitter. Nothing in her life had turned out well. Like everyone else, she had striven all her life to achieve happiness. Yet it seemed to her that she had never been happy.

And now Luke had rejected her. She had expected that they would become lovers. She had fully expected it even after the shattering news of his marriage had reached her. Marriages between aristocrats rarely meant anything in terms of sentiment, after all. Even after she met Anna and saw her beauty and vitality, she expected it. She remembered the power of Luke's love for her and the terrible depths of his anger and grief when he lost her.

But he had rejected her. For now, anyway. Perhaps in time . . .

Henrietta had had lovers. How could she not have when George had never once bedded her after their marriage? She had needs. It would have been impossible to remain celibate all those years. George had taken her frequently to London and she had taken lovers there. He must have known but he had not cared. Not George.

She had never had a lover in the country. And never a lover outside a comfortable bed in a comfortable boudoir. And certainly never a lover whose face and body she had not seen and approved. Looks and physique mattered a great deal to Henrietta.

Her masked highwayman made love to her for the first time—it was during their third weekly tryst—on a pile of not perfectly clean straw in a drafty barn. The day was chilly. He remained fully clothed apart from the essential adjustment to his breeches. He even wore his boots and his mask. And she remained clothed, the skirt of her riding habit bunched rather untidily at her waist.

He made love without foreplay and without finesse, pumping swiftly, almost violently into her, his whole weight bearing her downward.

She really was not sure why she enjoyed it so greatly and why over the coming weeks she went back eagerly for more. He would never tell her his name. He never removed his mask or his cloak. She knew nothing about him except that he was an older man—ten or fifteen years her senior at a guess—and that he knew how to flatter and that he favored swift and lusty sexual encounters.

Of course, she recognized almost from the start, it was the very mystery of the man that was his main attraction. Perhaps if she saw him, if she knew his name, if she knew something about him, she would lose interest.

She did try. "How do you know Anna?" she asked him. "What is your interest in her?"

"'Tis nothing to concern you, Henrietta," he told her. "'Tis in your interest, my dear, to work with me so that you may in time gain back the position you so covet."

Working with him meant supplying him with trivial and seemingly meaningless details about Anna's appearance and daily activities. And yet perhaps not meaningless either. She had noted a change in Anna. Her smiles were fewer, her complexion was paler, she was more reluctant to go outside the house or even from room to room. Her eyes sometimes darted about as if she thought herself observed.

"And yet," Henrietta said, "you say you have no personal interest in her."

He laughed softly. "You have no reason for jealousy, madam," he said.

"Jealousy!" She bristled. "La, sir, 'tis not likely I would ever be jealous of such as Anna. What has she done that you stalk her?"

"'Tis not your concern," he said again. "But I will rid you of her, Henrietta. You wish that, do you not? And more to the point, I will rid Harndon of her. By the time I take her away he will be ready to turn back to you again and you will once again be the Duchess of Harndon. 'Tis what you want more than him, I believe. And in the meantime you have our weekly trysts to comfort you."

"Oh, la," she said, "I can live without *that*, sir, I am sure."

But he backed her against the trunk of an ancient oak, lifted her skirts, adjusted his own clothing, and proceeded to prove her wrong. He laughed at her panting eagerness.

And so her appetites were fed, and her pride and her hopes. Only her curiosity was not—curiosity about her highwayman and about Anna. And her as-yet-unsatisfied curiosity was in itself an appetite that took her back to him week after week, to meet in whatever place he had appointed.

She began to play games with Anna. She contrived to be seen alone with Luke and then excused herself anxiously to her sister-in-law.

"'Tis just that we grew up together," she explained on one occasion, "and that we always enjoyed each other's company. We still do. There is no more to it than that, Anna, I promise you. You do not mind? If you do, I will stay away from him even at the expense of good manners."

"Oh, do not be foolish," Anna said, linking her arm through Henrietta's. "Come up to my sitting room and have tea with me."

"I do not want you to think that I have anything to hide, Anna," Henrietta said on another occasion. "You must know Luke loves you. He talks incessantly about his love for you. He loved me once but that is long in the past."

"You must not feel guilty, Henrietta," Anna said. "Come to see Emmy with me?"

Henrietta made careful mental notes of various trinkets displayed in Anna's sitting room and of the sort of gestures she and Emily made to communicate with each other.

Anna's eyes were beginning to look haunted.

When would her highwayman take Anna away? Henrietta wondered. But she was not sure she wanted it to be soon. He excited her.

• • •

*The* letters kept coming, as she had known they would. Sometimes they confined themselves to reminders of the past and assurances of future happiness and a demand for payment of an outstanding bill. Sometimes their sole purpose appeared to be to blind her with terror—and they always succeeded. He knew the inside of her home, even the inside of her sitting room. He knew her clothes and her trinkets. He knew what she said and what she did. He knew what others said to her.

It was pointless to remain indoors, though she did so as much as possible. He was indoors with her. He was in every room with her. He was always just behind her shoulder. Sometimes she even opened her eyes when Luke was making love to her to look furtively and fearfully about the bedchamber beyond the bed. She imagined—she felt—that he saw everything. Everything.

She preferred the letters that demanded money, even when she did not have enough with which to pay. Once she had to go to Luke to ask for an advance.

"Certainly," he said, crossing the room to unlock a drawer. He handed her the full sum of next quarter's allowance. "But not an advance, Anna. A gift if you will. Might I be permitted to know the occasion?"

She had come prepared with a story about a wedding gift for Victor and new dresses for Agnes and Emily. But she could not lie. She stared at the money in his outstretched hand.

"Secrets?" he said, his voice unaccustomedly harsh. "Again, Anna?"

She looked up into his face. "There have been no secrets," she said. There, she had lied after all. His eyes, steely and cynical, looked back into hers.

"Secrets are one thing, madam," he said. "Lies are something else again. Here, take the money, and take yourself from my sight. I am busy."

He might as well have slapped her face. She winced, took the money, and turned away. But his voice stopped her before she reached the door.

"Anna," he said, "you are my wife. I am never too busy for my own wife. Come and sit and I will order tea. Will came calling earlier. I do believe he fancies your sister. Certainly he blushes and stammers enough for ten lovelorn suitors. If she ever accepts him you must persuade her to tease him out of his atrocious bob wig and into a more fashionable bag wig instead. The sight of his head pains me. All of Paris would fall into a collective swoon at the sight of him."

She sat, clutching her money foolishly in her hands until he fetched a stool for her feet and took the money and set it on the desk. And she wished she could go back and answer his question honestly. *It is to pay one of my father's gambling debts,* she could have said. Would it have sufficed? Would he have wanted to know more?

She longed to tell him more. She longed to tell him everything. But she could not. She dared not risk it. There was a child in her womb, an innocent child who might well be cast out with her. And thrown into prison with her. And . . .

"I believe," she said, "that Agnes likes him as he is, Luke. She gazes at him as if he were Prince Charming come to life. It amazes me, I must confess. Myself I always looked for a . . ."

"Yes, madam?" His eyes were intent on her. She was reminded suddenly of the way he had looked at her across the Diddering ballroom.

"For a handsome face," she said and blushed.

"Indeed?" He raised his eyebrows. "And is that what you got?"

"Yes." Her cheeks were on fire.

"As for me," he said, "I always looked for a pretty face. And I got it, I might add."

They were on familiar ground, flirting and teasing each other. She kept her eyes averted from the money on the desk.

Anna learned over the weeks and months following that first letter to live deeper within herself. She did not neglect either her duties or her social obligations. But there was a private inner world to which she retreated whenever terror approached.

• • •

*Luke* knew about the letters. He had seen a few of them being delivered, but even when he did not see them, he always knew. He knew her far better than she could possibly realize, far better than he had known any other woman. He always knew.

He knew, too, that the letters did not come from anyone local or concern any local crisis. They were letters that were deeply personal and deeply disturbing to her. They were letters concerning her past, perhaps. Letters from her former lover. Though he felt he knew Anna rather too well to suspect that she would carry on such a clandestine correspondence. And he suspected that blackmail was somehow involved. There was that rather large advance she had asked for on one occasion.

What was it that she felt she had to hide? What could be so serious that she was willing to pay to keep it hidden? Something to do with that former love, perhaps? Was someone threatening to give him the details? Could they be so very bad?

He tried eventually to talk to her. It was on a day when one of the letters had come, though he had not seen it this time or the messenger who had brought it. He was in his study, dealing with some correspondence of his own, when there was a knock at the door. He ignored it, thinking that it was probably Henrietta, but the door opened anyway. He did not look up.

"I am busy," he said curtly. "Perhaps later."

But then he felt a hand touch and then smooth over his shoulder and looked up sharply. He smiled, set down his pen, and covered the little hand with his own.

"Emily," he said, "what can I do for you, my dear?"

She gazed into his eyes, her own sorrowful.

"What is it?" He took her hand between both his own. He felt a deep fondness for the child, a fact that had taken him by surprise at the beginning. There was so much person behind the silence, he suspected. Her eyes were the only window to that person, and her smiles. Today she was not smiling.

She pointed upward and he found himself looking up to the ceiling.

"Upstairs?" he said. "What is up there, my dear? Or who is up there?"

She stared at him mutely.

"Anna?" he said and she nodded.

He knew she had had a letter today. He had seen the truth in her face. "She is unhappy?" he asked. "She needs me?"

Emily nodded.

He did not immediately turn away from her. He found himself searching her eyes, almost as if he expected to find answers there. And almost seeing answers.

"You know, do you not?" he said. "You know what it is that is making her unhappy."

Her eyes grew luminous.

"'Tis something from her past," he said.

But she would neither confirm nor deny it. She pointed upward again.

"I will go to her," he said. He squeezed her hand between both his own and then brought it to his lips. "Thank you, Emily. You are a good sister. You love her dearly, do you not?"

But she turned, drawing her hand away, and ran lightly across the room. She had opened the door and was through it before he could open it for her. She ran ahead of him up the stairs, pausing a few times to look back to make certain that he followed. She stopped outside the door to Anna's sitting room, waited until he had caught up to her, and then turned back to the stairs. He watched her run lightly up to the nursery floor.

Yes, he thought, raising a hand to tap on the door, it was time he tried talking with her.

She was sitting beside the fire and was in the process of opening a book, which she had reached for in response to the knock at the door, he guessed as he opened it and entered. She had not invited him to come in though she smiled now and closed the book again.

"Oh," she said. "I was reading and lost track of time. Have I forgotten something? Is it teatime?"

"No," he said, seating himself and looking at her.

The incongruity of the smile on the one hand and the pale face and bleak eyes on the other was chilling. She was wearing a morning gown wrapped loosely about her and looked more than six months pregnant. Even in her stylish sack dresses, worn loose in front, French fashion, as well as at the back, which he had suggested to her after forbidding her to wear stays, she looked noticeably pregnant. His mother was scandalized by the fact that she was no longer laced and had suggested that she stay out of the public eye until after her confinement. Anna had told her gently but firmly, as only Anna knew how, that she went unlaced at her husband's bidding and would honor her social obligations for as long as he saw fit. Or so Henrietta had reported to him. Henrietta had also suggested that he have a quiet word with Anna and persuade her to behave in a more seemly manner. As if there were something unseemly about being with child.

"What is it?" Anna's smile had slipped somewhat. "Why do you look at me like that?"

"Emily just came to me in the study," he said, "to tell me that you were unhappy."

She looked at him blankly for a moment and then laughed. "*Emily* told you?" she said. "Emily cannot speak."

"Oh, yes, she can," he said. "Her eyes are more eloquent than many people's tongues."

"And with her eyes she told you that I was unhappy?" she said.

"Yes." He watched her keenly and waited.

A few times she looked to be drawing breath to speak but said nothing. He watched her swallow. He watched her hands on the arms of her chair. So much could be learned about people's emotions from watching their hands, he had learned when he was receiving instructions on swordplay and shooting. Anna's were plucking at the upholstery.

"I have been feeling heavy," she said at last, "and a little unwell. I have the misfortune to be one of those women who grow very large with child." She laughed briefly. "And I have three months still to go.

I have been feeling a little depressed. A little u-unattractive. It is foolish, I know."

"Have I made you feel unattractive?" he asked, his eyes narrowing.

"No," she said almost in a whisper. "No, Luke."

"Come here," he said.

She looked at him uncertainly for a few moments, but then she rose to her feet and came obediently to stand before his chair. He undid the sash that held her gown closed at the waist and pushed back the silk fabric. The swelling of her womb pushed against her shift. He spread both hands over it and looked up at her.

"Do you remember what I once told you about how you would appear to me when you were large with child?" he asked.

"Yes," she said.

"I spoke the truth," he said. "I still come to your bed at nights, Anna. I claim my marital rights there two or three times a week though I am careful these days not to burden you with my weight. You must know, I believe, that I still find you desirable."

"Yes." Her lowered eyes watched his hands.

"But perhaps, madam," he said quietly, "you wish to be attractive to others as well as to your husband?"

She looked up into his eyes and shook her head slowly.

"Let us have done with this nonsense about your feeling unwell and unattractive, then," he said. "We once agreed that plain speaking was essential to a workable marriage. I allowed you to retain one secret. I did so on the understanding that it belonged in your past and would forever remain there. But it encroaches on the present. That I cannot allow. There have been other secrets, Anna."

Her eyes had widened. His hands, resting firmly on her hips, prevented her from taking a step back.

"No," she whispered.

"Yes," he said. "You are mine, Anna. Body and soul. I will have all of you now and for the rest of our lives." He was surprised by the fierceness of his tone, by the power of his feelings. He had not intended to speak this way. "No more secrets."

"Ahh!" Her hands came up to cover her face though even so he could see its chalky whiteness. "Not those words, Luke. Not body and soul. Not like a bird in a cage, robbed of all freedom, robbed of all privacy. Not body and soul."

But he had grown angry. Even as he had spoken he had felt the impossibility of possessing her soul. And the undesirability of doing so. But even so he felt shut out, totally excluded from all the deepest meanings of her life. He realized suddenly how little he knew her even after six months of marriage. There was a whole aspect of her life from which she had excluded him and from which she would continue to exclude him.

The realization made him angry. He had never wanted such knowledge of her. What had changed? He got to his feet, keeping his hold of her.

"Who was he?" he demanded. "I need a name, madam."

A great blankness descended almost visibly behind her eyes, like a curtain. She stared at him, her face turning paler, if it were possible.

"Your lover," he said. "The man who had you before you married me. Who was he? Who is he?"

"No." Her voice was a whisper. "You said . . ."

"He is the cause of your unhappiness, if I am not greatly mistaken," he said. "Are the letters from him? Or from someone who writes of him?"

"The letters?" There was terror in her eyes.

"You must think me a fool, madam," he said.

She shook her head. "I sometimes have letters from Mrs. H-Hendon," she said. "She needs help with her—with her father. He is elderly and infirm. I sometimes go to help."

He looked at her steadily without saying anything and finally her eyes closed and she bit her lip.

"His name, Anna," he said. "He has already had the virginity that should have been mine to take. He will have no more of you. He will die if he thinks to try."

Her eyes came open. "He did not," she said. "He did not. I have only ever been yours. I have lain with no man except you. There has only ever been you."

"Ah, pardon me," he said. "Clearly my experience was not sufficient enough to enable me to know the difference between a virgin passage and one already opened for sexual activity. It seems I have done you an injustice, madam."

She bit her lip again. And she drew breath. "And what about you?" she said, her voice rising. "You kept a secret from me. You told me you could not remember the cause of the quarrel with your brother, as if that were possible. You told me nothing of Henrietta. And you have told me nothing of your numerous meetings with her since we came here. You could not marry her, could you, because she was your brother's widow. And you could not come here without a wife because then it would not have seemed proper for you to be so much in her company. But all is cozy for both of you now. Is that why you married me, Luke? Not just for sons but for respectability while you rekindle the past with your old love?"

Good God. "Madam," he said coldly, "you are out of order."

"Oh, yes," she said. "Yes, of course. We live in the real world, do we not? The real world where there is one set of rules for men and another for women. I must be condemned because I was apparently not a virgin on my wedding night. But you can freely admit to enough experience to have made the detection of my secret very easy. I must live without memories and bind myself to you body and soul while you can indulge, not only in memories but in a reenactment of those memories. Do you sleep with her, Luke? Or is a wife not permitted to ask such questions of her husband?"

He clamped a hand on her wrist and drew her toward the door. He was not consciously aware of where he was taking her or for what purpose until they were in her bedchamber and he was stripping off her gown and her shift and pushing her down onto the bed. He watched her as he stripped off his own clothes, feeling angry and frustrated. She looked back at him with pale, set face and hard jaw.

He knelt between her spread thighs and drew her legs up over his. He lifted her with his hands and pushed himself slowly and firmly inside. He held still there while he leaned over her, setting his hands on either side of her head, and joined his mouth to hers. He opened it with his own and thrust his tongue deep inside before withdrawing it and lifting his head to look into her eyes.

"You are mine, Anna," he said. "This is an act you will perform only with me for the rest of your life. 'Tis an act I will perform only with you for the same period of time and an act I have performed only with you since our wedding. Have I answered your question?"

She closed her eyes and lay submissive and unresponsive beneath him.

"You are my wife and I am your husband," he said. "If those facts make you feel like a bird in a cage, without freedom and without privacy, Anna, then so be it. 'Twas your choice to marry me."

He watched her during all the minutes while he worked in her with steady rhythm. But for once his expertise failed him. Not that he was using any great expertise. He was doing only that which was intensely satisfying for a man but far less so for his woman unless her body had been prepared in advance or was worked on as part of the process. He was touching her only with the one intimate touch. But he could bring no response. And he was not even sure he had ever intended to. He was not making love to her, he realized as his climax approached. He was stamping her with the seal of his possession, reminding her that there was no part of herself that did not belong to him and was not his for the taking.

He released into her and knew for the first time as he did so that physical satiety and emotional satisfaction were two quite different experiences and did not always come together. He wondered if he had just ravished his wife—though that was rather a contradiction in terms. He drew himself out of her and got off the bed. He gathered his clothes from the floor.

"If it is freedom and privacy you crave, Anna," he said, hearing the coldness in his voice, "you may have them in some small measure. Your private sitting room will be just that. I will not come there again uninvited. And I will not come to your bed again until after your confinement, until it is time for you to conceive again. Shall we say six months after this birth? Perhaps four if this is a daughter?"

Her eyes were closed. He had neglected to cover her when he got up from the bed. He dropped his clothes and did so now and then stooped for his clothes again.

"If you wish to discuss your letters with me at any time," he said, "you will find me ready to listen. I cannot imagine you guilty of anything so very heinous. But you will remember, Anna, that you are mine. That that is an unalterable fact."

She did not move. He went through her dressing room and into his own room, in which he had never slept. He leaned back against the door and closed his eyes. He had gone to her because she was unhappy. He had gone to try to bring her some comfort, some aid.

God!

He should have known that he was incapable of bringing comfort to anyone. He had known for a long time that he was no longer capable of loving. He had not known he was capable of cruelty. When she had needed comfort and understanding, he had been cruel.

He had allowed himself to become frustrated by her refusal to confide in him and angered by her accusation that he had been unfaithful with Henrietta. And that was something else he must do something about. He had allowed Henrietta to draw comfort from his company, always steering the conversation away from personal matters. But Anna had become suspicious. Could he blame her? He must see to it. He had hurt her and he did not want her hurt.

He opened his eyes and looked at his bed. Not so long ago he had guarded the privacy of his sleep, seeing to it that he never slept with the woman to whom he made love. Now he wondered if he was going to be able to sleep alone in that bed. For how long? Six months, he had said, four if this child were a girl. Plus the three months that remained of her pregnancy. Nine months, then. Perhaps seven.

Nine months of loneliness.

He heard the last word, verbalized in his mind, and he felt chilled. Loneliness? Was he becoming attached to her, dependent upon her, then? Was it really loneliness he was facing and not just sexual deprivation?

It was loneliness.

•  •  •

*Ironically,* the letters ceased soon after Luke had confronted Anna with his knowledge of them. There was only one more. It arrived a few days after the previous one and informed her that the remainder of her father's debts could remain unpaid until after her confinement. "I would have your mind free of anxiety as you enter the last three months before giving birth, my Anna," he had written.

She went with Luke and Agnes and Emily to Victor's wedding just before Christmas after assuring her husband that she felt quite well enough to travel. She even shared a bedchamber with him at the home of Constance's parents. They slept at opposite sides of the bed and did not once touch during the three nights they slept there. Seeing her brother and his bride, so very young and so very happy, Anna could not feel sorry for the burden she had taken on so that they could be free and so that they could have a home and a future.

No, she could not feel sorry.

And then at Christmastime, during a large gathering at Bowden Abbey, William, Lord Severidge, who had been uncharacteristically absent from home for a whole week and had returned only the day before, announced that he had called on Victor to make an offer for Agnes and had been accepted—by both the Earl of Royce and Agnes herself.

Agnes, blushing rosily, fixed her eyes on his face.

And what was more, William continued after a great deal of exclaiming and hugging and kissing had interrupted him, he was going to take his bride traveling after a spring wedding. They were going to travel about Europe for a whole year. He had met a fellow in London who was eager to lease Wycherly Park for a year.

There were more exclamations and much laughter over that particular part of the announcement. Lord Severidge's attachment to his home was something of a joke in the neighborhood, and Agnes's unadventurous spirit was well known to her family. But it appeared to be a decision they had made jointly and it appeared to please them.

Anna knew a few moments of terrified panic, which only long experience with such feelings enabled her to control.

"You are leasing Wycherly Park?" she asked William.

"To a fine fellow," he said. "Colonel Lomax. He has been with his regiment in America and is recently retired. You will all like him, as I live."

Anna exhaled slowly in relief.

She prepared herself quietly for her confinement, concentrating all her energies, all her love on the child inside her. She lived alone inside her own mind as she had done during those two years before her marriage.

And she missed her closeness to Luke with a gnawing emptiness.

## 19

HE dowager duchess sat in her own apartments, steadily working at her embroidery. Doris and Agnes walked outside—though not too far from the house—and then returned and sat together in one of the downstairs salons, wondering rather nervously, rather excitedly, what it must feel like. Perhaps, Doris said, Agnes would find out for herself in a year or so's time. Agnes turned pink-cheeked. Emily escaped from her nurse and found a corner of the conservatory in which to curl up. Ashley found her there and smiled gently at her, sat down beside her, and held her hand. After a while she tipped her head sideways to rest her cheek against his shoulder. Henrietta joined Luke in the library but withdrew to her own rooms when it became apparent to her that he was totally unaware of her presence.

Luke was pacing.

Anna was in her bedchamber, in her bed, in labor. It had started soon after she retired the night before. As soon as she was sure, she had gone through to Luke's room instead of ringing for her maid. He had leapt out of bed rather as if someone had poured scalding water over him and had carried her back to hers despite her protests that she was quite capable of walking. Soon her maid was with her and Mrs. Wynn, and the physician had been sent for. No one else had been disturbed. Anna had hoped that by morning they could all waken to the announcement that an heir had been safely born.

But in the morning she was still laboring and it seemed that it would never come to an end. She could hear the peevishness in her voice as she begged to have windows opened, to have a cool, damp cloth applied to her face, to have someone rub her back. But she could not alter the tone of her voice or the demands it made. It seemed to belong to someone else—someone out there. Anna herself seemed to be hiding far inside herself, hiding from the pain, from the anxiety, from the impatient excitement, and from the fear of dying or—even worse—the fear of the baby's dying.

And then about noon, not that Anna was in any way aware of time by that point, the nature of the pains changed and the voice that did not seem quite to belong to her was yelling in panic for the physician. And all became pain after that and frenzied pushing and great gaspings for air in the brief moments of respite. And somewhere beyond, soothing voices and instructions that she followed blindly.

And then the final burst of pain and pressure and the warm gush and the indignant squawking.

Anna found herself crying helplessly and laughing and reaching out her arms for her blood-streaked, crying, ugly, beautiful child.

Luke stopped his pacing when the library door opened and Mrs. Wynn appeared and curtsied. He glared at her, pale-faced.

"Her grace has been safely delivered," she said, smiling at him, "and mother and child are ready to receive you, your grace."

He stared at her for a moment, wondering if the buzzing in his head was what people felt when they were about to faint. And then he strode past her without a word and took the stairs up to the next floor two at a time, something his grace had not done in fifteen years, Cotes observed to Mrs. Wynn as they watched him go.

The bedchamber was quiet except for the unfamiliar fussing sounds of a newborn child. Luke did not see his wife's maid curtsy and leave the room. He was standing very still just inside the door, his eyes on the bed, where his wife lay looking at him with wide eyes, a blanket-bound bundle in the crook of one arm.

"Luke." Her voice trembled slightly and her eyes slipped from his. "You have a daughter."

A daughter. He heard that buzzing again for a moment and felt air cold in his nostrils. A daughter. He kept his eyes on his wife.

"You are well?" he asked.

"Yes. Just tired." Her voice was flat.

A daughter. He approached the bed cautiously and shifted his gaze to the bundle. Through the opening of the blanket he could see a fat little slit-eyed face, blotched with red. Dark, wet-looking hair. One little hand. Tiny but perfectly formed with five little fingers and five fingernails. Blotched like the face.

His daughter. His and Anna's. He was a father. No longer alone and a law unto himself. No longer even just part of a couple, responsible for the well-being of the woman he had taken to wife. He was a father. Head of his own family. With a daughter who was his own flesh and blood.

He reached down as in a dream, slid his hands beneath the bundle, one spread beneath the little head, and lifted it. There was no weight at all. None except the weight of the blanket, it seemed. But it was warm and soft and it made those fussing noises and the unfocused eyes examined the world through the narrow slits.

God! Oh dear Lord God. There was life between his hands. Human life. A life he had helped create. A life for which he would be responsible for years and years to come.

His child.

His daughter.

Love, Luke found, though he was not fully conscious of the thought, returned in a powerful rush and grabbed his heart in a vise and did not let go. Love was the most intensely exalting emotion life had to offer, and the most frightening. Fear and exaltation mingled and were indivisible, the one a part of the other. Love was what made life worth living. Not the pursuit of pleasure, but love. Love, which involved the full spectrum of human emotions.

Love came surging back to him in the form of a little bundle of humanity held in his hands. Not even a particularly beautiful little bundle. But his and Anna's. Their daughter. Their treasure beyond price. After a few moments, slightly turned away from the bed, he could no longer see what he held—it had blurred before his eyes. He could only feel the warmth and the miraculous featherlightness of love and hear its mutterings.

"Luke." The trembling voice behind him was thin with misery. "I am so sorry."

"Sorry?" He blinked his eyes and looked over his shoulder.

"Perhaps there will be a son next year," she said.

He understood her misery in a flash. And it was perfectly reasonable. It was why he had married her. He had made no secret of that at the time, fool that he had been. Could he have ever been so incredibly stupid?

"Anna." He turned fully toward her. His voice was little more than a whisper. "I cannot begin to think of next year. Only of today, of this moment. We have a daughter. She is beautiful. Look at her. She is beautiful."

"You are not too disappointed?" She looked up into his eyes at last, her own filled with hope and pleading.

"Disappointed?" He set the baby carefully back in the crook of her arm, seated himself on the bed, and touched the back of one finger to a fat little cheek. "Anna, I wanted a girl. Duty dictated that I hope for a boy. Inclination had me secretly wanting a little girl. This particular one."

She was crying then, one hand spread over her face, making clumsy attempts to muffle her sobs.

"Did you really believe," he asked her, "that I would be disappointed in her and perhaps even reject her because she is the wrong gender?" And yet she had no reason to believe that he would feel anything for any of his children, even his sons, beyond a satisfaction at having perpetuated his dynasty. He had told her repeatedly that he was incapable of love.

How could even he have known that he would love again? That he would love his own child almost from the moment of its birth? How could he have known that that miracle—and that terror—awaited him?

"I was so h-happy," she wailed. She swallowed. "I was so very happy when she was born and when I saw her and held her. It did not even matter to me, only that she was alive and whole. I wanted you to come and see her, and then I remembered."

"I believe you need to sleep, Anna," he said. "You are exhausted. But know that I am pleased with our daughter, that I could not be more pleased if you had been delivered of triplet boys." She sputtered into unexpected and shaky laughter. "There will be time for sons, my dear, but if we have none I suppose the world will somehow keep on turning. What are we going to call her?"

"I have not thought of girls' names," she said. "I was foolishly convinced 'twould be a son. Catherine? Elizabeth? Isabelle?"

"Joy, I believe," he said. "Lady Joy Kendrick with a few lengthy middle names to add consequence. Do you like it?"

"Joy?" She bit her lip and then smiled at him for the first time. Anna's smile, a little teary-eyed and tremulous, but full of sunshine. "Yes. Joy."

He touched a knuckle to his daughter's cheek again before getting up and leaning across her to kiss his wife on the mouth. "Thank you, Anna," he said, "for Joy. She is a precious gift. Sleep now. I shall send your maid to you."

*She* was exhausted, Anna thought after he had left. But she was not sure she could sleep just yet. There was too much of a tumult of emotions still churning inside her. She turned her head to gaze at the baby. At her daughter.

Joy. He had named her Joy. He had called her a precious gift. He had said that he had hoped for a daughter. He was neither disappointed nor displeased.

And he had looked at his daughter, at Joy, with a light in his eyes she had not seen there before. He had not been lying just to make her feel better. He had meant what he said.

He loved their daughter.

Perhaps, she dared to think, oh, perhaps there was hope. Perhaps there was a future. A future with Luke and with Joy and with more sons and daughters, though she could not at the moment contemplate a repetition of last night's and this morning's ordeal.

But she would go through it again and again if she could have Luke back. There had been such a distance between them in the past three months. Today was the first time he had kissed her in three months. Perhaps now he would come back to her. And perhaps that other was all at an end. She was a wife and a mother. Perhaps *he* would leave her alone now.

Perhaps there was hope.

"Oh lawks, madam," her maid said, tiptoeing across the room toward the bed a few minutes later, "don't weep, then. Was his grace harsh with you? 'Twill be a boy this time next year, I vow and protest. And her such a quiet little thing, poor mite. Just arrived too soon, she did, alack. She should have waited for a brother to come first."

Anna smiled through her tears at her little bundle of joy.

"*Whoever* ordered the ringing of the church bells this afternoon must be severely reprimanded," the dowager duchess said at the dinner table the evening after her granddaughter was born. "I trust you have seen to it already, Lucas."

He looked at her keenly. "I ordered the ringing of the bells, madam," he said, "to announce the birth of my firstborn child."

"You should have consulted me first, Lucas," she said. "The church bells are only ever rung at Bowden to announce the birth of sons. A wrong message was sent today."

"No," he said, "'twas the right message. The message that a child has been born here to the Duchess of Harndon. You, madam, have said nothing to me today beyond an enquiry about Anna's health. Ashley shook my hand and Doris kissed me and Agnes made her curtsy to me, but all three of you looked warily at me as if afraid of appearing too delighted. Henrietta actually commiserated with me. The servants have been subdued, almost as if there had been a death in the house. Only Emily hugged me and kissed me and cried all over my cravat and then smiled at me and told me with her eyes how happy she was for me."

"Emily does not understand," Henrietta said gently, "how important it is for a man in your position to have an heir, Luke. Poor Anna. She must be feeling very sad. I will have to try cheering her up."

"It is to be hoped," the dowager said, "that she will do her duty next year."

"Do you mean, Mama," Doris asked, "that the church bells rang when George and Luke and Ashley were born, but not when I was born?"

"They will ring for your wedding, Dor," Luke said and watched her eyes widen in astonishment at his unconscious use of the old shortened form of her name that he had used when she was a child. "And they will ring for every child of mine regardless of gender. There is a child upstairs with Anna. Our daughter, whom we would not exchange for a dozen sons. I shall send to Theo and Lady Sterne and Royce and Anna's other sister with the announcement and with the hope that they will be able to attend her christening."

"After all, Luke," Ashley said, grinning, "you do have an heir. Not that I covet the position, I make all haste to add."

"I have no immediate plans to marry," Doris said, eyeing Luke warily.

"But you will," he said. "It has ever been my observation that the loveliest and most eligible of ladies fall prey to Cupid's darts sooner or later. And you are both, Dor."

She flushed with pleasure and looked down at her plate.

"Cotes," Luke said, addressing his impassive butler, who stood at the sideboard with a footman, "you will open three bottles of wine for the servants' dinner following this, and you will have the health of Lady Joy Kendrick toasted. You will inform my servants that it is a birth they are celebrating. If I see one long face on the morrow, it will be dismissed from my service along with its owner. Is that understood?"

"Your grace," his butler murmured with a dignified inclination of the head.

And with that, Luke rose from the table with the rest of his family—he never allowed the ladies to depart first unless they were entertaining. He had made clear to them all that duty was not going to rule his life and rob it of all joy—an apt word to use. Joy was a far better word to use than pleasure. Pleasure brought empty, emotionless enjoyment. Joy brought . . . well, everything. It brought love and happiness and fear and pain and vulnerability.

He understood clearly that love had broken through all the barriers he had built so carefully and deliberately about his heart in ten years—almost eleven now. And one moment of time—the moment in which he had gazed at his daughter for the first time—had shattered the work of years. He loved her, his little Joy, with such an intensity of emotion that it almost frightened him.

Yes, it frightened him because he felt the unfamiliar urge to share his feelings. He had had the church bells rung, though he had not been near the church since his return to Bowden, he had scolded the family for the coolness of their congratulations, he had already planned a christening party. And he had felt a certain tenderness for Ashley and Doris, from whom he was estranged, and a need to set things right with them somehow. He had spoken to them and they had spoken to him for one of the few times in the past eight months.

And Anna . . . he had been all but estranged from her for three months. They had been courteous and distant with each other. Duty had remained; pleasure had gone. He wanted the pleasure back and perhaps, too, a little . . . joy. There surely should be more to their relationship than just duty and pleasure.

A small child had found a chink in his armor this morning and had blown it apart. But he felt naked without it and afraid. And not at all sure he did not want to drag it about himself again and reserve his newfound capacity to love for his child.

*Luke* excused himself after drinking tea with his family in the drawing room and went upstairs to his wife's room. There was a sliver of light visible beneath the door. He tapped lightly on it and waited until her maid opened it.

"You may go and have dinner with the other servants, Penny," he said.

She bobbed a curtsy and left as he stepped into the room, quietly in case his wife and his daughter slept. But Anna was propped up in bed against a bank of pillows and she had the child to her breast. She flushed and smiled at him as he crossed the room toward her and sat down carefully on the bed. His eyes lowered from her face.

And love constricted his breathing again.

"She was fussing," Anna said. "I thought perhaps she was hungry, but I do not believe she is."

His daughter's mouth was about Anna's nipple, but she was not sucking. "She is quiet," he said.

"I believe she likes the comfort of being here," she said. "Luke, I am sorry you came at such a moment. You are looking so grand. You are wearing the clothes you wore when I first saw you."

Though no one had remarked on his appearance at dinner, he knew that several of them had looked askance at him for wearing the most splendid of his evening clothes for a family dinner. They had not understood, perhaps, why he had felt constrained to wear his best. Indeed, he had only just resisted applying his cosmetics. He had had to make some small concessions to country living, alas.

"While I am . . . like this," Anna said with an apologetic laugh.

"You appeared beautiful to me in your green and gold ballgown on that evening, madam," he said. "Tonight you appear ten times more lovely."

"Oh." She laughed again, delight in the sound. "Where did you learn such gallantry, your grace? Do you hear your papa flatter your mama, Joy?"

Their daughter gave no sign of having done so. She appeared too content to be where she was.

"The church bells rang in the village for half an hour this afternoon," he said. "The servants are drinking wine with their dinner in the servants' hall this evening. Invitations will be sent tomorrow to our absent family members and to your godmother to attend the christening. And I donned my scarlet coat and gold waistcoat. 'Tis not every day that one becomes a father for the first time."

She rested her head back against the pillows and smiled at him. "Luke," she said. She drew breath to say more, but merely shook her head slightly and smiled again.

"May I?" He reached out hands that trembled slightly, as they had not done, surprisingly, the first time, and took the baby into his own arms. He held her in the crook of his arm and gazed down at her. And smiled.

"Her skin has lost some of the red patches," Anna said.

"Has it?" He continued to smile. "She looks just as beautiful to me as she did earlier."

Anna, resting against her pillows, raised her eyes from the baby to his face. She kept them there, gazing at him in wonder and with some wistfulness.

He was smiling.

*Laurence* Colby had not been happy since Luke's return to Bowden Abbey. For five years he had had almost a free hand in the running of the estate, during the first three of those because George, Duke of Harndon, had been an unhappy man and had shown little interest in the day-to-day workings of his inheritance, and during the last two years because Lucas, Duke of Harndon, was living in Paris and seemed totally unconcerned with his home or his lands.

It was difficult to adjust to the homecoming of the duke and to the unexpected fact that he took a keen interest in the affairs of Bowden and had his own very distinctive and very unshakable ideas on how things should be run. Ideas that involved the spending of money that had been carefully hoarded over the past years. Ideas that involved improvements that would profit the tenants far more than the duchy itself.

Colby was an honest man, but he had been a disgruntled one for almost a year. When an opportunity presented itself to him in the form of the offer of employment fifty miles away, he took it though it offered no improvement in his salary. Money did not mean everything to Bowden's steward. Control did. And so he left with no more than a week's notice, in the middle of March, just when spring was coming and with it one of the busiest times of the year on the farms.

Luke was at a loss. Although he had concerned himself since his return with the workings of his estate, in truth he knew little about the business aspects of it. He walked into his office one morning and grimaced. He had had all the books and ledgers brought over from Colby's and stacked on his desk and on the floor beside it. He scarcely knew where to start. What he really needed was a new and experienced steward. But where was one to be found at a moment's notice? He should ride over to Wycherly, perhaps, and see if Will could suggest someone. Will seemed to know everything there was to know about farming.

But his thoughts were interrupted by the arrival of his wife in the room.

"She is sleeping?" she asked.

"What?" he said and then looked down at the child he held cradled in his arms. His family and servants had been confounded by the fact that he often carried his daughter about with him. Apparently fathers were under no obligation to see their children for more than a few minutes a day, if that—or so his mother had explained to him after he had received visitors one afternoon while holding Joy. "Ah, yes. She must have nodded off from boredom when I forgot to continue conversing with her. Have you ever in your life seen such a mess, Anna?" He frowned at his desk and the floor beside it.

She took the child from his arms. "I'll take her up to the nursery," she said. "You know what Mother says about spoiling children by holding them too much." She smiled at him. "Poor Luke. It was very bad of Mr. Colby to leave so abruptly. Have you thought of Ashley?"

"Ashley?" He frowned blankly at her.

"Doris told me that he used to trail about after Mr. Colby during his holidays after you went away," she said. "And you know that he spends a great deal of his time with William."

He knew no such thing. And how the devil had she got Doris to tell her that?

"You suggest that I call on my brother for help?" he asked.

"What is family for?" she said.

But this was no normal family. Not like hers. How could he ask Ashley of all people for help? And yet perhaps it was the very opening he had been looking for for months now. And in the three weeks since Joy's birth he and Ashley had been warily circling about each other, figuratively speaking. Luke could not forget the way his younger brother had grinned at him on the evening of her birth and reminded him that he still had an heir. And the next day Ashley had shaken his hand more warmly than he had done the day before and told him he was truly happy for him.

"He will not do anything to help me," he told Anna now.

"Perhaps not," she said, lifting the baby to her shoulder and rubbing one hand gently over her back. "But you will not know if you do not ask, Luke. Ask him. Please?"

He might have known that she was going to do this to him—act as his conscience, wheedle him into doing things that he had no particular wish to do. She was quite as bad as Theo.

He found Ashley outside, walking across the lawn from the woods with Emily. He was holding one of her hands. In her other she held a bunch of daffodils. They were both laughing, Emily in her strangely appealing though ungainly way.

"I would talk with Ashley," Luke said when Emily was close enough to listen to his lips. "You may go up and see the baby before Anna leaves her, if you wish."

She gave him her wide, happy smile and went running off toward the house.

Ashley was looking at him warily. "What have I done?" he asked. "You look grim. Are you sure you would not prefer to be seated behind your desk with me standing on the other side, Luke?"

"I would not be able to see you over the stack of Colby's ledgers," Luke said. "I need your help, Ash."

His brother raised his eyebrows. "Egad," he said, "I have not been called that sooty name for a long time." And then he frowned. "What sort of help?"

"Have you ever fancied yourself as a steward?" Luke asked.

"You want me to take Colby's place," Ashley said, surprise in his voice.

"If you think you can do it," Luke said, "and if you want to do it. You are under no obligation to me."

"That is the trouble with my whole bloody life," Ashley said. "I am under no obligation to anyone. Everyone is obliged to look after me. Sometimes I think it would be as well to put a gun to my temple."

"Don't," Luke said curtly.

"I suppose," Ashley said, "I should have settled for the church or the army when they were suggested to me."

"Not if they do not suit you," Luke said. "We must talk about it, Ash, and find something that really will suit you and give you a sense of purpose. In the meantime, will you help me out until I can get someone to take Colby's place?"

Ashley nodded slowly. "As a matter of fact," he said, "I have always had an interest in business, Luke. I mentioned the East India Company to Papa once and he exploded in my face. No son of his . . . You can guess the rest. I fancied going to India."

Luke looked keenly at him. "Past tense?" he said.

Ashley shrugged.

"Then 'tis an idea we must explore without further delay," Luke said. "If 'tis what you really want, Ash. But will you help me while we wait for some answers?" He raised his eyebrows.

Ashley grinned. "Everything is on your desk?" he asked. "I'll take a look. I used to get Colby to explain everything to me, you know. Yes, I'll do it for you, Luke."

Luke reached out his right hand and his brother took it after a moment's hesitation. They clasped hands firmly and warmly.

"Ash," Luke said, "I have made a devil of a mess of several things since my return. Give me a second chance?"

Ashley laughed. "If it had been Papa last year," he said, "or even George, I would have been bent over the nearest desk and soundly walloped. And I would have deserved every stroke. Your contempt was worse in a way because it was so unexpected, but it had its effect, Luke, as the walloping might not have. Give *me* a second chance?"

Luke clapped a hand on his shoulder. "Yes, this very minute," he said. "In my office, my dear. Sorry—in my office, *brother.*"

## 20

*I*T seemed to Anna during the two months following the birth of her child that she lived almost with bated breath. They were a busy two months and a happy two months.

And there were no letters.

Perhaps he had grown tired of taunting her, she thought. Perhaps he had admitted defeat, knowing that she was to have Luke's child. Perhaps she realized that he had lost her.

She did not believe it for a moment.

But she tried, she pretended to believe it. And sometimes she almost succeeded.

Agnes's wedding was to take place one week after Joy's christening. It had been arranged thus so that the guests who had traveled some distance for the one event would be able to stay for the other. Anna looked forward to seeing Victor and Constance again, and Charlotte and her husband, and Aunt Marjorie. And Lord Quinn, Luke's uncle.

But it was not just the busy preparations and the absence of letters that accounted for her happiness. The long and terrible estrangement from Luke seemed to be at an end. Their child brought them together. Often when she went to the nursery to feed Joy, she found him there before her, playing with the child or vainly trying to soothe her if she was very hungry. Once—to the nurse's obvious consternation—he was changing the baby's nappy. Almost always he stayed to watch his daughter being fed.

He loved their daughter. Anna ached with the happiness of knowing that it was so, but at the same time she felt a certain wistfulness. If only he would look at her as he looked at Joy.

And yet there was happiness. He talked to her more than he had ever done before. He talked about more than just trivialities. She wondered sometimes if he realized that he was treating her more like a wife than he used to do.

He talked about Doris's going back to London with the dowager after the christening and about his efforts to find a new steward so that Ashley could join the East India Company. And on one magical afternoon he took her and Joy for a walk to the falls and sat with them there telling Anna about his childhood.

"We were always up to mischief here," he said. "We were strictly forbidden to go near the water, so of course we had to wade in it to see if we could descend the falls without losing our footing. I used to encourage Ashley to do it when I was old enough to know better."

"And George encouraged you?" she asked.

There was a short silence. "I suppose so," he said.

She had noticed that he never spoke of his elder brother.

"They were happy days," he said quietly. "I would have our children as happy, Anna."

She hugged the words to herself almost as if they were a declaration of love, almost as if they guaranteed her a future. And then he got to his feet, set the baby in Anna's arms, and strolled away to gather a bouquet of daffodils.

"Madam." He bowed formally though he was dressed in an informal frock coat and breeches and his hair was unpowdered. "The blooms almost match the sunshine of your smile." He set them along her free arm and took Joy from her again.

"Your grace." She set a hand over her heart. "You flatter me." She laughed lightly, but in truth her heart was crying with pleasure.

It was an afternoon she hated to see come to an end.

*Luke* enjoyed the hectic days surrounding the christening of his daughter and the wedding of his sister-in-law and Will. Anna's brother and his wife and her sister and her husband arrived together one day, Lady Sterne and his uncle on the following day. The house seemed suddenly filled with laughter and raised voices.

It surprised Luke that he enjoyed it all. It was true that he had been much in society in Paris and had always chosen the most glittering, most crowded entertainments. But he had enjoyed it all in a somewhat detached manner. His heart and his very being had never been involved.

But now he was with his family and his wife's family and he was enjoying the sense of involvement. The sense that he was part of it all, that he belonged.

"Pox on it, lad," his uncle said the first time they were alone together, slapping him on the shoulder, "but I am proud of you. I always knew you would come back here with a little encouragement and do your duty."

"There are those, my dear," Luke said, taking a pinch of snuff and sniffing it delicately up each nostril, "who would say it was lamentably undutiful of me to beget a daughter as my firstborn."

Lord Quinn laughed heartily. "Nay, but it takes practice like all else," he said. "A gel this time and a boy next. There is time, lad."

Luke felt rather as if he had lost his daughter. She was always in some female's arms being cooed over while other females crowded about awaiting their turn. But only he—and Anna, it was true—was able to make her smile. It was merely wind, his mother told him when he was unwise enough to boast of the fact. But he knew—and Anna knew—that their daughter smiled for her mama and papa.

Sometimes Luke looked back on his Parisian self and wondered if he could possibly be the same person.

He spent his time—as fathers were expected to do, it seemed, when there were enough aunts and great-aunts available to amuse their children—either at work or with his brother and brothers-in-law and uncle. And with Will, who was looking these days rather as if his cravat was always tied too tightly.

There was one meeting with Henrietta a couple of days before the christening. She met him on the bridge when he was returning from some business beyond the village. She was standing gazing

into the water, making a pretty and rather melancholy picture. He
felt obliged to dismount from his horse and speak to her. She seemed
to have been depressed for some time. He supposed the birth of Joy
would have reminded her of the stillbirth of her own son.

He felt sorry for Henrietta and a little guilty that he had returned to make her unhappiness more acute. He stood talking with
her for a few minutes and plucked a single daffodil for her from the
bank of the river and gave it to her before proceeding on his way.

He wondered if he would have continued loving her if all that
business with George had not happened. Perhaps he would have.

*Henrietta* stood looking after Luke. She crushed the bloom of
the daffodil in one hand, not looking down at it.

There was only one bright point in her life at the moment. And
even that was small comfort enough. She was fiercely glad that the
child was a girl. Anna had failed. And perhaps there would be no
next time. Perhaps before she could conceive again . . .

But Henrietta's highwayman had disappeared several months
ago, as suddenly and mysteriously as he had come. They had met and
made love as usual one week and had made a tryst for the following
week. But he had not come, though she had waited longer than an
hour. She had neither seen nor heard from him since.

And Anna was still here. And still mistress of Bowden.

Luke was still distant and polite.

But she refused to go to London for the Season with Doris and
her mother-in-law, though Luke had suggested it. Would he not love
it if she married someone else, she thought bitterly. No, she belonged
at Bowden. Bowden was hers. It always had been.

She was not going anywhere.

*Luke* went back to church for the christening of his daughter. He
walked up the winding stone path from the carriage with Anna, his
eyes on the baby in her arms, gloriously splendid in the family christening robes. Only when he was inside did he lift his head and look
about him.

He was surrounded by family, by his and Anna's. And he had his own family within reach of his arms—his wife and his daughter. He tried to remember his aversion to marriage when he lived in Paris and his reluctance in London to take a bride—until he set eyes on Anna and the decision had seemed to be taken out of his hands.

He was not sorry. He held the thought in his mind, weighed it, considered it while the service went on about him, largely unheard. But he could find no fault with it. He was not sorry.

Yet another thought nudged at his consciousness but was kept ruthlessly at bay. The family was not complete. There were two other members of the family outside. Outside in the churchyard. His father and George.

George. *How could you do it, George? I loved you. You were my hero.*

Joy stirred as water was poured on her head, and began to protest. Her father looked down at her and smiled, his heart aching with a love that was almost painful.

*He* went back to church the following week for the wedding of his sister-in-law to Will. It was easier the second time. This time the event did not concern his own family—only Anna's and Henrietta's.

The wedding breakfast was held at Bowden Abbey. It was a dazzling and gay and noisy affair that extended well into the afternoon. Agnes—quiet, timid little Agnes, whom Luke had scarcely noticed during the year she had spent at Bowden Abbey—glowed with happiness and gazed at her new husband with open adoration. Will, smart and clearly uncomfortable in satin full-skirted coat and embroidered waistcoat and buckled shoes and bag wig—all purchased with Luke's aid—was preening himself and looking fondly back at her.

Agnes and Will were to spend their wedding night and the night following at Wycherly before setting out on their wedding journey the day after. The new tenant of Wycherly, Colonel Henry Lomax, was to take up residence there within the week. But before the wedding day ended, there was to be a ball at Bowden Abbey. Guests from the neighborhood returned home to dress for it while family and friends at the house relaxed for a few hours before dressing.

Luke and Anna spent the time in the nursery, though Anna left early to go to the ballroom to make sure that everything had been prepared to her liking. It would be the first full-scale ball they had attended since they were in London, Luke thought. There had been a certain magic about the balls there. Yes, there really had. He wondered if any of it would be recaptured tonight.

*Luke* dressed for the ball in burgundy and gold, new clothes he had had made in Paris and sent from there. Although he had made concessions to English country fashions for daytime wear, he still did not trust English tailors and was frequently pained by their creations as worn by men of his acquaintance. His eyes strayed to an upper shelf when he had finished dressing and he pursed his lips. Should he? But his neighbors would be scandalized by the sight of patches and cosmetics on his face. And since when had he cared what his neighbors thought? His Parisian days seemed long in the past. However, as he turned to Anna's dressing room to lead her downstairs, he paused with his hand on the knob and smiled. Ah, yes. If his guests were shocked into a collective apoplexy, then that was their problem. At least Theo would be amused. And Anna too.

He turned back to search for his ivory fan—he had already dismissed his valet. He slipped it into a pocket.

Anna was dressed in a deep pink open mantua over wide hoops, with silver embroidered robings and stomacher. There was lace at her cuffs and edging her cap. Her hair was carefully curled and powdered. She smiled dazzlingly at him as she rose from her dressing stool and dismissed her maid.

"Madam." He took her hand in both of his and bowed over it. "Your beauty quite robs me of breath."

"And you, your grace," she said, her eyes sparkling at him, "have been shopping in Paris again. 'Tis not fair to the other gentlemen who will be at the ball. They will be dressed according to the fashions of the English countryside."

"But then, madam," he said, "I have never followed any fashions at all. I have my tailor's word for it that the design of this coat and waistcoat are three months in advance of what even Parisians are wearing."

"You have forgotten your fan, alas." She smiled.

"Not so, madam." He drew it out of his pocket and touched the end of it lightly to the tip of her nose. "Shall we join our guests?" He made her a courtly bow and offered his arm.

He was not falling in love, he told himself as they descended the stairs together, her arm along his sleeve. He was surprised that he had even thought of his reaction to her appearance in those terms. It was just that she was gorgeously dressed and looking her most beautiful and that he was on familiar territory with her. He wondered if she would flirt with him this evening as she had used to do in London and hoped that she would. And he wondered if they would take flirtation to its natural conclusion at the end of the evening.

He turned his head as they descended the stairs and looked at her with hooded eyes. Her lips were parted and her eyes were shining. She looked like a girl about to attend her first ball.

*It* was one of those magical nights that Anna would remember afterward with bitter nostalgia. There had been dances at Bowden and at the homes of some of their neighbors since she and Luke had come there, but nothing on the scale of this ball. The chandeliers were bright with myriad candles and the ballroom was laden with spring flowers from the gardens and other blooms from the hothouses. Their perfume made the ballroom smell like an indoor garden. And there was a full orchestra in the minstrel gallery.

Her whole family was there, and all of them happy. Agnes, the new Lady Severidge, seemed lit from the inside with excitement and happiness and nervousness. Even Emily was in the ballroom, seated beside Charlotte, whose husband pronounced her unable to dance because of the interesting state of her health. Emmy gazed about her with bright and wondering eyes, but eyes that nevertheless grew even brighter on the occasions when Ashley came to her for a few minutes at a time and talked to her, an indulgent, brotherly smile on his face.

But what made the evening magical for Anna was that Luke played with her again the game of flirtation they had always played in London. Although they danced the opening set together, their position as host and hostess of the ball forbade them to spend any more of the evening in each other's company. It might have been a disappointing fact but was not. Anna danced all evening with a variety of partners. So did her husband. And neither neglected to converse with their partners or to circulate among their guests between sets. And yet they contrived to look at each other almost constantly, Anna with bright smiles, Luke with deceptively lazy eyes.

And she shamelessly used her fan, fluttering it when she caught his gaze across the room, raising it to her nose when she had his full attention. And he used his, waving it indolently before his face as his eyes did shameful things to her body.

It was ridiculous, she told herself several times in the course of the evening. If they were observed—and Luke's appearance tonight, more gorgeous than he had yet appeared in the country, doubtless ensured that they were—they would be thought to be out of their wits. They had been married for almost a year. They had a two-month-old child in the nursery upstairs. And yet they were flirting with each other as if they had just met. It was ridiculous. And wonderful beyond imagining.

"Faith, child," Lady Sterne said to her at one point in the evening, linking her arm through Anna's, "whose wedding day is this, pray? I vow that anyone who was not sure would swear it was yours and Harndon's."

Anna flushed. So someone really had noticed. "Aunt Marjorie—" she began.

But her godmother squeezed her arm and interrupted her. "It does my heart good, child," she said. "I promoted the match. Theodore and I between us. But I have worried about it. You were set against marriage. Harndon was set against it. It does my heart good, I vow, to see the two of you so deep in love."

Oh, it was not quite that way, Anna thought wistfully. There was love on one side, and flirtation and perhaps a little affection on the other. But even that fact was not allowed to dim her enjoyment of the evening.

After supper, before the dancing resumed for another couple of hours, the bride and groom left for Wycherly, William's carriage streaming with ribbons that Ashley and a few of the other young men of the neighborhood had attached to every conceivable projection. Everyone spilled out of doors to give them a rousing farewell.

Anna hugged a rather tearful and clearly nervous Agnes and then a blushing and hardly less nervous William. He would not have been her choice for Agnes, she thought, but clearly it was a love match. Her second sister was safe and headed for happiness. Her vision blurred as Agnes was assisted into the carriage by her new husband, and she felt a small hand creep into her own—Emily's—at the same moment as a larger, warmer hand came to rest on her shoulder—Luke's.

Perhaps neither of them realized fully just what it meant to her to have her brother and sisters safely established in life. Perhaps both of them thought that her tears resulted from mere sentiment. She squeezed Emmy's hand and smiled at her husband.

And then the dancing resumed. Anna stole away to give Joy her night feed, but was able to dance the last two sets, one with Ashley and the other with Lord Quinn.

"Egad," Lord Quinn said, "I will never forget that night when I had three lovely ladies to escort and only two arms. And now two of those gels are wed and have deserted me."

"But not Aunt Marjorie, Uncle Theo," she said, smiling.

"Zounds, no," he said, chuckling. "You are in the right of it there, lass."

Anna had the very improper suspicion that her godmother and Luke's uncle enjoyed a relationship that was somewhat closer than mere friendship.

And then the ball was over, far too soon, it seemed, though it had extended well past the normal hour for such entertainments in the country. Luke and Anna saw all their outside guests on their way and bade good night to their houseguests and then returned to the ballroom to commend their servants on a job well done and to direct them to go to bed and leave the cleaning up until morning.

Everyone else had gone to bed long before Anna finally climbed the stairs, her arm on Luke's. There was a tension between them. Surely the night could not be at an end. She did not want it to be over. Not yet. She wondered if only she felt the tension.

But he paused outside her dressing room and bowed over her hand as he had done at the start of the evening.

"You are tired, Anna?" he asked.

Oh, yes, but not too tired. "A little," she said, smiling at him.

"I promised you privacy and freedom," he said, "for another two months."

"Yes." She scarcely heard her own whisper.

"Do you wish me to honor my promise?" he asked, his eyes looking very keenly into hers.

"No."

He raised her hand to his lips. "I may come to you in a short while?"

She nodded and he opened the door of the dressing room. Penny was waiting inside. Anna stepped in without another word or a backward glance. Drawing breath into her lungs took a conscious effort.

*Except* for her wedding night Anna had always waited naked for her husband. She wore her nightgown tonight and felt as nervous as a bride. She spared a brief thought for Agnes, but Agnes would be a wife by now. And she loved her William and he her. All would be well with them.

She stood at the window and turned to watch Luke when he tapped on her dressing room door and came inside. He was wearing a blue silk dressing gown. His hair had been brushed free of powder and had been left to fall free about his face and shoulders in long, dark waves. She was glad he did not follow the fashion to shave his head and wear a wig. She loved his hair.

"Anna." He took her hands and squeezed them. "You will be thinking me a devil of a nuisance keeping you up later than late." And yet his eyes wooed her.

"No," she said. She did not even try to hide the naked love and longing in her eyes.

He drew her hands down against his sides so that she had to take a step forward. She touched him from breasts to hips to thighs. She could feel that he was already aroused. He set his mouth, opened, over hers and parted her lips with his tongue. It had been such a long time. Ah, it had been so long.

"I have missed you," he said.

"And I you." The touch of his tongue had sent raw desire shooting downward into her breasts and into her womb.

"It was to be for duty and pleasure, this marriage of ours," he said. "There has been too much of duty and too little of pleasure lately, Anna."

"Yes." She longed for a third dimension to be added to their marriage. She longed for him to talk of love. But he wanted pleasure of her, and it was enough. She had feared that perhaps he would not look for it with her ever again.

"Will it give you pleasure to be kept awake and hard at work until dawn?" he asked her, his eyes gazing lazily into hers. "Or will the pleasure be mine alone?"

He was wooing her with words. By now he must know her answer beyond any doubt. But words could be as erotic as lips or hands or body. That downward stabbing of desire had reached her knees. "It will give me pleasure," she said. "I never did mean for you to go away entirely, Luke. I never meant that. My bed has felt empty."

He kissed her again, pushing his tongue inside her mouth for a few moments. "Perhaps, madam," he said, "we should lie down on it and discover if it feels more occupied tonight."

"Yes, your grace." She smiled at him.

It felt simply filled and wonderful. They both agreed to that after the first swift, lusty coupling. The bed really did not feel empty at all any longer, she admitted to him after the second skilled, agonizingly slow yet thoroughly satisfying lovemaking to which he subjected her. It was an infinitely more comfortable bed than his own, he told her after the third leisurely, almost languorous joining of bodies and sharing of pleasure—warmer and softer.

"I could be persuaded to spend all my nights here for the next fifty years or so," he said, his breath warm against her ear. "And some of my afternoons too."

She sighed sleepily against his throat. "How might you be persuaded?" she asked.

"By your promising to spend those nights and those afternoons here with me," he said.

"So it is not just the bed?" she said. "'Tis the woman in it too?"

He blew into her ear. "I believe 'tis entirely the woman, madam," he said. "You might have a straw pallet dragged in here and I would be none the wiser, provided the woman was the same."

She chuckled. It was the closest he had come to a declaration of love, and probably the closest he would ever come. But it was enough. They had loved the night away, giving and taking pleasure. She would be fortunate to snatch an hour of sleep before it was time to feed Joy again. But she would not exchange a few hours of deep sleep for what they had just shared.

She loved and she felt almost loved in return. She felt safe and warm and drowsy in her husband's arms. Perhaps part of him could not let go of the past, but she was giving some pleasure to his present. And perhaps she feared the future, but there was love and the illusion of security in the present.

It was enough. For now it was enough.

"Good night and good morning, my duchess," he murmured into her ear.

"I am asleep," she muttered.

"Ah," he said and bit her earlobe until she wriggled, protesting sleepily, out of reach of his teeth.

She had descended too far into sleep to hear his chuckle.

## 21

*C*OUNTRY living could sometimes be monotonous even when
neighbors made the effort to be sociable and to both host and
attend various entertainments. The main problem was that one
tended to see the same faces wherever one went.

The return of the Duke of Harndon with his new bride and her
sister had brightened the summer and autumn months at Bowden.
Then the christening of their daughter and the marriage of Lady
Agnes Marlowe to Lord Severidge added excitement to the spring,
bringing as they did a whole host of fashionable guests to Bowden.

And then, just when the neighborhood might have expected a
return to rather dull normality, the new tenant arrived at Wycherly.
Colonel Henry Lomax was a single gentleman—a point of interest
to the single ladies of the neighborhood and their parents. And he
was a retired army colonel and thus could be expected to bring with
him many stories of adventure and gallantry. After he had been in
residence at Wycherly for a day, Colonel Lomax began receiving a
steady stream of callers and a warm welcome.

Luke and Anna were among the first to call, together with the
dowager and Henrietta. It seemed strange, Henrietta remarked as
they descended from the carriage and she looked up at the house, to
be coming to Wycherly as a visitor when it had been her childhood
home.

One group of neighbors was already in the drawing room with
the colonel. But he rose to greet the new arrivals with a warm charm.
He was a tall, slim man in his late forties, still handsome. He

was fashionably dressed in brown and cream, his bag wig neatly powdered.

"I am honored indeed," he said when the introductions had been made and he had favored his new visitors with a deep bow. "But, Harndon, 'tis unfair, I vow. Most dukes of my acquaintance are allowed only one duchess apiece. Yet you have three, all equally lovely." His smile crinkled his eyes attractively at the corners and revealed white and even teeth. Everyone gathered in the room laughed at the witticism.

The dowager duchess was not amused by his gallantry and showed her displeasure by inclining her head stiffly and regally to the colonel, taking a seat next to Mrs. Persall, and engaging her in conversation.

Henrietta smiled and extended a hand, which the colonel took and fetched to his lips. "La, sir," she said, "I am but a widow, a dowager though not in name. My late husband was Luke's elder brother."

"A dowager?" he said, retaining her hand in his and seating her beside him on a sofa after Luke and Anna had sat down. "Your youth and beauty would make a mockery of the title, madam." He released her hand.

Henrietta continued to smile at him.

He turned his attention to Anna. "I have been told, your grace," he said, "that you have recently presented your husband with a child. A son, 'tis to be hoped?"

"A daughter," she said.

"Ah." He smiled kindly. "I am sure she is a treasure to you, madam, and to his grace." He inclined his head to Luke. "Your husband already has his heir in Lord Ashley Kendrick, I believe?"

"Yes," she said.

Conversation became general and the tea tray was brought in. The party from Bowden took their leave after half an hour had passed and more callers had arrived.

"I can see," Colonel Lomax said with a laugh when he stood out on the terrace with them, "that I have been fortunate enough to take up residence in a hospitable part of the world. It means a great deal to me to have amiable neighbors." He handed Henrietta into the carriage after Luke had done the like for his mother. "I shall look forward to furthering my acquaintance with all of you who have been kind enough to call."

He smiled appreciatively at Henrietta and turned to Anna, hand extended. But she already had her hand in Luke's and ascended the steps and seated herself with his assistance.

"I shall also look forward to meeting your young daughter, your grace," he said. "I am inordinately fond of children."

Anna inclined her head to him but said nothing as Luke seated himself beside her and their coachman closed the door and climbed up to his seat again. Colonel Lomax smiled and raised a hand in farewell as the carriage started on its way back to Bowden Abbey.

"Oh, la." Henrietta laughed. "I cannot say I am sorry William has taken Agnes on a wedding journey. I vow the colonel is a most charming man. Would you not agree, Mother?"

"A little too free in his manners, perhaps," the dowager said. "But he made an effort to make himself agreeable. When he returns our call, Lucas, you must invite him to dinner."

"You may be sure I shall do all that is correct, madam," Luke said.

Anna smiled brightly. "What a beautiful day it is," she said. "And what a shame that we have had to spend a part of it inside a carriage and paying a call."

"Duty is something that must be done regardless of the weather or one's personal inclinations, Anna," her mother-in-law reminded her.

Anna smiled warmly at her. "Yes I know, Mother," she said. "That is why I am here. I wonder where Agnes and William are at this very moment. They were going to Paris first? You gave them introductions there, Luke, did you not? But 'twould not surprise me at all if neither of them calls on anyone you recommended to them."

"Madam?" He raised his eyebrows.

"They will take fright, imagining that any friend of yours must be alarmingly grand," she said. "And I daresay they would be right."

She laughed at his look of surprise and chattered brightly for the rest of the journey home.

*At* first Henrietta had not been sure. It had seemed too incredible. But there had been no mistaking those intent eyes and that perfect smile and the distinctive smell of his cologne. And he had squeezed her hand more tightly than a stranger would have done.

She brimmed over with excitement. He was a wonderfully handsome man. More handsome than she had imagined. And charming. All the other ladies there had devoured him with their eyes. While he had devoured her with his.

And Anna had known him. Oh, yes, indeed she had, clever as she had been at disguising the fact. She had known him yet not acknowledged the acquaintance. There had been fear in Anna, well contained but quite visible to Henrietta's eyes.

It was all a glorious mystery, which was to be uncovered at last.

He had come back. And somehow—she had no idea how—he was going to destroy Anna. And perhaps Luke too.

Suddenly the world seemed a brighter place again.

*Normally* Anna would have made haste to the nursery after returning from an afternoon call. Joy was usually awake at this time of day even though she was not due for a feed for more than an hour yet. She had started to smile, though she was usually more willing to oblige for her father than for her mother. And she was a good child, placid and cheerful.

But today after excusing herself and hurrying upstairs, Anna did not turn in the direction of the nursery, but rushed instead into her sitting room and closed the door firmly behind her. She leaned back against it and wished there were a lock on the door, but it did not matter. Luke never came there now, and it was unlikely that anyone else would call on her there for a while. They would all assume she was with Joy.

Her hands were cold and clammy. She held them out in front of her and watched them tremble out of control. She was so breathless that for a few moments she was afraid she would not be able to suck in enough air to keep herself conscious. There was a coldness and a buzzing in her head. Her knees felt as if they would buckle under her at any moment. She sat down heavily in the nearest chair.

She might have expected it. Why had she not expected it and prepared herself? She had thought of it, of course, when William had first mentioned at Christmas that he was going to lease his house to a tenant, but she had been instantly reassured by his mention of the man's name. She had gone to Wycherly today quite unsuspecting. She had entered the drawing room with a smile on her face.

Oh, dear God, dear God, dear God. She spread icy, shaking hands over her face and lowered it into her full, hooped skirt. Dear God. But there was nothing particularly dear about God to her these days. He had not helped her at all in the last three years unless it was in the gift of Luke and Joy. It was a cruel gift—one that had brought illusions of happiness and security. One that was about to be snatched away from her.

He had behaved exactly as he had always behaved at Elm Court and in its neighborhood. He had behaved with warmth and charm and had made everyone like him and feel an eagerness to have him return their calls, to have him become part of their social life. He had looked exactly as he had always looked there—handsome, fashionable, virile, attractive. Henrietta had fallen under his spell. Even Luke's mother had thawed noticeably after that first and only mistake he had made in trying to flatter her.

Anna sat up again and set her head against the cushions at the back of the chair. It was all going to start again in earnest, then. It was going to be just as it had been at Elm Court. There would be the visits and the demands for money in payment of her father's debts, as there had been by letter in the months following her marriage. And perhaps demands that she help him in other ways—help him to cheat and steal from her neighbors and friends. No. She gripped the arms of the chair tightly. Not that. Never that again. There at least she would draw the line.

What was she to do? Her instinct at this very moment was to go to Luke and tell him everything, every sordid detail. She tried to imagine the overpowering relief she would feel at being able to unburden herself to her husband. To the man she had grown to love more than life. She tried to imagine it, but all she could see behind her closed eyelids was Luke's face, first disbelieving, then disdainful, and then cold and thin-lipped. And she pictured him taking their daughter from her and hiring a wet nurse. And having her carried off to a magistrate elsewhere, far away, so that the scandal would be somewhat lessened.

Her breathing quickened again. She would never see them again. Ever.

The imaginings were ridiculous, she thought. Luke would never react that way. She was his wife. Lately he had made her his friend. He felt . . . surely he must feel some affection for her. Surely he would listen with sympathy. Surely he would help her.

But she thought of how he had reacted on a previous occasion to someone who had offended and hurt him. His brother George. Not only had he never forgiven his brother in this life, he would not even go near his grave.

Oh, no, she could not risk it. She could not risk losing everything. The stakes were so much higher now. There was Joy now as well as Luke.

But she was going to lose everything anyway. She felt that the final denouement was somehow near. At some time, perhaps soon, perhaps far in the future, he was going to take her away—away from Luke, away from Joy, perhaps away from England. Was she going to go meekly? Or was she going to fight? But how would she fight? Tell Luke? If she was going to tell him when the time came, why not tell him now?

Why had she not told him that day he came to propose marriage to her? Or better still, why had she not just refused his proposal? By now she would be with Sir Lovatt wherever it was he planned to take her. She would know what he had in store for her—as his mistress, as his wife, as neither. But at least she would know. And she would not have allowed herself the treacherous luxury of happiness. And hope.

Anna's mind teemed with conflicting thoughts and emotions and decisions. Her body fought against the urge to send her hurtling into her dressing room to vomit.

*Luke* was in the library, thumbing through a book he had drawn from a shelf but not really seeing it. He, too, would normally have gone up to the nursery at this time of day. The lure of playing with his daughter when she was awake was usually irresistible. Under other circumstances he would probably have suggested that he and Anna take her outside for a walk. It really was a lovely day.

But he had come to the library instead and shut the door firmly behind him.

Colonel Henry Lomax was a gentleman of some refinement. He had presence and conversation and a fashionable appearance for an Englishman. He had displayed an easy amiability toward his male guests and charm toward the ladies. He would doubtless be much in demand through the summer until the novelty of his presence in the neighborhood had worn off, and perhaps even beyond that. Henrietta had been noticeably drawn by his charm. That at least was a promising sign.

Luke frowned and snapped the book shut. But what the devil had the man been doing standing half hidden behind a tree in the middle of the square outside the church on the day of his wedding to Anna? Had it been pure coincidence that he had been there and curiosity that had held him there to watch? But if that were so, would he not have commented this afternoon on the strange fact that he had seen the duke and duchess on the day of their wedding? There had not been a flicker. of recognition in his eyes when they had entered his drawing room.

Luke himself had not mentioned it either, of course. Perhaps the colonel was too embarrassed to admit the fact that he had stood and watched a wedding party, like an uninvited guest, just like the people of the lower orders.

Luke replaced the book on its shelf and absently drew out another. That was not the only peculiar fact, though. There was also his strange conviction—but surely he must be wrong—that Colonel Lomax was the man who had walked with Anna at Ranelagh. He had been cloaked and hooded and masked. It had been impossible to gain anything more than an impression of height and slimness. There were probably a few thousand tall, slim men in England. It was foolish to imagine that he had recognized the same man in the new neighbor he had called on this afternoon. Lomax and Anna had shown no sign of having recognized each other.

But Luke could remember on both occasions—outside the church and at Ranelagh—that fleeting feeling he had had that he should know the man, though he had made no connection at the time between the two incidents. He had had the same feeling this afternoon. Lomax, Lomax . . . the name meant nothing to him, and physical recognition, if that was what it was, had eluded him.

It was all very foolish, he thought now, pushing the second book back into place impatiently and turning resolutely away from the bookshelf. If Lomax was the man outside the church—and Luke was almost sure he was—then his appearance there had been coincidental and of no significance whatsoever. And Lomax was surely not the man from Ranelagh—he could not be. If Luke had seen him before— possibly in France—then it had been so fleetingly that the memory of the occasion would not come back to him. It was quite unimportant.

He sat down behind the desk, rested his elbows on its top, and steepled his fingers, tapping them absently together. He realized that he had not taken the simple step of asking Anna if she had any previous acquaintance with Lomax. And he realized too, with some unease, that he would not ask her.

Was he afraid of the answer? Or the lack of an answer?

He frowned across the room. Why the devil had he not asserted his full authority from the start? Why had he permitted her to retain a secret that had deprived him of one of his marital rights? Why had he not forced her to tell it right then at the start?

His frown deepened. And what the devil connection was he imagining between her secret and the arrival of a perfectly amiable neighbor whom he had spotted once before, quite by accident, on his wedding day and whom Anna had never seen in her life before this afternoon?

*With* the coming of spring there were changes at Bowden Abbey. Luke had found a new steward, Howard Fox, who came well recommended. He was to begin work within a few weeks, as soon as he had served out his notice at his previous employment. Ashley was to join the East India Company and to leave for India as soon as he was called. He was enthusiastic about his future, and Luke was happy for him. There he would be able to make his own way in life, as Luke had done. But things would be different for Ashley. He would know that he had the love and support of his family behind him—though his mother thought he was disgracing his name by associating himself with a business enterprise. Ashley would know that he could come back at any time.

And with the coming of spring Doris was returning to London for the entertainments of the Season. Indeed, she would have been on her way there sooner if the christening and the wedding had not kept her and her mother at home. Luke had not done quite as well at making his peace with Doris as he had with Ashley, though they had at least been able to treat each other civilly for a few months.

He wished for her happiness. He hoped she would have better experiences this year to obliterate the bitter memories of the year before. Nevertheless, he would probably have been content to let her go without any private or personal word had Anna allowed him to get away with it. But she would not.

"Doris will be leaving the day after tomorrow," she told him two nights after they had made their visit to their new neighbor.

He grunted a reply. He was only half a remove from sleep, having just finished making love to her.

"Are you going to have a word with her?" she asked.

He resigned himself to staying awake for a few minutes longer. "A fatherly admonition to behave herself and not repeat last year's indiscretion?" he said. "Hardly, Anna."

"I would hope not," she said fervently. "Have you ever told her that you love her?"

"Not since I was twenty," he said. "I believe she has passed the age of craving an outpouring of love from a mere brother, Anna."

"Oh, there you are wrong," she said. "And I know you love her, Luke. There is no point in reminding me that you know nothing of love as I am sure you are about to do. She needs to hear that you trust her, that you desire her happiness, that you love her. 'Tis what she has waited for all year."

He considered her words. Did it matter to Doris? She seemed to have done very well without him for the past year. Except at the beginning, she had not appeared either sullen or moping as he had fully expected. But he knew that Anna was right. He had felt the rift himself. And fleetingly—just fleetingly—he felt the old resentment at the responsibilities and obligations that he had been burdened with though he had not asked for any of them.

"Yes, madam," he said with an exaggerated sigh. "May I go to sleep now?"

"Yes, you may," she said, snuggling closer, but he thought he detected disappointment in her voice. Just as he had felt the suggestion of desperation and clinging in her arms and her body while they had made love. The same sort of desperation, but more controlled, as he had experienced on two previous occasions. But he did not want to consider the reasons for it just now.

"I shall have a word with her tomorrow," he said. "And I shall have a word with Theo next time I see him about talking me into marrying you."

This was better, he thought when he heard her chuckle against his shoulder. And yet he was learning something about himself. He had not suspected himself capable of cowardice before. But he had teased her instead of confronting the issue that was in the forefront of his mind.

And he no longer felt sleepy at all.

Damnation.

• • •

*Doris* looked at him in some surprise the following morning when he strolled into the breakfast parlor and asked to have a word with her when she had finished eating. But he did not make the mistake he had made on a previous occasion. When she came into his office a short time later, looking rather wary and defiant, he did not remain behind the barrier of his desk.

"'Tis a little cloudy outside this morning," he said, "but not cold. Shall we stroll in the garden?"

She looked even more suspicious than she had before.

"I know what you are going to say," she said when they were in the formal gardens and he had tucked her arm through his. "I am not going to try to write to him or see him, Luke. I told you I hated him and I meant it. And I am a year older than I was then and a year wiser. I do not need you to act the part of stern father."

"How about concerned and affectionate brother, then?" he asked.

"Affectionate?" She looked at him and laughed.

"Do you remember what you were going to ask the king one day?" he asked her.

She frowned. "Ask the king?"

"You were going to ask him to allow you to marry me," he said, "because you loved me more than anyone. More than Papa and George and a little more than Ashley. Do you remember?"

She looked incredulous for a moment and then burst into genuine laughter. "No! Did I really?" she said.

"You were five years old," he said. "But as soon as you were grown up you were going to ask him. I let you down, Dor."

"By not taking me to the king?" Her look had become wistful.

"By acting without either wisdom or compassion last year," he said, "in that affair with Frawley."

"That." She flushed. "You did quite right, Luke. I would have been dreadfully unhappy with him. I believe I hinted of my plans to Anna at Ranelagh in the hope that someone would stop me. Though I did not admit that to myself at the time."

"I should have hugged you tightly and refused to let you go until you had promised not to give my favorite sister's affections to a damned fortune hunter," he said.

"I am your *only* sister, Luke," she said.

"Precisely," he said, "and a sister I have been without for far too long. Don't ever do it again, Dor, or I will kill the man, whoever he is. You may marry whom you will with my blessing—within reason, of course—provided he loves you more than five thousand pounds or fifty thousand or five hundred thousand."

"Within reason?" She had stopped walking and was smiling at him.

"Words I should not have added," he said ruefully. "Pardon me. The weight of responsibility is sometimes heavy on my shoulders. I worry about you. But I do trust you, Dor, now that you are twenty years old and have a wiser head on your shoulders than you had last year. I trust you to make a choice that will be for your lasting happiness."

"As you did when you chose Anna?" she asked.

The question caught him off guard. "As I did," he said and realized as he said it that it was at least partly true. But lasting happiness? His mind touched on that desperation he had felt in his wife last night.

Doris put her arms about his neck then and kissed him, first on one cheek, and then on the other, and finally and smackingly on the lips. There were tears in her eyes when she drew back her head.

"How sorry I am now," she said, "that I made you speak first. All year I have been wanting to tell you how sorry I was for my childish behavior and how glad I was that you had freed me from what would have been an intolerable situation."

He smiled at her.

"You do that too rarely," she said. "When you smile, you look just like the brother I remember. Oh, la, I believe now that you really are my brother Luke."

He chuckled, and she linked her arm through his again and drew him along the path through the gardens, away from the house.

"I am very glad," she said, "that you did not marry Henrietta, Luke. I wish George had not married her either."

He stiffened. "George had no choice," he said. "If he was unhappy, 'twas no more than he deserved."

"Oh, fie," she said, "you do not believe that, do you, Luke?"

"This is not a subject I choose to discuss," he said.

"Oh, nonsense," she said. "You do not believe that George ravished Henrietta, do you?"

He had no wish to talk of the matter with anyone, least of all his sister. Somewhere, long filmed over but still very capable of being ripped open again, was a deep and painful wound. There had been his loss of Henrietta in the past. There had been another loss too, perhaps worse. There had been the loss of George, his beloved brother.

"There was a baby, Dor," he said stiffly. "And George married Henrietta. You do not suggest it was mine, do you?"

She tutted. "Children see a great deal they are not supposed to see," she said. "I saw a great deal, Luke. She had an eye to George as soon as he came home from his Grand Tour, looking very handsome and very dashing. And of course he had a marquess's title and was Papa's heir. She flirted with him whenever your back was turned. She wanted to be a marchioness and a duchess one day."

"Doris!" His voice was like cold steel. "You speak of your sister-in-law, I would have you remember. You will be silent now or change the subject."

But she would not be cowed. "And I speak, too, of my brother," she hissed at him, "and of yours. You cannot have believed such evil of him all these years, Luke. You cannot. There was seduction between George and Henrietta, 'tis true. But 'twas Henrietta who was the seducer, I swear. George merely gave in to a moment's weakness and suffered for it the rest of his life. Poor George!"

Luke felt himself turn cold. "We will speak no more of this," he said. "I would not quarrel with you when we are newly reconciled."

"Luke." She looked at him with tear-filled eyes. "'Twas because of Henrietta you stayed away for two years after George died, was it not? You still loved her? You still love her? Oh, poor Anna."

"No, I do not love Henrietta. But I said we will speak no more," he said quietly, his eyes flashing dangerously, and at last she obeyed.

He did not know if what she said was true. He did not know if he wanted it to be true. But it did surprise him that he had not thought of it for himself before now. He had grown a hard shell of cynicism during his ten years in France. And yet somehow Henrietta had been held outside that shell, the one inviolable piece of perfection in his past. The one object of love in which he had continued to believe even though it had not survived into the present.

And yet believing in her, he had had to bear the deep wound of his brother's cruel betrayal. And it was the need to take away the pain of that wound that had forced him to kill all love in himself.

"Shall I tell you what kind of husband I shall look for in London this spring?" Doris asked after a few minutes of silence.

"Yes, do," he said, covering her hand with his.

## 22

COLONEL Henry Lomax paid a courtesy call at Bowden Abbey the same afternoon. He shook hands warmly with Ashley, was charmed to make the acquaintance of Lady Doris and disappointed to learn that she was to leave for London the following day with her mother. Disappointed for himself, that was, and dared he speak for all his new acquaintances in the neighborhood? For the gentlemen in town, of course, the arrival of two such lovely ladies would be a fortunate event indeed.

Doris, blushing and laughing, was won over by his gallantry.

Henrietta was clearly interested in this handsome and attractive new arrival to the neighborhood. "La, sir," she said when they were all seated in the drawing room, taking tea, "'tis hard to believe that there will be a stranger in my girlhood home for the next year."

"A stranger, madam?" he said. "I trust that very soon that word will be changed to neighbor and friend."

Henrietta blushed. "'Tis just that I have so many fond memories associated with that house," she said.

"Then you must be no stranger to it during the coming year, madam," he said. "You must come as often as you wish—with her grace, your sister-in-law, for company, I would hope."

"Oh, la," Henrietta said, laughing, "you did not believe I would dream of coming alone, sir? But your offer is most generous. If Anna cannot accompany me, I shall bring a maid."

"'Twould be my pleasure, madam," he said, "to see you make free with your former home."

Luke watched with some interest. In many ways it would be a relief to find that Henrietta was taking his advice and putting the past behind her. A new man in her life might be just the thing for her. And Lomax, though a good deal older than she, was quite personable enough to be attractive to women, he supposed. The man was all charm and amiability. Luke was not quite sure why he could not like him, unless it was those foolish thoughts he had had after that first call.

"You served for a long time with the army, Colonel?" he asked. "With which regiment?"

Lomax answered all his questions. He gave a good deal of detailed information on military matters, but at the same time engaged the interest of the ladies by including interesting little anecdotes, especially as related to the years he had spent in America. He was a skilled and a courteous conversationalist, Luke was forced to conclude.

"You have lived in France?" Luke asked him.

"Alas, no." The colonel laughed. "Unlike you, your grace, I lack the polish in both appearance and manners that only a long sojourn in Paris can give a man. My visits to France have all been of lamentably short duration."

A fact that did not preclude the possibility of Luke's having seen him there at some time. But memory of the specific occasion still eluded him.

"You have been back from America for some time," Luke said. "You were in London last spring? My wife and I were there too as well as my mother and brother and sister. 'Tis surprising we did not meet you then."

"Not as surprising as it might seem," Lomax said with a shrug and a smile. "After such a long absence, your grace, it took me a while to become reacquainted with old friends."

Luke had half lowered his eyelids over his eyes, a habit he had acquired in France during his months of serious gambling. Watch keenly while appearing to be lazily daydreaming, an older and experienced gambler, who had taken an interest in him, had once told him. But Lomax met his eyes and hesitated a moment.

"You married in London last spring, your grace?" he asked, frowning. "I have the strangest notion that 'twas your wedding I observed from outside the church. In an aimless walk about town I came upon a group of people waiting outside a church and at the same moment the doors opened and I realized that a wedding party was about to emerge. Curiosity caused me to pause and to gaze in what I must confess was an unmannerly way. And I do believe"—he paused to glance at Anna and smile—"yes, I do believe you were the bride and groom. What a curious coincidence!"

"Yes, indeed," Luke said, raising his eyebrows in feigned surprise. So there was his explanation, perfectly reasonable, the sort of explanation he had imagined for himself a few days ago. It had been coincidence, and Lomax had not immediately recognized them here almost a year later. Why should he? They had been total strangers to him. Or else the man was being very clever. He had seen something in Luke's eyes and had adjusted his behavior according to what he had read there.

Or perhaps it was Luke who was being too clever. Was there anything whatsoever of which to be suspicious?

Colonel Lomax set down his empty cup and saucer on the table beside him and showed signs that he was about to take his leave.

"The formal gardens of Bowden Abbey are famous, sir," Henrietta said, "as perhaps you have heard. And there is color in them again now that spring is well advanced."

"Indeed, madam," the colonel said, getting to his feet and making her a bow. "I caught tantalizing glimpses of their beauty from the window of my carriage as I approached the house."

Henrietta smiled warmly. "'Tis a beautiful day, sir," she said. "Far too lovely to be spent entirely indoors or inside a carriage."

"You are quite right." He smiled at her. "At least a part of the day should be enjoyed in a stroll amid beautiful surroundings with a beautiful companion." He turned and bowed to Anna. "Would you do me the honor of showing me the gardens before I leave, your grace?"

Luke only half noticed Henrietta's quickly hidden look of chagrin. His full attention focused on his wife, who rose gracefully to her feet, smiled, and informed Colonel Lomax that she would be delighted.

Was there any sign in her face, Luke asked himself, watching her keenly, that this whole situation was not exactly as it appeared on the surface? Any sign that she had a previous acquaintance with this man? Any sign that she was either pleased or displeased by his request? There was nothing that he could detect unless there was a certain blandness in her smile, a certain lack of her usual warmth. But he might well be imagining that, twisting the facts to suit his groundless suspicions.

But Lomax? Had he not almost openly snubbed Henrietta? A man would have to be as insensitive as a brick not to have seen that she had set her cap at him and had been hinting that he take a walk alone with her. And it seemed to Luke that there had been something almost deliberate, almost theatrical in the snub, as though Lomax had deeply relished administering it.

And yet again, it could be imagination. Could it not be conceived of as a courtesy to turn to the mistress of the house to show one the gardens or a part of the house?

During his years in France, Luke had learned to follow his intuition. More than once it had enabled him to avoid a nasty situation. He could never remember an intuition that was as strong as this one, that nagged at him so persistently. He could ask Anna. That would be the simplest course. But Anna, he knew, would look blankly at him and deny everything. There was another way, perhaps, one that would at least give him a little more information about the handsome and charming Lomax.

After the colonel had stepped outside, Anna on his arm, Luke watched them for a while from the window of his study. They were strolling and talking, just as one might expect a guest and his hostess to be doing. Lomax was dressed in a full-skirted blue coat with gray knee breeches, white stockings and buckled shoes. His bag wig was carefully powdered. He carried his tricorne hat correctly beneath his arm. It was impossible to say for certain that it was the same man who had walked with Anna at Ranelagh, cloaked in black from head to toe.

Except for one thing. There was a way he had of leaning slightly sideways, bent solicitously over his companion, listening to what she said. It was an elusive something, not anything Luke could have described with any conviction in words. But it was something that turned him cold.

It was the same man. He would swear an oath on it.

He sat down at his desk, drew paper toward him, and tested the nib of a quill pen before dipping it into the inkwell and beginning to write. Theo, he did not doubt, would get him the information he needed. He wanted to know everything there was to know about Colonel Henry Lomax, starting with his military record.

*It* does my heart good to see you again, my Anna," he said. "It has been far too long. Motherhood must agree with you, as I knew it would when I allowed you to become a mother. You are more lovely than ever."

For perhaps the first time anger was stronger in Anna than fear. "I am not your Anna," she said curtly. "And you have no business coming here under an assumed name and duping innocent people."

"You have courage and spirit," he said. "I have always admired that in you, Anna."

"What is the sum total of my father's remaining debts?" she asked, knowing even as she spoke that it was quite hopeless. "What does my family still owe you? Give me the sum, sir, and I shall have my husband pay it. And there will be an end of the matter. You may return to your life and I may resume mine."

"But you are my life, Anna," he said, chilling the fire of her anger. "Does he love you that well? He appears to be a cold and a proud man, and has a reputation as such. But I can understand that you have been seduced by a handsome appearance. Would he enjoy knowing that he has a thief and a murderer for a duchess?"

"You know I am neither," she said.

"I may believe in you," he said, "because you are my life, Anna.

But alack, there are those more objective and thus more reliable than I who can swear to your guilt."

She clutched her anger to her like a cloak. "I can perfectly understand what has happened," she said. "I would have to be an imbecile not to realize. From the first you marked me as your victim and set your trap. And like a foolish innocent I walked right into it. I understand that. The only thing I do not understand is why. Why are you doing this to me? 'Tis not the money. What, then?"

"Ah, Anna," he said softly, leaning his head closer to hers, "'tis that I love you."

"Love!" Fury exploded in her, but in time she remembered where she was, in the formal gardens at Bowden, in full sight of anyone who cared to watch from the house. "I would have married you after Mama died and you were so kind and understanding. I would have loved you. Did you realize that?"

"There could never have been marriage between you and me, Anna," he said. "'Tis not that kind of love between us."

"There is no love between us," she said. "Only a sick kind of obsession on your part. You would not have me as wife or mistress and yet you marked me so that no other man would have me—or so you thought. I hate you. If there were a stronger word to express what I feel for you, I would use it."

"'Tis because you do not understand," he said. "You will, my Anna. In time, a little while yet, you will understand all and you will see the rightness of spending the rest of your life with me. You will be more happy than you can possibly dream."

"I am happy now," she said. "I have a husband and child and a home and family and friends."

"Family," he said softly, a note of wistfulness in his voice. "You have a daughter. I was glad to learn 'twas a girl, Anna. 'Tis better so. I would like to see her some time soon."

Her blood ran cold. "No," she said.

"The gardens are as lovely as your sister-in-law said they were," he said, turning back and looking at the house. "The perfect setting for such an old and splendid house. There is beauty of design in

America, Anna, but not the feeling of history and antiquity one senses in old British houses. Shall we stroll back? I would not outstay my welcome."

"How did you get inside the house?" she asked him suddenly, chilled by memories of terror that she had suppressed for several months. "Or even into the park? How did you get inside the houses of my neighbors when I was there without anyone seeing you?"

"Anna," he said softly, "I am the air you breathe."

"Was it a servant? You bribed a servant?" She had considered the possibility before, but servants did not hear her private conversations or attend entertainments in other houses.

"I am as close as your heart, my Anna," he said. "And you will be as close as mine when you understand all."

His carriage had been brought up to the door. He entered it when they reached the terrace after bowing over her hand. Anna did not stay to watch him on his way. She hurried inside and upstairs to the nursery, where Joy was mercifully alone with her nurse. Anna picked her up, sent the nurse for tea belowstairs, and set about coaxing smiles from her daughter.

There had to be a way out, she thought. There had to be. She could not be his abject slave for the rest of her life. There had been no demands today. But there would be. From now on she would have to live in constant fear of his visits and his demands. But she was reaching the end of her tether. She would not tolerate this for much longer.

Even if she must kill him.

The thought terrified and fascinated her.

She turned her head sharply to look over her shoulder at the empty room.

*I am the air you breathe. I am as close as your heart.*

*Emily* never went downstairs for tea although she was now fifteen years old and very nearly grown up. To her family, she knew, she would never be quite an adult. She would always be different, a little strange. They loved her, Emily knew, as did Luke and Ashley and Doris, but she would always be something of a child to them.

And so at teatime she was usually outside wandering or in the gallery if the weather was bad, looking at the portraits, or in the conservatory smelling the plants and fingering the varying textures of their leaves and petals.

Today she had walked among the trees on the opposite side of the house from those that led to the river and the falls. She liked the walk on this side too. The trees led through to meadows that were always prettily carpeted with wildflowers. But she was coming back early. Ashley would be returning to his office after tea. He would be leaving soon for India and was trying to get the books in order and ready for the man who was to be Luke's steward. There was so little time left with Ashley. Emily did not care to think how little. But she would spend every possible moment of the remaining time with him.

Anna was walking in the formal gardens with a gentleman. Emily was some distance away, but even so she shrank back instinctively into the protective covering of the trees. It was impossible to see clearly from this distance who it was that walked with Anna. But Emily knew. There was something quite distinctive about his form and about his bearing. It was him. He had found Anna again. But of course he had found her. There had been those letters. But now he had come in person.

Emily felt physically sick as she hugged a tree trunk and gazed at the distant figures of her sister and Sir Lovatt Blaydon. They were moving back in the direction of the house, and a carriage was being drawn onto the terrace.

There was evil in the man, Emily knew, and evil in his presence here. His appearance would bring misery and perhaps even disaster for Anna. Emily did not know quite why she was so certain of it, but she was.

As soon as the carriage had left, taking Sir Lovatt with it, and Anna had disappeared into the house, Emily emerged from her hiding place and raced across the grass. Ashley. Oh, pray God he was back in his office. Pray God. She was sobbing with panic by the time she got there.

Ashley looked up, startled, from his books and then jumped to his feet and came around the desk to clasp her by the shoulders. "Little fawn?" he said, frowning. "What is it?"

She gazed earnestly into his face and pointed off in the direction of the formal gardens.

"Something happened outside?" he asked. "Something to frighten you?"

She nodded and pointed again.

He ran his hands down her arms and held her hands while his eyes swept down her body. "You were not hurt?"

She stared at him mutely and he searched her eyes with his own.

"Zounds," he said, and she read frustration in his expression, "there should be a language. Some way you can talk more eloquently than just with your eyes. You should be able to read and write, little fawn. There must be a way of teaching you. You understand spoken language. If I were staying, I vow I would teach you myself."

She bit her upper lip. No, there was no way of telling him. And even if she could do so, what then? What could he do? Tell Luke? But what could Luke do? Sir Lovatt Blaydon made Anna very unhappy and he had some hold over her, but Emily did not understand what. Even if she could explain, there was very little to explain.

Ashley cupped her face with gentle hands and touched his thumbs to her cheeks, blotting two tears that had spilled over. "Don't cry," he said. "I will not let anyone hurt you, little fawn. You are safe now. Come here."

He drew her against him and wrapped strong arms about her. He forgot, of course, that she could not hear him unless she could see his lips. She could tell by the vibrations of his chest that he was still talking. But she knew, even without seeing his lips, that he was murmuring soothing words to her.

How was she going to live without him? She would surely die. She would want to die.

He was holding her at arms' length again. "Better?" he asked.

She nodded. Her heart was breaking for Anna and for herself, but she smiled at him. At her dear, beloved Ashley.

"I need you to mend my pen for me," he said, grinning at her rather sheepishly. "I have been scratching too hard with it again and ruining the nib. No one mends a pen better than my little fawn. Will you?"

Emily nodded and continued to smile.

*Colonel* Henry Lomax was smiling as his butler closed the door of the drawing room behind Henrietta.

"Ah, duchess," he said. "How pleased and gratified I am that you have accepted so soon my open invitation to visit Wycherly. Only an hour after my own return here."

She smiled coquettishly and crossed the room toward him. "'Tis a face that does not need to be masked, sir," she said, "and a form that does not need to be hidden beneath a cloak."

"Now whatever can you mean?" he asked her as her hands splayed themselves lightly against his chest.

Henrietta pouted. "'Twas unkind of you," she said, "to ask Anna to walk with you in the garden when I had all but offered. Was it that you wished to protect my reputation? But perhaps I do not please you any longer."

Colonel Lomax chuckled softly. "You wish to please me, do you, madam?" he said, grasping the skirt of her riding habit at both sides and lifting it upward. "A gentleman must bow to a lady's wishes." He backed her toward the wide sofa behind her.

"Here, sir?" she half shrieked. "But there is no privacy."

"Any servant who enters a room in my house unannounced is instantly dismissed," he said. "Come, please me, Henrietta."

He turned her so that he could sit on the sofa, and held up her skirts with one hand while he adjusted his own clothing. He drew her down astride him, grasped her hips, and pulled her down hard onto him. She gasped.

"Come whore for me, then," he said, continuing to smile at her. "You do it with such panting enthusiasm, duchess."

"Sir?" Henrietta looked indignant and tried to get up onto her knees away from his penetration.

But he laughed and held her hips with firm hands. "Enjoy it,

Henrietta," he said. "Everything you want will be yours soon. I will be taking Anna away before too much time has elapsed. But it may take a little while for Harndon to recover from her loss and to turn to you for comfort. Enjoy it while you may."

He held her firmly down on him and took her quickly and ungently. Henrietta gasped and whimpered. And lowered her forehead to his shoulder when he had finished.

"But perhaps 'tis you I want and not Luke," she said. "Perhaps I do not want you to take Anna away. Perhaps I would prefer that you took me."

"You have been deprived too long of a man's part, Henrietta," he said, "and have forgotten what you prize most in life—position and power. You connived for them, did you not, and still connive? You brought me all that information about Anna, who can have done nothing to offend you, in exchange for a weekly mount. No, my dear duchess, you must not lose sight of what is important to you. I have no use for you but this, and this is sometimes tedious. 'Tis not something I crave with any frequency."

"Only with Anna?" she said bitterly, lifting her head.

He jerked her off him and dumped her onto the sofa beside him. He stood, his back to her, and buttoned his breeches. "Never with Anna," he said. "You will not sully her name by suggesting any such filth, madam. I will have your help when the time comes. You will return here next week at the same time for instructions and each week after that until I am ready to make use of you."

Henrietta was shaking out the skirt of her habit. Anger sparked from her eyes and sharpened her voice. "And why should I?" she asked him. "Why should I return where I have been insulted?"

He turned to look at her, his eyes amused. "I have servants, madam," he said, "who have seen you here today, alone without maid or chaperone. I have a servant who walked into this room to see you rutting with me on that sofa, your skirts about your waist, so mindless with pleasure that you did not even notice him."

Henrietta's eyes widened. "No one—" she began.

"And there are two or three witnesses to your lusty goings-on with a mysterious masked man several months ago," he continued. "Witnesses who may yet recover from their embarrassment sufficiently to begin gossiping."

"Why, you—"

Henrietta went for him with clawed fingernails. But he caught her wrists and held them.

"Besides, your grace," he said, "you will come back if only for this, will you not?" For the first time he kissed her, hard, pulling on her wrists until she came against him, opening her mouth with his and thrusting his tongue deep inside before withdrawing his head and smiling at her. "You need it, just like a drug, do you not? I will give it to you again next week, Henrietta. The very thought has you aching between your legs, does it not?"

She stared at him mutely, anger and desire mingled in her face.

"Yes." He smiled again. "Perhaps we will do it in a bed next week. Without the nuisance of clothes. Next week, my dear." He stepped back from her, released one of her wrists and lifted the other to his lips. "You must leave now. We would not wish any breath of scandal to attach itself to your name, would we?"

Henrietta stared at him while he released his hold on her wrist. Then she whisked about and hurried toward the door.

She hated and feared him. Her breasts and her womb throbbed with desire for him.

## 23

COLONEL Henry Lomax drew attention to himself and became a great favorite wherever he went. No dinner, no dance, no evening party was complete without the presence of the colonel. Men liked him; women adored him. Even some of the younger girls giggled and blushed when he paid them compliments, as he frequently did.

Luke found himself contemplating pleasurable and original ways to kill the man.

Wherever he went he singled Anna out for attention. Oh, never enough to cause a breath of gossip or a hint of scandal. He usually maneuvered matters so that he sat beside her at meals and then punctiliously divided his attention between her and whatever lady was seated at his other side. He always joined her group in a drawing room, and then talked more with the other members of the group than he did with her. He always danced with her at assemblies—only once—but with no one else. Yet he always spent the rest of such evenings charming all the other ladies and protesting the debilitating effects of old wounds, which prohibited him from dancing as much as he would like. He always smiled in such a way when he talked thus that the ladies never believed that those wounds also detracted from his virility.

There was nothing improper in his behavior to Anna. Luke found himself wishing that there were. He would know how to deal with any man who made indecent advances to his wife. There was nothing indecent about Lomax and his attentions could hardly be called advances.

Of course, they upset Henrietta.

"I am surprised," she said to him one evening at the Pierces',
when he was dancing with her and Anna was dancing with Lomax,
"that you of all people will put up with it, Luke."

"Madam?" He raised his eyebrows and focused his gaze on her.

"'Tis very clear," she said, "that he fancies her. And she does
naught to discourage him."

No, she did not. That was part of what made him feel murderous.
But then there was nothing to discourage.

"I assume you speak of my wife and Colonel Lomax?" he said.
"You are out of line, Henrietta."

"You cannot see it, can you?" she said. "She married you for your
fortune, Luke, but she is not above taking a lover, I vow. She told me
that first day he visited that she found him irresistibly charming and
handsome. And she warned me that if I thought to flirt with him
myself, she would give me competition. La, as if I would flirt with a
man of such indiscriminate tastes!"

Luke's look was so icy that she faltered to a stop and lowered her
eyes. "You will say no more, madam," he said from between his teeth.
"You have already said too much."

She had become a bitter and a spiteful woman, he thought with
some regret. She had seemed perfection itself once upon a time. And
perhaps she had been. Poor Henrietta. Life had not been kind to her.

Luke waited in some impatience for a reply from his uncle to the
inquiries he had made about Lomax. It came finally and chilled him
to the heart, though it was the answer he had anticipated. The army
had no records of a Colonel Henry Lomax. It seemed that the man
did not exist, at least not in any military capacity. And Theo, with
all his considerable connections, had been able to find no trace of him
in any nonmilitary capacity either.

Colonel Henry Lomax, it appeared, since he was a very real
flesh-and-blood man, was living at Wycherly under an assumed
name.

He was someone from Anna's past. Someone who had known
about her wedding plans and had come to watch from afar. Someone

who had followed her to Ranelagh and had taken the first opportunity that had presented itself to walk apart with her there. Someone who had written to her several times during the first six months of her marriage and even drawn her into clandestine meetings. Someone who had gone to the trouble of making Will's acquaintance, perhaps of talking him into taking his bride on an extended wedding journey, and of persuading him to lease out Wycherly for a year.

Someone whose feelings for Anna were so powerful that he could not let her go.

Her secret lover.

Luke sat at the desk in his study, absently turning his uncle's letter about and about on its surface while staring into space.

And what about Anna? Was she finding it equally hard to let him go—Lomax, or whatever his name was?

She was not being unfaithful. Luke did not know why he was so sure of that since he did not spy on her and could not account for her every move during every hour of every day since he had married her. But he was sure nonetheless. One could not live intimately with a woman for a year without being certain of some facts about her. Anna was a faithful wife. And a devoted mother.

But what of her inner feelings? What had her distress after Ranelagh and after her receipt of that first letter indicated? Fear at the renewal of an acquaintance she did not want renewed? Fear of her own feelings? Had she clung to her husband and made love to him with such desperate passion out of guilt? Guilt over the fact that she did not love him but did love another man?

He remembered—he could never stop remembering—the look in her eyes and her tears on the morning after their wedding when he had asked her if she loved the man who had taken her virginity.

Luke crumpled the letter almost viciously in one hand and got abruptly to his feet. One thing was certain. The time for secrets was past. He was going to find out the truth. Not from Anna—he doubted he would get it from her. But he was going to find out the truth. Himself.

Not Theo this time, but himself.

• • •

*Luke* and Ashley were out riding. They had no particular destination but somehow they ended up at the top of the slope a few miles behind the house and stopped by unspoken consent to turn their horses' heads and look down on the panorama of park, gardens, and house. It was Ashley's last day at home.

"I will think of this when I am in India," he said, "and wonder what the devil I am doing there. 'Tis said that Englishmen always appreciate their own country best when they are out of it. Did you find that?"

"I had reason not to want to remember England," Luke said quietly. "You have not changed your mind, Ash? 'Tis not too late."

Ashley laughed. "When I am packed to leave for London tomorrow and to leave for India within the week?" he said. "No, I have not changed my mind, Luke. Thought of the future excites me. 'Tis just that I will miss all this and all of you."

"Fox comes here well recommended," Luke said. "But he cannot do a better job than you have done, Ash. Any time you want to come back . . . But no matter. I will miss you too—my only brother." They had grown close again in the months since Joy's birth.

'There was another brother," Ashley said. "Have you even been to see his grave, Luke?"

"No," Luke said curtly, "and 'tis not a topic I wish to pursue, Ash."

"There is something you should know," Ashley said abruptly. "Mama said 'twas something no one should ever know except her and Henrietta and me. But it has troubled me, especially now that I am leaving. You have the right to know."

Luke turned his horse again and proceeded down the far side of the hill. "If it concerns George," he said, "I have no wish to know."

Ashley came after him. "He killed himself," he said.

Luke stopped so abruptly that his horse reared and it took a few moments to bring it under control. By the time he had done so, his face was deathly pale. "What?"

"He fell on a knife," Ashley said, looking equally pale. "Deliberately. Fortunately—I suppose it was fortunate—there was some cholera in the village and we put it about that it was of that he died. He would not have been given a Christian burial if the truth had been known, Luke."

Luke felt that buzzing in the head he had felt once before. "But why?" he asked.

"He could never forgive himself, I suppose," Ashley said. "He loved you. He sent you money once, did he not, and you sent it back? He drank for two weeks without stopping after that. Even Papa could do nothing with him."

God!

"She got what she wanted," Ashley said. "Can you see her clearly enough by now, Luke, to know that it was all her doing? She put him through hell. He could do nothing right. She even blamed him for the death of the child. They hated each other. I think she perhaps had feelings for you, Luke, but you were only a second son and George was available. Ironic, is it not? He used to take her to London and she had affairs and flaunted her lovers before him. I heard about it when I was at university. And then he killed himself."

"God, Ash." Luke rode onward, neither knowing nor caring which direction he took.

"He wronged you," Ashley said, "but as I live, Luke, he suffered for it a thousandfold."

*I sent back the money,* Luke thought, unconsciously increasing his horse's pace to a canter. *I sent back the money. I sent back his peace offering.*

"Perhaps I should not have told you." Ashley sounded miserable. "But you did have another brother, Luke. And I loved him."

And now Luke was about to lose the other brother too. Not so cruelly or so permanently. But it would be a loss. He eased back on the reins and looked across at Ashley. "You did right, Ash," he said. "Thank you."

Ashley shrugged. "Let me ask something of you," he said. "I am going to be in the devil of an emotional mood tomorrow morning. I want to leave as if I were running an errand into the village. I do not want you and Anna on the terrace hugging and crying all over me and waving me on my way."

Somehow they were close to the stables. Ashley must have been steering their course.

"I'll stay out of the way, then," Luke said reluctantly. "And I will ask Anna to do likewise."

Ashley breathed an audible sigh of relief. "Thank you," he said, grinning. "I'll write, Luke."

"See that you do," his brother said, leading the way into the stables. "Orders from the head of the family, Ash."

*It* had not been easy to say good night to Ashley just as if it were any other night and not to wring his hand as if to crush every bone in it or hug him closely as if to break ribs. Luke had been away from his family for ten years and had neither expected nor wanted to come back to them. And yet now, knowing that his brother was going far away for an indeterminate number of years, he mourned those last years. Ten years, or some of them anyway, in which he might have known his brother.

Anna did not have as much fortitude. After excusing herself early from the drawing room in order to go up to the nursery to give Joy her night feed, and after bidding Ashley her usual warm and cheerful good night, she had turned back at the door, rushed back across the room to him, and given him all the hugs and shed over him all the tears he had hoped to avoid in the morning.

Ashley had emerged from the embrace looking sheepish and damp-eyed.

Luke breakfasted early and left the house before Ashley came down. He had had a sleepless night and had even wandered into his own bedchamber so as not to wake Anna. He had renounced his family, all of them, and had lived with deadened emotions for ten peaceful years. Now they were back, his family and his emotions. He loved Doris and Ashley. He was still hurt by his mother's rejection— he would admit it now. He still hated his father and George.

George. George had thrown himself on a knife and killed himself.

Luke left the house early, saddled his horse himself, and rode slowly and reluctantly to the only place he could go. He had a visit to pay, a long overdue visit.

He had always liked to wander in the churchyard as a boy. It had fascinated him to know that his own ancestors from generations back and those of the neighbors and villagers he knew were buried there. It had not been a morbid fascination. He had felt all the mystery and wonder of the continuation of life.

But he had come this time to see two particular graves, ones he had not seen before. He stopped at his father's first. His father had been a stern man. There had been love in him too—love for his boys and his girl. But clearly there had been limits to that love. Luke had passed those limits. The twenty-year-old Luke had been bitter about his father's rejection. The thirty-one-year-old Luke finally found it more understandable. He had tried to shoot his brother—or so it would have seemed—and had very nearly succeeded.

Luke wondered if his father had felt any regrets during the final five years of his life.

*Father,* he said silently. But there were no words. Only a suddenly remembered image of his father teaching him, with endless patience, to ride his first pony. *Papa.*

There was a small grave for the stillborn child. He had even been named: Lucas.

Luke stared at the little headstone for a long time, perhaps afraid to take that one more step to the side that would bring him to the other, most recent family grave. But he finally took the step.

George. Dead at the age of two-and-thirty. Killed by his own hand. Because he could not forgive himself. Because his brother would not forgive him. Because his brother had returned the money.

Hurt and bewildered and angry and proud, Luke had sent the money back and the paper on which only his brother's signature had been scrawled.

A peace offering.

A love offering.

Scorned and rejected.

In all the selfishness of youth, Luke thought now, he had believed that only he suffered—he and Henrietta. And so he had rejected the love offering. And love itself. He had killed all love in himself and torn out his own heart so that no one would be able to hurt him ever again.

And yet he had hurt someone else so deeply that he had killed himself. He had hurt his brother. He had killed George after all.

He hunched his shoulders as the cold breeze knifed between his shoulder blades. He had not brought a cloak. It looked as if it might rain at any moment. Everything around him looked suitably gray and gloomy.

"George," he said aloud. "George." *Forgive me. I have forgiven you. Forgive me. Forgive me.* "I love you."

Love came in pain, in unalloyed pain, and was not turned back. Luke went down on one knee and rested one hand on the top of the gravestone and the other on the earth over where his brother's remains lay.

"Forgive me." Tears plopped unheeded onto the grass. "Forgive me." And then he rested his forehead on the hand that held the gravestone, and he wept with deeply painful, racking sobs.

A long time passed before he got slowly to his feet and turned again in the direction of home, leading his horse, not riding it. No one had disturbed him though more than one person, the rector included, had seen him.

*Ashley* had told her yesterday that he was leaving today. He had set his hands on her shoulders after doing so, smiled cheerfully at her, told her to be a good girl, and gone striding away. It had been a very brief meeting. He had been riding all afternoon with Luke.

Emily did not want to see him today. She would not be able to bear seeing him actually leave. And yet when she had eaten her breakfast—or rather when she had not eaten it—she could feel nothing but panic. Had he left? Was he gone already? Gone forever and she had not seen him go?

She sat at her window and tried to draw calmness from the sight of the lawns and trees outside. But it was a gray and gloomy day. And perhaps even now he was at the door and entering the carriage that would take him away.

She would never see him again.

Her nurse would come for her soon and take her to the nursery, where she would try to interest her in some needlework or painting. She could not do any stitching today or any painting either. Not when her heart was breaking. She leapt up, ran into her dressing room for a cloak, flung it about her shoulders, and ran from the room while there was still time.

If there was still time.

But there were trunks and boxes in the hall. No carriage at the door. No sign of Ashley. He would be at breakfast. He had not left yet. But she could not go to him. She did not want to see him today. Oh, yes, she did. She must see him. But she did not want him to see her.

She ran outside and down the steps onto the upper terrace of the formal gardens. She ran fleet-footed through the gardens, across the wide lawn, over the bridge, and down the driveway, until she stopped, gasping for breath, among the trees. She set her back against one tree trunk so that she could see the driveway but not be seen. But all she would see was the carriage. It was unlikely that he would be looking through the window, and if he were he might see her. She did not want him to see her.

She wished her cloak was not red. Why had she not thought of bringing a different one?

She was shivering with cold by the time she heard the carriage approach. Not that she *heard* it, of course. But she was far more aware of vibrations than other people seemed to be. She knew the carriage was coming before it came into sight. And panic hit her. He was leaving forever and all she would see was the carriage. She leaned forward, desperate for one last sight of him.

But the carriage rolled on by and she saw nothing. And then it slowed and stopped and the door opened and Ashley jumped to the driveway and turned back to where she was standing, clutching the tree trunk behind her back.

He came to stand in front of her, very close to her, before he said anything. There was a sadness in his eyes.

"Little fawn," he said.

But if he said any more she did not hear it. Her vision blurred.

His weight came against her, pressing her against the tree, though he did not immediately touch her with his hands. When she looked up at him, she saw that his head was thrown back and his eyes were tightly shut. And then he lowered his head and looked into her eyes, only inches away.

His mouth, when it touched hers, was warm and soft and wonderful. And it stayed against hers for a while. She pushed her own lips back against his for comfort.

He framed her face with his hands, one of them still, the other smoothing back her hair. "I will be back, little fawn," he said. "I will be back to teach you to read and write and to teach you a language you can use."

*All I want to be able to say is I love you. I'll always love you. Forever and ever I will love you.*

"Ah," he said. "Those eyes. Those eyes, Emmy. I'll be back. I'll not forget you. I'll carry you here." He stood away from her and touched a hand to his heart.

And then he was gone.

Some time after she had closed her eyes, the carriage was gone too. She felt the vibrations again.

Emily stood where she was for many long minutes until she pushed herself away from the tree and began to run recklessly, heedlessly through the woods, faster and faster, as if all the fiends of hell were at her heels.

*Anna* was in the nursery playing with Joy when Luke came in. The baby, who had been insisting to her mother for half an hour or more that she was just not in a jovial mood this morning, smiled brightly as soon as she set eyes on her father.

"Rascal," Anna said to her.

"She has your smile," Luke said, setting a hand on Anna's shoulder.

"When she decides to use it," Anna said. "Little imp." She turned her head to look into his face. He was pale. He looked almost as if he had been crying. "What is it?" she asked. "You saw Ashley after all this morning? It was very hard to stay up here, I must confess. It seemed unnatural to let him go without a proper farewell."

"Ash is very young," he said. "Too young to want to be seen shedding tears, Anna. No, I did not see him today though I have been told that he has gone. I'll miss him."

"I know." She smiled at him.

His hand tightened on her shoulder. "Invite me to your sitting room?" he asked.

She never had since he had told her it would be her private domain, though she had often wanted him there, just the two of them together. She handed him the baby, who smiled at him again, and rang for the nurse. When the woman came and took charge of the baby, Anna led the way to her sitting room.

"What is it?" She seated herself beside him on a sofa and took one of his hands in both of hers. She was surprised—and rather horrified—to see tears spring to his eyes.

"I have been visiting my other brother," he said, leaning his head back against the cushions and turning it so that he could look into her face. "I went to the churchyard to see George's grave."

"Ah," Anna said quietly. "I am glad, Luke." And she could see from his face that there had been some reconciliation, absurd as that sounded when his brother was dead. But she knew that Luke had needed this, that he had needed to have all his family back after years of bitter estrangement.

"He killed himself, Anna." He closed his eyes while she turned cold, and then he told her everything Ashley and Doris had told him between them. He finished with what she knew was the most painful fact of all. "He sent me that money as a sign that he still loved me, that he was sorry for what he had done to me. And I sent it back. I rejected him. I failed to kill him with that bullet—did you know that I aimed for a tree six feet to one side of him and hit him one inch from the heart?—but I killed him by returning that money."

"No, Luke." She lifted his hand to her cheek and held it there. It was so rare to see her husband weak and vulnerable. "Of course you did not kill him. You must not think that. Both of you suffered dreadfully. You had the strength to come through it. He did not. He might have written a letter to send with the money. He might have gone to Paris looking for you. You cannot blame yourself for what he did or did not do. And if you did reject him once, then he had rejected you too. Unfortunately, people do that to each other. People hurt each other, especially those closest to each other. And some people lack the inner strength to endure that others have. They cannot help it, perhaps. My f-father appeared strong to me all my life until he discovered that Mama had consumption, and then he fell all to pieces. Many people blamed him. It would have been easy to have stopped loving him."

"I loved George, Anna," he said. "He was always everything I ever wanted to be. He was my idol."

"He loved you too, Luke," she said. "To the end, else he would not have suffered so much. He would not want you to suffer now. He would not want to know that he had hurt you in death perhaps more than he hurt you in life."

He turned his head to look at her again. "Love is never the soft and easy emotion it is sometimes made out to be," he said. "I should be able to have him back so that we could make our peace with each other, but he is dead. Love hurts, Anna."

"Yes." She turned her head to kiss the lace at his wrist.

"Anna." He was looking closely at her. "Has Henrietta always been your friend?"

She considered answering vaguely. But she knew that he was struggling to put his life together again, to reconcile the past with the present. He needed honesty, on this point at least. "No, not really," she said. "She has always been at pains to describe her meetings with you and to make me understand how much you and she still love each other. And I have come to believe, perhaps unjustly, that it is deliberate, that she dislikes me. I avoid her company whenever I can."

"'Tis not true, what she has insinuated, Anna," he said. "I will confess that I was afraid to come back, afraid that my feelings for her would be revived if I ever saw her again. And after my return I was afraid to be alone with her for the same reason. She maneuvered all our meetings. It did not take me long to understand that what I felt for her was no longer love but pity."

Anna drew a breath and let it out slowly. She lowered his hand to her lap again.

"Anna," he asked her, his eyes searching hers, "do you have any regrets about marrying me?"

"No," she said, closing her eyes. And then she opened them to look at him and spoke more fiercely. "No, none."

"And I have none," he said. "You are the best thing that has happened in my life."

She bit her lip hard. What had he just said about love hurting?

"Is there anything . . . ?" he began almost hesitantly. He started again. "May I be of service to you in any way, Anna?"

How often the most momentous decisions of one's life have to be made in a moment, she was to think afterward. With no prior warning. With no more than a few seconds of time in which to weigh one's answer. Why had she not told him? she thought later. He was in a mellow, almost tender mood. He had just told her that she was precious to him. He had just been confessing to her his own terrible mistakes. He would have listened sympathetically to her own confession. He would have set her free.

But she had only a moment. She answered from instinct—the instinct for self-preservation.

"You are always good to me." She smiled at him.

"And there is nothing—?"

"Nothing," she said firmly, holding on to her smile.

He nodded. "I have to go to London on some business," he said more briskly. "It should take a week or so."

Her heart leapt with gladness, though of course any idea of escape was merely illusory. "We will go together?" she asked. "Soon?"

"No." He reached out with his free hand to brush his fingers across her cheek. "I will go alone, Anna. 'Twill be easier than packing up Joy and her nurse and taking you all with me. I will come home as soon as 'tis possible."

"Oh," she said.

"You have no . . . fear of staying here alone?" he asked her, his eyes keen on hers.

Fear? Terror, perhaps, was a better word. "No, of course not." She smiled at him. "But we will miss you, Joy and I. I shall count the hours until your return."

"Anna," he said. "Ah, Anna."

He was in a strangely pensive mood. His eyes were unusually wide and defenseless. But he returned suddenly to his more normal self and rose to his feet.

"I must have a word with Fox," he said. "And with my valet."

She smiled at him, resisting the urge to grab for him, to cling to him, to beg him not to leave her alone. But she stayed where she was as he left her room. Perhaps being alone, without the semblance of safety to hide behind, was what she needed more than anything. Perhaps when she was alone she would find the courage to do something in her own defense.

Perhaps—the thought came unbidden again—she would find the courage to kill him.

## 24

N hour or so later Luke was in the office of his new steward, Howard Fox, listening with some satisfaction to the man's praises at how well ordered the ledgers and records were and giving him some instructions on what was to be done during Luke's absence from Bowden. But they were interrupted by a knock on the door, followed by the appearance of Anna. She looked worried.

"Emmy has disappeared," she said with an apologetic glance at Fox.

Luke nodded at his steward and left the room with her. "'Tis but early in the afternoon," he said. "She is in the habit of wandering, Anna. Is there need to worry?"

"But she has been gone since early this morning," she said. "Her nurse has only just reported her absence, foolish woman. She has been gone a long time, Luke. Ashley left early. I suppose she saw him leave and went off somewhere to grieve alone. I blame myself for not giving her my company this morning. I should have known how 'twould be. Goodness knows where she has gone."

"Poor Emily," he said. "She will come home when she is ready." But he looked into his wife's face and saw agitation there. "You want me to look for her?"

"I have to feed Joy," she said. "It will be half an hour or more before I will be free to go."

"I will find her and bring her home safely to you," he said. "Was she at least wise enough to take a cloak with her? 'Tis a raw day."

"Her red cloak is missing," she said.

"Ah, then she should be easy to spot," he said. But he would wager a bundle that the child had gone running off to the falls. It appeared to be one of her favorite places.

He found her there, lying facedown on the flat rock that jutted out over the water, her cloak fanning over her.

"Emily?" he said softly as he scrambled up the other rocks toward her. Poor child. He had been so wrapped up in his own powerful emotions this morning that he had not spared her a thought. "Emily?" He touched a hand to her shoulder and kept it there.

He had not frightened her as he had feared he would. She turned her head to look up at him with dull, reddened eyes, and then hid her face on her arms again.

He sat down beside her and patted her shoulder for a while. She was not crying any longer. She was utterly passive. Poor child. She had loved Ash more devotedly, more singlemindedly than any of them. And she was fifteen years old already, was she not? It was probable that she loved Ash not as a sister loves a brother or a child loves a hero, but as a woman loves a man. It was so easy because of her affliction to think of Emily as a child rather than as a girl budding into early womanhood.

What would happen to her? he wondered. Would he and Anna be able to find her a husband who would be kind to her when the time came? But she would be quite unable at this moment to look forward to a possibly contented future. She was too absorbed in the agony of the present.

He turned her over eventually, scooped her up in his arms, and set her on his lap. He cradled her as she huddled against him, crooning comforting words to her even though he realized that she could not hear them.

"You saw him leave?" he asked her when she looked up at him at last with wide and unhappy eyes.

She nodded.

"Did you speak with him?" he asked. "He said good-bye to you?"

She nodded again.

He wondered if Ashley realized that the child loved him. "I am sorry," he said. "I am sorry for your pain, Emily."

She rested her head on his shoulder again and lay against him for a few minutes longer before getting to her feet and arranging her cloak carefully about her, eyes lowered. He offered his arm and she took it.

"Emily." He bent his head to her as they walked until she looked at him. "Anna and I love you very dearly. I know that knowledge will not help ease the pain, but 'tis true, my dear."

She smiled wanly at him.

It was when they were halfway across the lawn to the house that he had an idea. He slowed his pace and bent his head toward her again.

"Emily," he said when she looked up, "do you know Colonel Lomax?"

She looked at him blankly.

"Our new neighbor," he said. "The man who is living at Wycherly."

He saw awareness come into her eyes. And something else. Definitely something else.

"Do you know him?" he asked. "Had you seen him before he appeared here?"

She nodded, her eyes huge with a message he could not read.

"Where?" he asked.

She pointed in a vague, wide gesture and then shrugged helplessly.

"At home?" he asked. "At Elm Court?"

She nodded vigorously.

"But his name was not Lomax?" he said.

She shook her head.

He had known, of course. But there was a certain stab of bleakness about the heart to have his suspicions finally confirmed.

"Did you like him?" he asked.

She shook her head and her eyes told him that her feelings for Lomax were just the opposite of liking. But why? And did Anna like him? But he would not ask the question of Emily. It would not be fair. Though what fairness had to do with anything he did not know.

He squeezed her hand. "Thank you," he said. "I will find out the truth for myself, my dear. Do you believe I should?"

She nodded and there were tears in her eyes. He squeezed her hand once more as he led her toward the house. Yes, he would find out for himself. It was time. And he had the feeling that the whole future of his marriage depended on his finding out the truth.

A marriage that had gradually—so gradually that he had hardly noticed its happening—become very dear indeed to him.

*If* only one could go back, Henrietta thought as she rode alone up the driveway to Bowden Abbey, and order one's life differently. If only she had stayed with Luke—dull, unfashionable, bookish Luke with his dream of a career in the church. She might have been a bishop's wife now. Or perhaps the reigning Duchess of Harndon, though George might still be alive if . . . He might be married with sons.

She had just come from Wycherly, where she had been thanked for the news she had brought of Luke's intended journey. Thanked in the usual way. It had become more and more insulting. Never in a bed, as he had once half promised. It had been in a stall in the stables this afternoon, the door closed but not locked, grooms clearly audible just beyond the thin wooden barrier. He had laughed at her protests.

And yet she could not seem to live without it.

If only he took Anna away—she had stopped wishing he would take her instead—she would be free again. She would have her pride back. She would have Bowden to rule again. And Luke. She had never had Luke. But if half the stories about him that had come from Paris were true . . .

And there was a look in Anna's eyes some mornings . . .

Henrietta clamped her teeth together as she strode from the stable block to the house. Cotes met her in the hall, bowed, and told her that his grace wished to have a word with her.

Henrietta raised her eyebrows in some surprise but followed the butler across the hall to the study and swept past him when he had knocked and opened the door for her.

Luke was seated behind his desk. He got to his feet but stayed where he was. He motioned to a chair on the other side. "Henrietta?" he said. "Have a seat."

She smiled at him when they were both seated. He looked steadily and silently back at her for several moments. How different he was, she thought. How much more handsome and commanding. How much more attractive.

"What has happened?" She leaned forward in her chair and set one delicate hand on the far side of the desk. "Has Anna—?"

"Henrietta," he said, "we are going to have to make arrangements for you to live somewhere else. Permanently."

She stared at him blankly for a moment, while what remained of her world began to fall about her ears. But perhaps she had misunderstood. Her eyes softened and saddened. "Poor Luke," she said. "You feel it too? The constant tension? The constant temptation? You cannot bear it any more than I can?"

"You have done your best," he said coldly, "to ruin my marriage, madam. I will have no more of it. My marriage is very precious to me."

Her lips compressed suddenly and her eyes sparked. "What has Anna been saying?" she asked. "What lies has she been telling about me? She is naught but a slut, Luke, and you—"

"Silence!" Luke said, not loudly, but so coldly that she instantly obeyed and stared at him.

"I have to be away from Bowden for a week or so," Luke said, "as I announced at luncheon. I will be leaving tomorrow. By the time I return, madam, you will be prepared to leave. I will send you to Harndon House until we can make more permanent arrangements. You will decide whether you would like your own establishment in town or whether you would prefer a house in the country somewhere. Somewhere that is not close to Bowden. I will honor your wishes in the matter."

She realized then the extent of her loss, the extent of her foolishness. There were tears in her eyes. "Luke," she whispered, "is this what has come of our love?"

"I loved you once," he said. "But I doubt you know the meaning of the word, Henrietta. Frankly I have no wish to debate the matter with you. But you have been a force of destruction in my family for too long. You are my sister-in-law, my brother George's widow, and as such you are entitled to be housed in some luxury for the rest of your life and to be generously supported by the estate. But once you have left here, you will not return under any circumstances, madam. At least not during my lifetime."

She got to her feet and looked scornfully at him. "You always were a weakling," she said. "Wanting to be a clergyman, running away to France and fearing to return, marrying a slut for whom you have no feelings at all so that you could hide behind her skirts when you returned to me, fearing now to admit to your continued attraction to me. You were always weak. I am glad I took George instead of you. Of course, he would probably still be living if I had not, and I would be sitting in a church pew every Sunday morning, pretending to gaze adoringly at you as you delivered the sermon."

Luke took his snuffbox from a pocket and opened the lid with one thumbnail. "You are dismissed, madam," he said, looking up with cold eyes.

Too late she realized what her flash of temper had accomplished. She had lost him forever, lost Bowden forever. But then he was going to lose too. She could scarcely wait. She snapped her teeth together, turned sharply away from him, and flounced to the door, head high. Then she turned and glared at him.

"He would not lie with me after our son was stillborn," she hissed at him. "What was I to do but hate him? He deprived me of my rights. He would not risk having any more children by me. The dukedom had to be preserved for Luke. Always his precious Luke. And finally he gave it to you—on the end of a knife, so to speak. Did you know that? Did you know that your brother, my husband, took his own life? So that no son of mine would succeed him, but his precious Luke?"

• • •

*Luke* took snuff with a steady hand until she had turned again and left the room. And then he allowed the final piece of the puzzle to fall into place. All those years he had thought himself cruelly betrayed. Yet all those years he had been dearly, dearly loved.

Yes, Anna was right. George would not want him to suffer now from pangs of guilt. George had loved him and had done all in his power to make amends, finally—foolish, foolish man—giving his life in order to do so.

Greater love hath no man than this . . .

*She* did not want Luke to go. Even for a week. A week was seven days long. Seven endless days. A great deal could happen in seven days. He would surely find out soon enough that Luke was gone and would take full advantage of the fact. So far he had been content merely to seek out her company wherever they went. There had been no demands. But that would change. It would probably change this week.

She had this week, too, in which to do something about the situation herself. To put an end to the terror. Or perhaps to begin it . . .

She did not want Luke to go. If she begged him, would he take her and Joy? Or stay at home and send Mr. Fox on whatever business there was to do? But she would not beg him. Clearly he felt compelled to go himself and preferred to go alone. Anna tried not to feel hurt at the realization.

When he came to bed and took her into his arms, she tried not to cling. But she knew immediately and with some relief that it was one of the nights when he would make love to her. She tried not to appear overeager. But she was always excited when she knew he was going to love her.

He kissed her mouth warmly and lingeringly. She opened it wide and arched against him.

"Mmm," he said. "What is it, Anna?"

He always knew. Sometimes she thought he knew her better than she knew herself. It was so hard to deceive him.

"Nothing," she whispered. "I am going to miss you, 'tis all."

"Let us make the most of tonight, then, shall we?" he said, returning his mouth to hers.

"Mmm," she said.

He loved her slowly. Very slowly, melting her into warm relaxation, stirring her by degrees to excitement, letting it subside into warmth again, building it once more, over and over again. His hands and fingers, his mouth and tongue and teeth, his legs, his body—he used them all with marvelous skill. After a year of marriage it might have seemed that there would be no new way of touching or arousing her. And yet always there was something new. And her own hands and mouth and body had learned to give pleasure in skilled and varying ways.

She lost her fears and anxieties and gave herself up to the moment, to the giving and receiving of pleasure. And when it came time for their bodies to join, she opened herself to him and lifted to him and sighed as he came deeply inside. She was panting with arousal, very close to the brink. Had he moved in her, even just once or twice, she would have gone shuddering over.

But he held still, and raw sensation subsided yet again. She lay still and relaxed beneath his weight, knowing that soon, in his own time, and at his own pace, he would move them both into the entwined dance of bodies that would take them to a shared ecstasy. She felt no anxiety as excitement waned. He would bring it back again with even greater intensity with one withdrawal and inward thrust.

"Anna." He had lifted himself to his forearms and was gazing down into her face. With the curtains drawn back both from about the bed and from the windows, she could see his face almost clearly, though his hair hung about it and over his shoulders. There was a light in his eyes that made her heart lurch. "Anna."

She lifted both hands and smoothed his hair back from his face and tucked it behind his shoulders. She cupped his face with gentle hands and gazed back at him. She loved him so tenderly at that moment that she was close to tears.

"I love you," he whispered.

And then the tears did spring and trickle down her cheeks.

"I love you," he said again, his lips light against hers.

There was a moment's pause before he deepened the kiss, perhaps to give her the chance to return his words.

And then he loved her with his body, as he had loved her innumerable times before, with firm, deep inward strokes and gradually increasing rhythm until every nerve ending in her body was raw with need and she tumbled with him beyond need into that temporary heaven where all was fulfillment of needs and dreams.

As he had loved her innumerable times. As he had never loved her before. For there was a difference. Both her body and her heart recognized it. He had given her pleasure countless times before. He had never before given love with the pleasure. Conscious, tender love.

He had made love to her, and she floated in heaven as he disengaged his body from hers, turned her onto her side against him and covered her with the bedclothes, as he usually did. She was sexually satiated, as she usually was. She also felt loved—as she never had before.

She would not even consider, she thought sluggishly, why she had been unable to return his words.

He found her mouth with his and kissed her lingeringly.

"I love you," he said once more.

It was because she could not yet give herself completely to him. There were secrets, barriers of her own making. Secrets that must be told, barriers that must be torn down. And then . . . But there was no knowing what lay beyond that point.

No, she could not speak the words yet. Perhaps never.

And yet she loved him as she loved her soul. She loved him more than life. She had loved him since she had set eyes on him, all scarlet and golden and Parisian affectation, that first evening. She would love him until she had taken her last breath and perhaps even beyond that.

The journey from Bowden Abbey to Elm Court usually took three days. Luke did it in two. He felt uneasy being away from Anna. Perhaps he had done the wrong thing to leave her alone, though he could not believe she was in any danger. If Lomax was her former lover, however—and Luke was almost convinced he was—perhaps he was putting temptation in her way by leaving her at home alone. Perhaps he was presenting Lomax with just too good an opportunity.

He could not shake from his mind the fact that Anna had failed to respond to his declaration of love three times. They had not married each other for love. She was not obliged to love him, and he certainly did not want her to fake a love she did not feel.

But he had hoped and even believed . . .

There had been a special tenderness about their lovemaking the night before his departure. Or so it had seemed to him. He had found it impossible to believe that only he felt it. What they did to each other that night had not been just physical. They had not been two separate entities giving and receiving pleasure. They had been man and wife, making love. One body, one heart.

Or so it had seemed to him.

He had not paused to consider how horrifying or how laughable—depending on how he looked upon it—such a notion would have appeared to him just a year ago. A year ago he had not known that love in its many forms could possibly return to him. A year ago he would have resisted such a possibility.

But love had returned. Including love of his wife. Especially love of his wife.

But perhaps it was something he alone had felt. Anna had not returned his words.

And yet there had been the silent tears.

Yes, he had had to leave her. He had to find out the truth. He had to know what was between her and Lomax, whether it was love or something else.

Heaven help him, Luke thought, if it was love.

The Earl and Countess of Royce were not expecting him and greeted him in some astonishment, though warmly enough. They were disappointed, of course, to find that he had come alone and had not brought Anna and Emily with him—and Joy.

Lomax? Henry Lomax? Royce frowned over the name when Luke finally began asking his questions an hour or two after his arrival. No, he had no acquaintance with anyone of that name.

It was the expected answer, of course.

"Emily told me she had seen him here," Luke said. "He is now living at Wycherly Park, Severidge's home, while Will and Agnes are away. He is close to fifty years of age, at a guess. Tall, slim, distinguished-looking, even handsome. Well liked by all. Charming to the ladies."

But Royce responded only to the first words. "*Emily* told you?" he asked, and he looked at his wife and chuckled.

"Yes," Luke said, not stopping to explain. Surely her own brother must have discovered that the child could communicate certain facts?

Royce frowned again. "But why did you not just ask Anna?" he said. "If Emily saw him here, then so did Anna. Am I missing something?"

Luke drew a deep breath. He hated to voice any of his suspicions when Anna did not even realize that he was here. But Royce was her brother. And they had always appeared to him to be a close family.

"Anna will not admit to knowing him," he said. "But she does, and he makes her unhappy somehow. I want to find out the truth."

"Perhaps," the very young and idealistic Constance said, her voice atremble, "you should trust my sister-in-law, your grace."

"Connie!" her husband said in mingled embarrassment and admonition.

"No," Luke said, holding up a staying hand. "She is quite right, Victor. I have explained myself poorly, my dear. Will it help if I explain that I love Anna very dearly? That I want to help remove the burden that is clouding her happiness if I may? I fear she keeps a secret that for some reason she is afraid to disclose."

"Perhaps 'tis that she is fond of this man," Constance said. Her voice still trembled and she glanced apprehensively at her husband. His youthful sister-in-law was a woman with backbone, Luke thought approvingly.

"Perhaps so," he said. "But if 'tis so, my dear, this man who calls himself Lomax has no business following her to the home where her husband has taken her. It would be more honorable and more compassionate to go away and to allow her heart to heal. That is what I shall tell him if that indeed is Anna's secret."

"Yes," Constance said rather sadly, looking down at her hands and then up to gaze so adoringly at Royce that Luke almost smiled. "Yes, your grace, you are quite right. Forgive me."

"I will always honor a woman who will speak up for the rights of others, madam," he said and watched her flush with pleasure at the compliment.

"I believe," Royce said, "that this man might be Blaydon. Sir Lovatt Blaydon. He leased a house close to ours soon after my mother died and stayed for a year. After my father's death he went to America, I believe. I had not heard of his returning, but then there is no reason that I should have."

Sir Lovatt Blaydon. The name hammered on a door in Luke's memory that had remained stubbornly closed for a year, and the door suddenly flew open. Luke had been at a notorious gaming hall in France during that first year of his exile, heavily inebriated, when one of the other patrons had been tossed out on his ear—almost literally—for beating insensible one of the whores upstairs and then cheating at cards. It had struck Luke at the time as an interesting point that the latter offense was the one that had got the man—Sir Lovatt Blaydon—tossed out, the former misdemeanor merely adding fuel to the fire of indignation against anyone who would dare to cheat and get himself caught. Luke had not seen the man before or since that incident—until the morning of his wedding.

"Blaydon?" he said and raised his eyebrows.

"He was very good to us," Royce said, "and especially to Anna. She bore all the burdens of our family problems, you know, after Mama died. And Papa was"—he flushed—"well, I suppose Anna has told you."

Luke nodded.

"There were debts," Royce said. "Mostly gaming debts. Blaydon bought them all and allowed us to pay them back in our own time. I suppose he did not charge interest either. I do not know. I was at university and let Anna take care of everything. I have been ashamed since, but she always seemed so capable, and she always insisted that I complete my studies and not worry about anything else. She must have paid off the debts, for I was not presented with any bills after Papa died. We thought at one time Anna would marry Blaydon. They seemed fond of each other. 'Twas something of a surprise that he went away just when perhaps she needed him most. Papa's death was a terrible shock to all of us."

There were debts. Paid off? Luke doubted it. He doubted it very much. He knew something about how huge gaming debts could be, especially when they were incurred by a man who also drank to excess.

Was that what it was? Was that all it was? Luke allowed himself to feel the luxury of a huge relief. She owed the man money? Or rather, Royce owed him money, but Anna, true to form, would not put the burden on her brother's shoulders but kept it on her own. The foolish woman! His poor foolish, brave, wonderful Anna. Why in heaven's name had she not come to him? He would have paid all the debts twice over if necessary to have released her from the burden of the hold a ruthless man had over her.

Why had she not told him on that very first morning after their wedding instead of keeping the secret to herself?

But thinking of that morning brought back a more chilling memory. Anna had had a lover. Or more accurately, since he was not certain of the truth of that, someone had had her virginity. Blaydon? In payment of some of the debts? Rape?

Luke's blood ran cold and quite unconsciously his hand strayed to the hilt of his sword.

"Do you think, Vic," Constance asked timidly, "that perhaps some of your father's debts still have not been paid? Is that why he has followed Anna to Bowden? Is that why she is not quite happy?"

"My thoughts exactly, madam," Luke said.

Royce looked grim and somewhat pale. "Zounds," he said, "if

that is true, she will have the length of my tongue, begging your pardon, Luke, and he might well have the length of my sword if he has been harassing her. Those debts, if they still exist, are mine."

"I will get to the bottom of it," Luke said quietly. "Can you tell me anything else about Blaydon?"

Royce thought but he shook his head. "I was away most of that year," he said. But he brightened at a sudden thought. "Perhaps Charlotte will know more. She was here all the time. She married only just before Anna and Agnes went to Aunt Marjorie's in London, you know."

Charlotte. Perhaps she would be able to fill in some of the gaps in the story. If there were still gaps. Perhaps everything was just the way it seemed.

Luke turned suddenly cold again. If Blaydon had raped Anna once—or more than once—perhaps . . .

He was going to have to get back to Bowden Abbey just as soon as possible, Luke decided.

## 25

Anna knew she had made a mistake when she let three
days pass after Luke's departure and Sir Lovatt Blaydon came calling on her. Of course he had found out that Luke had
gone; it would have been difficult to keep such a thing secret in a
country neighborhood even if she had tried. And so in some way she
had let the initiative stay with him. She should have gone and confronted him on the very first day, she thought as soon as a servant
came to the nursery to announce that Colonel Lomax had been
shown into the drawing room.

Anna handed Joy reluctantly to Emily and smiled. "I have a visitor," she said.

And of course it had to be on an afternoon when there were no
other callers, she thought as she went downstairs with firm steps and
shrinking heart. But then perhaps he had known that too. The man
seemed omniscient in many ways. At least she was fortunate enough
to find that Henrietta was at home and in the drawing room entertaining their guest. Relations with Henrietta had been difficult lately,
but Anna was very thankful to see her on this particular occasion.

It was a relief that was short-lived. Henrietta got to her feet even
as Sir Lovatt rose to make his bow to Anna. Henrietta smiled dazzlingly at him as she gave him her hand, and then turned her head
to look archly at Anna.

"I would not be *de trop*," she said. "I can see when two people
prefer to be alone together. I shall leave."

Anna froze.

Sir Lovatt bowed over Henrietta's hand, brought her fingers to his lips, and smiled at her. "Ah, you are perceptive, my dear duchess," he said. "Anna and I thank you."

Henrietta, on her way out of the room, her back to Sir Lovatt, smiled again at Anna. A rather unpleasant smile.

"My Anna," Sir Lovatt said, reaching out a hand for hers as soon as they were alone. "We have an ally in your sister-in-law. We are fortunate indeed."

"I believe," she said icily, staying where she was, just inside the door, "in my vocabulary, she would be called an enemy, sir. I shall ring for tea."

But he stepped into her path as she moved. "Anna," he said, "the time will be soon. The time when we will be happy together, though I know you do not believe so now. It should be this week since a perfect opportunity has presented itself in the absence of your husband. But the child is not weaned?"

Anna wished suddenly that she was sitting down. She felt dizzy. There was darkness somewhere at the outer edges of her vision.

"No," she said curtly.

"I would wait until it is," he said. "That has always been my plan. You see how I consider the interests of your daughter as well as yours, my Anna? We will wait a while. But there must be a token of good faith. There has not been one since I came to Wycherly, has there?"

"No," Anna said again.

"Your poor papa was experiencing particular bad fortune on this particular evening," he said, sympathy in his eyes and voice as he held out a voucher with her father's signature scrawled at the bottom. A drunken, unsteady signature, but unmistakably his.

Anna glanced at the amount and then stared at it more fixedly. The darkness was approaching closer to the center of her vision. "One thousand pounds," she said. "I do not have that much money."

"Ah, Anna," he said, "there are other valuables in this house apart from money. There are jewels."

All the most valuable jewelry, even her own, was kept in a safe and private place in Luke's room. Anna knew where it was. She even knew where the key was. Luke had never made a secret of its hiding place from her. He kept her jewels there, not to hide them from her, but to keep them safe. Yes, there were more than enough jewels there to pay off this particular debt.

"I do not have access to any of the jewels or other valuables here," she said. "You must give me time."

"I shall do that, my Anna." He smiled at her. "The morning after tomorrow—one day longer than usual? The usual place? You would wish to wean your own child, would you not? You would not like to think of a wet nurse doing it for you?"

The darkness closed in completely and cold air rushed into Anna's nostrils. She stumbled and felt hands on her arms and heard a voice talking to her from a long way off.

Luke. Luke.

"Luke!"

"It is I, my dear," Sir Lovatt's voice said. She was seated and his hand was firm against the back of her head, forcing it downward so that the blood would return to it. "How foolish you are not to trust me. Do you not realize that all the money you have given me and all the jewels you will bring me have not gone to supply my own greedy needs but have been set aside for your future happiness?"

He stooped down on his haunches and rubbed her hands, one at a time, in an effort to restore warmth to them. She found the energy to snatch them away when he lifted one to his lips.

"I cannot steal from my own husband," she said.

"Anna," he said reproachfully. "'Twould not be theft, my dear. Are the jewels not your own? Can you steal from yourself?"

"They are mine in my capacity as Duchess of Harndon," she said. And she realized what she was doing in her weakness. She was arguing with him. She was not confronting him as she had sworn she would. And she had not brought a weapon to the drawing room with her. How satisfying it would be at this moment to whip out a knife from among the folds of her skirts and plunge it into his black heart. She would almost gladly hang for such a crime.

"I will take my leave now," he said gently, straightening up before her chair. "You are in no state to entertain a guest for tea, my Anna. The morning after next you will do as you have been instructed and the largest of your father's debts will be paid."

Anna laughed.

After the drawing room door had closed behind him, she continued to laugh. And the laughter, quite beyond her power for the moment to control, horrified her far more than hysterical tears would have done.

*Henrietta* was waiting among the trees far down the driveway when Sir Lovatt Blaydon rode homeward. He touched his tricorne to her and she smiled, as she had smiled at Anna earlier.

"Well?" she said. "When is it to be? Soon, I hope."

"Your good wishes for my future happiness and Anna's are touching, madam," he said. "'Twill be when it will be. You will come to me in three days' time, as usual."

Henrietta's smile faded. "Oh, la," she said, "you are not going to take advantage of Luke's absence? I begin to believe you merely play games with us all, sir."

Sir Lovatt leaned forward from his horse's back, set the tip of his riding whip beneath Henrietta's chin, and raised it. "You have enjoyed our little games immensely, my dear," he said. "You enjoy degradation. We will see what near-public place we can find next time for our carnal delight. Perhaps I will arrange for a servant to be present. Yes, I believe I will. Other games I choose to play, madam, are none of your concern. And your opinion is unsolicited and unwelcome. I trust you will remember not to offer it again?"

The point of his whip was pressing rather uncomfortably against Henrietta's neck. She disdained to take a step back, but she dared not answer. She swallowed.

"You are wise," he said. "Another part of this whip would feel a little more painful against another part of your person, duchess. Good day to you."

He straightened up, touched his whip to his tricorne, and rode on his way.

Henrietta looked after him, burning with hatred and with painful and unrequited desire.

*At* first Charlotte, complacent and plump with pregnancy, was able to tell Luke no more than her brother had known. Sir Lovatt Blaydon had been particularly attentive to Anna. Everyone—not just her family but the entire neighborhood—had expected that they would marry, though Charlotte and her sisters had thought him too old for Anna.

"But he was very well-liked," Charlotte explained. "We all admired him a great deal, except Emily, perhaps. But Emily has always been a little strange. She cannot help it, poor dear. 'Tis her affliction. She used to run away when Sir Lovatt called."

Luke felt convinced that Emily, if only she could talk, would be able to tell him a great deal more than the others had noticed. He felt frustrated in his efforts to piece together a story.

"Blaydon appeared here soon after your mother's death?" he asked. "Did he ever explain why he came here? And why he came at that particular time?"

"He was looking for a place in the country," Charlotte said with a shrug. "And that particular house was for lease. I suppose he might have chosen any of a dozen different places."

Luke did not believe so somehow. He frowned. What was it he was not seeing or not understanding? What was the missing clue? Had Anna met Blaydon somewhere even before that? Had he followed her to Elm Court then as he had followed her to Bowden now?

"Did Anna go away to school?" he asked. "Was she ever from home for any length of time before your mother's death?"

Charlotte thought, but she shook her head. "Mama was ill for several years," she said. "Anna was like a mother to us. She was always at home."

It seemed, Luke thought, that he would have to take his interpretation of what had happened back to Anna and hope that she would finally confide the truth to him when confronted with what he already knew.

"'Twas a pity," Charlotte said, "that Sir Lovatt did not arrive a little sooner than he did. He just missed the chance to become reacquainted with Mama."

Luke regarded her from hooded eyes.

She looked a little disconcerted for a moment. "His family had an acquaintance with Mama's," Charlotte explained. "He and Mama knew each other as children."

It was strange, Luke thought, how sometimes the most pertinent information on a subject could come out quite by accident. Charlotte had let out this particular piece of information as an aside, as something that had no particular relevance to the matter at hand. And yet to Luke it had enormous significance, suggesting as it did that the arrival of Sir Lovatt Blaydon at Elm Court had been no more accidental than his appearance at Bowden.

But how could he find out what the significance of that particular piece of information was? Had there been some sort of family feud that he was continuing? Had Anna's mother at one time done him some harm that he wished to avenge? Had he been in love with Anna's mother?

How could he find out? Who would know?

The answer came to him almost as soon as he had asked himself the question.

"Lady Sterne," he said to Charlotte. "She was your mother's friend?"

"Oh, yes," she said, blinking at the abrupt change of topic. "She is Anna's godmother, you know. We all call her Aunt Marjorie though she is not really our aunt."

"How long were they friends?" Luke asked. "All their lives?"

"They met in London as girls," Charlotte said, "when they were both presented to the queen. Mama often told us about it. They remained friends ever after though Mama would not allow Aunt Marjorie to come visiting after she became so sick. She did not want to be seen pale and thin and ugly, she used to say. Poor Mama."

There was a chance. Just a chance that Lady Sterne would have known Blaydon or at least that Lady Royce had talked of him. It would mean going to London, of course, and delaying his return home by another day at least. He was becoming more uneasy about being away from Anna. But he needed to learn the truth, or as much of it as he could possibly piece together. More and more he was beginning to feel—partly with elation and partly with fear—that whatever it was between Anna and Blaydon, it was not love.

He left Elm Court for London early the following morning, one day after his arrival there.

*Anna* was careful to tell a number of people where she was going. It might not seem very proper that she was going alone, with only a maid for company, but she was not concerned with appearances. She just wanted some people to know. She told Mr. Fox and Cotes and Mrs. Wynn, and she took with her a coachman, a footman, and her maid.

She was paying a morning call on Sir Lovatt Blaydon.

At the time when his man would be waiting among the trees to watch her set the money and jewelry beneath the stone outside the gamekeeper's cottage so that he could retrieve them without delay, she was being driven through the gates of Bowden and along the road to Wycherly. She was paying a morning call because it was unlikely she would encounter any other visitors at that time.

"Wait here for me," she told the coachman and footman when the latter handed her down outside the doors of Wycherly. They looked disappointed that they would not have the anticipated visit and ale in the kitchen, but both bowed their acquiescence.

"Wait here for me," she told her maid when Sir Lovatt's butler offered to escort her to a visitors' salon leading off the hall, and Penny nodded and bobbed a curtsy though she looked as disappointed as the men had looked.

Anna stood inside the salon for ten minutes, gazing out the window, drawing some strength from the sight of her own carriage and servants before the doorway. She slipped a hand beneath the robings of her open gown and through the slit at the side of her petticoat to the pockets taped about her waist beneath her hoops. Her fingers touched cold steel and suddenly felt as cold as the metal. And for a few moments she was breathless and the darkness threatened the edges of her vision again.

But she was not going to faint today, she decided. Never again. She was not going to be a victim ever again. She should never have allowed him to gain such power over her. When he had talked of witnesses to various crimes, she should have invited him to use them. She should have gambled on pitting her honesty against their lies. Except that there had been so much to lose then, both for herself and, more importantly, for her family.

No, she thought now, she must not blame herself for the weakness of the past. In the past it had been necessary. But no longer. Now, giving in to the endless demands protected only herself, making her into an abject, cringing creature.

She would not do it any longer.

The door opened behind her. She did not turn immediately.

"Anna." He sounded genuinely pleased. "What a very pleasant surprise. You have brought your bundle in person instead of leaving it beneath the stone? I would have asked it, my dear, if I had realized you had the courage to come here alone and risk your reputation. Do take a seat. I shall have refreshments brought."

She turned at last to look at him. He was wearing a morning gown of gray silk over his shirt and breeches. Without the padding of waistcoat and skirted coat, he looked thin rather than slim. His wig had not been freshly powdered. She guessed it was yesterday's powder. He looked older than usual.

"I want neither a chair nor refreshments," she said. "And as you see, I carry no bundle." She spread her empty hands to the sides. "There is no bundle beneath the stone outside the cottage."

He looked sympathetic rather than angry. "He has hidden away the valuables and the keys, my Anna?" he asked. "What sort of a husband is that, I ask you? Not one who loves you as you deserve to be loved, my dear."

*I love you.* She had a vivid image of Luke's face above hers on her bed, the tender light of love in his eyes to prove the truth of the words he spoke. She thrust the memory back whence it came.

"I will not pay any more of my father's debts," she said, "until they have been presented in full to either my husband or my brother. And I will not allow you to make any more threats to me. If you wish to bring any charges against me, you may speak to the appropriate authorities. My husband will be home soon. When he returns, I shall tell him everything. Every single sordid little detail. Perhaps you can make life difficult financially for my brother, sir, and perhaps you can destroy me. Perhaps you can even put a rope about my neck. But I will not allow you to harass and intimidate me ever again. Your power over me is ended as of this moment."

He looked at her silently for a few moments, his hands clasped at his back. And then he smiled slowly. "Anna, my dear," he said at last, "you are magnificent. You are finally becoming the woman I always knew you could be."

"I will be returning home now," she said. "I have three servants with me, sir, and several more at home know where I have come this morning and what time I expect to be home. If you try to detain me, there will be trouble."

He laughed. "You are wonderful, my dear," he said. "I kiss my hand to you." He proceeded to do so. "You are free to leave whenever you wish."

She stood looking steadily at him for a while, trying to make sense of his reaction. Was it possible that he would let her go so easily? Had it been as simple as this all along, if she had only had the courage to stand up against him?

She did not believe it for a moment.

She walked past him to the door and was relieved when he stepped well to one side of her path.

"Anna," he said softly as she passed. "My dearest Anna."

Her back prickled as she stepped into the hallway and summoned Penny. It bristled as she stepped outside and allowed her footman to hand her into the carriage. It crawled during the seemingly interminable time it took him to climb to his place beside the coachman.

And then the carriage lurched into motion. After a few minutes they were off Wycherly land and on the road back to Bowden.

She was free. It was all over. At last. She was free.

But she did not believe that, either, for a single moment.

$\mathcal{D}oris$ was delighted to see Luke. She hugged him when he arrived at Harndon House and looked beyond him for Anna. He had come on business for a day or two and had left her at home with Joy, he explained. Doris was enjoying the entertainments of the spring Season in town and had an even larger court than she had had the year before.

"But if you do not mind being burdened with me for a while longer, I do not believe I will choose a husband from among them," she explained to him. "There is no one for whom I feel a particular fondness."

Last year, Luke thought, that argument would probably have meant nothing to him. This year it did. He smiled at her.

"Then you must wait until there is, Dor," he said.

He arranged matters so that he could have a few words alone with his mother.

"I have learned the truth, you know," he told her. "About George's death, that is. You should have told me, Mother. 'Twas something I needed to know."

"No," she said, her face stiff and pale. "You did not need to know anything so shameful. You thought badly enough of him as it was."

"I have learned the full truth," he said. "I have been to his grave, Mother, and wept there. He continued to love me even though he thought I had tried to kill him. I was angry enough to challenge him, to make a point, but I loved him too dearly to kill him. I aimed well to one side of him, but I hit him."

"He knew it," she said. "He always argued with your father that 'twas so."

Luke went down on his haunches suddenly before her and took both her hands in his. "Mother," he said, "Papa and George are dead, more is the pity. I will grieve for them for the rest of my life. But there are still you and Ashley and Doris and me. Let us love one another while we are alive and have the chance. I was without my family for ten years and convinced myself that 'twas better so. But I have learned in the past year that family and love are the most precious possessions anyone can own."

His mother sat staring woodenly at the floor. "So many decisions," she said, her tone flat, "have to be made without time to reflect and without knowledge of what the consequences will be. I had to decide, Lucas, between you on the one side and your father and George on the other. Duty led me to choose them. I have always put duty first since my marriage. I have always put duty before love. What is love, after all, but an emotion to cause us pain and bring us loss? I always loved you best, shameful as the admission is. But I put duty before love."

"Mother." He warmed her stiff, icy hands with his own. "Mother." He raised her hands one at a time to his lips.

"I love all of you," she said. "I worry about all of you. With my lips I try to persuade all of you to be dutiful. With my heart I am afraid that you will all love and be hurt by love."

"Mother." He kissed the palm of the hand he held to his lips. "Mama."

She looked up at him. "I cannot change, Lucas," she said. "But know that I love you and wish for your happiness. You made a wise choice in Anna."

"Yes." He squeezed her hands once more and released them as he got to his feet. "I have to call on Lady Sterne with a message from Anna. And then I must hurry home to her. All is well with Doris?"

"All is well," his mother said. "She is a year older in age than she was last year and five years older in experience, I vow."

*Luke* called on Lady Sterne without delay and was fortunate to find her at home—with his uncle. They were seated quite respectably in her drawing room. Luke knew that they were lovers. He knew too that they were ever discreet and would not have dreamed of making love to each other in the home of either.

"Mercy on me," Lady Sterne said, coming across the room to Luke, both hands extended. "As handsome as ever, Harndon. But you left Anna and the child at Bowden? For shame."

"Hark ye, lad," Lord Quinn said sternly, on his feet too, "I'll not have the two of you drifting apart merely because the first year of marriage is past. Pox on it, but marriage is the damnedest thing."

"Oh, pshaw!" Lady Sterne said. "Pay him no heed, Harndon."

"I need some information that I hope you can supply, madam," Luke said, taking the offered chair.

Lady Sterne raised her eyebrows in enquiry.

"The late Lady Royce, your friend," he said, "grew up knowing a family by the name of Blaydon. In particular a boy of about her age named Lovatt. The father would have been a baronet, I believe. Did she ever mention this man or this family to you?"

"Egad, Luke," his uncle said, "you ask some strange questions."

"The man took up residence at Elm Court immediately following Lady Royce's death," Luke said, "and he has leased Wycherly Park from Severidge under an assumed name. Anna pretends not to know him, but Emily does know him and she does not like him. I have just come from Elm Court, where I spoke to Royce and to Charlotte."

"Lud," Lady Sterne said almost in a whisper, "Anna is harboring a secret?"

"Lookee, Luke," Lord Quinn said, "you may bring naught but grief on yourself by prying into your wife's secrets."

"Anna is not happy," Luke said. "And I love her, Theo. Oh, yes, the two of you can congratulate each other on the total success of your schemes. I love her. Therefore, I must find out the truth."

"But as I live, I have never heard the name," Lady Sterne said. "Blaydon." She frowned in thought. "You are quite sure it is not Blakely? Lowell Blakely?"

Luke stared at her. "Perhaps," he said. "What do you know of him, madam?"

"He was a handsome lad," Lady Sterne said, "tall and slender and dark. Or so Lucy said. I never saw him myself. He was quite in love with her and she had been infatuated with him when she was very young. She had promised—when she was just a young girl—to marry him. But even before her papa brought her to London she had grown tired of his persistence and his ardor and his jealousy. He used to smuggle letters to her quite shamelessly after she came here. She used to complain of them to me. She started to return them unopened. And then she met Royce and no man ever existed for her after that."

"And she never heard from Blaydon—from Blakely—again?" Luke asked.

"Only once, as far as I know," Lady Sterne said. "She was married in London. I remember her telling me afterward that he was standing outside the church, silently watching, when she came out on Royce's arm. Lud, it quite gave me the shudders when she told me that."

Luke felt it now himself—a deep inward shudder. "The man who now calls himself Colonel Henry Lomax," he said, "was standing outside the church when I brought Anna out after wedding her."

"Mercy on us!" Lady Sterne said.

"Zounds!" Lord Quinn said.

"I believe," Luke said, getting to his feet, "I had better return to Bowden as quickly as I can." He bowed. "You will excuse me, madam?"

"Egad." Lord Quinn jumped up too. "I'll come with you, lad. I can still shoot a pistol and hit my target, I warrant you. If this Blakely-Blaydon-Lomer or whoever he is thinks to lay one finger on that gel, he will find himself staring down the barrel of a gun with my itchy finger on the trigger. Devil a bit! I'll not be able to escort you to the Minden soirée tonight, Marj, m'dear."

"Oh, do go with Harndon, Theo," she said, her hands pressed to her mouth. "Oh, Anna. My dear little Anna."

Luke did not argue. For almost ten years in France his sword and his pistol had been the only friends and the only defense he had felt need of and both had been quite adequate in protecting him. But for those ten years he had not had love to protect. Or Anna. He felt sick with worry.

Why in heaven's name had he left her there alone? He had seen only unhappiness. He had not dreamed of danger.

## 26

ANNA returned to Bowden Abbey late in the morning the day after her visit to Sir Lovatt Blaydon. She had been visiting the wife of one of her husband's laborers, a woman who had just given birth to her eighth child.

Anna was feeling happy, quite lightheartedly happy. Luke had been away for six days and should be home tomorrow or the day after. There was a little sick lurching of the stomach when she thought of all she must tell him on his return. But only a little. He knew her well enough by now, surely, to believe that she was neither a thief nor a murderer, and to understand why she had become involved in some shady dealings. And he would understand about that other ugly deed too, though the thought of telling him the details of that made her shudder. It seemed almost better to let him go on believing that she had had a lover. But she would tell him. She wanted everything off her mind and her conscience. Everything.

Surely Luke would believe her story. And surely he would be able to protect her from anything Sir Lovatt tried to do to her. Looking back now, she could not understand why she had not told him everything at the start, on that first dreadful morning when he had suggested that openness between them was essential to a workable marriage. Surely even then he would have helped her.

But it was hard now to look back on Luke as he had been then, and on herself as she had been. At that time he had not yet looked into her eyes with that special light in his own. At that time he had not yet told her that he loved her. He had told her quite the opposite, in fact. He had said that there would be no love between them. And she had seen steel in his eyes.

*I love you.* She could hear him saying the words the night before his departure. She could see the look in his eyes. And she quickened her steps up to the nursery, feeling so happy despite her anxieties that it was difficult not to break into a run. What would the servants think if they saw her do that? Anna smiled at the thought.

She stopped abruptly in the doorway of the nursery. The room was empty. What a disappointment! Where had Nurse taken Joy? It was a fine day outside, but the baby's nurse always avoided the outdoors unless she had been given direct instructions to take the child out. She had the strange notion that fresh air was harmful to a child below the age of one.

Anna crossed the room and jerked on the bell pull. If the nurse had Joy somewhere in the house, then Anna would take her outside herself. Perhaps she would take her all the way to the falls. Emmy could come with them. The outing would help fill in time so that the day would pass quickly. Though she must not expect Luke tomorrow, she told herself. If she did, she would be disappointed if he did not come.

She would be disappointed anyway. She smiled again.

The nurse came into the room alone.

"Where is Joy?" Anna asked. She must be with Emmy, though Emmy never took her out of the nursery.

The nurse smiled. "The duchess took her out for a picnic, your grace," she said. "I thought you would be pleased. She has never shown much interest in the child before. Packed a bagful of changing cloths, she did, and some extra clothes. As if she were going for a week, I told her." She laughed. "Though I told her, too, she could not keep Lady Joy out for very long because she would want her feed. That will be another hour, your grace."

Henrietta? She had taken Joy for a picnic? Alone with no nurse? With cloths that she would change herself? Anna remembered suddenly the smile Henrietta had given her when leaving her and Sir

Lovatt alone in the drawing room three days ago. She felt instantly uneasy, even frightened. Henrietta had never shown any interest in Joy.

"Where did she go for the picnic?" she asked.

"She did not say, your grace." For the first time the nurse looked uneasy herself. "But she did say that she spoke to you at breakfast."

Anna left the room without another word and hastened down the stairs. Though she stopped halfway and hurried back up to her dressing room, where she took the knife from the drawer where she had hidden it the day before and slipped it into her pocket again. The action frightened her and she tried to tell herself that she was being absurd. She rushed back down the stairs.

But where would she begin looking? And why would she need to look? In another hour or less Joy would be hungry and would first fuss and then cry lustily. Henrietta would come hurrying back when that happened even if she did not return sooner. She had done this deliberately, Anna thought, merely to be tiresome.

How she disliked Henrietta. And how sad she felt at the change in their relationship. There had seemed to be so much love and friendship at first.

Henrietta, Anna saw as she stood uncertainly in the doorway, was strolling in leisurely fashion through the formal gardens toward the house—alone. She stopped walking and smiled when Anna came hurrying toward her. It was that same smile she had worn in the drawing room a few days ago.

"Where is Joy?" Anna asked. She was seriously frightened now.

"Quite safe," Henrietta said. "She is with your lover."

"W-what?" The darkness threatened again.

"I value our friendship even if you do not, you see," Henrietta said, her eyes glittering with that strange look of triumph. "I still love you, Anna. I have been helping you, making your elopement easier. You have only yourself to take to the gamekeeper's cottage. The child is there already. You are fortunate that your lover is willing also to take the child. Many men would not. But he appears quite to dote on her."

"Oh, dear God." Anna gazed wildly at her sister-in-law. "What have you done, Henrietta? He is not my lover. And now he has kidnapped Joy. You must go for help. Please!" She clutched at the other woman's sleeve. "Go and tell Mr. Fox and Cotes. Get them to send as many menservants as possible. And quickly. Please, Henrietta. Please?"

Henrietta continued to smile. "Of course," she said. "Of course, Anna. You run along. Did I do wrong?"

But Anna did not stay to answer. In her panic she broke into the run that in her happiness she had resisted inside the house.

She dared not think as she ran, though thoughts and images teemed unbidden through her mind. Sir Lovatt with Joy in his arms. Sir Lovatt threatening to dash out her brains on the stone outside the gamekeeper's cottage unless Anna promised to bring the money and jewels and to keep her mouth shut when Luke came home.

She would do it too. She would sell her soul to get her child safely back.

She had to pause on the bridge, one hand pressed to her side as she gasped for air. *Oh, dear God,* she prayed as she stumbled onward. *Dear God. Please, dear God.* God had seemed her friend again lately. Was he to turn deaf ears to her pleas again now? But it was a child for whom she prayed now. A helpless infant. An innocent. *Please, dear God. Please, dear God.*

A man stood in the clearing before the cottage. A man she had not seen before. Undoubtedly the servant who had delivered the letters and left the bills beneath the stone and retrieved her money. Perhaps she had seen him once ride up to the house.

Anna came to an abrupt halt at the edge of the trees. "Where is she?" she demanded. "Where does he have her?"

The man set his fingers to his lips and whistled piercingly. Then he grinned at her.

A few moments later Sir Lovatt Blaydon stepped out from among the trees opposite, a blanket-bound bundle in his arms. The baby was still and quiet—*was she dead?*

Anna stumbled toward him, arms outstretched. "Give her to

me," she begged. "Oh, please give her to me." She did not even try to
control the hysterical sobs that came with the words.

But two strong hands clamped onto her upper arms from behind
before she could get close enough, and held her still.

"Dearest Anna," Sir Lovatt said, smiling tenderly, "the time has
come. There is a gate in the wall close by. My carriage awaits beyond. Do not worry that you bring no trunks or boxes. I have provided them for you. And I would prefer that you bring nothing that
he has bought for you. Come, my dear."

"What?" Hysteria gave place to frozen terror. "Where are you
taking me?"

"Home, my dear," he said. "I am taking you and the child to the
home I prepared for you more than a year ago. In America, my Anna.
Across the ocean, where we can be at peace together with no one to
pursue or find us."

"Oh, dear God," she said.

"Come," he said, and he nodded to the servant who still held her
arms from behind. "We will talk as we travel."

"No!" she shrieked. "You cannot take us to America. Not without
a word to my husband. And you cannot take Joy. She is his daughter."

"She belongs to you," Sir Lovatt said. His tender gaze was trans-
ferred to the sleeping child in his arms. "And to me now. She is
beautiful, my Anna. But come. No more delay."

Anna struggled against the servant, who urged her forward.
"Take me if you must," she said. She was sobbing again. "But please
send Joy home. Oh, please. She is his. She belongs here with him.
Please send her back home. I will come without a struggle if you will
but send her home."

But Sir Lovatt merely nodded curtly to his servant, who swept
her up into his arms and strode with her through the trees to the
gate she had never seen before and beyond it to a waiting carriage.
He thrust her inside, and Sir Lovatt climbed in behind her, the baby
still in his arms.

Anna moved to the corner of the seat and reached out her arms blindly. He set the baby in them and seated himself beside her. Anna bent her head over the warm bundle of her daughter and wept as the door was firmly closed from the outside. A moment later the carriage lurched into motion.

*Emily* clutched the gatepost and watched the carriage disappear along the road. She felt such panic that for a full minute she stood rooted to the spot. She could not decide whether to go running after the carriage or to race to the village, which she could reach in perhaps five minutes if she ran without stopping, or to run all the way back to the house.

But she stood rooted to the spot in despair. There was no point in trying to follow the carriage on foot. And if she ran into the village she would not be able to make anyone understand that her sister and her niece had been abducted. If she ran back to the house, a great deal of time would be wasted and she would still face the same problem.

Ashley. Oh, Ashley.

She started to cry in her fright and frustration and then turned back to the house. She had to make someone understand. She had to. But not when *she* was around—Henrietta.

Emily had seen Henrietta take the baby from the nursery and had been struck by how unusual an event it was, especially the fact that she also brought from the nursery a large bag of supplies. How foolish the nurse was, Emily had thought, letting the baby go so easily when Anna was not at home to permit it and Luke had gone away for a week.

Emily had followed, keeping well behind the woman and child, careful not to be seen. And to her amazement it had soon become obvious to her that Henrietta was taking the familiar route to the gamekeeper's cottage.

Emily had watched it all—the meeting with Sir Lovatt Blaydon, his taking the baby and smiling down at her, Henrietta smiling and happy and turning back to the house. But Emily had stayed where she was, sick with terror and bewilderment and indecision. Should she show herself and try to wrest the baby away from him? But that servant Emily had seen before was there too. It would do no good to show herself. It was her duty to keep herself hidden so that at the very least she could tell Anna where the baby had gone.

She had stood there long enough for despair to set in. Sir Lovatt had disappeared with Joy while his servant had remained, pacing up and down before the cottage. Waiting. Waiting for what? For whom? For Anna? But of course for Anna. Henrietta would return to the house and tell her about Joy and Anna would come for her. But surely not alone. Surely she would bring servants who could help get the baby back.

Emily had known that Anna would come alone.

And so she had stood hidden, helplessly watching the scene before her as Anna had struggled to reach the baby and as she had eventually been carried away by the servant. Sir Lovatt following with the baby. Emily had followed them cautiously and had discovered the gate, which she had never seen before despite her wanderings.

And she had seen the carriage drive away and had experienced the greatest frustration and despair of her life.

How was she to tell anyone? she thought as she hurried back in the direction of the house. Henrietta would doubtless have told some plausible story to account for the absence of Anna and Joy so that for many hours no one would even realize that they were missing. How was she, Emily, to convey that message? And even if she could, even if someone understood and believed her, how could she tell anyone where he had taken them?

To America. Across the ocean. She had seen his lips form the words. She remembered Anna's explaining to her—when Blaydon had left Elm Court after Papa's death—that America was far, far away at the other side of the world, across the vast ocean. Emily had known that Anna was glad he had gone so far away and had hoped he would never come back. Emily had hoped it too.

And now he was taking Anna and Joy there. How was she to explain this to anyone?

Emily could feel the pain of her breathlessness and her sobs as she hurried onward.

• • •

"*I* am *what?*" Anna stared wide-eyed at Sir Lovatt Blaydon, ignoring Joy's protests at being held so close and at not having her early hunger pangs satisfied. "I am what?"

Sir Lovatt chuckled and looked fondly back at her. "Yes, 'tis true," he said. "You see what a wonderful secret I have hugged to myself all this time, my Anna? You are my daughter. Mine and my beloved Lucy's."

"I most certainly am not," she said, indignation flashing from her eyes. "How dare you suggest such a thing, sir."

His eyes softened. "I know 'tis a shock to you, my dear," he said. "I know you were fond of the man you called father, worthless drunkard as he was. But in truth you are mine, Anna."

"Liar!" she spat at him.

"Anna," he said, not at all perturbed by her fury, "dearest Anna, do you know how many months after your dear mama's marriage you were born?"

Her eyes widened again. "She fell!" she said. "I was born a month early. I was so small that 'twas thought I would not live. And Mama almost did not survive."

"Ah, Anna," he said, "that was the story she told your papa, my dear. 'Twas fortunate you were small. He might have suspected the truth had you been larger."

Anna felt suddenly cold. And filled to the brim with horror. It could not be. Oh, it could not. Mama and this man? Papa cuckolded? Herself the daughter of the fiend who had stalked her and tormented her for three years? She would rather die than have it be true.

Only gradually did she realize what was causing unbearable aggravation to her anguish. Joy was crying lustily.

"See to the child, my Anna," Sir Lovatt said. "My dear granddaughter. She is hungry?"

"She is *wet* and hungry," Anna said.

"Ah. But I had the forethought to have supplies brought with her," he said, placing the bag of changing cloths and clean clothing on the seat opposite.

Anna changed the baby over her continued protests. And all the while, as she stood awkwardly, feet braced against the swaying of the carriage, she pictured the movements she would have to make to get at the knife in her pocket without his seeing and the way she would have to swing around and stab with it. Stab hard enough to kill. But the space was too confined, and if she was not successful all hope would be finally gone. Besides, Joy was in the carriage. It would be far too dangerous to try to wield a knife while she lay on the carriage seat.

"Here." Sir Lovatt smiled as she sat down again with the furious baby. "A shawl to guard your modesty in the presence of your father, Anna."

He wrapped it about her shoulders, a beautiful cashmere shawl that enabled her to loosen her clothes at the front and set Joy to her breast without the embarrassment of exposing herself to a man who was not her husband.

Oh, Luke!

The child suddenly fell silent. It seemed strange to Anna at this particular time and in this particular place to feel the pleasurable suction of her baby's mouth drawing milk from her. Strangely normal in a situation that had no other normality about it.

Sir Lovatt chuckled. "She was hungry," he said. "I did not want you to marry, Anna. You know that. Since we were forced to live apart during your growing years, you and I, I thought 'twould be enough for both of us to have only each other for the rest of my days. But I allowed you to marry after all so that we could have a child in our home. Your child, my grandchild. Three generations together. The two of you to gladden my heart through old age until my passing. And then you will still have the comfort of little Joy when I am gone, Anna."

"I am not your daughter," Anna said firmly. "And my child is not your granddaughter. This is absurd. Bizarre. Even if 'twere true, your behavior is incomprehensible. Why have you done all these things to me in the past three years? Why do you want me all to yourself? Any normal father would be delighted to see his child happily wed and happily producing more grandchildren for him."

"You were attached to people who were no concern of yours, Anna," he said. "To that worthless man who would have brought ruin to his own family if I had not come to his rescue. And to a boy and girls who are only your half-brother and sisters—one of them not even quite human. It hurt, Anna. And to know that my Lucy, your dear mother, was torn cruelly from my arms by parents who insisted she marry an earl. Anna, all your life you have been kept from me. You were even given his name. But no more. You are Anna Blakely—my real name—and my granddaughter is Joy Blakely. Joy indeed. I am glad you gave her that name. At last we are all together. Do not blame me for wanting us always to be together. I will make you happy, my Anna. Happier than you have ever dreamed of being."

"I am happy with my husband," she said. "I love him. This child is his. Ours." She disengaged her nipple from Joy's mouth and lifted the child to her shoulder. She rubbed her back gently and patted it to dislodge any wind she had swallowed.

Mercifully he fell silent while she finished feeding her child. Anna tried to keep her mind calm. She tried to think coolly and rationally. She tried to plan ahead. Were they close enough to the coast to board ship today? What were the chances anyway that there would be a ship in port that was bound for America and ready to be boarded? Would they put up somewhere on land for the night? At an inn? Would she have a chance there to enlist help from the landlord or another guest? Would there be an opportunity to use her knife and make her escape with Joy?

But there was the servant who had carried her to the carriage. And a coachman.

And then a thought struck her out of nowhere. Of course. But of course!

She turned her head and tried to keep the triumph out of her face and her voice. "I am not your daughter," she said. "I can prove it."

"Dear Anna," he murmured.

"My father," she said, emphasizing the words, "used to keep a miniature of his mother, my grandmother, in his room. I now have it in mine at Bowden Abbey. I am so like her that it has always been a source of wonder and amusement to my family. It looks as if I dressed up in clothes of an earlier era for the portrait painter, everyone who sees it agrees. If you were to look at that portrait, you would be in no doubt whatsoever that she was my grandmother, that Papa was my father."

For the first time there was something of an ugly look on Sir Lovatt Blaydon's face. "'Tis easy to imagine likenesses within families," he said. "Lucy, your mother, was mine, my Anna. Mine! Ours was a love rarely encountered in this world. A love that she carried to her grave. A love I shall carry to mine. A love that will reunite us for eternity. And you are a product of that love."

"Even without the portrait as proof," she said, "I would not believe it of Mama. She would not have done such a thing. She would certainly not have deceived Papa with another man's child. And when it comes to love of a rare intensity, sir, then such a love was shared by my mama and papa. I am ashamed that I doubted Mama and half believed you for even a single moment. Take me back home. I am not yours. There is no relationship whatsoever between us."

His eyes glittered with a light that frightened her. But he spoke pleasantly enough. "Shock usually brings denial with it at first, my Anna," he said. "You will believe the truth eventually. When you see how I love you and how I have provided for you and my granddaughter, you will believe it. America is a beautiful country. New and vast. A place for fresh starts. A place for freedom."

Freedom! It had been a slim hope that he would be convinced by her words and would take her back home. But Anna was now convinced that there was not even the possibility of his story being true. Her mother just had not been the type of person to have given herself to another man a scant month before her marriage. And her mother had clearly loved her father very dearly. Sir Lovatt Blaydon must know, then, that she could not possibly be his daughter. But did he know that he lied? Was he mad? Had he convinced himself of the truth of the lie?

The possibility that he was mad caught at Anna's breathing and threatened to bring panic and hysteria. But she would not give in to either. It would do no good at all. If there was any shred of hope left—and she had to cling to hope—it was essential that she stay calm and keep thinking clearly. She must keep looking about with her eyes and her mind for any small opportunity for escape that presented itself.

Joy, satisfied by her meal, refreshed by her long morning sleep, was eager to play. Anna smiled at her, love constricting her heart, and played while her captor looked on, chuckling indulgently.

## 27

*I*T was the middle of the afternoon. Full daylight. A pleasant day with blue sky and white scudding clouds. Clawing fears and wild imaginings seemed foolish somehow when one descended from the carriage and stood on the terrace and looked about at the peaceful beauty of Bowden Abbey.

Luke looked somewhat apologetically at his uncle. "I believe we will find that you have been dragged away from the pleasures of town for naught, Theo," he said.

But he hurried up the steps and through the doors into the hall and immediately demanded to know where he might find her grace, his wife.

"The duchess is from home, your grace," Cotes said with a bow for Luke and another for Lord Quinn, who had hurried in behind him.

"Ah," Luke said. "And where might she have gone, Cotes?"

His butler inclined his head in another bow. "She took Lady Joy out for a picnic, your grace," he said. "Despite the fact that the child's nurse feels that so much fresh air will be harmful to her lungs."

Luke turned to look at his uncle, eyebrows raised. "Out on a picnic, Theo," he said. "So much for our fears. I have a mind to join them after being so long cooped up inside the carriage. Will you come too? Did her grace say where she was going. Cotes?"

But even as the butler shook his head, Henrietta appeared in the archway that led to the staircase. She was smiling and looking beautiful and happy—as if they had not had words before his departure, Luke thought, making her a stiff bow.

"Henrietta?" he said. "I trust we find you well?"

"Very well, I thank you," she said. "You have brought Uncle Theo with you. How lovely it is to see you, sir." She crossed the hall-way toward him, one hand extended graciously, just as if she were still mistress of Bowden, and he bowed over it.

"As lovely as ever, I see, m'dear," he said. "You did not join Anna for the picnic?"

Henrietta smiled archly. "I would have felt quite out of place, Uncle," she said. "Anna has more congenial company than mine. She is picnicking on Colonel Lomax's land at his invitation. I declare he quite fancies her, though Anna is all propriety, of course."

"She is at Lomax's?" Luke said, exchanging a glance with his uncle. All his anxieties returned. God, but he should not have left her. He should not have assumed that she would be safe at Bowden Abbey without him. "Cotes, send orders to have my horse saddled immediately. Theo?"

"And one for me, Cotes, if you please," Lord Quinn said. "Egad, but I do not like it."

"But 'tis merely a picnic," Henrietta said, all wide-eyed innocence.

And then another figure came hurtling through the arch and launched itself at Luke, making noises that seemed not quite human.

"Emily?" He touched a hand to the back of her head as her arms came about his waist.

She tipped back her head almost immediately and looked at him so piteously that he frowned.

"Something is wrong?" he asked.

She nodded vigorously, but Henrietta spoke from behind her back. "Anna would not allow her to go on the picnic," she said. "The poor girl could not understand the reason. She has come to you for comfort, Luke."

Luke fixed his eyes on the wild face that gazed up into his. "I must go and bring Anna home," he said. "She has gone to Wycherly with Joy for a picnic. We will talk when I return."

But Emily shook her head fiercely and tightened her arms about his waist.

"What is it?" he asked, frowning. "Anna is not at Wycherly?"

Again the headshake.

"Where is she, then?" he asked.

Emily had to take a step back in order to use her arms. She pointed wildly, first in one direction and then another and then she gestured furiously away from herself with both arms.

"Ah, we are losing time," Luke said in some frustration. "I do not understand you, my dear. Henrietta says that she has gone on a picnic with Colonel Lomax."

And then Emily was shaking her head wildly again and turning to point accusingly at Henrietta. She made a cradling gesture with her arms, pointed at Henrietta again, and gestured toward the outside door before gazing imploringly back into Luke's face.

Luke frowned again. "Henrietta had the baby?" he said. "But Anna went out alone with Joy."

Emily shook her head.

"Hark ye, Luke," Lord Quinn said. "I believe the child is trying to say that Henrietta took the child somewhere."

Emily, who had realized somehow that he was talking, had watched him intently. She nodded her head eagerly now.

"I took the baby?" Henrietta laughed lightly. "La, how ridiculous. You know, Luke, that I have never had a great deal to do with your daughter. I am reminded too strongly of the child I lost. The girl should be locked up for indulging in such insane fantasies."

But Luke was beginning to feel a return of the panic that had brought him dashing home a day earlier than planned, bringing his uncle with him.

"Emily," he said, taking her by the upper arms and speaking very distinctly, "what does Colonel Lomax have to do with this? Did Henrietta take the baby to him?"

Emily nodded and Luke felt all his insides perform a somersault.

"This is preposterous!" Henrietta said.

"To Wycherly?" Luke asked Emily.

She shook her head and gestured outward, away from the house.

"Somewhere fairly close to here?" he asked. "On Bowden land?"

She nodded.

"And Anna was not with them?"

No, she told him with her head.

"So Lomax had the baby," Luke said, willing panic down so that he could think straight and find the truth as fast as possible. "Is Anna with them now?"

A nod.

"How did she find out?" Luke asked. "Did Henrietta come for her?"

Another nod, and Emily turned to point at Henrietta again.

"The girl is mad," Henrietta said scornfully. "You are not going to believe a half-wit, Luke—"

"Egad, madam," Lord Quinn said, "if you do not hold your tongue until you are invited to use it, I vow I may forget that I am a gentleman."

"So Anna went to them," Luke was saying to Emily. "You saw this?"

Tears brightened her eyes and she blinked them away.

"And she went away with him?" Luke said. "He forced her, Emily?"

Yes, her nodding head told him.

God, but why had no one—himself, for example—ever tried to teach the girl a more adequate language to use? Why had no one ever tried to teach her to read and write?

"Emily." Unconsciously he grasped her arms more tightly. How could she possibly answer his next question. "Where did he take them? Do you know?"

Yes, she told him.

"To Wycherly?"

No.

God! "To London?"

No.

Where would he be likely to take them? Somewhere safe from pursuit. A place where a frantic husband was unlikely to find them.

Emily had already indicated that the place was not London. But she knew where the place was.

"To France?" he asked.

No.

"Zounds," Lord Quinn said, "did you not tell me the scoundrel went to America after Royce's death, lad?"

America. Of course! "To America, Emily?"

She nodded, and the tears spilled over and her face crumpled into misery. Luke drew her close and set his arms about her. And over her head he looked directly at Henrietta.

"You, madam," he said very softly, "will stay just where you are until I have a moment to deal with you. Say a prayer of thanks while you wait that it will be only a moment. Perhaps, if I bring my wife and daughter safely home with me, my temper will have cooled before I deal with you more thoroughly."

"Egad," Lord Quinn said, "the villainy of the woman. Confine her to her room, lad, with Cotes to guard her. You will be going in pursuit. I will come with you."

"No," Luke said. "I would rather you stayed here, Theo, to protect Emily from that witch. Devil take it, where would he have taken them? Southampton, do you think?"

"Most likely, lad," his uncle agreed.

"Fresh horses for the carriage, Cotes," Luke said. "And quick about it."

Emily was gazing up at him again, with reddened eyes and untidy hair and frantic hope.

"I am going after them, my dear," he said. "I will bring them back safely, never fear. You will stay here. Lord Quinn will see to it that you are safe. I will bring them back." He raised her hands to his lips and forced himself to smile.

Lord Quinn took the girl by the hand and smiled at her with avuncular gentleness, and led her toward the stairs. "You understand lips do you, gel?" he said. "Up we go, then. A cup of tea 'twill be for you and me."

Henrietta lifted her chin and looked at Luke. "I did it because I love you," she said. "I have always loved you, even though pride and misery caused me to imply otherwise the last time we spoke. I did it because they are lovers and she is not worthy of you. How do you even know that child is yours?"

"Madam," he said, his voice and his eyes so icy that there was a flicker of alarm in her own eyes, "be thankful for three things. First, that my time is very limited. 'Twill not take long for fresh horses to be brought up. Second, that you are not a man. If you were, you would be feeling a horse whip about your shoulders. Third, that I do not hold with the chastisement of women. If I did, you would find that I have a heavy hand."

"You never loved me," she said. "I was deceived in you. I thought you the love of my life."

"If you wish to see the love of your life," he said, with cold contempt, "I suggest you look in the mirror, madam. You seduced my brother for his title and wealth and set a distance between me and him that was never breached. You lied to me and killed a part of me for ten years. You effectively killed my brother. You have used friendship during the past year to try to put doubts and misery in Anna's mind and have tried to seduce me. And now you have put the lives of my wife and child in grave danger. I will not make the excuse for you that perhaps you did not realize that. I believe you know it very well."

She opened her mouth to speak but closed it again.

Cotes coughed from behind Luke. "The carriage is ready to leave, your grace," he said.

Luke kept his eyes on Henrietta a moment longer. "You will escort her grace to her apartments, Cotes," he said, "and see to it that a guard is kept outside her door at all times. She is not to leave her rooms under any circumstances."

He did not wait to see his orders carried out. He strode from the house.

He had promised Emily he would bring Anna and Joy safely home. He felt very much less certain when he was back on the road, alone inside his carriage this time, on a trail that might well be cold by this time, traveling in a direction that he was not at all sure was the correct one.

Anna, he thought, setting his head back against the cushions and closing his eyes and feeling immediately dizzy. My God, Anna.

And Joy!

*They* were indeed close enough to the coast to reach it before nightfall. And there was indeed a ship bound for America in port. But it would not sail until the morrow and could not be boarded until first light. They were forced to take rooms at an inn close to the waterfront—a single bedchamber with a private sitting room.

Anna must be a good girl, Sir Lovatt warned her before he took her inside the inn. Any attempt to draw attention to herself might well result in harm to the child—he took the baby into his own arms as soon as they left the carriage. And she would accomplish nothing else. The innkeeper had been well paid to ignore her. And his servant would be stationed outside the door of their rooms for the rest of the evening and all night.

"You will be happy enough once we are on our way," Sir Lovatt told her. "'Twill be a wondrous adventure, my Anna. But 'tis natural that now you look back in some regret."

And so she found herself late in the evening, pacing the floor of the sitting room, ignoring her captor's suggestion that she sit down and relax or retire to the bedchamber for the night.

"We make an early start in the morning, my dear," he told her.

Her knife was still where it had been from the beginning. But gradually through the evening she had nudged back the robings of her gown and widened the slit in the side of her petticoat and arranged the haft of the knife so that it was tilted toward the edge of the pocket. She could draw it quickly.

But having done so, would she be able to kill with it? To jab for the heart with such force that the blade would not simply become entangled with the fabric of coat and waistcoat and shirt but would penetrate flesh? The thought of killing was frankly terrifying. But to save Joy? To save herself? To give them a chance to see Luke again?

Oh, yes, she could do it. And she would do it, too, as soon as a chance presented itself. The trouble was that he would not allow her to take Joy into the bedchamber although she had been asleep for more than an hour and would probably sleep all night. Anna could not risk having an unsheathed knife in the same room with her daughter. What if she failed and he punished her by stabbing the baby with her own knife? The thought sent a deep shudder through her.

And so she procrastinated.

When would be a good time? Would a good time ever present itself as though on a platter? Would it not have to be created? But when? There would be only one chance. Only one. She had no other weapon. No one would come to her rescue. No one knew where she was. The only help she could expect must come from herself. And from her knife.

Oh, dear God. Oh, Luke.

But there was no point in giving in to panic or self-pity. And so she paced.

Until a sound outside the door had her stopping abruptly and straining to hear. It was not loud, but it sounded like a scuffle.

She was not mistaken. Sir Lovatt, too, was suddenly alert. He was half out of his chair by the time a grunt outside the door was followed almost immediately by the crash of the door opening inward and colliding with the inner wall.

"I regret to inform you, Blakely," Lucas Kendrick, Duke of Harndon, told Sir Lovatt, all cold formality, "that your servant has met with a little accident. I believe he is—to put the matter bluntly—dead."

The unsheathed sword he held in his right hand was red to the hilt and dripped onto the worn carpet.

Anna's trembling hands went to her mouth.

*Dear God, thank you. Dear God, let me not be dreaming. Not unless the whole thing is a dream.*

𝓛𝓾𝓴𝓮 had been sick with worry throughout the journey. There were several ports from which one might sail to America, including

London itself. What if Blakely had not made for the nearest one? And what if he had, and had had the good fortune to find a ship about to sail? And how was Luke to find them in Southampton anyway? Blakely, he remembered now that he thought about it, had always ridden in a plain carriage. Luke doubted he would recognize it even if he saw it.

It was evening by the time he reached Southampton. But as it turned out, tracking down his quarry proved almost unbelievably easy. There was a ship bound for America the next day. The captain was on board and confirmed the fact that Sir Lowell Blakely had booked passage for himself and for his daughter and her child. They were to board soon after first light on the morrow. Given that fact, it was unlikely that they had put up at an inn very far from the quay, the captain gave as his opinion. There were four inns within a stone's throw, so to speak.

They were not at either the White Horse or the Dolphin. The landlords of both watched the gold coins Luke jingled absently in one hand with some wistfulness but could give him no information. The landlord at the George was a different story. He licked his lips at sight of the coins and glanced with shifty eyes in the direction of the stairs. He had already denied knowledge of the travelers. Luke casually added two more coins to the others.

"Well, there is a gent with a lady and a babe in number twelve, an' it please your worship," the man said. "But I vow I do not know if 'tis your man."

"Who else is with them?" Luke asked, the coins suspended over his closed fingers halfway across the taproom counter.

"A manservant," the innkeeper said. "He is on guard outside the room, your worship. He has a pistol. But I will have any damage to my good house paid for in full, d'ye hear?"

Luke looked steadily into the man's eyes as he dropped the coins into his open palm. The landlord licked his lips and turned shifty-eyed again.

"As I was a-saying," he said, "you should find the gent in number twelve, your worship."

The man who was sitting outside room number twelve, looking bored, was the same man who had refused to deliver Anna's letter into Luke's hand one morning at the gates to Bowden Abbey. He lost his look of boredom as soon as he caught sight of Luke, bounded to his feet, and assumed a posture of defense, both hands clenched into fists and raised menacingly before him.

Luke would have been content to knock the man insensible, but even as he moved in with his fists, evaded his opponent's guard, and landed one satisfying punch to the jaw, the servant drew a pistol. It was a mistake he would not live to regret. Luke's sword was drawn and through his stomach even before he could get his finger on the trigger. He moaned, but he was dead before he measured his length on the floor.

Luke opened the door of the room and flung it inward. One glance assured him that there were three occupants. Anna was there, standing at one side of the room. Joy was lying in a sleeping bundle on a sofa at the opposite side. Blakely was between them.

And it was on Blakely, alert and half out of his chair, that Luke's eyes and all of his attention focused.

"I regret to inform you, Blakely," he said, "that your servant has met with a little accident. I believe he is—to put the matter bluntly—dead."

His mind assessed the fact that his wife and his daughter were widely separated and that the other door—doubtless leading to a bedchamber—was close to Anna but far away from Joy. There was no chance to get them out of the way.

Sir Lowell Blakely finished getting to his feet, his sword scraping free of its scabbard as he did so. "Harndon," he said, eyeing Luke's sword with some distaste, "this is a rude interruption to a quiet evening I am spending with my Anna."

"You sully her grace's name by permitting it to pass your lips," Luke said. "It were better to make use of that weapon if you know how."

"I wonder if you realize," Sir Lowell said, smiling, "what a strumpet you have for a wife, Harndon. It were best to let me take her away with me. You would not want her if you knew all."

"Perhaps you noticed," Luke said softly, "that I call you Blakely, not either Blaydon or Lomax. I am not in utter ignorance of the facts. On guard, Blakely."

"The baby," Anna moaned. "Oh, dear God, the baby."

But Luke could not afford to have his attention diverted by the very real danger to his wife and his daughter on either side of him.

Blakely was not a worthy opponent. Luke realized that early in the fight, at the first clash of swords. He fought defensively and wildly, trying to take his opponent by surprise and end the bout quickly. But he was a desperate man, and desperate men are ever dangerous. Luke fought with care and with intelligence, parrying wild thrusts and patiently setting up his opponent for the inevitable opening that would take his sword in for the kill.

He was aware that Anna had not stayed where she was but was edging her way around the room in an attempt to reach the baby. But he could not spare a moment's attention either to look at her or to advise her to stay still. He could only ensure that she stayed out of range of either his sword or Blakely's.

But Blakely had noticed her too. And Luke had made the mistake of assuming that he, too, would ignore her and keep his full attention on the fight to the death in which he was involved. Blakely suddenly whirled about, dropped his sword with a clatter to the carpet, whipped an arm about Anna and turned back so that her body was a shield between him and Luke. He drew a pistol from his pocket. A moment later its muzzle was resting against Anna's temple.

Sir Lowell was smiling and breathless. "It might be advisable to set the sword down on the floor, my dear Harndon," he said. "You may not enjoy seeing your wife's brains spattered all over the room. Now, if you please."

For the first time Luke's eyes rested fully on his wife. She was deathly pale. She was looking directly back at him. "I am sorry," she said. "I am so sorry." And she closed her eyes.

Luke leaned slowly down and set his sword on the floor at his feet. He straightened up again. What now? What the devil was to be done now? He cursed himself for not anticipating that very obvious move of Blakely's.

"Luke," Anna was saying, "you had best go back home. He will not kill you or me if you agree to go. I do not love you, you see. I never have. And I have no further wish to live with you. I am going to America with Sir Lowell. He has a home prepared for me there. And although I have been reluctant all day, I know now that I have seen you again that I really want to go."

Luke's eyes focused on her as her words lashed at him. But her eyes were sending him a different message entirely. And from the edge of his vision he could see her hand inching its way beneath the folded back portion of her gown to the side of her petticoat. There was a slit there through which she could reach into a pocket. What was in the pocket? What the devil was in it?

"Strumpet?" he said, eyes blazing, voice dripping scorn. "Aye, 'twas well said, Blakely. Strumpet indeed. Is this what I get for coming after you to claim my own? America, you say? Go, and good riddance, madam." His nostrils flared. And his knees felt suddenly weak. He had seen what Anna was sliding free of the petticoat slit.

Anna turned her head slowly so that the muzzle of the pistol moved from her temple almost to the center of her forehead. She smiled. "Shoot him instead of me," she said. "Dear Father. Dearest Papa."

Sir Lowell's eyes turned to her in some surprise and the gun shifted position slightly so that it was no longer against her head— or pointing at any other occupant of the room.

Luke watched, his heart in his mouth, as Anna's hand whipped up and she stabbed the knife sharply downward into Sir Lowell's leg.

He howled with shock and pain, Anna whirled away, and Luke snatched up his sword from the floor and embedded it in Sir Lowell Blakely's heart.

Sir Lowell stared at him for a moment, a ghastly smile on his lips. Luke withdrew his sword before the man pitched forward, dead, onto his face.

Anna had the baby, still miraculously asleep, in her arms. Luke dropped his sword as she stumbled toward him, and opened his arms. He held them both against him, his eyes tightly closed. Neither he nor Anna spoke.

"Lawks a-mercy," the voice of the landlord said from the doorway. "Two dead bodies, and more blood than will wash away with a dozen pails of water, forsooth. And who is to answer for these two deaths, your worship?"

"The Duke of Harndon," Luke said with weary haughtiness. "You will send for the nearest magistrate without delay, my good man. Standing there gawking will accomplish nothing."

A group of curious servants and guests had gathered in the hallway to witness the fascinating spectacle of a dead and bloody body stretched on the floor there. Several of them peered into the room for the extra satisfaction of seeing the phenomenon repeated—but this time the body belonged to a gentleman, the murmur went.

"Anna," Luke said, leading her to the doorway into the bedchamber, "there is no need for you to have to look further on this. Wait in here with Joy."

"Yes," she said as he opened the door and stepped into the inner room with her. She raised a face to his that was even more ghastly pale than before. "Luke, thank you for coming. Thank you for killing him for me. I did not come willingly. I swear it."

"I know." He bent his head and kissed her quickly. "I know, my love. And I must treat you with care for the rest of my life. I will live in fear and trembling of that knife hand of yours."

She laughed shakily and bit her lip.

"Stay here for now," he said, looking down at their oblivious daughter and bending his head to kiss her too on the forehead. "I'll be back, Anna. We will leave here tonight, late as it is. We will go home."

"Yes." Tears sprang to her eyes. "Yes, please, Luke."

# 28

I T was close to midnight when he came back into the room. She had lain on the bed the whole while, having removed only her hoops, staring upward. Joy, beside her, had not stirred. Sometimes Anna had stilled her thoughts by listening to the child's quiet breathing. She had tried to ignore the sound of voices in the other room and the line of light beneath the door.

She had plunged a knife into living flesh and had heard the howl of agony she had caused. And she had exulted in the feeling of power and triumph. She would have pulled the knife out and stabbed it into his heart if she could have done so and felt even more triumphant. She shivered.

And then eventually the door opened again and Luke came in. She turned her head to watch him as he approached the bed. The light was behind him so that she could not see his face.

"Do you want to stay here for the night, Anna?" he asked. "It is very late."

"No." She sat up. The thought of staying, of trying to sleep in this room, even if he stayed there with her, was nauseating. "I want to go home."

"The carriage is ready," he said, looking down at their daughter. "She is wrapped warmly. Those are your trunks?"

Anna shook her head. "They are what he brought for me," she said. "I do not want them. Only Joy's bag of supplies."

But he stooped over one of the trunks, opened the lid, and came out after a brief rummaging with a new and warm-looking cloak. He wrapped it about her when she got to her feet. "We will burn it when we get home if you wish," he said.

"Yes." She shivered despite the increased warmth the cloak brought.

The landlord was still up. He bowed obsequiously to them as they passed through the taproom. A few guests, who were sitting up late drinking, perhaps discussing the exciting events of the evening, gazed at them silently. And then they were in the blessed darkness and familiarity of their own carriage.

Anna sank down onto one of the seats and watched as Luke set the baby down opposite and wedged her carefully with the blankets so that she could not roll off.

"How wonderful," Anna said, "to have the kind of innocence and the sense of security that would enable one to sleep through such an evening."

Luke sat down and took her hand in his.

"How did you know?" she asked him. "How did you know he had taken us? How did you know where to look for us? Did Henrietta tell you?"

"Emily told me," he said. "She saw all, Anna, and somehow managed to tell me all, even to the fact that he was taking you to America. Theo is at Bowden to protect her from Henrietta, so you need not worry about her. Henrietta will be sent away tomorrow. You will never see her again."

Anna did not comment. There was nothing to say about Henrietta, whom both she and Luke had loved at different times. They sat in silence for a while.

"You called him by his real name," she said at last. "Even I did not know it until today."

"'Twas the business that took me from home," he said. "I needed to find out who Colonel Henry Lomax really was, Anna, and what hold he had over you. Your brother and sister and Lady Sterne helped me to piece the story together. You called him Father."

"He told me today that that was what he was," she said. "I felt that he almost believed it himself."

"But 'tis not true." He squeezed her hand. "You do not need to carry about that burden, Anna. He had an obsession for your mother long after she had turned him off as a girl and even after she had fallen in love with your father and married him."

"I know," she said. "I know he was not my father. There is the portrait of my grandmother I have hanging in my room."

"Ah, yes," he said. "The portrait that looks for all the world like you masquerading as your paternal grandmother. I am glad you resemble her so closely, Anna. There will be no lingering doubt in your mind."

She closed her eyes. She wanted to tip her head sideways to rest against his shoulder, but she could not do so. Not yet.

"Luke," she said, suddenly finding it difficult to speak, "you do not know the half."

"I know," he said, "that he was obsessed with you, Anna. I know that he bought all your father's debts and so gained power over you. I know that he has demanded gradually that you pay off those debts one at a time. And I know that you love your brother too much to have burdened him with the debts. And that you were too proud to come to me so that I could pay them for you. Why did you not trust me? Even at the beginning? Did you not realize that I would have honored rather than censured you?"

"You do not know the half," she said again, her heart heavy. A fiendish voice in her head was telling her to let it go at that. He need never know the rest. But she had to tell the rest. All of it. She had to give him the whole truth.

He lifted her hand to his lips. "Tell me, then, my love," he said.

"Perhaps you will not call me that when you know," she said. And she told him all the things she had done to redeem some of those debts in addition to the payment of money. And about the witnesses he had hired to perjure themselves if necessary and swear that she was both a thief and a murderer.

"Anna," he said with gentle reproach when she fell silent. "Ah, Anna, why did you not tell me? What foolishness to think yourself guilty of crimes you were forced to witness. And how foolish to believe that he would have brought you to court when he was so very guilty himself. My love, I could have eased your mind in a moment. You have lived through this hell for three years? I could have put an end to it a year ago if you had only confided in me."

"I thought you would not have the power," she said. "Worse, I thought perhaps you would believe it all and turn me away."

"Anna." He released her hand in order to set his arm about her shoulders and turn her toward him. "What a scoundrel you must have thought me." He tilted her chin with his free hand and kissed her deeply.

She sagged against him and kissed him back. The numbness was gradually leaving her mind. She was only just beginning to realize that it was all over, the nightmare of three years. That she was free. That she was going home with her husband and their daughter and that she would be able to live with them there without fear for the rest of their lives.

He was looking into her eyes from a few inches away. She could see his face clearly from the light of the moon and stars.

"He called himself your father, Anna," he said, "yet he raped you? It was him, was it not? Was it once or many times? Talk about it, my love, so that we may put it behind us and let the healing begin."

And yes, there was that. One more barrier to happiness. She did not want to think about it. She did not want to remember.

It had not really been rape, though in a way it had been. It had been as ugly and as sordid and as demeaning as rape could possibly have been. And she had not understood it at all, either at the time or afterward. Only now did she understand, now that she knew he claimed to be her father.

He had lured her to his house on some pretext—not difficult when she dared not disobey his every whim. They had taken her upstairs to a bedchamber, his two servants, when she had refused to go there herself. One on each side of her, they had half dragged, half carried her, while he had walked behind, talking soothingly to her. And then they had tied her to the bed by her wrists and her ankles so that she was spreadeagled and helpless and feeling quite robbed of dignity and personhood.

The woman servant had folded back her petticoat and her shift to the waist so that Anna had closed her eyes tightly and sobbed with shame. And then the servant had taken something—Anna had not seen it but it had felt hard and cold and greasy—and pushed it slowly inside, twisting it as she did so.

There had been blinding terror, screams above that constant soothing voice, and sharp pain. Anna had thought she was about to die. She had thought they were going to impale her until they had killed her.

But the woman had withdrawn whatever it was she had used and Anna had felt a hot gush between her legs.

"There is the blood," the woman had said, sounding satisfied. "It has been done, sir."

She was no longer a virgin, he had told her afterward. No man would want her as a wife now. She must never think of marriage.

Anna was sobbing. Dry, painful sobs that hurt her chest and robbed her of breath.

"Shh," Luke was saying, cradling her head against his shoulder, freeing it of cap and pins so that he could run his fingers soothingly through her hair. "My love, forgive me. Please forgive me."

He was crying too, Anna realized suddenly. She stayed where she was for a while until the echo of his words finally took meaning in her brain.

"Forgive you?" she said. "For what?"

He swallowed. "I can see myself sitting behind that desk," he said, "the morning after our wedding, telling you that you had some explaining to do. Interrogating you. Demanding to know how many times, with how many lovers. Demanding to know if you had loved him. Ah, my sweet love, forgive me."

She drew back her head and looked into his face. "Yes," she said, "if 'twill make you feel better. But I was very foolish not to tell you all then. I realize that now. I was afraid to, Luke. I was afraid of losing you."

"So soon?" he asked. "But why? We hardly knew each other. We had had a week's acquaintance. Not even. The fact constantly amazes me when I look back."

"But I loved you from the moment I first saw you," she said, "looking more gorgeous than any other gentleman I had ever seen. With your cosmetics and your fan that should have made you seem unmanly but somehow had just the opposite effect. I was dazzled. And I was lost from that moment on. And so I was unwise enough to give in to temptation when you came to offer for me. I would have done anything after that to avoid the risk of losing you. I was foolish."

He sighed. "And I talked so sensibly of duty and pleasure," he said. "Anna, Anna, what a very foolish man I was."

"No." She raised a hand to cup about one side of his face and let all the tenderness she felt show in her eyes. "Just a very unhappy and a very hurt person, Luke. Hidden skillfully behind a facade of splendor and a reputation for ruthlessness and heartlessness. I believe some of the pain has gone away, has it not?"

He touched his lips to hers. "All of it," he said. "All of it, Anna. I was dead for ten years, my love, and you have brought life back to me in one."

She smiled and then snuggled her head against his shoulder. She suddenly felt very tired.

*It* was still dark when he woke up. He guessed that he had not slept for very long. The carriage was still moving at a steady pace. They were fortunate that it was a light night. His coachman had assured him that he would have no trouble seeing well enough to drive. And neither the coachman nor Luke had any particular fear of highwaymen.

Joy was settling into sleep again. He realized that it was her slight fussing that had woken him. But she stilled and fell silent even as he watched. Anna was sleeping against his shoulder.

He had killed four men in his lifetime—two of them this very night. It was a heavy burden knowing that he had deprived men of life, though in each case he had felt fully justified and in each case the killing had seemed unavoidable. But he knew at this moment that he had only one regret about killing Lowell Blakely. The regret was that he had been able to do it only once.

One other thing of which he was glad. He was thankful that Blakely was not in fact Anna's father and that she had proof that would satisfy her beyond any doubts. For a long time, perhaps for the rest of her life, she was going to live with bad memories. At least she would not be burdened by the knowledge that her father had so used her and that she had helped kill her father.

There were still hours to go before they would be home. It would be daylight by the time they reached Bowden and there was not the faintest sign of dawn yet. He was impatient to be home.

Home! A feeling of almost unbearable longing and love swept over him. Bowden Abbey—where he belonged, where he lived with his wife and his daughter, where their other children would be begotten and born and nurtured. Where he would live surrounded by family and warmed by the love he gave them and received from them for the rest of his life. Where he could be with Anna, the two of them living there together until a ripe old age, God willing.

Unconsciously he tightened his arms about her.

"Mmm." She sighed deeply and burrowed closer for a few moments before drawing her head back and smiling sleepily up at him. "Are we almost home?"

"I see my wife here before my very eyes," he said, "and feel her in my arms. I have but to turn my head to see my daughter asleep within a few feet. Are we not home already, love?"

She smiled slowly at him. "Yes," she said. "Oh, yes, Luke."

He chuckled suddenly. "Do you remember going home from Ranelagh?" he asked her. "I suppose 'tis not a very pleasant memory for you, Anna, as you were very frightened on that occasion and had turned to me for comfort, I believe. But the memory is very pleasant indeed for me. And very tantalizing."

Her smile deepened and became fully Anna's smile—sunshine in the middle of the night, with a touch of mischief added to it.

"What memory would that be?" she asked, getting to her feet, and turning awkwardly in the confined, swaying interior of the carriage to sit on his lap.

"It started like this," he said, his lips light against hers while his hand explored one of her breasts through the fabric of her stomacher and then pushed beneath it to fondle smooth and warm flesh. "Mm, Anna, they feel so good when there is milk. I have never sucked them since you gave birth. Tonight I will."

"Memory is returning," she said in a whisper. "But 'tis sluggish."

"And then there was this," he said, his hand moving sensuously beneath her petticoat and up her legs until his fingers could fondle and arouse her. "Though I believe my memory is hazy too, my love. I believe at the time we both had such voracious appetites that we moved immediately to the main feast."

She moaned. "I am voracious now," she said.

"Ah, me too, love," he said, lifting her and bringing her astride him, pushing her skirts up out of the way as he did so and unbuttoning the flap of his breeches. "Come to the feast, Anna. Let us gorge ourselves together."

"Yes." It was half gasp, half sigh as he brought her down onto his hard length and let her settle there for a few moments. He pressed his mouth to her one exposed breast, took the nipple into his mouth, and sucked hard. Her milk was warm and sweet . . . and infinitely exciting. "Ah, Luke, Luke, you are so beautiful."

He chuckled and lifted his head. "But manly, too, I believe we are agreed?" he said. "Tell me I am manly as well as beautiful, Anna. Come, my dear, I must not have my self-esteem shattered."

She was laughing quietly and helplessly then against his hair. "Oh, yes," she said. "Oh, yes, you feel manly, Luke, I must confess. So manly that I marvel there is room for you there."

And so after all it was a joyful feast in which they indulged together and on which they gorged themselves over the next several minutes. Passionate and joyful and healing and life-giving. There was pleasure in plenty and ecstasy for the taking at the end. But more than that, there were happiness and self-giving and love. And the promise of an ever-abundant and ever-joyful feast for the rest of a lifetime.

They did not sleep afterward but sat side by side, their arms about each other, gazing with shared affection at the child who was sleeping the night away on the opposite seat, quite ignorant of the fact that her safety had been seriously threatened for a number of hours.

And now they would take her home together and give her the security of their shared love until it came time for her to pass on the love she had been given to someone else and begin her own family. They would take her home and give her brothers and sisters if they were fortunate.

"Luke," Anna said, "I have always been fortunate enough to be able to enjoy happiness when it presented itself. I have always had hope and I have always had the ability to see and appreciate the little things that can make life worth living. But I know now that it has been years and years since I have felt totally happy. I am happy now at this moment. Totally, wonderfully happy. No matter what the future has in store for us, I want to remember that there has been this moment. And that even this moment, with no more preceding and no more to come after, would make the whole mystery of living worthwhile."

He rubbed his cheek against the top of her head. "We will live life from moment to moment," he said, "thankful for each one we have together. Look, Anna, the world is turning gray beyond the windows. Dawn is coming."

"Ah," she said, "daylight and hope."

"And sunshine and laughter," he said. "Let us watch the sun come up, shall we? Together?"

She sighed with contentment. She did not need to answer in words.

Read on for a look at Lord Ashley Kendrick
and Lady Emily Marlowe's story in

*Silent Melody*

Available in trade paperback from Signet Eclipse
in August 2015.

*I*T was hard to leave. But it was impossible to stay. He was leaving from choice because he was young and energetic and adventurous and had long wanted to carve a life of his own.

He was going to new possibilities, new dreams. But he was leaving behind places and people. And though, being young, he was sure he would see them all again some day, he knew too that many years might pass before he did so.

It was not easy to leave.

Lord Ashley Kendrick was the son of a duke. A younger son, and therefore a man who needed employment. But neither the army nor the church, the accepted professions for younger sons, had appealed to him and so he had done nothing more useful with his twenty-three years than sow some wild oats and manage the estate of Bowden Abbey for his brother, Luke, Duke of Harndon, during the past few months. Business had always attracted him, but his father had forbidden him to involve himself with something he considered beneath the dignity of an aristocrat—even of a younger son. Luke felt differently. And so Ashley, with his brother's reluctant blessing, was on his way to India, to take up his new post with the East India Company.

He was eager to go. Finally he was to be his own man, doing what he wanted to do, proving to himself that he could forge his own destiny. He could hardly wait to begin his new life, to be there in India, to be free of his dependence on his brother.

But it was hard to say good-bye. He did it the day before he left and begged everyone to let him go alone the following morning, to drive away from Bowden Abbey as if on a morning errand. He said good-bye to Luke; to Anna, Luke's wife; to Joy, their infant daughter; to Emmy . . .

Ah, but he did not really say good-bye to Emmy. He sought her out and told her he was leaving the following day, it was true. But then he set his hands on her shoulders, smiled cheerfully at her, told her to be a good girl, and strode away before she could make any reply.

Not that Emmy could have replied verbally even if she had wanted to. She was a deaf-mute. She could read lips, but she had no way of communicating her thoughts except with those huge gray eyes of hers—and with certain facial expressions and gestures to which he had become sensitive during the year he had known her, plus others they had agreed upon as a sort of private, secret, if not entirely adequate language. She could not read or write. She was Anna's sister and had come to Bowden soon after Anna's marriage to Luke.

Emmy was a child. Though fifteen years old, her handicap and her wild sense of freedom—she rarely dressed or behaved like a gently born young lady—made Ashley think of her as a child. A precious child for whom he felt a deep affection and in whom he had been in the habit of confiding all his frustrations and dreams. A child who adored him. It was not conceit that had him thinking so. She spent every spare moment in his company, gazing at him or out through the window of the room in which he worked, listening to him with her wonderful, expressive eyes, following him about the estate. She was never a nuisance. His fondness for her was something he could not put satisfactorily into words.

He was afraid of Emmy's eyes the day before his departure. He did not have the courage to say good-bye. So he merely said his piece and hurried away from her—just as if she were no more to him than a child for whom he felt only an indulgent affection.

He regretted his cowardice the following day. But he hated good-byes.

He got up early. He had been unable to sleep, his mind tossing with the excitement of what was ahead of him, his body eager to be on the way, his emotions torn between an impatience to be gone and a heaviness at leaving all that was familiar and dear behind him.

He got up early to take a last fond look at Bowden Abbey, his home since childhood. But not his, of course. It was true that he was heir to it all, that Luke and Anna's firstborn had been a daughter. But they would have sons, he was sure. He hoped they would. Being heir was not important to him, much as he loved Bowden. He wanted his own life. He wanted to build his own fortune and choose his own home and follow his own dreams.

But he loved Bowden fiercely now that he was leaving it and did not know when he would see it again. If ever. He strode away behind the house, watching the early-morning dew soak his top boots, feeling the chill wind whip at his cloak and his three-cornered hat. He did not look back until he stood on top of a rise of land, from which he had a panoramic view down over the abbey and past it to the lawns and trees of the park stretching far in all directions.

Home. And England. He was going to miss both.

He descended the western side of the hill and strode toward the trees a short distance away and through them to the falls, the part of the river that spilled sharply downward over steep rocks before resuming its wide loop about the front of the house.

He had spent many hours of the past year at the falls, seeking solitude and peace. Seeking purpose. Seeking himself, perhaps. A little over a year ago, he had been in London. But Luke had returned from a long residence in Paris, rescued him from deep debts and a wild and aimless life of pleasure and debauchery, and ordered him to return to Bowden until he had decided what he wished to do with his life.

He climbed to the flat rock that jutted over the falls and stood looking down at the water as it rushed and bubbled over the rocks below. Emmy had spent many hours here with him. He smiled. He had once told her that she was a very good listener. It was true, even though she could not hear a word he said to her. She listened with her eyes and she comforted with her smiles and with her warm little hand in his.

Dear, sweet Emmy. He was going to miss her perhaps more than any of them. There was a strange ache about his heart at the thought of her, his little fawn, like a piece of wild, unspoiled nature. She rarely wore hoops beneath her dresses and almost never wore caps. Indeed, she did not often even dress her hair, but let it fall, blond and loose and wavy to her waist. Whenever she could get away with doing so, she went barefoot. He did not know how he would have survived the year without Emmy to talk to, without her sympathy and her happiness to soothe his wounded feelings. He had felt despised and rejected by Luke, his beloved brother, and his own sense of guilt had not helped reconcile him to what he had considered at the time to be unwarranted tyranny.

He drew a deep breath and let it out slowly. It was time to return to the house. He would have breakfast while the carriage was brought around and his trunks were loaded, and then he would be on his way. He strode back through the trees in the direction of the house. He hoped everyone would honor the promise not to come down to see him on his way. He wished that he could just click his fingers and find himself on board ship, out of sight of English shores.

He wished there did not have to be the moment of leaving.

*Ashley* had told her yesterday that he was leaving today. It had not been unexpected. For weeks past he had been excited over the prospect of joining the East India Company and going to India. There had been a new light of purpose in his eye and a new spring in his step, and she knew that she had lost him. That he no longer needed her. Not that he ever avoided her or turned her away. Not that he stopped talking to her or smiling at her or allowing her to walk about the estate with him or to sit in his office while he worked. Not that he stopped holding her hand as they walked or stopped calling her his little fawn. Not that any of the affection had gone out of his manner.

But he was going away. He was going to a new life, one that he craved. One that he needed. She was glad for him. She was genuinely glad. Yes, she was. Oh, yes, she was.

Lady Emily Marlowe curled up on the window seat in her room and gazed out on a gray and gloomy morning. She tried to draw peace from the sight of the trees and lawns. She tried to let them soothe her aching heart.

Her breaking heart.

She did not want to see him today. She would not be able to bear seeing him actually leave. It would hurt just too much.

And yet instead of peace, the only feeling that would come to her was panic. Had he left yet? She could not see the driveway or the carriage house from her room. Perhaps even now the carriage was before the doors. Perhaps even now he was stepping inside after hugging Anna and Luke— would they have taken Joy down too for him to kiss? He would be looking about him for her. He would be disappointed that she was not there. Would he believe she did not care? Perhaps he was driving away—now. At this very minute.

It could well be that he would be gone forever.

It was possible she would never see him again. Ever.

She leapt up suddenly and dashed into her dressing room. She shoved her feet into a pair of shoes and grabbed the first cloak that came to hand—her red one. She flung it about her shoulders and rushed from the room and down the stairs. Was she in time? She felt that she would die if she were not.

Ashley. Oh, Ashley.

There was only one footman in the hall. And a mound of boxes and trunks by the doors, which stood open. There was no carriage outside.

Emily sagged with relief. She was not too late. Ashley must be at breakfast. She took a few steps in the direction of the breakfast parlor, and the footman hurried ahead of her to open the doors. But she stopped again. No. She could not after all see him face-to-face. She would shame herself. She would cry. She would make him uncomfortable and unhappy. And she would see the pity in Anna's and Luke's eyes.

She ran outside and down the steps onto the upper terrace and on to the formal gardens. She ran fleet-footed through three tiers of the gardens and then down the long sloping lawn to the two-arched stone bridge over the river. She ran across the bridge and among the old trees that lined and shaded the driveway for its full winding length to the stone gateposts and the village beyond. But she did not run all the way to the village. She stopped halfway down the drive, gasping for breath.

She stood with her back against the broad trunk of an old oak and waited. She would see his carriage as it passed. She would say her own private good-bye. She would not see him, she realized. Only his carriage. He would not see her. He would not know that she had come to say good-bye. But it was just as well. Fond as he was of her, to him she was just a type of younger sister to be indulged.

She could remember her first meeting with him, the day she arrived at Bowden Abbey to live with Anna, feeling strange and bewildered. She had instantly liked Luke, though she had learned later that her sister Agnes was terrified of his elegant appearance and formal manners. But he had been kind to her and he had spoken with her as if she were a real person who had ears that could hear. And incredibly she *had* understood most of what he said—he moved his lips decisively as he spoke and he kept his face full toward her. So many people forgot to do that. But she had felt uncomfortable during tea in the drawing room until Ashley had arrived late and demanded an introduction. And then he had bowed to her and smiled and spoken.

"As I live," he had said, "a beauty in the making. Your servant, madam." She had seen every word.

Tall, handsome, charming Ashley. He had gone to sit beside his sister, Doris, and had proceeded to converse with her after winking at Emily. He had taken her heart with him. It was as simple as that. She had adored him from that moment as she had adored no one else in her life, even Anna.

Ashley had a loving heart. He loved Luke, even though they had been close to estrangement for almost a year. He loved his mother and his sister, who were now in London, and he loved Anna and Joy. He loved her too. But no more intensely than he loved the others. She was Emmy, his little fawn. She was just a child to him. He did not know that she was a woman.

He would forget her in a month.

No, she did not believe that. There was nothing shallow in Ashley's love. He would remember her fondly—as he would remember the rest of his family.

She would hold him in her heart—deep in her heart— for the rest of her life. He was all of life to her. He was everything. Life would be empty without Ashley. Meaningless. She loved him with all the passion and all the intense fidelity of her fifteen-year-old heart. She did not love him as a child loves, but as a woman loves the companion of her soul.

Perhaps more intensely than most women loved. There was so little else except the sight of the world around her with which to fill her mind and her heart. She had somehow made a life of her own dreams before meeting Ashley. It had not always been easy. There had been frustrations, even tantrums when she was younger—when perhaps she had remembered enough of sound to be terrified by its absence. She had no conscious memories of sound since it had been shut off quite totally after the dangerous fever she had barely survived before her fourth birthday. Just some fleeting hints, yearnings. She did not know quite what they were. They always just eluded her grasp.

Ashley had become her dream. He had given her days meaning and her nights fond imaginings. She did not know what would be left to her when the dream was taken away—today, this morning.

She was beginning to think that she must have missed him after all. Perhaps he had gone ahead and his luggage was to follow later. She was almost numb with the cold. The wind whipped and bit at her. But finally she heard the carriage approach. Not that she could hear it in the accepted sense of the word—she often wondered what sound must have been like. But she felt the vibrations of an approaching carriage. She pressed herself back against the tree while grief hit her low in the stomach like a leaden weight. He was leaving forever and all she would see was Luke's carriage, which was taking him to London.

Panic grabbed her like a vise as the carriage came into sight, and despite herself she leaned slightly forward, desperate for one last glimpse of him.

She saw nothing except the carriage rolling on past. She moaned incoherently.

But then it slowed and came to a full stop. And the door nearest her was flung open from the inside.

Eager for a look at the next book
in Mary Balogh's Survivors' Club series?
Read on for a sneak peek at Imogen and Percy's story in

## *Only a Kiss*

Available from Signet in September 2015.

$\mathcal{P}$ERCIVAL William Henry Hayes, Earl of Hardford, Viscount Barclay, was hugely, massively, colossally bored. All of which descriptors were basically the same thing, of course, but really he was bored to the marrow of his bones. He was almost too bored to heave himself out of his chair in order to refill his glass at the sideboard across the room. No, he *was* too bored. Or perhaps just too drunk. Maybe he had even gone as far as drinking the ocean dry.

He was celebrating his thirtieth birthday, or at least he had been celebrating it. He suspected that by now it was well past midnight, which fact would mean that his birthday was over and done with, as were his careless, riotous, useless twenties.

He was lounging in his favorite soft leather chair to one side of the hearth in the library of his town house, he was pleased to observe, but he was not alone, as he really ought to be at this time of night, whatever the devil time that was. Through the fog of his inebriation he seemed to recall that there had been celebrations at White's Club with a satisfyingly largish band of cronies, considering the fact that it was very early in February and not at all a fashionable time to be in London.

The noise level, he remembered, had escalated to the point at which several of the older members had frowned in stern disapproval—old fogies and fossils, the lot of them—and the poker-faced waiters had begun to show cracks of strain and indecision. How did one chuck out a band of drunken gentlemen, some of them of noble birth, without giving permanent offense to them and to all their family members to the third and fourth generation past and future? But how did one *not* do the chucking when inaction would incur the wrath of the equally nobly born fogies?

Some amicable solution must have been found, however, for here he was in his own home with a small and faithful band of comrades. The others must have taken themselves off to other revelries or perhaps merely to their beds.

"Sid." He turned his head on the back of the chair without taking the risk of raising it. "In your considered opinion, have I drunk the ocean dry tonight? It would be surprising if I had not. Did not someone dare me?"

The Honorable Sidney Welby was gazing into the fire—or what had been the fire before they had let it burn down without shoveling on more coal or summoning a servant to do it for them. His brow furrowed in thought before he delivered his answer. "Couldn't be done, Perce," he said. "Replenished consh—constantly by rivers and streams and all that. Brooks and rills. Fills up as fast as it empties out."

"And it gets rained upon too, cuz," Cyril Eldridge added helpfully, "just as the land does. It only *feels* as if you had drunk it dry. If it *is* dry, though, it having not rained lately, we all had a part in draining it. My head is going to feel at least three times its usual size tomorrow morning, and dash it all but I have a strong suspicion I agreed to escort m'sisters to the library or some such thing, and as you know, Percy, m'mother won't allow them to go out with just a maid for company. They always insist upon leaving at the very crack of dawn too, lest someone else arrive before them and carry off all the books worth reading, which is not a large number, in my considered opinion. And what are they all doing in town this early, anyway? Beth is not making her come-out until after Easter, and she cannot need *that* many clothes. Can she? But what does a brother know? Nothing whatsoever if you listen to m'sisters."

Cyril was one of Percy's many cousins. There were twelve of them on the paternal side of the family, the sons and daughters of his father's four sisters, and twenty-three of them at last count on his mother's side, though he seemed to remember her mentioning that Aunt Doris, her youngest sister, was in a delicate way again for about the twelfth time. Her offspring accounted for a large proportion of those twenty-three, soon to be twenty-four. All of the cousins were amiable. All of them loved him, and he loved them all, as well as all the uncles and aunts, of course. Never had there been a closer-knit, more loving family than his, on both sides. He was, Percy reflected with deep gloom, the most fortunate of mortals.

"The bet, Perce," Arnold Biggs, Viscount Marwood, added, "was that you could drink Jonesey into a coma before midnight—no mean feat. He slid under the table at ten to twelve. It was his snoring that finally made us decide that it was time to leave White's. It was downright distracting."

"And so it was." Percy yawned hugely. That was one mystery solved. He raised his glass, remembered that it was empty, and set it down with a clunk on the table beside him. "Devil take it but life has become a crashing bore."

"You will feel better tomorrow after the shock of turning thirty today has waned," Arnold said. "Or do I mean today and yesterday? Yes, I do. The small hand of the clock on your mantel points to three, and I believe it. The sun is not shining, however, so it must be the middle of the night, though at this time of the year it is *always* the middle of the night."

"What do you have to be bored about, Percy?" Cyril asked, sounding aggrieved. "You have everything a man could ask for. *Everything.*"

Percy turned his mind to a contemplation of his many blessings. Cyril was quite right. There was no denying it. In addition to the aforementioned loving extended family, he had grown up with two parents who adored him as their only son—their only *child* as it had turned out, though they had apparently made a valiant effort to populate the nursery with brothers and sisters for him. They had lavished everything upon him that he could possibly want or need, and they had had the means with which to do it in style.

His paternal great-grandfather, as the younger son of an earl and only the spare of his generation instead of the heir, had launched out into genteel trade and amassed something of a fortune. His son, Percy's grandfather, had made it into a *vast* fortune and had further enhanced it when he married a wealthy, frugal woman, who reputedly had counted every penny they spent. Percy's father had inherited the whole lot except for the more than generous dowries bestowed upon his four sisters upon their marriages. And then he had doubled and tripled his wealth through shrewd investments, and he in his turn had married a woman who had brought a healthy dowry with her.

After his father's death three years ago, Percy had become so wealthy that it would have taken half the remainder of his life just to count all the pennies his grandmother had so carefully guarded. Or even the pounds for that matter. *And* there was Castleford House, the large and prosperous home and estate in Derbyshire that his grandfather had bought, reputedly with a wad of banknotes, to demonstrate his consequence to the world.

Percy had looks too. There was no point in being overmodest about the matter. Even if his glass lied or his perception of what he saw in that glass was off, there was the fact that he turned admiring, sometimes envious, heads wherever he went—both male and female. He was, as a number of people had informed him, the quintessential tall, dark, handsome male. He enjoyed good health and always had, knock on wood—he raised his hand and did just that with the knuckles of his right hand, banging on the table beside him and setting the empty glass and Sid to jumping. And he had all his teeth, all of them decently white and in good order.

He had brains. After being educated at home by three tutors because his parents could not bear to send him away to school, he had gone up to Oxford to study the classics and had come down three years later with a double first in Latin and Ancient Greek. He had friends and connections. Men of all ages seemed to like him, and women . . . Well, women did too, which was fortunate, as he liked them. He liked to charm them and compliment them and turn pages of music for them and dance with them and take them walking and driving. He liked to flirt with them. If they were widows and willing, he liked to sleep with them. And he had developed an expertise in avoiding any and all of the matrimonial traps that were laid for him at every turn.

He had had a number of mistresses, though there was none at the moment, all of them exquisitely lovely and marvelously skilled, all of them expensive actresses or courtesans much coveted by his peers.

He was strong and fit and athletic. He enjoyed riding and boxing and fencing and shooting, at all of which he excelled and all of which had left him somehow restless lately. He had taken on more than his fair share of challenges and dares over the years, the more reckless and dangerous the better. He had raced his curricle to Brighton on three separate occasions, once in both directions, and taken the ribbons of a heavily laden stagecoach on the Great North Road after bribing the coachman . . . and sprung the horses. He had crossed half of Mayfair entirely upon rooftops and occasionally the empty air between them, having been challenged to accomplish the feat without touching the ground or making use of any conveyance that touched the ground. He had crossed almost every bridge across the River Thames within the vicinity of London—from underneath. He had strolled through some of the most notoriously cutthroat rookeries of London in full evening finery with no weapon more deadly than a cane—*not* a sword-cane. He had got an exhilarating fistfight against three assailants out of that last exploit after his cane snapped in two, and one great shiner of a black eye in addition to murder done to his finery, much to the barely contained grief of his valet.

He had dealt with irate brothers and brothers-in-law and fathers, always unjustly because he was always careful not to compromise virtuous ladies or raise expectations he had no intention of fulfilling. Occasionally those confrontations had resulted in fisticuffs too, usually with the brothers. Brothers, in his experience, tended to be more hotheaded than fathers. He had fought one duel with a husband who had not liked the way Percy smiled at his wife. Percy had not even spoken with her or danced with her. He had smiled because she was pretty and was smiling at him. What was he to have done? *Scowled* at her? The husband had shot first on the appointed morning, missing the side of Percy's head by a quarter of a mile. Percy had shot back, missing the husband's left ear by two feet—he had intended it to be one foot but at the last moment had erred on the side of caution.

*And*, if all that were not enough blessing for one man, he had the title. Titles. Plural. The old Earl of Hardford, also Viscount Barclay, had been some sort of relative of Percy's, courtesy of that great-great-grandfather of his. There had been a family quarrel and estrangement involving the sons of that ancestor, and the senior branch, which bore the title and was ensconced in some godforsaken place near the toe of Cornwall, had been ignored by the younger branch ever after. The most recent earl of that older branch had had a son and heir, apparently, but for some unfathomable reason, since there was no other son to act as a spare, that son had gone off to Portugal as a military officer to fight against old Boney's armies and had got himself killed for his pains.

All the drama of such a family catastrophe had been lost upon the junior branch, which had been blissfully unaware of it. But it had all come to light when the old earl turned up his toes a year almost to the day after Percy's father died and it turned out that Percy was the sole heir to the titles and the crumbling heap in Cornwall. At least, he assumed it was probably crumbling since the estate there certainly did not appear to be generating any vast income. Percy had taken the title—he had had no choice really, and actually it had rather tickled his fancy, at least at first, to be addressed as Hardford or, better still, as *my lord* instead of as plain Mr. Percival Hayes. He had accepted the title and ignored the rest—well, most of the rest.

He had been admitted to the House of Lords with due pomp and ceremony and had delivered his maiden speech on one memorable afternoon after a great deal of writing and rewriting and rehearsing and re-rehearsing and second and third and forty-third thoughts and nights of vivid dreams that had bordered upon nightmare. He had sat down at the end of it to polite applause and the relief of knowing that never again did he have to speak a word in the House unless he chose to do so. He had actually so chosen on a number of occasions without losing a wink of sleep.

He was on hailing terms with the king and all the royal dukes and had been more sought after than ever socially. He had already patronized the best tailors and bootmakers and haberdashers and barbers and such, but he was bowed and scraped to at a wholly elevated level after he became *m'lord*. He had always been popular with them all since he was that rarity among gentlemen of the *ton*—a man who paid his bills regularly. He still did, to their evident astonishment. He spent the spring months in London for the Parliamentary session and the Season, and the summer months on his own estate or at one of the spas, and the autumn and winter months at home or at one of the various house parties to which he was always being invited, shooting, fishing, hunting according to whichever was most in season, and socializing. The only reason he was in London at the start of February this year was that he had imagined the sort of thirtieth-birthday party his mother would want to organize for him at Castleford. And how did one say no to the mother one loved? One did not, of course. One retreated to town instead like a naughty schoolboy hiding out from the consequences of some prank.

Yes. To summarize. He was the most fortunate man on earth. There was not a cloud in his sky and never really had been. It was one vast, cloudless blue expanse of bliss up there. A brooding, wounded, darkly compelling hero type he was *not*. He had never done anything to brood over or anything truly heroic, which was a bit sad really. The heroic part, that was.

Every man ought to be a hero at least once in his life.

"Yes, everything," he agreed with a sigh, referring to what his cousin had said a few moments ago. "I do have it all, Cyril. And that, dash it all, is the trouble. A man who has everything has nothing left to live for."

Photo by Sharon Pelletier

**Mary Balogh** grew up in Wales and now lives with her husband, Robert, in Saskatchewan, Canada. She has written more than one hundred historical novels and novellas, more than thirty of which have been *New York Times* bestsellers. They include the Slightly sestet (the Bedwyn saga), the Simply quartet, the Huxtable quintet, and the ongoing seven-part Survivors' Club series.

marybalogh.com
facebook.com/authormarybalogh